Fatal Beauty

Also by John Godey

Nella
The Snake
The Talisman
The Taking of Pelham One Two Three
The Three Worlds of Johnny Handsome
Never Put Off Till Tomorrow What You Can Kill Today
A Thrill a Minute with Jack Albany
The Fifth House
The Clay Assassin
This Year's Death
The Man in Question
The Blue Hour
The Gun and Mr. Smith
The Crime of the Century and Other Misdemeanors (nonfiction)

Fatal Beauty

John Godey

Methuen

First published in Great Britain in 1985
by Methuen London Ltd
11 New Fetter Lane, London EC4P 4EE
Copyright © John Godey 1984
Reproduced, printed and bound in Great Britain
by Redwood Burn Limited, Trowbridge, Wiltshire

British Library Cataloguing in Publication Data

Godey, John
   Fatal beauty.
   Rn: Morton Freedgood   I. Title
   813'.54[F]   PS3556.R383/

   ISBN 0 413 58490 9

Italia! O Italia! thou who hast the fatal gift of beauty.
—Lord Byron

Even her sneeze—it's like a Puccini aria.
—Zayde

Fatal Beauty

The Ambush

Faint narrow ruts, the latent imprint of a road, bled off the edge of the macadam beneath a tangle of tall brush. Carlo, whose parents had once owned a villa nearby, and who had roamed these parts as a child, theorized that the ruts were the last remaining traces of a forgotten road that had first been worn into the earth by Roman wheels, winding down to some stream that had run dry centuries ago.

Nobody gave a second thought to Carlo's theory; it was irrelevant. The ruts were a convenient landmark, and that was all. Adriana backed and filled on the macadam until the front of the van lined up with the ruts. She hit the gas pedal. The wheels spun, meeting resistance from the tough springy undergrowth, and then caught hold and plowed straight through. A car's length down the shallow slope she braked the van to a stop.

Everyone piled out and set to work dressing up the brush, coaxing it erect, tidying it, reweaving it into a mat where that seemed necessary. Federico supervised with fussy efficiency. Adriana felt the sun warming her back, although it was barely nine o'clock. It would be one of those exceptional October days: *estate di San Martino*, or Indian summer as the Americans and English called it. The dry perfume of the vegetation reminded her of the autumnal fields of her childhood.

When Federico was satisfied with their groundskeeping, he ordered young Giorgio to take up his post in a tall pine tree a hundred meters along the winding macadam country road. Giorgio asked Federico if it was necessary for him to be in place approximately two hours ahead of time. He wasn't disputing Federico's judgment; to the contrary, he was respectfully seeking enlightenment from the man—the legend—who had planned the kidnapping of Aldo Moro.

"Yes," Federico said. "One can't be too careful."

Giorgio nodded his head vigorously in agreement. Little sheep, Adriana thought, lapping up Federico's platitudes like mother's milk. Federico patted Giorgio's shoulder, and Giorgio trotted off to his tree, cradling the walkie-talkie to his chest. It was one of a pair they had taken from the two cops they had executed in front of the Stazione Centrale in Milan. At eight thirty in the morning, height of the rush hour! Looking back, it struck Adriana as having been unacceptably risky. Yet they had pulled it off and earned points for their boldness. THE AUDACIOUS KILLERS, the headlines had screamed.

But that was almost six months ago, and they had done little since then.

They all piled into the back of the van. They were quite secure now, well hidden from any cars passing by on the macadam. There would be few enough of these, in any case. The road was barely used except for weekends, when people drove out from the cities to hunt pheasant and the occasional fox. And any car unlucky enough to happen by when the action began would not be a problem. The people of Italy were, one might say, educated: terrorist activity had molded a national mood.

Federico spoke into the transceiver. "Van to Lookout. Do you receive me?"

"Lookout to Van. I am in place."

"Report, please."

"From here I command a perfect view of the countryside, a full 360 degrees. God, it's a lovely landscape."

Adriana threw back her head and laughed.

Michael, toying with his croissant, watched Bering sail zestfully through a vast American breakfast. The morning room, typically, was the most modest of the hotel's elegant public rooms. Breakfast was simply not regarded as a serious meal. Besides themselves, there were only a handful of diners—some tourists, a few businessmen, an assembly of Japanese eating stolidly and silently. Two bored and sleepy-eyed waiters, assisted by a very young apprentice, were staff enough to serve the entire room.

As usual, with the last cup of his second pot of coffee, Bering produced his cigar with a ritual flourish, a huge showy Cuban. Both waiters—who, however amused they might be by Bering's uncivilized breakfast, had great respect for his cigar—hurried over to light it. Bering puffed out a cloud of thick blue smoke, his face blissful. Michael wished that he could dislike him, but it was impossible. He was a rarity—a fat, successful, self-indulgent person possessed of unlimited and effortless charm. He was also, as Michael had discovered in the months he had spent working for him, a cunning and efficient businessman.

Bering pointed the lighted tip of his cigar downward at Michael's setting, where his crumbled croissant lay untasted on his plate. His barely touched coffee was covered by a membranous skin of milk.

"You're a rotten eater," Bering said. "Can I say something? You eat like a man in love. Still and all—would you believe it—I envy you."

But he didn't, Michael thought, except in some remotely sentimental way that didn't really touch his heart. "I'm not hungry."

"How can anyone not be hungry?"

They were the exact words, with almost the same intonation, that his parents had used when he was a child, although his father would have added, "Don't you want to grow up big and strong and have hair on your chest like me?" Well, that was exactly how he *had* grown up. He was a mirror image of Jerry Sultan, a few inches taller but with the same broad-shouldered, powerful, heavy-torsoed build. And a luxuriant mat of black curly hair on his chest.

"Girl trouble." Bering was regarding him with a mixture of shrewdness and compassion. "I recognize the symptoms—after all, I was young once myself, I had pizzazz in my veins instead of schmaltz. You go through hell. But it doesn't last forever, you get over it. Count on that, Mike—everything passes, and life goes on."

But suppose you don't want it to pass? Suppose getting over it is an intolerable alternative? He said, "I'm fine, I just slept badly last night."

"That's another thing—it keeps you awake. Mark my words—everything passes." Bering looked upward at the waiter who was hovering over him. "What's up, Tony?"

The waiter knew English, but before he could respond, Michael said, "*Che cosa vuole?*" After all, Bering was paying him to be an interpreter.

"*La sua macchina è qui, signore.*"

"The car is here," Michael said to Bering.

"Right on time," Bering said. "Who said Italians aren't punctual? At least here, in the north." He stood up and handed the waiter a few thousand lira notes. "It's like doing business with the Germans or the Japanese, everything right on the nose. Except Italians know how to make it fun, too."

Everything passes, Michael thought, I'll try to keep that in mind. He followed Bering's bulk out of the room.

The limousine was drawn up in front of the hotel entrance. It was a Cadillac, by Bering's whimsical choice: "Everything is Mercedes here, so Cadillac isn't vulgar but different." The morning was bright, for a change free of the habitual morning fog that shrouded the cities of the Po Valley. The flowers banking the oval driveway were fresh and moist and fragrant. The chauffeur, horsefaced, enormously tall, opened the rear door. Bering got in and Michael followed. The chauffeur closed the door ceremoniously and circled the car to the driver's seat.

"*Verona, non è vero?*" he said, looking back over his shoulder.

"*Sì,*" Michael said. "*Avanti!* Get going."

The chauffeur cranked up the glass partition, and the car rolled smoothly out to the street. They headed in a generally northern direction, avoiding the main thoroughfares, trying to circumvent the crush of Milan's hectic morning rush hour.

"How do you like the size of the chauffeur?" Bering said. "He reminds me of Primo Carnera."

"Who?"

"Before your time." Bering waved his cigar. "He was a heavyweight fighter, a giant, but the poor fellow couldn't fight."

Through the window, Michael took note of the green and white signs denoting the route to an *autostrada*. When he had been taken to Italy for the first time at the age of fifteen, on one of his father's summer business trips, he had been prepared to find Italian roads and Italian drivers the worst in the world. Even now he wasn't so sure about the drivers, but he had learned to respect the highway system, an elaborate network of *autostrade,* express routes that crisscrossed the length and breadth of the peninsula.

The chauffeur turned into the approach ramp at the Tangenziale Ovest interchange, picked up his ticket at the toll booth, and edged into the speeding traffic of the A4, the major artery of the north. Through the glass partition the chauffeur's back conveyed that air of proprietary calm that seemed to characterize people who drove expensive cars belonging to other people.

In the rear, Joe Bering's cigar smoke hung in the air like a becalmed cloud. Michael stifled a cough.

"Smoke bothering you, Mike? Roll the window down."

Michael shook his head. The fume-laden air of the highway was just as bad. "I'm all right."

"You ought to learn to smoke cigars," Bering said. "Business people respect somebody who smokes expensive cigars. They equate it with being successful."

"I'm not really a businessman yet. I'm just a beginner."

"You'll get there. The thing to keep in mind, dealing with Canetti, is that he wants to sell us his cappuccino machines as badly as we want to buy them. It's all settled but the price, and price is everything. He knows we'll give a little, but not how much. The one who comes closest to guessing the answer wins the game. If you need some help, I'll come off the bench and help out."

Bering regarded his work as a form of mock battle, in which nobody was killed and the winner counted his victory in a few dollars or even a few cents gained. He had a shrewd instinct for merchandise that would sell in the United States. In earlier years he had sought out his wares in places like Hong Kong, Calcutta, Sydney, Kenya, Sri Lanka, but now he confined his trips to a Europe he knew as well as he did his own country.

Michael opened an attaché case and took out a file containing printed specifications for the cappuccino machines, a series of memos from Canetti, and two pages covered with Bering's briskly written figures. The specifications, which were in Italian, posed a challenge to his knowledge of the language. He became so engrossed that he was unaware that the chauffeur had turned off the *autostrada*.

"Where's he going?" Bering said. "This can't be the Verona exit so soon, can it?"

Michael shook his head. He rapped on the glass partition, and when the chauffeur rolled it down, said in Italian, "The boss wants to know if this is the Verona exit."

The chauffeur said, "Tell him there's an overturned truck up ahead. Tell him I'll make a detour and then get back on the highway after I bypass the tie-up."

Michael translated for Bering, who said, "How does he know about it?"

"*Come sa del' incidènte?*"

"*Dalla radio.*"

"Heard it on the radio," Bering said. "I got it. Remind him we have to be there by eleven."

Michael translated for the chauffeur, who said, "*Lui dice non si preoccupi.*"

"He says no sweat."

Federico studied the face of his watch, then shook the cuff of his jacket over it with an air of finality. "Let's put our masks on, please."

Adriana looked at her own watch. "Why? They're not due for at least a half hour."

"And suppose they were to arrive early? Put them on."

Adriana glowered at him, then, with pursed lips, drew the ski mask slowly down over her face and tucked in her honey-colored hair. She straightened the material to adjust the eye holes. The wool was itchy. With everyone masked, they looked like a family of sorts.

"It was understood," Federico said, "that we would be thorough down to the last detail. Our preparation, our discipline, our execution must all be absolutely German. Think of how stupid it would be if we had to pull our masks on at the last minute."

Adriana fought back her irritation with Federico's pedantic tone. She was already beginning to sweat underneath the mask. Over the past hour it had become oppressive in the van—heat aggravated by tension, by the rankness of sweating bodies, and, a crowning touch, the stink of garlic coming from Gildo, the Sicilian who didn't consider any meal complete, including breakfast, that lacked a few cloves of garlic.

Carlo cleared his throat. When he spoke his voice was pinched, strained, but his vowels remained as faultlessly enunciated as a classical actor's. "I admit we discussed it freely, and reached a unanimous democratic decision, but still..."

"Oh, God," Adriana said.

"...but is it necessary? I mean the killing."

"We know what you mean," Adriana said. "Just shut up, Carlo."

Federico gave her a stern look before speaking to Carlo. "Yes, it's necessary. We can't take even the slightest risk of betrayal. In the long view, his life is meaningless."

Carlo said earnestly, "I understand the proposition intellectually, I'm fervently committed to the dialectics of terror, and in the case of the two cops, as you know, I pulled the trigger..."

"And then balked at giving them the *colpo di grazia*," Adriana said. "If you didn't have the stomach for the hard realities of terrorism, Carlo, you should have joined the Boy Scouts instead of the Forze Scarlatte."

"*Basta!* That's quite enough," Federico said sternly.

"And you," Adriana said, swinging around to face him. "You and your German thoroughness. What the devil is wrong with Italian thoroughness? To say German thoroughness is denigrating. Italians aren't all *dolce far niente*, you know. We ourselves are a good example of that, aren't we?"

"I used German merely as a metaphor for precision," Federico said.

"You ought to be more sensitive about your choice of metaphors. It was you yourself, wasn't it, who broke with the Brigate Rosse over bringing in the Baader-Meinhoff Germans in the Moro kidnapping?"

"We quit the Brigate because of serious differences in revolutionary philosophy. The matter of the Germans was a by-issue."

Carlo began an involved rationalization of his reluctance to finish off the cops. Adriana put her hands over her ears to tune out his fear-thinned voice. Through a slit in the curtained rear window of the van the sun was a brilliant white, edging up a sky of dazzling blue.

Opposite her, slouched against the side of the van, Gildo was drumming his fingers on the stock of his *lupara*. They had tried to talk him out of using the weapon, with its Mafia associations, but he had refused to give it up, and in the end they had dropped their objections. After all, it hardly mattered whether death issued from the muzzle of a peasant shotgun that had been killing wolves and men for hundreds of years, or from Carlo's elegant, silver-chased hunting rifle.

Gildo shifted his attack on the stock of the *lupara*. Now, instead of using the balls of his fingertips, he tapped with his hard stubby nails. Adriana flared up.

"Stop that, you imbecile!"

Gildo's white teeth appeared in the mouth slit of his mask. "Certainly, *duchessa*, anything your highness wishes. I am only a poor proletarian from a benighted island, and if the *duchessa* from the enlightened north commands, I bow my head in obedience."

"You black hairy ape, *contadino*, Sicilian clown!"

Gildo burst into raucous, derisive laughter.

Federico stared at both of them in turn. "Can we have an end to this childishness?"

Beneath her ski mask Adriana's face was burning, but she said nothing.

"Thank you," Federico said. He looked at his watch. "I'd like you to get behind the wheel now, Adriana."

It was too soon, but it would be a welcome relief from the tension, from the stink of Gildo's breath and Carlo's fear. She rose and moved toward the doors of the van.

"From this moment on," Federico said, "we must be ready to strike."

Carlo began a spasm of nervous coughing. Gildo laughed. "Look at it this way, Carlo, we're being very conservative. There's three of them, and we're only killing one."

Adriana hopped down, slammed the doors shut, and waded through the knee-high tangle of weeds to the cab.

After leaving the state road the chauffeur had made a bewildering series of turns. Their course seemed improvised and capricious to Michael, but he couldn't doubt that the chauffeur knew exactly where he was going. His driving was smooth and relaxed, and the solid set of his enormous shoulders inspired confidence.

Now he eased the Cadillac through a tight right turn into a macadam country road. It was narrow, with a high crown in the center, surrounded by fields on both sides, bordered by trees and a heavy growth of head-high brush. The fields had already been harvested, although there were still signs of late crops which Michael couldn't identify. Once, in a break in the foliage, he caught a glimpse of distant hazy hills. There were a few widely spaced dwellings, farm houses, set far back from the road. In a field, he caught a glimpse of wild flowers, spread out like a pink carpet.

The chauffeur held to the exact center of the road, even on curves, as if he was certain there would be no oncoming traffic. Once, a pheasant crossed the road, and the chauffeur, laughing, tried to run it down. The pheasant scurried across the road in a panic, lost a few feathers, but escaped annihilation.

Bering was dozing, with his head nodding. His cigar was still clenched between his teeth and still lit, kept alive by his soft breathing, the ash almost an inch long. Michael leaned toward him, tapped the cigar gently with his finger, and caught the ash in his palm.

"Are we there?"

Bering had an eye open, the lid fluttering. Michael shook his head and the lid slowly closed down. The end of the cigar glowed, and another ash began to form.

"They should have been here"—Federico tapped the crystal of his watch with a long fingernail—"five minutes ago."

The sun beating down on the roof of the van had turned it into a sweat box. Federico and Carlo kept mopping their pink faces, groaning with discomfort. Gildo didn't seem to mind; after all, he was *meridionale*, and a southerner thrived on heat.

"A tie-up in Milan," Carlo said. "You know what a mess traffic is like in the city."

"Next time we ought to do Germans," Gildo said solemnly. "They're always on time."

"I allowed for unforeseen delays in my projection," Federico said. He looked at his watch again. *"Cristo!"*

Abruptly, the walkie-talkie crackled. Giorgio's voice: "Lookout to Van. They're coming. About two kilometers down the road. Do you read me? Over."

"Read you," Federico said. "Come back to the van."

He scrambled to his feet and rapped at the cab window. Adriana looked back and nodded. The van's motor started up.

Bering was catnapping again, dreaming of food, when the Cadillac bucked to a sudden stop. The cigar was jarred from his mouth. He groped for it on the floor, and, when he straightened up, saw masked black-clad figures tumbling out of a van that was slewed diagonally across the road. Beside him, Michael's face was white as paper. Bering reached under his coat for the automatic, but the door was yanked open, and the barrel of a pistol cracked across his knuckles. He yelped in pain. The automatic fell from his fingers, but he still clung to the cigar with his left hand.

He was hauled out of the car by two of the masked figures. One of the men twisted his arm behind his back in a hammerlock, not painfully but purposively, and he knew that if he resisted the grip would become punishing. Then he was being shoved toward the open rear doors of the van. From the tail of his eye he saw Michael, between two other black figures, also moving toward the van. Both groups arrived at the same time and caused a jam. The masked men shouted at each other and jostled, and finally Michael's two backed off and Bering was lifted off his feet, hoisted, and dumped into the back of the van.

He landed on all fours, and a moment later Michael followed and the doors were slammed shut. He became aware of a throbbing pain in his right hand. He put his hand to his mouth and blew on it. He noticed a window between the front wall of the van and the cab, and a head framed in it, with a mask drawn down low over the neck.

He raised himself on his haunches and duck walked to the rear doors. There were two small windows there, covered by bits of monk's cloth on curtain rods. Steadying himself with his good hand, he peered through a corner of the curtain. There was a masked figure at the wheel of the Cadillac, backing it away out of view. The remaining three were standing beside the chauffeur, who was talking animatedly, smiling and gesturing, the brim of his peaked cap pushed back off his long horse's face. The Cadillac reappeared, turned sharply to the left, and plowed into the heavy growth at the side of the road.

Michael was standing behind him. He was sweating. Bering could smell him. His breathing was shallow and rapid.

Bering took his hand out of his mouth. The forefinger was gross, swollen. "I think I've got a busted finger."

In a pinched, thin voice, Michael said, "I didn't know you carried a gun."

"Someone told me it was a good idea. It was dumb. I never fired one in my life."

Through the window, Bering saw the fourth masked man join the group talking to the chauffeur. He was carrying a shotgun. The chauffeur greeted him with an expansive gesture. The man with the shotgun fired point blank into the chauffeur's chest. The chauffeur flew over backward. His long legs kicked up high, then fell back, twitching.

"My God," Michael said. "They shot him! Why did they have to shoot him?"

When the man with the shotgun stepped forward, aiming the weapon downward, Michael made a whimpering sound and turned away. Bering shut his eyes. The shotgun boomed. When Bering opened his eyes, two of the masked men were dragging the chauffeur's body off to the left. The chest was bloody, the head was a jelly. On the macadam, there was a pool of blood, glossily red in the sunlight.

The doors of the van opened and two of the masked men clambered in. They spoke rapidly in Italian to Michael. One of the men slapped him on the back and the other embraced him. Bering put his hurt finger in his mouth and began to suck on it.

"I'm sorry," Michael said.

Bering sucked his finger.

Michael spoke to the two masked men, his voice querulous. One of them answered him, and there was a sharp exchange. Without understanding the words, Bering knew they were discussing the shooting of the chauffeur.

"Why did they kill him?" Bering asked Michael.

"It doesn't concern you."

"I'm curious."

"All right," Michael said. "They didn't trust him. He sold you out for money, so he could sell them out for money, too."

"What about you, Mike—what did you sell me out for?"

In English, one of the masked men said, "Enough talking, you."

"Not for money," Michael said, "but for a cause I believe in."

The rear doors opened, and the two men who had carried the chauffeur's body away jumped in. They pulled the doors shut and latched them. The van began to back and fill. Through the window to the cab, Bering saw the driver's hand pulling at the ski mask. It lifted away, and a fall of sleek long hair tumbled down over the black-clad shoulders.

"Ah," Bering said to Michael, "the cause you believe in."

The man who had spoken before said, "Quiet, CIA bastard!"

"Oh boy," Bering said, "have *you* guys made a mistake."

The man made a threatening gesture. Michael restrained him. The van had straightened out, and now it was getting up speed.

"Don't make them mad," Michael said. "Just sit quietly."

Bering took his finger out of his mouth and put his cigar in instead. He drew on the cigar, trying to bring it back to life.

He said to Michael, "Ask them if they have a match."

Michael stared at him.

"You're paid up till the end of the month. Ask them."

"They don't smoke."

"Wouldn't you know it?"

Bering sucked at the wet end of the cigar. It tasted of cold ashes.

One

Zayde, her grandfather, would have called it *potchkying,* a Yiddish verb blithely combined with an English participial ending, which translated as doing aimless, mindless busywork. It was not Juno Sultan's nature to *potchky,* but today she was teetering on a knife edge of tension—and what else would you expect of someone who, please God, was about to make a fool of the government of the United States of America?

So she fussed nervously, standing in front of the full-length mirror in the bedroom, calling into question for the tenth or twentieth time this or that detail of her disguise.

She glanced at her watch. More *potchkying;* she had looked at it a few seconds ago. It was ten minutes of three, about a half hour before Luis was due to come for her. She checked over her reflection in the mirror again, squinting through the steel-rimmed eyeglasses at her image, willing herself to see it as a stranger might: a dowdy woman with black hair ("What do you want to buy *that* color for, when you have such a gorgeous color of your own?" the salesgirl had said) escaping in wisps from under the cheap gray felt hat with its broad floppy brim; beneath it a shapeless dull brown dress with blue trim, falling to an unflattering hemline between the calf and the ankle, an old woman's dress with the sad air of being a hand-me-down (which it was—she had bought it for two dollars at a rummage store); a short summer coat of a dusty melancholy pink, illogically pleated in the back, which she had scavenged from the incinerator floor, pouncing on it as another woman might a new mink coat; heavy support nylons that bagged at the ankles; clodhopper shoes. But the heart of her disguise was the atrocious posture—shoulders bent toward a caved-in chest, head inclined on a downward bias that bespoke shyness, recessiveness, resignation from the pleasures of life.

Closer to the mirror, bending her head toward it, she caught a sudden glint of violet. Damn! The violet eyes were a giveaway. She had thought of wearing dark glasses, but that would have made her conspicuous; one didn't wear sun shades at night. She adjusted the brim of the hat, pulling it down to mask her eyes.

Then, all at once, she was swept by despair. The figure in the mirror was totally transparent, unmistakably Juno Sultan in masquerade, as unlikely to fool anybody as a child wearing her mother's high heels. How had she ever hoped to bring it off? What experience did she have with intrigue, how could she dream of prevailing against professionals? Then a spark of violet flashed in the mirror. She wasn't a quitter, she never had been, and when the fate of her own dear Michael was at stake . . . She straightened up with resolve. No! Not that! She let her body go slack, shoulders turned inward, chest hollow, and she was a frump again. Simply because she could see through the disguise herself didn't mean that others could.

She turned away from the mirror and surveyed the room. Neat as a pin, nothing lying around. If burglars broke in in her absence they would have no complaints about her as a housekeeper. Her bags—the valise tagged with the airline label, and the roomy shlep bag—were in the entry hall, together with the shoddy black plastic pocketbook she had bought. When Luis came, everything would be at hand, waiting. She had even watered her plants, though God knew if they would survive until they got their next watering.

The face of her watch barely showed any change from her last inspection of it. She sighed and went to the window. On this warmish late October afternoon the street, viewed from her eighth floor window, preserved its air of East Side elegance: a handsome lady walking an expensive dog, a doorman who had opened a taxi door pausing for a moment to feel the sun on his back, the cars going by sedately where they might have rushed through a meaner street. And, of course, the gray car—occupying its space beside the fire hydrant, flaunting its exemption from the rules.

The car never followed her when she went out; there were others who did that. It was simply there as a reminder to her that she was being watched and that the watchers were implacable in their intention of seeing that she stayed put. As for the two men in the front seat, they too were formidable in their way, they and the interchangeable teams who replaced them to keep a round-the-clock vigil. *See, lady, we never sleep.* However bored or restless or cramped they might become in the car, she had never seen them stretch, or yawn, or slouch in weariness, or smoke. *See how incredibly disciplined we are, lady? See how foolish it would be to try to pull something funny?*

Well, at the risk of being foolish, something funny was exactly what she was trying to pull. And if it worked she would soon be sheltering Michael in her arms.

Below, the men in the car appeared to be chatting, facing each other at opposite ends of the seat. What could they have left to say to each other after two weeks of close confinement? They were both neat and clean-cut and well dressed, and their gestures were reserved and sparing. In a confrontation they would be polite and correct with her, but no less firm or, if it came to that, ruthless.

She had read all of that in the man who called himself Fernald, who had arrived two weeks ago, the day she had heard about Michael's kidnapping, and, on the television news broadcasts, proclaimed her determination to go to Italy in an effort to see Michael. Who "called himself" Fernald? How easy it was to slip into the language of melodrama. Actually, his name had been on his credentials. She hadn't paid any attention to them, except to take note of the seal of the United States and his name, so she still didn't know who they were, what agency of the government they represented, except that they weren't the New York City police.

If she had had any doubts about that, they had been dispelled by an incident she had observed from her window. Shortly after they had begun their surveillance—another word in the lexicon of melodrama; since when were ordinary matrons kept under surveillance?—a police car pulled up beside the gray car. Two uniformed cops got out and signaled to the driver of the gray car that they wanted the window rolled down. Without haste the window opened, and a hand came out, proffering, with an air of boredom, a wallet or card case. While the two cops studied it, the hand remained outside the car, palm up, twitching slightly with an impatience that bordered on insolence. After a brief discussion with the man in the car (the second man never even turned his head toward the cops), one of the cops went back to his squad car and spoke on the radio. When he returned, he put the card case in the still upturned palm, and then both cops touched their hat brims and drove off. The palm withdrew lazily, and the window was rolled up.

That incident alone bespoke the presence of a government agency on a pretty high level. So did the fact that there was always a man hanging around in the garage beneath the house, and another near the delivery entrance. The board of directors of luxury cooperatives didn't lightly put up with such goings-on unless they were instructed. So she knew that the watchers—surveillers?—had both clout and manpower. She had become paranoiac of late, and begun to see them everywhere. When a new porter had appeared on the scene she was sure that he was a plant. But he had turned out to be Luis's cousin, newly arrived from Colombia.

The phone rang, as abrupt and startling as a peal of thunder. It was Jerry, she had no doubt about it, making his afternoon call from the hospital. And as always, the trilling of the bell revived her anxieties about him, even though his doctors kept assuring her that he was recovering from the episode in timely fashion. "Episode"—that repellent clinical word that was so coldly inadequate to describe the primitive, almost prophetic fright of a heart attack.

Jerry phoned her three times a day, morning, afternoon, and evening, even after she had spent hours at his bedside. Today she had not gone to the hospital. She had been unsure of her ability to dissemble, and feared that he would somehow read her secret. When you had been married for twenty-odd years you became as transparent as glass.

The phone continued to ring. She thought of escaping it by going to another room, but, excepting the bathrooms, there wasn't a room that didn't have a phone. "Take the phones out of this place," Jerry always joked, "and AT&T would have to file for bankruptcy." The phone rang, and she let it go on. She knew that the phone was bugged, and the phone in Jerry's hospital room as well, and the room itself. That insight had occurred to her almost inadvertently, ironically from something Jerry had said.

It was the evening of the day she had gotten the note from the Forze Scarlatte. She had gone to the hospital at night, bursting with the news. But she had been sidetracked by a series of irrelevancies. First, Jerry had scolded her for coming at night. He thought it wasn't safe, even though she took a taxi.

"I had to come here. I couldn't talk over the phone. You know why."

Jerry looked exasperated. "How many times do I have to say it? Nobody bugs people like you and me."

But nobody parked a car in front of a house for twenty-four hours a day, either, or had teams of men following her wherever she went. To defuse the possibility of an argument, she said jokingly, "For people who can park permanently in front of a hydrant the sky is the limit."

He adverted to another familiar theme. "They're professionals, it's their trade. Try to get it through your head that these people are using all their skill and bending every effort to *help* Michael."

"Effort and skill, yes, but not passion. I'm his mother. Nobody has as big a stake in Michael as I do."

Jerry was hurt, and it took her a moment to realize why.

"Except you. Naturally. You're his father."

But he wasn't yet ready to be mollified. "Yes, me too, you ought to keep that in mind. I love him very much."

It was true, of course. Jerry had a fierce capacity for affection, and never mind that he and Michael disagreed on practically everything. Surely she didn't love Sharon any the less because they quarreled. It was just that she didn't *adore* Sharon, merely loved her very much, as Jerry didn't *adore* Michael, but loved him very much. Yet she was sure it was the kidnapping that had been responsible for Jerry's heart attack.

She said, "That's just the point. If you weren't in bed with a heart attack..."

"I'm not in bed. I'm sitting up in a chair. Can't you see I'm sitting in a chair?"

Ever since the heart attack Jerry's usual good nature had turned *kvetchy*. He was an active man, and the enforced bed rest had made him ill-tempered. Moreover, his illness seemed to have leeched something vital out of him, The old Jerry would never have defended the authorities, but defied them.

She said, "Never mind." She moved closer to him and lowered her voice. "I've got something to tell you."

"What are you whispering about?"

"They got in touch with me—the terrorists."

While he stared at her, shaking his head slowly in disbelief, she told him how the letter had been slipped into the pocket of her coat as she was going into Bloomie's. Feeling the slight tug, her first thought had been that somebody had tried to pick her pocket. By the time she found the envelope and saw its inscription: *SIGNORA SULTAN, a mano,* whoever had given it to her must have been long gone, and in any event would have been impossible to pick out in the crowds pushing in and out of the doors. She had had the presence of mind to go through the motions of shopping—mindful that *they* would be watching her—and then hurried home, double-bolted the door, read the letter, and looked longingly at the picture.

"Let's see it," Jerry said. He was pale.

She handed him the envelope. He removed the letter, glanced at it, and put it aside. It was written in Italian. He devoured the picture with his eyes. It showed Michael, facing head on, in a rather stiff pose, sitting in a chair with a newspaper. He had let his beard grow out; it was dense and black. In the picture of Bering and Michael that the Forze Scarlatte had sent to the newspapers immediately after the kidnapping, Michael had been clean shaven.

"The paper is the Paris Tribune," Juno said. "The date on it is October twenty-second, ten days after he was captured. I read it with a magnifying glass."

Jerry's lips twitched in a forlorn smile. "He's got a beard just like mine. Ten days and it's already flourishing." He picked up the letter. "What does this thing say?"

"It says that if I can get to Italy they'll let me see Michael."

"You believe that crap?"

"It doesn't matter. My watchers won't let me get away."

And that was the small beginning of her series of lies, though technically it wasn't a lie at all. While it was true that they didn't want her to get away, she had already made up her mind to try.

"I want you to promise me that you won't do anything dumb."

Promise? That was something else. She didn't say anything.

"Juno," Jerry said quietly, "come here." She got up and took his hand, and he leaned forward and rested his head against her stomach. "That's all I would need. Michael gone, and then you too. You know what that would do to me?"

She disengaged herself gently and went back to her chair and picked up the letter. "Listen to what they say." She read silently for a moment, recasting the letter into English. " 'We have seen the television wherein you called out your determination to see your son at all costs. We have heeded this cry from the heart which has moved us deeply. The Forze Scarlatte do not make war against the tenderness of motherhood. It is the most stirring of all emotions, the very root of humanity.' They're Italian, they're a little flowery. 'Our struggle is against the forces of repression, of colonialism, of authoritarian darkness, which is merely another way of declaring our affirmation of the basic goodness of mankind—' "

She stopped. Jerry wasn't listening; he was tilting the picture of Michael on a slant, studying its edge. "The picture is cut."

She was surprised that it had taken him so long to notice it. She had worked out what she would say, but to her relief Jerry said it for her.

"I guess there was something in it they didn't want to be seen." He put the picture down. "What else does the letter say?"

"That's about it. Just more of the same kind of thing."

"You're whispering again. For God's sake, Juno, you're not talking on the phone. Or have you got it into your head that the goddamned room is bugged too?"

Yes, she thought, I've been dumb. Yes! If they had the resources to bug the phones they could bug a hospital room as well; in fact, it was a certainty, if they were at all thorough, that if they did the one, they would inevitably do the other. She picked up the picture, put it back into the envelope with the letter, and returned it to her bag.

"You're holding out on me," Jerry said. "There *has* to be something in the letter about how to contact them."

Calmly, and with a cunning that surprised her, she said, "They want me to come to Milan, to the Duomo. . . . But what's the difference if I can't get away?"

Lying, she thought, was like diving into an icy pool. Once you got wet, it wasn't bad at all.

The phone had stopped ringing.

She went back to the bedroom and stood in front of the mirror again, backing off for a full-length view, willing herself to be objective about her image. She squinted her eyes to eliminate the violet beam. Yes, fine, she was facing a dowdy woman of indeterminate middle age, a *shlump*, a person with a gray, uninflected life. . . .

A ringing again. But it wasn't the phone, it was softer—the chime of the doorbell. She slammed the closet door shut and strode out of the bedroom in her erect, long-limbed way, until she remembered and let her shoulders cave in. She opened the door.

Luis was there, dark and plump, still in his street clothing, checked trousers and a white short-sleeved shirt with a blue and yellow collar. He looked somber, in contrast to his usual cheeriness. He was worried; she should never have accepted his offer to help, never have let him become involved.

"Good day, Mrs. Sultan."

She could almost feel the downward drag of her mouth, the near appearance of tears in her eyes. Luis looked at her in alarm.

"Mrs. Sultan, you are all right?"

"You knew me right away."

"No, no." Luis was quick, and a born diplomat. He shook his head emphatically. "If I meet you on the street, I never know it is you. But when I ring the bell in 8B, it has to be Mrs. Sultan, no matter how she look. On the street, I pass you by, I never know. Never!"

She smiled at him—not the pursed-lip twitch she had been practicing but her own generously wide smile. "Thank you, Luis, you're very nice."

"Nothing. It is the truth. You are ready?'

She nodded, suddenly excited, feeling a pleasant thrill of adventure- someness. Luis slung the tote bag over his shoulder and picked up the valise. The phone rang. Luis looked at her inquiringly. She hesitated. It was Jerry again. He was a bulldog, he never gave up. Luis started to set the bags down.

"Never mind," she said. "Let it ring."

"We go?"

She nodded. The phone trilled on. Luis opened the door a crack and peered out into the hallway. "Is okay. Nobody."

It was typical of a luxury building, Juno thought, that you rarely saw anyone in the hallways, unlike the dowdy low-rise apartment houses of her childhood where people were constantly coming and going. It was a phenomenon she didn't understand, but it was a fact. There was a treatise there somewhere; maybe she would ask Sharon, the budding sociologist, about it one day. What—and risk an exasperated "Oh, Mother, *please*..."?

The door to the service elevator stood open. She followed Luis inside and he shut the door. The elevator was much larger than the passenger cars, lined with tan quilted pads and smelling of must. Luis started the elevator downward.

"Even now," he said earnestly, "I have hard time recognizing it is you."

He was watching the lights flicker on the indicator above the door. The elevator reached the lobby floor, beyond which the passenger cars would not descend as a security measure. She watched the indicator: SC (for subcellar) one through six. At SC2 the car stopped. Luis peered out cautiously when the door opened.

He nodded. "Okay. I am late, so nobody will be here."

The day men left at three, and the new crew came on. At twenty past three the cellar would be clear of both the departing and the arriving crews.

She said, "I'm worried about your getting into trouble on my account."

He motioned her to follow him out of the elevator. "No, no. I told the super I would be late. I said my little boy was sick."

She followed him through winding passageways, gray cement floors the color of dust, calcimined concrete walls. They skirted a pile of coiled wire and electric cable, then a workshop with a single bulb lit over a table heaped with tools. Luis paused for a brief instant to show her a large room paneled in imitation knotty pine, furnished with armchairs, a long table strewn with magazines and newspapers, a sofa, a break-front, a television set and, against the rear wall, a cluster of metal lockers. It wa a combination of clubhouse and dressing room.

"This is our place," Luis said. "For the help only."

She said it was very nice, and they went on. More winding passageways of whitewashed walls and gray floors. Surely the house couldn't be this big; surely Luis had lost his way and doubled back. But then they came to a vast enclosure of slatted wood reaching to the ceiling. Inside was a warren of bins, each enclosed by its own slats, each crammed with household goods. It was the storage area, a honeycomb of private cells; one to a tenant, containing surplus furnishings: sofas, chairs, lamps, tables, outdoor furniture, valises—things that were not wanted in the apartment but were considered too valuable to be thrown away, yet not valuable enough to be worth selling, and so were left, perhaps out of lethargy, to molder in the damp subcellar. Her own rationalization, which was probably shared by many other tenants, was that the stuff might come in handy one day—when one of the children married, or, as they did more often these days, established a live-in relationship. Michael had corrected her mischievously one day. "Relationship is stuffy, Mother, we call it shacked up." Of course, she was sure that when Sharon got married, or shacked up, as the case might be, she would absolutely refuse to touch a stick of it—and there was no question in Juno's mind that "stick of it" was precisely the phrase Sharon would use. As for Michael, he would accept everything she offered, whether he wanted it or not, graciously though with a mildly barbed joke that always made her laugh, even when it stung a bit.

Oh, God, Michael, my poor Michael in the hands of murderers, and so far from home...

Luis unlocked the main enclosure, and she followed him through a narrow aisle. At the rear of the enclosure he stopped before a door hidden behind the back partition of one of the indivudial bins. The door was brown, thickly painted over, bolted by a heavy iron bar running through steel hasps embedded in the wall.

Luis said, "When we still had the incinerator, we took the cans out here, up to the street. But when it was changed to a compactor, they put in the lift to bring the bags up. So they shut this door up and made more bins. Most of the workers here do not know about it. But I remembered."

He was quietly prideful. He had been at the house a long time, fifteen years, perhaps more. With the door in mind, knowing her desperation and wanting to be helpful, he had rung her bell a few days ago. She had been deeply moved and grateful. After all, what did he owe to the well-to-do tenants of the building? Did they ever spare a thought for him, ever imagine his evenings with his large family in their tiny rooms in East Harlem? Her fingers touched the bills in her pocket, and she almost felt ashamed to offer money for something that had come out of a wellspring of sympathy and kindness.

There were a few articles of furniture against the wall—an overflow from one of the bins—and dust on the floor near the door, and she understood that Luis had moved furniture to clear the door, and would move it back again when she had gone. She watched him pry the iron bar out of its hasps, first the left side, then the right, then the left again, and push the door open. He brushed rust particles from his hands and picked up the valise and the shlep bag.

She followed him up the long enclosed incline, gloomy and smelling of long-forgotten ashes, to the street level. They stopped in front of another door. There were flakes of paint on the floor; he had worked it free before this, so that it would open easily. He removed the bar and turned to her. "They don' watch this side of the building because they do not know about this door, they think there is not a way out. You understand, Mrs. Sultan?"

She took the wadded roll of money out of the pocket of the pink coat. "Luis, I don't know how to thank you."

He drew back. "No, Mrs. Sultan."

"I'd like you to have it, Luis."

He shook his head, his lips thinned. "I do not do it for money."

She tried to push the money into his hands, but he wouldn't take it. His face was impassive, but she knew that she had offended him. She put the money back into her pocket.

"Will you let me tell you how grateful I am, Luis?"

"Thank you." He relaxed. "God be with you, lady."

"And you, Luis."

"I hope you will have success."

He handed her the valise and tote bag. He pushed the door open, peered out, and then stepped back. She slipped by him and the door shut behind her. There were a few pedestrians further up the street. She moved out of the shadow of the building to the sunlit curb. She set the bags down. There was a cab across the avenue, stopped by a red light. She started to wave to it, but another cab swung around the corner. She signaled and it pulled in to the curb. She opened its rear door, threw her bags onto the seat, then climbed in herself.

"Kennedy Airport," she said.

As the taxi took off she looked back through the rear window. No sign of them. I've made it, she thought exultantly, I've made it. She thought of the two men sitting in the gray car on the wrong street and smiled. Maybe her escape would temper their arrogance, splinter their self-confidence. It might even drive them to smoke.

*　*　*

The driver pushed his meter flag down, closed his glass partition, and picked up the radio microphone. He said, "Going to Kennedy."

"Fine, take her to Kennedy."

"And then?"

"And then see if you can pick up a passenger back to town, and then turn in the cab. Mission accomplished."

"Is this some kind of a joke?"

"Sorry. The game has been changed. We *want* her out."

"*They* want her out, you mean. Fernald wants her out. Why couldn't somebody tell me, chrissake?"

"Need to know—you're just a taxi driver. Take her to Kennedy."

"I *hate* the way those high-toned bastards operate," the driver said. "I hate the idea of the Bureau reduced to doing their donkey work."

"Well, we're all working for the same country, aren't we?"

"Sometimes I wonder about that."

"Don't be bitter. Over and out."

Two

From time to time, when the lobby was empty, Diebold would walk from his niche behind the doorman's desk to the bank of elevators, and study the indicators showing the location of the two passenger cars and the freight elevator. Now, at a quarter past three, the freight car was stopped at the eighth floor, and he became immediately alert. Suspicion was his natural mode—his stock in trade, he might have called it—though he defined it for himself as "creative curiosity."

For Diebold, action ratified thought: he punched the signal buttons and when one of the passenger cars came down to the lobby, got in and rode it up to the eighth floor. He paused for a moment to check the freight elevator. It was no longer at eight; the indicator was clicking, the car was descending.

He sprinted along the carpeted hall to 8B and pressed his ear to the door. A phone was ringing. He waited for four more rings before running back to the elevator banks. He pressed the signal button for the passenger cars. The freight car was no longer moving. It was stopped at SC2.

A passenger car arrived and took him down to the lobby. He got out, jostling a woman who was waiting to enter, and dashed across the lobby to the doorman.

"Give me the key to the cellar staircase. Hurry, please."

With his usual thoroughness, he had found out about the staircase from the manager of the building on his arrival. He had taken an early morning plane up from Washington yesterday morning, although his instructions were to meet Fernald at the safe house at three thirty this afternoon. It was his credo—by which he meant a combination of technique and life-style—to do more than was expected of him and, at the same time, to assert his independence of the chain of command without overtly flouting it: nobody had told him *not* to arrive a day early.

"I asked you to hurry."

The doorman raised his eyebrows. Diebold was familiar with his type—he had probably been with the house since it had been built, and had an inflated sense of his own importance. He was proprietary about his lobby, and had in fact told Diebold that it reflected on the quality of a house to have someone hang around in the lobby, even though he was more or less hidden in the niche. Diebold had given him one of those cold gray looks that were a part of his arsenal of intimidation, but said nothing.

The doorman was fishing in his pants pocket, but he was taking his own sweet time. Diebold stepped closer to him and said in a low voice, "If I don't have that key in five seconds, I'm going to smash the bridge of your nose."

The doorman's eyes turned watery, and he produced the key. Diebold snatched it away and strode back to the polished brass security door to the right rear of the lobby. He unlocked the door and found himself on a suspended steel staircase that vibrated springily under his feet as he ran down. At the second landing he went through a black-painted door marked SC2. A few steps inside he found the empty freight elevator. The cellar branched off to the right and left. He went right, running swiftly and lightly, through a maze of narrow calcimined passageways. He saw and heard nothing. Ending up at a blank wall of concrete blocks, he retraced his steps to the elevator and then struck off to the left branch. When he saw a faint light coming through an open door, he stopped, edged up to it, and peered around the jamb. The room was a workshop. It was empty. He moved on until he saw another spread of light. This time it came from a sort of improvised lounge, and there was a man inside, partially concealed by an open locker door. He was stripped to the waist. A sign over the locker was lettered LUIS.

Diebold slipped into the room and eased up behind the man. "Where is she?"

Luis whirled around, startled, his brown eyes wide. "Who are you? What are you doing here?"

"Never mind who I am. Where is she?"

Luis turned into the locker and lifted out a gray shirt with his name picked in red thread over the pocket. His lips were shut in a thin tight line. Not the sign of a man who knew nothing, Diebold thought, but one who would say nothing.

Speaking very slowly, deploying his gray eyes like a pair of matched threats, he said, "I'm going to ask only once more, and then I'm going to hurt you. Where is she?"

"What's the matter with you, man? You crazy?"

Diebold hit him in the mouth, slamming him back against the steel locker. Before he could straighten up Diebold hit him again, in the same place, and split his lips open. Luis sagged, his eyes blurred with pain and fear. Diebold grabbed his shirt front and pinned him against the locker. Blood was dribbling from his mashed lips onto his chin.

"Where is she?" His voice was flat, almost monotone.

"I don't know what you talking—"

Diebold slammed him against the locker. "Listen to me, you dumb monkey. I know you took her out of her apartment and down in the freight elevator. You understand what I'm saying?"

Grimacing with pain, Luis shook his head, but when Diebold tapped his jaw with a clenched fist, just hard enough to jar him, he shrank back and changed the movement to a nod.

"Mrs. Sultan, that's who we're talking about—right?"

"Yes." Luis touched his pulpy lips, and stared at his bloodstained fingers. "Mrs. Sultan. Yes. Don't hit me no more."

"Where did Mrs. Sultan go?"

"I don't know," Luis said. Diebold slammed him against the locker. Luis's face screwed up in pain. He said, "She is gone."

"I know that. Where did she go?"

"She din' tell me. I don' know."

Diebold hit him a short jolting blow to the ribs. Luis let out a sharp cry and doubled over.

"Where did she go?"

"You hurting me bad. Please." A trickle of blood came out of one of his nostrils. His eyes were filled with tears.

"Where did she go?"

Diebold hit him in the ribs again, a short thudding blow. Luis's eyes fluttered shut and he started to sag. Blood was spraying from his nose in a fine mist. Diebold held him erect, propping him against the locker, waiting for his eyes to open.

"Where did she go?" He tapped his clenched fist lightly against Luis's jaw. Luis recoiled, sobbing.

"Don' hit me no more. I tell you."

"Yes?"

"She go to the airport."

"Kennedy?"

"Yes."

"Which airline?"

"Pan Am."

He was ripe now, Diebold thought, it was just a question of shaking the tree by asking the right questions. "She has a ticket to Milan?"

"Yes, yes, she go to Milan."

"You're lying," Diebold said. It was standard procedure, just an extra turn of the screw as a precaution.

"No, no, it is true. I swear to you."

But there was a hint of panic in his voice, and his shifting eyes might have been animals scurrying for cover. Diebold jabbed him in his sore mouth, not too hard; he was close to going out. "Talk to me."

His eyes were crazed with fear, and it poured out of him in a babble of English and Spanish, but Diebold knew enough Spanish to piece it together. When he started repeating himself Diebold knew there was no more to be told. He stepped back and Luis slumped to the floor.

"Get up," Diebold said.

"No, you hit me again."

"I won't hit you again. Stand up."

Slowly, fearfully, Luis pushed himself to his feet, his back pressed against the locker, not so much for support as to keep at a distance from Diebold. Tears were flowing down his cheeks, diluting the seepage of blood from his nose and mouth.

Diebold studied him critically. He was a hospital case, no question about it. He would talk, spill his guts, and there would be a police investigation. There was no way of explaining this to the man, nor any need for it, so he simply said, "You gave me a very hard time."

Luis, reading his eyes, tried to scream, but there wasn't enough time for it. Diebold spun him around, knocked away his arms, and broke his neck. The sound of snapping bone was sharp and crisp. Diebold lowered him to the floor.

It was now eight days that Strawberry had been sitting at the airport and he was sick of it. But he understood the problem. They were unable to watch the subject's house because of the presence of the opposition's agents there, and so were obliged to cover the terminals of each of the four airlines that flew to Italy. Therefore, they were stretched thin.

Strawberry did not know why the lady was important, other than that Grigoriev had said so, but that was reason enough. At least he knew her name, which was more than could be said for some of the people he had liquidated in the line of duty.

However you looked at it, it was an extremely boring assignment, the only relief—if you could call it that—being that they rotated terminals every second day in order to avoid being conspicuous. Given the nature of airport waiting rooms, it was a distinction without a difference.

He had risked making a complaint to Grigoriev the other night, and Grigoriev, predictably enough, had been unsympathetic.

"They also serve who only sit and wait, Zemlyanika."

That was one of Grigoriev's tags. Pushkin, perhaps? He wasn't sure, and feared to risk a wrong guess that would invite Grigoriev's scorn. It had been friendly of Grigoriev to use his nickname, Strawberry, but beyond that he had been abrupt.

"You know, Comrade Grigoriev, this really isn't my métier. I would much prefer—"

"We have discussed this before. It doesn't matter what you prefer."

"But my entire career, my specialty—"

"Goodnight, Zemlyanika."

And that was that. But it was nonetheless true that he was unsuited for this dull detective work. He had been trained to kill, which was the area of his competence as well as the work that was congenial to his temperament. When he had been given this assignment he had pleaded with Grigoriev, even protested being asked to perform work that he thought of as menial. He had grumbled that it had been many months since he had last been asked to perform his specialty, and, incidentally, Comrade Colonel, executed—a little joke—his task in an exemplary fashion. Grigoriev had replied that to anyone with an ounce of sense it should be obvious that there wasn't much need for killing these days, and that they just couldn't let him sit around and do nothing. One way or another he had to earn his keep.

Strawberry understood that Arabs were being used for killing, but he was too discreet to say so. He regarded Arabs as crude, emotional, ideologically unsound assassins. He hoped that their use was just temporary, a matter of policy for the moment, and that professionals like himself would soon be restored to full duty. Otherwise, his aptitudes would atrophy, and eventually he would become technologically unemployed. Another little joke, and not half bad. He would have to try it on one of the others, perhaps even Grigoriev, if he should happen to catch him in an exceptionally good mood.

It was stuffy in the terminal. He would have liked to loosen his tie and open the button of his collar, but to do so would expose the strawberry marks spattered on his neck and collarbone. His nickname was known to the opposition and the tiny pink dots would be a giveaway.

So he sweated uncomfortably in the terminal, with the specially made high-rise collar tightly buttoned, amid sprawling groups of young Americans, most of them standby passengers, and their clutter of backpacks and cheap suitcases and guitars. Many of them, men and women alike, smoked pot constantly. When they weren't falling into blank silences they would talk and laugh a great deal, usually at nothing. Their conversation was infantile—it dealt with popular songs and singers, with sex in a joking way, with where to get good quality marijuana, or "dope," as they called it. Never a serious topic, never politics, never philosophy. They struck him as being imbeciles.

Yet he chose to sit among them. By studying their manners and their mode of speech he could learn much. His English was excellent but tended to be academic; he was shaky on idiom and puzzled by slang. By listening to these young fools he had already improved his vocabulary in the vulgate. Less seriously, he enjoyed looking at the young women. They were quite attractive, and their candid, casual sexuality excited him. Few of them wore brassieres, and since they were young they were very well formed. Frequently he had been aroused, and allowed himself to dwell on the thought of having one of them. With his rangy blond good looks—more than once he had been told he resembled a certain prominent baseballer—a conquest would have been simple, but in the circumstances it was out of the question. Where could he have taken a young lady—to Grigoriev's office in the Mission?

He smiled at the notion of profaning Grigoriev's somewhat tatty Tabriz rug by performing a sexual act on it. He shut his eyes to visualize the happy scene and presently dozed off. When he opened his eyes, he saw the subject coming through the entrance to the terminal—in person, not a motion picture, as the Americans said. It occurred to him, in dismay, that if he had not waked at this point he might have missed her altogether, although he was practiced at taking catnaps and rarely dozed for more than a minute or two at a time.

She was carrying a valise and a large canvas bag. He recognized her immediately, although he had never seen her, except for her picture, or, more accurately, many pictures, taken from many angles. Her disguise had not fooled him for an instant. Like the amateur she was, she had tried methodically and predictably to camouflage each of her salient features. Which, of course, was to give herself away to the practiced eye. But the disguise was a failure in another, more basic way: all the poor posture, the dowdy clothing, the diffident attitude couldn't conceal the fullness of her figure and the distinctiveness of her carriage. A Thoroughbred race horse in the traces of a cart remained a Thoroughbred. Making her, as the American police put it, had been laughably easy.

He lit a cigarette in a leisurely way, rose from the plastic bench, and picked a route through the sprawled young bodies and their litter. Stretching languidly, he observed her as she presented her tickets to the clerk at the check-in counter. He glanced up at the departure board. No delay: the plane for Milan was scheduled to leave at 6:30.

Strawberry was pleased, now that he had seen the subject, that his assignment was not to kill. How much more attractive she was than the young women whose breasts he had been admiring; even at her age and in her ridiculous disguise, she put them to shame. Yes, he was glad that he did not have to kill her. Much more to his taste would be to have her on Grigoriev's Tabriz. True, Grigoriev had told him, perhaps as a sop to his complaints, that his instructions were provisional, that in the end he might yet be called on to eliminate her.

If so, of course, he would perform efficiently, as always. But perhaps his enjoyment would be tempered by a tinge of regret?

Nonsense, Strawberry, a job is a job, and there is no place in a technician for bourgeois sentimentality.

The stooping, self-effacing posture was in a sense a retrieval from Juno's past. For almost a year in her life she had tried to disguise her figure, particularly her breasts, by caving herself in around them. She had been barely twelve, but already her body had bloomed in a sudden eruption of womanliness. "Wonderful *zaftig,*" Zayde had said with approval. Her early development had been a source of embarrassment to her, even of shame, although she was aware, at the same time, that she was attractive to boys (and, to her horror and disgust, observing the quickening of their eye as they glanced at her, to grown men, too). What troubled her was that her maturing body made her conspicuous among her contemporaries. At that age one wanted desperately to be like everybody else. Being different was freaky.

And so, in a way, her past had reinvented itself in the present.

She crossed the crowded terminal waiting room to the check-in counter, where, unexpectedly, she had a bad moment. After the clerk tagged her valise for the flight to Milan, he picked up her shlep bag, which she had placed on the counter. With a little shriek, she snatched it away from him.

"Sorry, I didn't mean to grab. I'm taking it on the plane with me."

She walked away from the counter with her cheeks burning. She had almost made a scene and called attention to herself. Suppose somebody had been watching her? And here she was walking upright! Quickly, she lowered her head, hunched her shoulders toward each other, and, barely looking to left or right, threaded her way through the crowd to the ladies' room.

She placed the shlep bag on the floor between her feet and looked at herself in the mirror. The wire-rimmed eyeglasses, the black wig straggling out of the floppy hat, struck her once again as being utterly unconvincing, a costume for an amateur theatrical. The door opened, and from the corner of her eye she saw a woman range herself at the next basin. Juno turned on the tap and washed her hands. With her head bowed, she took a sidelong glance into the mirror. The woman was wearing a handsome salmon-colored silk pants suit, and she was patting her hair. But she wasn't looking at her hair; the woman was looking at her.

Juno turned off the tap and pulled a paper towel from a container. She dried her hands with her back to the woman. When she faced about, the woman was staring at her quite openly. In a panic she darted into the nearest booth, locked the door, and sat down. And then she felt a fool. The woman had probably seen her picture in the newspapers, or on that memorable television broadcast, and either recognized her or, more likely, was simply struck by a vaguely familiar face.

Juno leaned forward, hoping to hear the woman's footsteps, the sound of the door opening and shutting. But there was nothing; no sign that the woman was entering a booth or washing her hands. How long could a woman stand in front of a mirror and pat her hair? Maybe...She thought back to that long-ago summer when she had played the pro tennis circuit, and discovered to her surprise, innocent that she was, that she was attractive to women as well as to men, and had to fend off ardent admirers in the shower. But what could such a smartly turned-out woman find to covet in the frump she had been eyeing?

She thought of piddling to justify her being in the booth, but settled instead for flushing the toilet as a concession to verisimilitude. When she came out, the woman was still bent toward the mirror, but then she faced about and looked at her directly, with an open arrogant scrutiny. Juno became suddenly angry.

"Why are you staring at me?"

The woman calmly stroked a lapel of her suit. "That hat, honey. I simply can't believe it."

Just a bitch, Juno thought with relief, an astringent bitch who enjoyed making people feel uncomfortable.

"I'll tell you, though," the woman said thoughtfully, "if I had your chest I would stand up very straight. Just a little tip, honey."

The woman shrugged and went out. Juno looked at her watch. The airline should be announcing her flight before long, but it might be a good idea to wait in the safety of the ladies' room until then, rather than risk the waiting room, where she would be exposed to anyone who was watching for her. Meanwhile, there was a lesson to be learned from the encounter with the woman in the salmon suit: you could scare yourself to death without reason.

The door opened, and a pair of middle-aged women came in. Juno turned on the tap and began to wash her hands again. The women went into adjoining booths, and presently she heard the sound of piddling. Good, Juno thought, all's right with the world.

If Strawberry had been unable to buy a ticket he would have informed Grigoriev, who would have arranged to have someone pick the subject up at Malpensa Airport in Milan. Still, that would have removed him from the game, so he was pleased that there was a seat available.

He phoned Grigoriev. "I've got her, Comrade. She has a ticket to Milan, and so have I."

"Very good," Grigoriev said. "We'll have some backup for you in Milan."

"I don't need help. It's a simple matter. She was wearing a sort of disguise, you know, but the instant she entered the airport—"

"Zemlyanika?"

"Yes, Comrade Colonel?"

"Don't talk so much," Grigoriev said, and hung up.

Strawberry strolled casually through the terminal, but there was no sign of her. She was doubtless still in the w.c., where he had seen her go after leaving the check-in counter. It was the natural place for her to hole up if she was worried about the Americans' spotting her. He bought a sports magazine and took up a post at a distance from the ladies' room. He had extremely sharp eyesight, which, along with his height, was a virtue in surveillance work: you could maintain a good distance between yourself and your quarry, and still see what was going on.

He immersed himself in his magazine until he heard the Milan flight being announced. Then he focused on the door to the ladies' room. He picked her up at once when she came out, noting with a smile that, after starting out with a brisk stride, she suddenly remembered her disguise and altered her erect bearing to a slump.

There was no hurry. He followed her at a distance until she entered the passageway leading to the departure gate, then stopped at a quick food stand for coffee. Why sit in the airplane any longer than he had to?

The coffee was very hot and quite good, better coffee, one had to admit, without admitting anything else, than one could normally get in Moscow, although there wasn't much to be said for the degenerate Styrofoam cup it came in.

* * *

The crowd that had flowed into the passageway as soon as the Milan flight had been announced clotted up at the entry checkpoint. Juno was content to be in the center of it. After passing through the metal-detector device she started off down the long tunnel-like walk. The first waiting room bay was empty. The next bay was the designated gate for the Milan flight. She went by it without a glance, and turned into the third bay; it was a London flight, due to depart ten minutes before the Milan plane. The bay was full of waiting passengers. She pushed through the crowd to the glass wall that looked out onto the field. Through it she could see silvery planes cumbersomely taxiing or turning.

She pressed against the glass, with her back to the thickening crowd. She had no way of knowing whether she had been observed since she had left the ladies' room. There were unavoidable risks at every turn, and she could do no more than hope that she had been clever—or lucky—enough to have brought it off.

There was a delay in boarding the London plane, and the crowd in the bay became denser. When the gate to the plane was opened at last, and the crowd began to push through, she slipped out of the bay. In the next bay, the Milan flight was boarding; all but a few passengers were already through the gate. She walked by swiftly, and went back through the long passageway to the entry checkpoint. The two attendants—a young woman and a burly man—watched her approach.

"Something terrible happened, I have to miss the flight. I forgot to take my insulin, I'm a diabetic, it's a matter of life and death...."

She babbled on breathlessly. The attendants nodded sympathetically.

"I *never* go anywhere without it. I can hardly *believe* that I forgot it today of all days...."

The attendants looked understanding, but they really weren't listening.

Enough, Juno, no need for overkill. She sighed. "So I guess I'll have to try to leave tomorrow."

The attendants asked if she had boarded the plane before turning back, checked her name against their passenger list, and advised her to stop at the reservation desk on the way out. She thanked them and went through the passage into the main entrance hall and then out through the exit.

There was a short wait for a taxi. "The TWA terminal, please."

The driver groaned; he had expected a long profitable haul into Manhattan.

She said firmly, "TWA, please."

She would make it up to him with a very generous tip.

34

*   *   *

Diebold booked a first-class seat on TWA flight 45 for Rome, departure time 9:30, then phoned Fernald.

Fernald said, "Ah, Mr. Diebold. May I ask you where the hell you have been?"

"Sorry. I've been busy getting the operation sorted out."

"Have you? Well, in that case you're undoubtedly aware that Mrs. Sultan is taking off for Milan at six thirty, which is, as I reckon it, five minutes from now."

"I think not," Diebold said.

"How odd. Our Bureau friends drove her to the airport themselves."

Diebold could almost see Fernald's pinched nostrils, the lift of his lip in a stiff smile. Fernald never exploded, simply smiled that wintry smile and turned sardonic.

"And—I hope you won't mind my bringing it up?—you were supposed to have been here several hours ago."

"Sir," Diebold said, "may I report?"

"Why yes," Fernald said, "that would be nice."

Diebold told his story calmly, economically, without haste, almost without inflection. When he was finished, Fernald was silent; but his breathing, heavy and labored, was clearly audible. When he spoke, finally, it was in a subdued voice.

"You weren't supposed to have been anywhere near that house, you know."

"Yes, sir, that is so."

"But of course if you hadn't been..." Fernald's tone was grudging. "I suppose there's a limit to how annoyed you can get at a man who's ordered to bunt and hits a home run."

"Thank you."

"She fooled us," Fernald said. "By God, she was cleverer than I would have expected."

"By the way," Diebold said, "we'll want a clean-up job in the second subcellar."

"The subcellar?"

"The *second* subcellar, if you'll remember my report."

"Clean-up job? Look, if you mean what I think you mean—"

Uncharacteristically, Fernald was shouting.

Diebold said, "Ah, there she is. I see her arriving. Will you excuse me, sir?"

He hung up.

He hadn't seen her; it was simply that the conversation with Fernald had become unproductive. He left the phone booth and headed for the first-class lounge.

Strawberry made no attempt to locate the subject when he got on the plane. He settled in his seat, which was up toward the nose, and opened his sports magazine. He felt comfortable and relaxed. There was, after all, something reassuring about tailing somebody in an airplane—you didn't have to exert yourself; your quarry wasn't going anyplace.

After the plane took off he ordered a vodka, which he drank neat, and then a second one. Only then did he decide to reconnoiter. He strolled casually down the aisle. She wasn't in the forward part of the plane, nor, for that matter, in the rear. That is, she wasn't visible, which meant, of course, that she was in one of the w.c.'s. Considering her actions in the airport, he thought with amusement, one would have expected that she was all pissed out by now.

He checked out the first-class section as a precaution, then went back to his seat. No sweating, as the Americans said, she wasn't going anyplace.

Juno balked at the notion of hiding out in the ladies' room until it was time to board the Rome flight. Her success so far had instilled a heady sense of confidence; she had reason to believe that she had thrown off pursuit. But if she had failed, if someone had seen through her strategy and followed her here, there was nothing more she could do. Unless they tried to stop her by force, she would fly to Rome anyway and hope for the best.

So she didn't hide. After checking in, she behaved as a normal tourist would. She joined a long line of people waiting to change their money and bought lire; she browsed over paperback books and magazines, examined the wares for sale in the duty-free shop. An hour before the plane was due to board she climbed the stairs to a bar above the central concourse and ordered a drink and a sandwich. At the bar a man tried to pick her up.

After staring at her from his place two seats away, he moved over to the next stool and said, "Can I buy you a drink?"

She wouldn't have believed it. Wig, eyeglasses, caved-in posture, shlumpy clothes—and he wanted to buy her a drink. Not that he was any bargain himself—a man in his sixties, well-dressed but with washed-out, disappointed eyes behind octagonal-shaped lenses. Maybe that was it—he needed new eyeglasses.

She said, "No, thank you."

"What are you thanking me for? When I buy you a drink, *then* you thank me."

And a joker to boot. She looked at her wristwatch. Another twenty minutes or so and they would be announcing the flight.

The man tried again. "Going someplace?"

"I'm waiting for my husband. He'll be here any minute."

"Then why didn't you say that in the first place?"

He picked up his drink and returned to his original seat. But the mention of her husband reawakened her concern for Jerry. No question that he would have been dialing her every five minutes, fretting at the unanswered ring, fantasizing dire accidents—and so, when the announcement of Flight 45 to Rome came over the PA system, she slipped into a phone booth and called the hospital.

"Juno! For God's sake! I've been trying to get you—"

"I know. What happened is that Betty Straus invited me for a drink—"

"I called her house, there wasn't any answer. Do you know how many people I've called, trying to find you?"

"We went out for a drink at the St. Regis, and now we're having dinner together."

"At the St. Regis? Nobody eats at the St. Regis."

"We just had drinks at the St. Regis, we're not eating there."

"Where *are* you eating?"

"What's the difference? At a restaurant."

"For God's sake, Juno, I haven't seen you all day, I've been worried about you, and then when I ask you a simple question like what restaurant you're eating at, you're evasive. What's going on?"

"All right," she said, sighing, "you might as well know the truth. I'm having an affair with Robby Whiteman in a hotel room. You want to know what hotel?"

"Don't be so damn funny. I've been frantic. I hope you're not trying to pull something foolish."

"Nobody has mugged, raped, or kidnapped me. Take your pill and go to sleep. I'll be in touch. Good night, Jerry."

"Be in touch? Like a business deal? This is your husband, Jerry whatsisname, you remember him?"

She hung up. Another thirty seconds and she would have spilled the beans, and the bug in his phone would have picked it all up. She came out of the phone booth trembling. The man from the bar was waiting for her.

"The husband can't make it?" He tagged along as she started across the floor toward the gate.

"He can't make it. He's busy practicing."
The man was half-running to keep up to her. "What is he, a musician?"
"A linebacker."

The flight attendant had seemed a bit uncertain when she brought Strawberry his third drink, and when he requested a fourth, she looked concerned. He saw her talking to another attendant, and the two were throwing covert glances toward him. How idiotic, he thought, for two little twits to try to judge a man's capacity. How often had he downed half a bottle of vodka—good vodka, too, the Russian kind, not this horse urine they served here—and felt nothing beyond a warm glow? Milksops—they didn't have the faintest idea how a real man—a Soviet man—could drink. Well, they had better decide in his favor, or he would make a fuss.

He turned to the window and looked out at nothing, at darkness moving by, the black air above the Atlantic, the black sky. Black—that was the exact color of his mood. Presently the flight attendant was beside him in the aisle, carrying his vodka on a tray. Just as well, he thought, scowling, or I might have beaten her to death with my dick, her and her colleague, too, using it as a truncheon on their silly heads.

"Are you sure you wouldn't like some tonic with your drink, sir?"

"Thank you, no, miss, my malaria is perfectly under control."

The girl didn't smile. In fact she looked grave, worried about a passenger with malaria. Soviet girls weren't terrific at appreciating jokes either, but one of them might have managed a small smile, whether she understood or not. Strawberry put the little bottle of vodka to his lips, tilted his head, and let the liquor run down his throat.

Black. It would be just as well to be roaring drunk when he disembarked in Milan and made his phone call to Grigoriev. He could already hear Grigoriev, in his threatful voice, demanding a full explanation. But how could he explain what he did not understand? Even now it was difficult to believe that the woman was not on the plane, and merely thinking about it reanimated the disbelief and panic of the moment when he had had to admit to himself that it was true. The plane was two hours out over the water when he had decided to do another check, simply as a formality. She wasn't seated anywhere in the plane, so he had parked himself beside one toilet after another, watching with growing anxiety as each emptied in turn. And at last he was forced to admit to himself that the subject was not on the plane. Black. A triumph had turned into a disaster, a tremendous mistake.

But it was an honest mistake. When he spelled out the circumstances, Grigoriev would understand, wouldn't he? After all, he was a highly intelligent man. Strawberry felt a sudden icy draft in the plane. He shivered and was reminded of the time, a few years ago, when he had escorted a prominent dissident to Siberia. That incredible coldness, which—as he had told his colleagues after his return, exaggerating only slightly—froze your piss into solid ice before it hit the ground. Siberia? Come, come, Strawberry, don't be an ass, you're spouting imperialist propaganda.

An attendant was going by in the aisle. Strawberry caught her arm and asked her to bring him a blanket.

Three

In Paris, when he had first gone operational twenty-five years ago, Fernald had been called upon to help dispose of a corpse. The remains were those of a Yugoslavian exile whose excellent anti-Communist credentials went all the way back to the Second World War: he had fought with Mikhailovitch's Chetniks, and fled the country when the Titoists prevailed. He had worked mainly with the French Deuxième Bureau, but had also been helpful to the British and Americans. As if all of that hadn't been enough to keep a man busy, he had also been doubling for the opposition as well, until his luck had run out. In the middle of the night, Fernald had gone to the man's spiffy apartment on the Boulevard Haussmann (given his large and varied clientele, he could well afford it) with two agents from the Deuxième. They were going to take him to a safe house to see what they could wring out of him before shooting him, but one of the Deuxième agents queered it. Whether in a flush of patriotism or because he was incensed at having been duped for all those years, he whipped out a knife in a fit of insane rage and cut the Yugoslav's throat.

It had been—all too literally—a bloody mess. While the Yugoslav's life bled away into the Chinese carpet on his bedroom floor, the two French agents got into a screaming match; the second one had been outraged by his partner's unprofessional behavior, especially since it had taken place in the presence of a green American agent. *"Jamais devant les enfants!"* he had screamed. Fernald had complicated matters further by getting sick. But by the time he tottered out of the bathroom, French practicality had asserted itself. The Deuxième agents, having now accepted the Yugoslav's death as an irreversible fact, were busy on the telephone making arrangements. A tradesman's van arrived, the body was carried out of the apartment, and they drove to the Pont Neuf. There, beneath the bridge, after a handful of gendarmes had rousted some *clochards* from a sound boozy sleep and run them in, Fernald and the Deuxième men had tossed the carcass of the Yugoslav into the Seine.

Fernald had remembered for a very long time the unnatural chill of the Yugoslav's skin, the ashiness of the face and the stripped body, and the illusion that the splayed arms and legs were struggling frantically to keep the body afloat. The Yugoslav sank, did a turn in the water, then slowly came back to the surface before, half-submerged, he began to slip downstream. Fernald was sick again, this time in the car, and the two Deuxième men patched up the last of their differences with each other in mutual disdain of the weak-stomached American novice.

In some kind of irrational penitential throwback to that Yugoslav, Fernald offered to take the responsibility now for disposing of the body in the cellar. Of course the Bureau people wouldn't hear of it, and in fact looked at him as if he were dotty. People at his level of importance didn't do donkey work. And still he persisted, hearing himself, with astonishment, contributing a suggestion: Couldn't the body be dumped into the East River?

One of the Bureau men said coldly, "Look, sir, we said we'd take care of it."

He returned to the safe house, an apartment on the upper East Side, in a state of exhaustion. The phone was ringing. It was the agent in charge of the New York office of the Bureau, who expressed his displeasure at what he termed an inconvenient and indiscriminate murder, and made it ungraciously clear that the Bureau was depositing the occurrence for future withdrawal on demand.

"You know what the trouble with you guys is?"

Fernald didn't answer.

"You're so fucking tricky you fool each other."

Fernald hung up, loosened his tie, and made himself a drink. He took half of it down at a single swallow, thinking, I'm getting too old for this kind of work, I should stick to my desk. He finished his drink and made another. "Nonsense," he said aloud, "I'm only forty-eight years old." He thought about the parting shot of the Agent in Charge. Nothing new. It was a universally held perception that the Agency regarded simplicity as a disease and Byzantine complexities as a religion. Like all gossip, it was exaggerated, but the exaggeration was wrapped around a kernel of truth.

In the matter of Mrs. Sultan, the charge was fair, and yet, in an admittedly unplanned way, deviousness had paid off. The credit belonged to a combination of a serious breach of discipline with a stroke of pure luck. The philosophical conclusion, if there was one, might be that God helped those who fucked up.

At the beginning, Group Nine's brief—with the cooperation of the FBI—had been the rather routine work of surveillance: simply seeing to it that Mrs. Sultan didn't take off for Italy. Locksley had been trying for an extrication order, but the Director had demurred, opting for discreet, behind-the-scenes cooperation with the Italian police, and putting it out that there was money available for informers, something like two million dollars, which, translated into lire, was an astronomical figure. The policy was based on the Dozier experience of a few years back, when American dollars had greased the way to the rescue of the general and led to the arrest and conviction of seventeen members of the Red Brigades who had been implicated in the kidnapping. But from the first, it was Group's belief that this technique wouldn't work in the instant matter. For one thing, the Dozier affair, with its *penitenti*—Red Brigades people who blew the whistle on their comrades—had shaken out the weak sisters. Those who remained were a hard core who would resist both repentance and money. In an odd way, the Dozier fiasco, which had depleted the Red Brigades—and its rival sister groups, the Forze Scarlatte and the Prima Linea—in terms of numbers, had fortified the ferocity and daring of those who remained.

There was also the question of time. It had taken forty-two days to discover Dozier's hiding place in Padua, and that was something they couldn't afford.

Whatever benefit Group had hoped to gain from its surveillance of Mrs. Sultan—aside from keeping her out of Italy, where she might be a nuisance—it had not foreseen that the Forze Scarlatte would contact her personally. But the moment they had learned about it through the hospital listening post, everything had changed. Locksley was able to wangle an immediate extrication order; the broader Agency effort was not suspended, but the participation of Group Nine, from being peripheral, became central.

The motives of the Forze Scarlatte in contacting Mrs. Sultan could only be guessed at. It might be simply a gesture: *solo per mostra* as the Italian phrase had it—for show only. On the other hand, they might be serious about attempting to reunite Mrs. Sultan with her son, if only on a temporary basis, to win public relations Brownie points for their compassion, particularly with the sentimental, family-loving Italian populace. In the latter case, it offered a rare opportunity that might lead

Group to the Forze Scarlatte hideout; it might turn into a bonanza.

Fernald was prepared to defend against a charge of overtrickiness his tactics in allowing Mrs. Sultan to think she had escaped surveillance on her own. They might simply have pulled the watchers out, but then even a civilian like Mrs. Sultan might have turned suspicious. The thing had to be done convincingly. The Hispanic porter, Luis, solved their problem. When they had first established the surveillance they had run a routine check on the house staff. One had turned out to be an ex-con, and another was a pill popper, none of which signified. But Luis had been more promising. He was fidgety in the course of a lenient interrogation, so they'd turned up the heat, and something had come of it. He was from Colombia and he was illegal. The FBI had wanted to turn him in, but Fernald called them off. Better to save up the information against the possibility that Luis might eventually prove to be useful in a substantive way. They had the wherewithal to make him jump through hoops; he had a nice little family in East Harlem, and there was nothing waiting for him back in Colombia but poverty.

His foresight had paid off after Mrs. Sultan got the note from the Forze Scarlatte. Luis turned out to be a perfect fit: his knowledge of the old incinerator exit provided them with the means to effect a rather elegant getaway. They had put the fear of God into him with the threat of deportation, and reduced him to a whimpering mess. When they put the proposition to him, he was ready to do anything. They sent him up to Mrs. Sultan's apartment to volunteer the information about the incinerator exit. She went for the bait. That same afternoon she sent him off to a travel agency. When he returned, they made him show the ticket: one economy passage to Milan, Pan Am Flight 432, departure time 6:30, October 20.

Until Diebold found out about it—in his own inimitable way—they didn't know that Luis also had another ticket in another pocket: TWA to Rome, same day, departure time 9:30. It had been Diebold, the maverick, the near psychotic—yes, Fernald thought, that's my considered judgment—who had saved their bacon.

Fernald made himself a third drink, slipped the knot of his tie up in place, and phoned the head of Group Nine at his home in Georgetown.

"Alan is in the library, Tony. Please hold on."

Waiting, Fernald could visualize the scene: Mrs. Locksley ascending the stairs in her unhurried patrician glide, tapping softly at the leather-covered door (in that household, wife and husband took few liberties with each other's privacy). Inside, Locksley seated at his desk, frowning at the interruption, setting his magnifying glass down on the English sporting print he had been examining, and saying, "Yes? Who is it?"

Who is it? There were only the two of them in the house. When she entered, his arms would be folded across his chest, palms cradling the elbow patches on his tweed jacket. He would thank Mrs. Locksley for the message, wait until she had left, and then pick up his phone.

"Yes, Tony, what is it?"

"The lady is out," Fernald said, "and Diebold is with her." It was all right to speak in clear. Locksley's phone was swept daily for bugs.

"Very good. Is that all?"

"Not quite, Head of Group." Fernald paused, and in the silence heard Locksley tapping the stem of his pipe against his teeth. "There's been a minor fatality."

"You say minor?"

How we're different from God, Fernald thought: He merely counts the fallen sparrows, we classify them. Luis would undoubtedly have viewed his death in a different light. "The Hispanic porter, Luis Ortiz, was left dead in the cellar of the apartment house."

"Left by *whom*, please."

"It was the fellow we co-opted to sneak her out of the house."

"I understand. How did he die?"

"His neck was broken. Double-Oh-Seven broke it."

"Diebold? What on earth for?" Locksley was aware that Diebold was mockingly known inside Group Nine as Double-Oh-Seven, but he never used the nickname; he considered it to be frivolous and in bad taste.

"It was one of those death-dealing stunts he's always bragging about—you know, a hundred simple ways to kill a man with your bare hands."

"Was Diebold at the house on your instructions?"

"No. He was there on his own, in distinct contradiction of his orders, which were to report directly to me this afternoon."

"Well then, I shall see that a reprimand is entered in his personal file."

Fernald sipped his drink and his lips twitched in a minimal smile. "Yes, Head of Group."

"What reason did he offer for terminating the Hispanic?"

"He felt it was necessary to cover himself. Alive, Luis, the Hispanic, would have revealed that he had been tortured."

"Tortured? Dear me."

"In a way of speaking. Diebold gave him a bad beating."

"Yes," Locksley said, "but why?"

"Diebold wasn't aware that Luis was our asset, nor that he had been engaged to help the subject escape on our behalf."

"Well, why the devil *didn't* he know..." Locksley's voice, which had begun on a note of asperity, faltered. "Give me a moment, please."

"Yes, of course, Head of Group."

There wasn't anything to think about, so Locksley may have requested the pause to chew his lip in chagrin or relight his pipe. Diebold hadn't known about Luis because that information had been on a need-to-know basis. Locksley himself had ordered it. *You're so fucking tricky you fool each other.* Locksley's pipe stem was beating a staccato rhythm against his teeth. He would be leaning forward at his desk, his narrow elegant head supported by his long-fingered hand. Could Head of Group, perhaps, be pondering the ineluctable metaphysics of secrecy for its own sake? Head of Group. Locksley insisted on that form of address because it was the British mode. He was British by self-adoption. He admired the British, or their secret services at any rate, and sedulously modeled himself upon them. He spoke of the DCI, the Director of the Agency (the only man to whom he was answerable), as "our master"—broad *a*, of course. His suits were bespoke from Huntsman in Savile Row, shirts and ties from Turnbull and Asser in Jermyn Street, Lock for his Bowlers, Lobb for his boots, Dunhill pipes ordered directly from the London shop although they were more easily accessible on Fifth Avenue. He wore a Guards mustache and referred to its color as ginger. His professional demeanor—it was said by the uncharitable—derived from his shelf of Le Carré novels, which he studied as assiduously as the young ladies of an earlier generation read Emily Post.

In fairness, Fernald was compelled to admit that Locksley had the drill—as he would undoubtedly have put it—down pat, including such fine details as frequent use of the word "ackchully," an occasional "whilst," and rigorous avoidance of pronouncing the terminal *r*, which entailed a high degree of discipline, since he hailed from the Midwest. When he ate, his fork never changed over into his right hand.

Actually—ackchully—Locksley had spent a half dozen years as Chief of Station in London, blissfully unaware that it was the deep night of empire. It was thought that he hadn't been very well liked there.

The tap-tap of the pipe stem stopped. Locksley said, "It's a matter of vital importance, I needn't tell you, that we are not compromised."

"Yes. The FBI understand the seriousness of the situation, and they're cooperating fully, although they're quite pissed off, ah, discommoded. They claim they don't approve of murder."

"Yes, well, nobody approves of it, ackchully. Then we can count on being kept clean?"

"Yes, including Double-Oh-Seven."

"I do wish you'd stop calling him that. I would also have wished that we might have used someone else."

"We're shorthanded, I needn't tell you. And what he's going to do in Italy, well, his extrication record is spectacular."

Locksley sighed. "To sum up, then—barring the accident to the Hispanic, the essential element of the operation is in place. Mrs. Sultan is on the plane to Milan, and so is Diebold."

"No, Head of Group, they're on the plane to Rome."

"I don't understand."

"Luis, the porter, doubled on us."

"Doubled? With whom?"

"Mrs. Sultan. He bought her two tickets, one to Milan and another to Rome."

"Damn the fellow! And let her know we had arranged for her exit?"

"He said he didn't give us away, that the misdirection was entirely Mrs. Sultan's idea, and he simply bought the extra ticket on her instructions. Since he was speaking then under rather heavy pressure from Diebold, I'm inclined to think he was telling the truth. But since he misled us by not telling us about the second ticket, to that extent he was doubling."

"If it was her own idea," Locksley said thoughtfully, "she's rather more resourceful than we had calculated her to be. Would you agree?"

"Yes, a little," Fernald said. We teach people by our example, he thought. They learn to play by our rules, and because we're so sure that we're the sole masters of the game, we can be fooled. "She was also clever enough to plant the idea of Milan at the hospital listening post."

"She knows about the listening post?"

"She made an off-the-cuff guess about the room being bugged. She doesn't really *know* anything."

"As for Diebold—if he hadn't been at the house, never mind that he disobeyed his orders..." Locksley trailed off.

"Yes, Head of Group, we would have lost her."

"In light of the circumstances, I might reconsider the reprimand. As for the Hispanic, it's inescapable that if he hadn't doubled, he would still be alive. Wouldn't you say so?"

"Of course," Fernald said, though he had serious doubts about it.

"Nevertheless, although the termination of the Hispanic must be condoned, I'd like it made clear that harming the woman is not particularly in our interests. Diebold must be made to understand that. He isn't likely to want to hurt her, is he?"

"No, Head of Group," Fernald said.

At least, not to my present knowledge.

Four

Juno was nervous and on edge even when the plane taxied out onto the runway and revved up its engine for takeoff. She was convinced that the people who were trying to prevent her from going to Italy were undoubtedly powerful enough to stop a plane on the ground, on one pretext or another, and remove her from it. But not, she thought with relief, as the plane began its headlong dash down the runway, not now. The plane lifted away from the ground, and they were airborne, rushing up the incline of the sky. She let out a sigh, and said to herself: Be strong, Michael, be brave, Mama is coming!

The plane was an island of safety, a cocoon. She had a window seat in a row of two, beside the forward galley, with an oblique view of the bulkhead where the movie screen would eventually be unfurled. Her seatmate was a middle-aged Italian woman, dressed in black. She seemed shy and, perhaps, frightened by the airplane. She either spoke no English or so little of it that she wouldn't trust herself to say anything beyond "please."

The plane was about three-quarters full. It occurred to Juno that it was the first time she had flown overseas in economy class. Jerry didn't believe in it. That was exactly how he put his preference—he didn't believe in it. He didn't believe in public conveyances like buses, either, or in inexpensive restaurants or moderately priced hotels. What he did believe in was first-class accommodations, taxis, limousines, haute cuisine, de luxe hotels, and special treatment for which he was prepared to tip lavishly. He understood himself. "I am—like they used to say—a self-made man. As a class, self-made men are extravagant. Show me somebody who inherited and I'll show you a tightwad. Anyway, all my trips are business trips, and the government foots half the bill."

At the thought of Jerry she made an involuntary sound. The Italian woman said, "Please?"

"Sorry," Juno said. "*Mi dispiace.*"

The woman brightened. "*Lei parla italiano, signora?*"

Juno tried to compose the phrase, "A little, but I'm rusty," but she didn't know the word for rusty nor any appropriate synonym for it. So she said nothing, and the woman murmured an apology and faced to the front again.

When the flight attendant stopped beside them with her drinks cart, Juno ordered a Scotch and soda. The Italian woman unleashed a spate of very rapid Italian.

"I'm sorry," the attendant said. "If you can wait a while, I'll send our Italian-speaking steward to help."

"Please?" The woman looked helpless.

"I'll give it a try," Juno told the attendant. She said to the woman, "*La signorina chiede se desidera una bevanda*"—The girl asks if you want a drink.

"*Sì, sì,*" the woman said. "*Un bicchiere di vino rosso.*"

"A glass of red wine," Juno translated.

"Got some," the stewardess said.

As the girl poured the wine, the woman turned to Juno gratefully. "*Grazie mille, signora.*"

"*Prego.*"

Juno turned to the window, to the infinitude of blackness with nothing visible but the long back-slanted wing of the plane. She sipped her drink, and said in a whisper, "I'm coming, Michael."

"Please?" the Italian woman said.

Diebold had bought a first-class seat because that was how he was accustomed to traveling. If the subject had been in first class it might have been a bit awkward, but he had proceeded on the assumption that she would choose economy class because she would feel more secure among several hundred other people.

His seat was on the aisle. His seatmate was a standard issue businessman, already stripped down to his vest, and holding a sheaf of papers in his lap.

"Good evening," the man said as he sat down.

Diebold settled himself in his seat with great deliberateness before turning to face the man. He regarded him wordlessly, staring at him with his light gray eyes. The man tried a smile, which faded under Diebold's stare, and turned away, rattling his papers nervously. Nip sociability in the bud, Diebold thought. It would eliminate boring conversation and, hopefully, inhibit the man passing by him to take a leak as often as he might want to.

Diebold acknowledged that he had allowed anger to dictate his treatment of the businessman. Ordinarily, he would have been courteous but aloof, chilling only if it was necessary. He regarded emotional, as opposed to professional, anger as a weakness. He had killed the Hispanic in the basement because it was indicated, not because he was angry. But he was angry with Fernald. Not because of anything Fernald had said, not even because of his implied disapproval of the killing of the Hispanic, but because Fernald's withholding of essential information had almost been a disaster in terms of keeping the Sultan woman under surveillance. If it hadn't been for his efforts—if he hadn't performed at the high professional level he expected of himself—the whole operation might have gone down the drain.

Diebold realized that his own uncompromising standards of behavior, and unfashionable and uncomplicated patriotism, were not shared by his colleagues; that, in fact, they regarded him as something of a freak. Yet his outlook was simple: anyone who thwarted the will of Group Nine was an enemy of the Agency, which made him, in turn, an enemy of the United States, which earned him the undying enmity of Wilton Diebold. The present subject fell into this rubric: whatever her motivations (innocent but annoying, in the view of his colleagues) she was an enemy of Group Nine, of the Agency, of the United States, of Wilton Diebold.

Diebold was aware that he was something of a joke among his peers, and an occasional problem to his superiors. He believed that only his superior effectiveness and his willingness to do jobs others balked at kept him from being separated. He knew that he was satirically called Double-Oh-Seven. He also knew that his expertise in unarmed combat made him an object of derision. Once, in fact, it had come to a showdown. A Group Nine agent named Starmann had twitted him, suggesting that he was a fake, that it wasn't all that easy to kill a competent and alert adversary with his "secret" techniques. Quietly, he had offered to validate his claims by the simple expedient of killing Starmann. Starmann had blustered, but he had backed off and, ever since, been cool to him. But Starmann had known that if he had accepted the challenge, he would have been killed.

He had terminated seven men in the line of duty—eight with today's kill—and he would kill again, without a second thought, whenever it was necessary to do so. His colleagues regarded him as a freak—though they themselves were all cleared for wet work—because they thought he took sadistic pleasure in killing. The truth was that he took pleasure in the performance of his duty, and that was a quite different thing. Fernald professed to be repelled by the killing of the Hispanic, at the same time that he acknowledged that it was essential to avoid their being compromised. Diebold regarded Fernald's double standard, his hypocrisy, as despicable.

He drank the whiskey the stewardess had brought him and then wandered back into the economy section of the airplane. Despite her ridiculous disguise, he located the subject at once. He returned to his seat. The businessman studiously avoided looking at him; he busied himself with his papers.

After dinner, Diebold went to sleep.

When the dinner trays arrived, Juno's seatmate tore into her food with such gusto that Juno thought of offering her own tray, which she had barely touched. How could she eat in the circumstances? Were Michael's captors feeding him, at least? The Italian woman looked up with a shy smile. She had great luminous eyes and white even teeth against a tawny skin. Dressed differently, free of the disfigurement of that dusty-black dress, and with a rearrangement of the rat's nest of her hair, she might have been quite handsome.

Juno drew in her breath sharply and gave a start.

"Please?"

If *she* was wearing a disguise, couldn't the woman also be doing so? No, Juno, you're being paranoiac. Soulful dark eyes and good looks were a Mediterranean commonplace. She smiled vaguely and turned back to the window, watching the massive soaring diagonal of the wing cutting its way through the pervasiveness of the night. Then, reflected in the window, she saw the woman staring at her. She faced about abruptly.

"What are you looking at?"

The woman recoiled. "Please?"

"I'd like to know what you're staring at."

"Please?" And then, almost fearfully, she said, *"Mi scusi, signora, la parrucca. È storta."*

La parrucca—the wig. The woman was touching her own hair, pushing it to the side. *Storta.* Crooked? She touched her head; the black wig was awry. The woman was nodding, smiling in relief. Juno used the window as a mirror to set the wig straight. Oh, Juno, you're a beast, scaring the poor thing half to death when she was only trying to be helpful. How could she apologize?

The woman said, *"È meglio, signora."*

That's better. *"Grazie,"* Juno said. She pointed to her tray, working the verb form out in her head before speaking. *"Vorrebbe la mia pietanza?"* Would you like my dinner?

"No, no, no, signora."

"Non ho fame. Non posso mangiare." Not hungry. Can't eat. Make it a little stronger? She touched her stomach. *"Ho mal di stomaco."*

"Povera signora." The dark eyes were saddened. *"Posso aiutarla?"*

Can I help you? "No, thank you." She tried again. *"La prego di prendere la pietanza"*—Please, take the dinner. At least eat the broccoli, it's good for you.

The woman shook her head firmly, with a touch of hauteur.

Not a spy, Juno thought, nor a peasant from Calabria, but a *principessa* in disguise, and she had just insulted her. No, certainly not from Calabria, her accent was too refined. And suddenly her suspicions were aroused again.

In Italy, much more than in America, accents defined both region and social class. She recalled that when she had studied Italian, with the idea of making herself useful when she accompanied Jerry on one of his business trips to Italy, there had been much emphasis on learning a "classical" Italian pronunciation. Her teacher insisted on her students' acquiring an accent that was *raffinato*—"the speech of Tuscany, of Dante, of Florence, where I was born"—and was openly contemptuous of all other accents, particularly those of Naples, Calabria, and Sicily. By her reckoning, anyone who spoke other than good Tuscan Italian (though she grudgingly excepted a number of areas in the north) was a *contadino*, a peasant. The teacher's snobbery to one side, it was true that the more cultivated speech of the north was pleasanter to the ear than the southern—slower, more comprehensible.

Starting from scratch, Juno had had little trouble with pronunciation. But it was hard work for some of her classmates, Americans of Italian descent who, for one reason or another (two were singers with operatic ambitions), wanted to replace their regional dialect with what they termed "high Italian." She remembered an amusing but nonetheless revealing conversation with one of them, a young college math instructor of Sicilian ancestry. He had told her ruefully of a trip he had made upstate to visit his old grandmother. When he had mentioned his Italian lessons to her casually, his grandmother had been thunderstruck. "You? Studying Italian? You talk beautiful—I taught you myself when you were a little boy. You crazy!"

He tried explaining to her that the language they spoke in their family was a local dialect, and that he was trying to acquire high Italian, classical Italian, *la lingua di Dante.*

His grandmother listened to him in silence, rocking in her chair. When he was finished, she said, "Tell me, Nick, when you learn this classical language of Dante, who you gonna *talk* to?"

Although she didn't rank as an expert, Juno knew without question that the accent of her seatmate was not that of the southern woman in the telltale black dress that she appeared to be. Phrasing the Italian sentence in her head before speaking, she said, "May I ask what part of Italy you are from?"

"I am from near Orvieto, signora."

And again, the doubts in Juno's mind were settled. Orvieto was a wine-producing city not far from Rome, which would account for the Roman clarity of the woman's speech. "Was this your first visit to America?"

The woman responded eagerly. Yes, it was her first time in America, her first time out of Italy. A brother in New Jersey had sent her a ticket. She had not seen him in thirty years, but now he was very sick, and wished to see her before his death. Very sad, signora, he had been a powerful man—the lovely dark eyes moistened—and now he was frail and shrunken. America was so beautiful and prosperous, her brother lived in a noble house with an American wife, with beautiful children, and now he was to die. She would pray for him night and day, and perhaps her prayer would make his death easier.

"I'm sorry," Juno said.

The woman said that it was God's will. Then, after a pause, she asked if Juno had been to Rome before. Yes? Ah. She herself had been in Rome only three times in her life. It was so large, so crowded, so many treasures to see, so many cars, it frightened her a little. Still, when the plane landed, she would spend three days in Rome before returning home, and she hoped to have an audience with the Pope—not alone, of course, but with one of the groups. His Holiness gave audiences on Thursdays when he was in residence in the Vatican. She would stay at the house of a cousin, a lawyer. He lived on the outskirts, but she would learn about the buses, and travel by herself into the heart of the city each day to see the sights. . . .

"The signora will stay with a relative? No no, of course not, the signora will stay at one of the grand hotels of Rome. I have heard much about them, with the servants to wait on you, and the great marble bathrooms.

I have seen several—from the outside only, of course. I have seen such hotels as the Excelsior, the Ambasciatore, the Hassler. The signora will stay at one of these great hotels?"

Juno stiffened. The question might be innocent, surely it was in keeping with the character of a provincial woman, and yet . . . She said, "No, none of those. I don't know yet where I'll be staying."

"A marble bathroom," the woman said, smiling. "What richness!"

"The movie is starting," Juno said; the lights had been dimmed in the cabin. "May I offer you my earphones?"

"No, no, signora, I couldn't."

"Please take them. I'm very tired, and I would rather sleep."

The woman protested, but at length, when Juno pressed them upon her, accepted with profuse thanks. The main title of the film appeared on the screen. Juno showed the woman how to use the earphones and adjust the sound.

"The signora is so good."

"Enjoy the film."

"Thank you, thank you. *Dorme,* signora."

Juno leaned back and shut her eyes. Presently, she tilted her head toward the woman, who was gazing intently at the screen, cupping the earphones with her hands. But the dialogue of the movie was in English, Juno thought. Then why had she accepted the earphones, and why was she listening so raptly?

But in the early dawn, looking at the drawn, careworn face of the sleeping woman, Juno felt ashamed of her suspicions. When the woman woke, Juno offered her one of the moist traveling tissues she carried. Over breakfast, as they flew into a glowing pink dawn, she asked the woman if she had enjoyed the movie.

"Yes, although I could not understand what was spoken."

For the remainder of the trip the woman was silent, withdrawn, as if, with the approach of home, she was acknowledging that the accidental democracy of the plane was almost ended, and was preparing herself for the social differences that she felt existed between them.

When the plane landed Juno helped the woman gather her possessions, waited, and left side by side with her.

Diebold was the first passenger off the plane. Not that there was any rush; it would be at the very least five minutes before the subject, back in the crowded economy section, made it to the exit. After that, he could count on a minimum of a half hour while she made the long walk to the main concourse, collected her baggage, and cleared through customs. He himself was unencumbered; he carried no more than a change of linens and an electric razor. He would find some gofer at the embassy to shop for him.

Nevertheless, he was first off the plane because that was his nature. Nor did he dawdle through the interminably long corridor leading to the main area of the Fiumicino Airport. He remained far ahead of the other passengers, looking neither to left nor right. He came out into the huge concourse of the terminal and headed directly for an empty passport control lane. The official at his seat in the booth glanced perfunctorily at his passport, stamped his *Carta di Sbarco*, his disembarkation card, and waved him through. He headed for the customs lanes.

"Morning, Diebold."

Diebold's eyes brushed over the man in front of him, then went on to locate the baggage carousel for Flight 45. None of the passengers had yet arrived. To the left, a large restless crowd surrounded the carousel for a flight from Paris that had arrived earlier.

"Diebold? It's Tom Mackey."

Diebold looked at him squarely for the first time. "So it is," he said coldly. "You're supposed to be in Athens."

"I flew in last night."

"Last night. Did you have a nice flight?"

"I don't make the rules, you know," Mackey said. He held out his hand. "Welcome to Rome."

Diebold ignored Mackey's hand. He turned so that he could see the Flight 45 carousel. A few people had begun to circle it. One of them was his ex-seatmate, the businessman.

Diebold said, "Have you got a car?"

"Of course." Mackey pursed his lips and said, "But I'm not here as your chauffeur, if that's what you mean."

"What *are* you here for?"

Mackey flushed. "Lay off me, Diebold. You have any complaints, make them to Fernald. Me, I'm just a soldier."

"I didn't expect you, soldier."

"You're making it pretty obvious. But I'm here, and you might as well get used to it."

Diebold nodded. "I don't hold anything against you. I'm a soldier too."

"I can sympathize with how you feel," Mackey said. He shrugged. "*C'est la guerre.*"

Diebold saw the subject coming out of the corridor, talking to a shorter woman in a dowdy black dress. She pointed to the carousel, then approached it, followed by the woman in black, edging into the circle of waiting passengers.

"How are things in Greece?" he said pleasantly to Mackey.

"Good weather, terrible food, and Athens isn't Paris." Mackey looked at the crowd around the carousel. "Has she come through yet?"

Diebold shook his head. "She was in the back of the plane; Lots of time. Why don't we clear through and pick her up on the other side?"

"I've got an arrangement laid on," Mackey said. He took Diebold by the arm and steered him off to the right. At a customs control lane a man in uniform was sitting behind a desk. He smiled at Mackey. "This is Signor Stark, my business colleague."

"Welcome to Italy, signore. I see you have nothing to declare."

"My bag was stolen right off the curb at Kennedy," Diebold said. "You wouldn't believe what it's like."

"*Mi dispiace*," the customs man said, and pulled a sympathetic face. "Please pass through, signori."

"Thank you," Mackey said.

"*Prego. Arrivederla.*"

They moved on into the main terminal area. "Nice fellow," Diebold said. "Friend of yours?"

"Fifty thousand lire's worth of friend. I thought you might be in a hurry."

Diebold surveyed the area. People were running toward the far end of the shed, trying to find carts for their baggage. Porters were loading luggage onto their handcarts, reassuring anxious travelers, and then making toward the exit doors where taxi drivers waited in little groups. Large ungainly wagons, battery propelled, piled high with baggage, were crisscrossing the floor without regard for rules of right-of-way, narrowly avoiding colliding with each other, skimming by startled pedestrians with that penchant of Italian drivers for hairbreadth avoidance of calamity.

"Where's your car parked?" Diebold said.

"Right outside, at the curb," Mackey said, grinning. "Twenty thousand to a *carabiniere*."

"What make and color?"

"A light blue Alfa Romeo—what's the difference? Do you have a preference in colors? Four doors—is that all right?"

"Just getting the picture," Diebold said. "Habit. How much did Fernald tell you?"

"Broad strokes. He said you'd fill me in."

"That's all there is at the moment—just broad strokes. We'll follow the subject in to Rome. . . . Did he say you'd be working for me?"

"Not *for*," Mackey said. *"With."*

The ring of passengers surrounding the Flight 45 carousel was now six deep. The baggage had begun coming through. Diebold saw a man push his way out of the crush lugging two heavy leather bags.

"I'll be frank with you," Mackey said. "Fernald said that you'd be teed off, but that I wasn't to let you intimidate me."

"First reaction," Diebold said mildly. "You'd have been the same yourself if somebody arrived out of the blue. Actually, I don't mind, now that it's sunk in. In fact, I'm glad that you're going to assist me."

"Well, I'm not exactly going to *assist* you. Fernald was quite clear about that. I mean, let's get it straight, I'm nobody's assistant."

In a very quiet voice Diebold said, *"You* are going to run *me?"*

Mackey shifted his gaze to the floor. "Well, I wouldn't put it *quite* that way."

"Watch," Diebold shouted, reaching out toward Mackey as a clanking motorized wagon bore down on them. Mackey started to turn to face the danger, and the leading edge of the wagon struck him heavily on the hip and shoulder. He was jolted forward, his arms shooting upward out of control, and he fell heavily just out of the path of the wagon's metal wheels. His head struck the floor with a thud. Diebold jumped back to avoid being brought down by Mackey. The driver applied his brakes, looking back over his shoulder in bewilderment.

Diebold bent over Mackey. He lay in an awkward sprawl, unconscious. Blood was pouring from the back of his head. Diebold found the car keys in Mackey's right jacket pocket. He cupped them in his hand, straightened up, and shouted, "Help! There's a man hurt here. Help!"

People were staring, others were running toward them. The driver of the wagon was climbing down from his seat. Mackey was very still. His face was pale, the blood under his head was spreading.

"Help!" Diebold yelled. "Ambulance. *Ambulanza."*

He saw a couple of *carabinieri* heading toward them. He yelled *"Ambulanza"* once more before edging back and slipping away.

Five

At home the leaves had turned color, but here, through the window of the taxi, Juno could see palms, spreading their graceful green arms. It might have been a day in August or early September instead of late October. It was already quite warm under a brilliant sun blazing in the intensely blue Roman sky. She rolled down the window and removed the black wig, letting the breeze fluff up her flattened hair. There was no need for the wig now, or the eyeglasses. She had made good her escape, she had foiled the powerful agencies of government.

Then why was she glancing back over her shoulder through the rear window? There was a black car behind them, at a discreet distance. Why "discreet"?—more of the language of melodrama. Of course there was a black car, and behind the black car other cars, of all colors, all leaving the airport and heading for the center of Rome. Juno, you've got to be sensible, or you'll turn into a nervous wreck, and then you'll be of no help whatsoever to Michael.

The taxi sped out of the airport complex toward Rome, twenty miles to the northwest. The landscape was flat and bare, relieved by an occasional stand of tall graceful pines. It was ten thirty; even allowing for the heavy city traffic, the ride wouldn't be much over an hour. If she hadn't stopped at the baggage carousel with her seatmate she would have been away even earlier. Not that it mattered. There was a whole day to kill before her rendezvous on the Via Veneto.

The woman in the black dress had seemed so intimidated by the crowd at the carousel that she had accompanied her. And she might still have been there, waiting, if the woman hadn't offered to ask her *cugino*, who was to meet her, to drive her in to the city. At once her suspicions had flared up again. Why couldn't she have realized that it was a perfectly innocent and generous offer? But she had let herself become rattled; instead of simply declining the offer with thanks she had been abrupt and ungracious.

"No."

The woman had shrunk back at her brusqueness, and when she held out her hand it was hesitantly, as if she feared rejection. Juno took her hand and the woman said, *"Auguri, signora, tante belle cose"*—Good omens, all beautiful things to you.

"Auguri."

She had moved away swiftly from the carousel. At passport control her *Carta di Sbarco* had been stamped and her passport cursorily examined. She had passed quickly through a "Nothing to Declare" customs line—an officer barely glanced at her tote bag before waving her through—and moved across the main concourse toward the exit. She glanced back once: the Italian woman, looking small and defenseless, was watching the bags flow by.

If the truth had to be told, Juno thought, she hadn't left, she had *fled*. It wouldn't do, she had to get herself under control, stop being so jumpy, so *tsitterdik*, as Zayde would have put it.

Her taxi bypassed the *grande raccordo anulare*, the circumambular road around the city, and turned into the Via Trastevere, running alongside the Tiber. The driver had been one of a half dozen yelling *"Tassì"* outside the terminal. Behind her, as she came through the exit, she had heard someone shouting for an ambulance. For an instant, her driver had been intrigued and appeared on the verge of running inside to see what was happening, but in the end the prospect of a fat fare into Rome won out, and he grabbed her tote bag and led her to his car.

He gave her a demonstration of Italian driving style once he crossed the river and approached the center of the city. He drove at immoderate speed, leaping forward to occupy the least gap in the traffic, skimming pedestrians in the *passaggi pedonali*, the zebra-striped safety zones, challenging everything on wheels: Mercedes, tiny buglike Fiat *cinquecenti*, bicycles, motorbikes, motorcycles, buses, all of which vied furiously for pride of place. She looked through the rear window. The black car was nowhere in sight. She relaxed and began to note familiar landmarks: the Piazza Repubblica, the Turkish Embassy with a soldier armed with a machine gun on the steps sweeping the street below, the Via Bissoleti, a ghetto of obscure airlines—Zambian, Royal Jordanian, Saudi Arabian—the massive Renaissance pile of the Quirinale, once a papal palace and now the residence of the president of Italy.

By the time the taxi dashed into the Via Veneto she had become inured to the last-second escape from collision, to the pedestrian providentially spared from being run down. She took another look through the rear window. No black car. Another false alarm. They raced by the American Embassy, with its pink facade, frivolous palms, and white statues. At the end of the street, at the corner dominated by the massive Hotel Excelsior, the taxi made a left turn into the Via Ludovisi. She had considered trying to find a room at the Excelsior, but rejected the idea quickly. It was too active, too feverish, and always under siege by an army of paparazzi, attracted by the film people who liked to stay there. Jerry was intrigued by the ambience of the Excelsior; he was an easy mark for its hard-breathing glamour. She had told the driver to take her to the Hassler, at the top of the Spanish Steps. There would be no paparazzi there to sniff her out.

The taxi bore left, ran down the Via Francesco Crespi, and at the corner made a sharply angled turn into the Via Sistina, leading down to the Piazza dei Monti and the hotel. She paid off the driver, turned over her tote bag to a porter, and went into the lobby. From behind his desk the concierge broke into a smile and said, "Ah, *buon giorno,* Signora Sultan."

"*Buon giorno.*"

If he recognized her it was partially because it was his business to remember guests, and also because Jerry, immediately on arrival, would tip him as an earnest of even better things to come.

The clerk at reception recognized her, too. He smiled, and they shook hands, and then his brow knit. Could he have been so stupid as to have forgotten her reservation? She told him that, alas, it was she who was stupid; she had neglected to make one.

"It is very busy, signora, but—" His frown turned to a reassuring smile. "I'm sure we can arrange." He looked toward the entrance. "And the Signor Sultan?"

"He didn't come with me. I'm here... on business."

And then, from the sudden clouding of his eyes, she realized he had made the connection to Michael. "Yes, of course, signora. *Mi dispiace.*"

He changed the subject smoothly. She must set her mind at ease about the room. Crowded as the hotel was—"there are no longer seasons"—he would manage. It would be ready for her at one o'clock. Meanwhile, she could wash up if she wished, have a coffee and perhaps a sandwich at the bar, and by then...

"*Tante grazie.*"

It was his pleasure to accommodate the signora. She thanked him again, but did not tip him. A tip now might be construed as a bribe and offend him; later it would be a sincere tribute to his artfulness in accomplishing a difficult task, and as such be gratefully appreciated.

She went to the bar. The barman greeted her with a wide smile, and then he too remembered, and his eyes moistened.

"Can you make me a sandwich, Rinaldo?" She thought for a moment. "A toast." The Italian verson of a grilled cheese sandwich.

"At once, signora, with great pleasure."

He led her to a table, brought her a plate of nuts and another of potato chips. She asked him for a newspaper.

"*Pronto, signora...*" And then his eyes widened. "I forgot, signora. It is still too early for the newspaper."

She pointed. The paper he had been reading when she came in was spread out on top of the bar ."Please, Rinaldo."

He went off reluctantly. She watched him fold the paper. He didn't look at her when he put it down on the table. "I will make you a perfect toast, signora."

Her heart was thumping as she picked up the paper. A streamer across the top announced the formation of a new government. She turned the paper over and translated the headline below the fold: COMMUNIQUÉ #3 FROM THE FORZE SCARLATTE.

Driving Mackey's hired Alfa Romeo into Rome, Diebold got lost three times. He was in a rage. He screamed at the drivers of other cars, and they screamed back and made ferocious or lewd gestures. On two occasions he challenged drivers to get out of their cars, but of course they wouldn't. Italians were all show and no action. Once, at a red light, he jumped out of his car and ran back to the car behind him, whose driver had been honking his horn mercilessly. The driver laughed at him from behind his rolled-up window. He launched a kick at the side of the car. By this time the light had turned green, and a dozen cars were bleating their horns at him. He got back into the Alfa Romeo and drove off.

He knew that his anger had little to do with the traffic, and everything with what had happened at the airport. After walking away from the gathering throng around Mackey, he had taken up a position close to the customs lanes with a clear view of the baggage carousel. He couldn't make out the subject in the crowd, but he knew he would pick her up sooner or later. He turned for a moment to the *carabinieri* pushing back the circle around Mackey. One of them was blowing a whistle.

Watching as though he were waiting to meet someone, he checked each passenger who went off with luggage. He didn't try too hard to place the subject, but when the crowd had thinned by half he began to feel concerned. He spotted the woman in black who had come through the gate with the subject. She was by herself, standing next to the conveyor, watching the stream of luggage circulate. An alarm went off in his mind. He left his post and circled the carousel from right to left without seeing the subject.

She was gone.

He approached the woman in black. "Excuse me. The lady who was with you . . ."

"Please?"

"*La Signora*. The tall lady. Where is she?"

"Please? *Non capisco inglese, signore.*"

"No, you wouldn't," Diebold said. He turned to a heavyset man who was watching them. "Can you help me, sir? Do you speak English?"

"A little bit," the man said. "What do you want?"

"Would you ask this lady where the lady is who came off the plane with her?"

The man spoke to the woman in Italian, and waited for her response. He said, "She say the lady has gone away."

"Did she leave without collecting her baggage?"

After a rapid exchange the man said, "She say the lady did not have no baggages."

Without baggage, without having to wait at the carousel, she would have passed quickly through passport and custom controls while he was still speaking to Mackey, taking his time because the conveyor had not yet begun to bring the baggage out.

The heavyset man listened to the woman speak, then said to Diebold, "She wishes to know if you are friend of the lady."

"Yes, I am her friend."

He thanked the man and went back to the main concourse. He was furious. She was gone, and it was his own damn fault, no matter how obvious it might have seemed, for taking it for granted that she had baggage. He was angry with himself because he had no tolerance for carelessness, especially his own, and he was angry with the Sultan woman because she was the agent, however unwittingly, of his humiliation. Damn the bitch!

As he was leaving the building, two men in white, trundling a stretcher on wheels, came running in. They headed toward the crowd around Mackey. An ambulance stood at the curb. He thought of asking a group of taxi drivers if they had seen the subject come out, but they probably didn't speak English, and anyway it would be indiscreet. He located the blue Alfa Romeo a few yards to the left of the entrance.

By the time he arrived at the embassy on the Via Veneto he had more or less calmed down.

* * *

As Juno was finishing her sandwich, the reception desk sent word that her room was ready. The barman insisted that she must take the newspaper. She didn't want it; she hadn't read beyond the headline, and she knew that the barren ideological language of the "communiqué" would make her infuriated and frightened at the same time. But it was simpler to accept it than to hurt his feelings by rejecting his generosity.

She proffered a 20,000-lira note to the reception clerk who played out the expected charade. No, he couldn't think of it, please do not, signora. But when she insisted very firmly he succumbed, to avoid causing her distress, and took the note with a smile of pleasure that was only partly simulated. There was a style to receiving as well as to giving, and Italians were past masters: their joyous acceptance warmed the giver and made him feel that he had not only been generous but wise and discerning as well.

She followed the porter into the elevator and through the halls to her room. Fresh flowers in a bowl, an Oriental on the floor. The porter busied himself: placing her tote bag on a baggage rack, turning up the air conditioning, switching on the television set, lighting the bathroom.

She locked the door after he had left, kicked off her shoes, and lay down. She heard voices, and saw that the porter had left the television set on. On the screen, in a western saloon, a youthful John Wayne was pointing a huge six-shooter at three scowling villains and drawling, *"Mani in alto!"* Hands up! The villains were slow to oblige. *"Fate presto, buffoni, o la mia pistola parlerá"*—Make it snappy, you clowns, or my gun will speak.

She clicked the set off and went back to the bed. But she knew she was too keyed up to sleep. And she didn't really feel tired. Her store of energy and stamina were high, as they had been ever since her childhood. She had been a natural athlete, a runner and jumper as a child, and, later, a basketball player, a field hockey player, and pretty good at baseball and soccer as well, when the boys would allow her to play. It had distressed her mother, who thought it wasn't ladylike—"You'll make yourself muscles!" Despairing of discouraging her fondness for athletics, her mother had sought to channel it into something more socially acceptable and sent her for tennis lessons, which Zayde, however, who thought women should be cooks and cleaners, even his beloved Juno, had characterized as being "a roughneck game for men, and maybe a few *shiksas*, but not for a Jewish girl. A smart girl like her, I could teach her chess if she would let me."

Her mother's plan hadn't quite worked out. Tennis had turned out to suit her perfectly. She had made the high school tennis team while she was still taking lessons, and in college she had become the team's number-one player by the end of her freshman year. Her college coach had encouraged her to try qualifying for the women's tennis circuit after her sophomore year, and by the end of the summer she had achieved a national computer ranking of a hundred and forty-five. But she hadn't cared for the life. She wasn't cut out for the blind single-mindedness of a serious jock. She would undoubtedly have risen in the rankings if she had kept at it, but she knew that her progress would always be limited by a lack of dedication. So she had quit the tour after that first summer and confined her playing to her college team. But she still played regularly at the tennis club she and Jerry belonged to. She was able to beat the other women at the club, and all but the best of the men, as well.

In her forty-fourth year she was still, somewhat to her embarrassment, an all-around natural athlete, with fast reflexes and the right instincts. Any doubts she might have felt about it had been dispelled the previous winter when, with a group of neighborhood women, she had attended a class in anti-rape self-defense. None of the women had been raped, but several had been mugged, and the course had attracted a large turnout.

They met in a room at the police precinct set aside for them by the community affairs officer. The instructor was a physical education sergeant from the Police Academy.

"In a rape situation," the sergeant told his class of women clad in shorts or designer slacks, "you have a limited choice of options—scream, run, fight." He paused for an instant. "Or submit."

There was an outburst of indignation.

"I'm not recommending anything. I'm just laying out the alternatives. Submitting can sometimes be as dangerous as fighting, running, or screaming—especially if the rapist has a weapon."

One of the women suggested that, since they didn't need any instruction in screaming, running, or submitting, perhaps he ought to get down to the business of training them in self-defense.

The sergeant blinked, but took the cue. "If you must resist, fight dirty. Kick, scratch, step down on an instep, go for the eyes or the family jewels." He turned fiercely jovial. "Nothing discourages a perpetrator so much as to find an eyeball hanging down on his cheek."

After illustrating kicking, gouging, and crashing down on an instep with a grinning assistant, he put on a pair of aviator goggles and a catcher's shin guards. He was, as he told the assemblage, already wearing an aluminum cup. He invited the ladies, one at a time, to attack him. Perhaps because he was nettled by the woman who had spoken up earlier, he was a bit rough with his first pupils, and noted that, thus far, not one of them had laid a glove on him.

When it was Juno's turn she quickly lifted her knee toward the sergeant's groin, and when he lowered his hands reflexively, shot out the forefingers of both hands and struck him squarely on the lenses of his goggles, snapping his head back. After a moment of stunned silence the women cheered strenuously. The sergeant pushed his goggles back onto his forehead and looked at Juno sternly.

"Okay, you feinted me out of position. But you took me by surprise—I didn't teach you feinting yet."

The women jeered.

The sergeant flushed and said, "Try that again."

She retreated as he came toward her, then stopped abruptly and kicked him hard and accurately in the groin. The women went wild. The sergeant was staring at Juno.

"I'm sorry," she said. "I hope I didn't hurt you."

The sergeant shook his head. "Speed, reflexes, and surprise, that's the ticket. Who wants to be next?"

When the class ended, the sergeant asked Juno if she'd like to have a drink with him. But his tone was respectful, so he probably had no ulterior motive beyond admiration for her speed and reflexes.

Her classmates had practically carried her off on their shoulders in triumphal procession.

Actually, the experience had shaken her somewhat, and she never returned to the class. Her own violence, the physical pleasure she had derived from it, even allowing that it was a simulation, had troubled her. It reminded her of something she preferred to forget. A number of years back she had played in a "mixed" basketball game, which, from an innocent beginning, had degenerated into a travesty with rather nasty sexual overtones. There was a lot of groping, of "playful" roughhousing that turned into a kind of grubby saturnalia in which most of the men were running around with discernible erections under their shorts. The crux came, for her, when one of the men grabbed her around the waist from behind, held her against his stiffening front, and squeezed her breasts painfully. She broke free, whirled around, and smacked him squarely in the mouth, bloodying his lips and, as it turned out, loosening one of his teeth, which eventually required expensive dentistry to repair. The trouble was that her reflexes were too fast for her natural repugnance to violence.

She got up and went to the small antique desk near the window, where she had left the newspaper. COMMUNIQUÉ #3 FROM THE FORZE SCARLATTE. At the bottom of the page there was a reproduction of the end of the typed note. The last words read: *"Morte ai porci CIA!"*

She folded the paper and placed it face down on the desk. Death to the CIA pigs. Michael a CIA pig? Good-natured fat Joe Bering, with no children to howl for him as she howled for her Michael, no one but a sour wife twenty years divorced—Joe Bering a CIA pig?

Morte. But they couldn't mean it. Or else why had they taken the trouble to get in touch with her? It was just standard terrorist rhetoric. Don't worry, Michael, they won't harm you, it's all a lot of noise and fake ferocity, just don't worry, Michael, I won't let them harm you.

She got up from the desk and paced the room. She switched on the television set. John Wayne, still in the same saloon, or another just like it. *"Veesky, barista, e lasci la bottiglia"*—Whiskey, bartender, and leave the bottle. See, Michael, John Wayne is here in Italy, he'll help me find you, and our *pistola* will speak and all the Forze Scarlatte will bite the dust. . . .

She began to laugh at herself, but her laughter soon turned to tears. When her weeping stopped she washed her face, ran a comb through her hair, and went out.

Orlandi said, "Did you find her an intelligent woman?"

His office at the Questura looked out on a blank wall, and because of the bleakness of the view, perhaps, he usually kept the drapes drawn. Giuseppina Cavalera was grateful for it; the soft glow of the lamp on his desk was kinder to her than the raw natural light.

"Who could tell?" Giuseppina crossed her legs and took a cigarette out of her bag. Orlandi leaned across his desk to light it. "She was very nervous. She kept suspecting me on and off. But it was just nerves. She gave me her dinner."

Orlandi smiled.

"I must have looked as though I needed it. Airline food, mind you—I give my all for Italy."

"You're a good actress, Pina."

"Thank you." She plucked at the dusty black dress and touched the severity of her hair with distaste. "She also gave me her earphones. The film was worse than the food."

"It was clever of you to bring up the question of the hotel."

"A bit risky. It roused her suspicions again. It was careless of our tail to lose her on the way from the airport."

"Have you ever tried tailing anybody in Roman traffic? In any case, we'll locate her through the hotel registration cards."

"I wish you could have seen the wig she was wearing. *Molto brutta.*

Also a shapeless dress and an atrocious hat. But nothing could conceal her beauty. They call her Juno. She's well named. She's forty-four years old, exactly my age."

"You're beautiful too, *cara. Bellissima.*"

Five years ago they had been lovers. No hard feelings, to be sure; she had long ago given up on the idea that anything that was good could be permanent. She also knew that she hadn't aged well. Police work was hardly to be recommended as a beauty treatment.

She looked around the office. Orlandi had dressed it up with some things of his own to offset the deadly government-issue furniture: drapes with an imprinted Etruscan design; on the wall behind his desk a huge unframed Madonna and child by an unknown Umbrian artist that he had wheedled out of a *museo civico* somewhere; a majolica lamp his ex-wife had overlooked when she had cleaned out their apartment before leaving him; a chipped slab of an ancient pediment he had picked up in Greece.

There was a valise standing near the door. She said, "Going somewhere?"

"To Milan. Tomorrow morning. They think I can work wonders because of the bit of luck I had in the Dozier affair. The Milanese *polizia* won't welcome me with open arms. You know how they feel about Rome meddling in what they regard as their affair."

"With Americans involved it's a good deal more than local. But they'd rather fail on their own than succeed with help from Rome. And the *carabinieri?*"

"The usual rivalry. If they get a lead they won't tell the *polizia*, and the *polizia* return the compliment. How do we manage to survive, Pina?"

"We don't. We gave up the ghost two thousand years ago with the last of the Caesars, but we refuse to acknowledge it."

"Tell me about the man who questioned you at the airport."

"In his early forties, well dressed, well bred, about six feet tall, weight a hundred and sixty, black hair with some gray in it, face like the vice-president of an oil company, except for the eyes—gray, no depth to them, cold and cruel. CIA, I'll bet on it."

"He might be from the consulate."

"Consulate people don't have that kind of eyes unless they're CIA. His clothes were rumpled, as if he had slept on an airplane. I think he followed her from New York."

"And lost her at the airport." Orlandi grinned, then turned serious. "If he's CIA, he'll have resources available to him. He'll try to pick her up and follow her north." He made a gesture as Giuseppina started to speak. "No doubt in my mind that the FS are in the north, probably in the Veneto. That's their territory, that's where *their* resources are. Sending her to Rome was misdirection, to throw off any pursuit. They'll contact her here, and then she'll go north. I hope to see her there myself."

"You want to see her because she's beautiful? I'm jealous. Sorry, Alfredo, it's just a rather bad joke."

Orlandi smiled guardedly. "And what do we owe your informants, Pina, how much for the *bustarella?*"

"The one who passed her the instructions in New York—we must do what we can for his nephew."

"The nephew is a cop killer, Pina."

"His two friends did the shooting. He just drove the car."

Orlandi gave her a pained look. "Please, Pina."

"I know. He's red scum. But I made a deal for bigger game. I gave my word."

"And the other one? At the airline?"

"Just some money. I promised her a thousand dollars—about a million and a half lire—she had to displace somebody else in order to put me right alongside the woman."

"We'll take care of her. You're certain the courier in New York didn't know what was in the letter?"

"He swore on his mother. I believe him. The FS gave him the letter and told him to deliver it and not to open it unless he wanted his balls cut off. He's scared stiff of them. I'm sure he did exactly what he was told to do and nothing more."

"But he knew she was going to Rome."

"They told him that much, and he went to the airport to see that she got on the plane, then was supposed to phone and tell them."

"Where is he now?"

"Still in New York. He's a free-lance journalist."

"We can get our hands on him if we need him?"

Giuseppina shrugged. "Of course. But he won't be any help. He isn't even an *irregolare*, except by courtesy. He did this job on behalf of his nephew, and that's the extent of his connection."

Orlandi smiled. "Thank you very much, Pina. You'll be wanting to get some sleep."

"You don't want me to do anything else?"

"Nothing now, thank you."

"If you need me, I'm available." God in heaven, must even the most innocent thing I say sound suggestive?

"Yes, of course," he said gravely. "I know I can count on you."

"*Prego, dottore*," she said, matching his tone.

* * *

Coming from the cool dimness of the hotel lobby Juno felt assaulted by the brilliance of the sun. She walked across the Piazza dei Monti, past the taxi ranks. The drivers broke off their animated conversation to eye her appraisingly. She paused for a moment at the top of the Spanish Steps. To her right was the church, the ancient Trinità dei Monti with its twin bell towers; far below, at the foot of the Steps, the Piazza di Spagna and, emerging from the far end of the square, the Via Condotti, the great street of shops. Overhead, the Goodyear blimp floated serenely through the Roman skies.

She started down. The Steps still had their quota of tourists, of course, as they had had in the centuries since they had been built by a French king, but for the most part they had become a place for youth to "hang out." The marble steps were strewn with papers, empty Coke bottles, crusts of food, crowded with vendors selling a variety of wares from rickety folding tables: reproductions and paintings of questionable provenance, standard souvenirs of Rome, postcards, junk jewelry, and leather goods. There was a scent of pot in the air. The steps themselves were dirty and discolored, their edges chipped, rounded with the erosions of half a millennium. Here and there, young families, or fragments of families, were sprawled along the steps, sunning themselves, eating, keeping a more or less watchful eye on bored children. A vacant-eyed young woman sat beside her child, who was stretched out asleep on the hard stone, its angelic blond head uncushioned, its forehead wrinkled with mysterious worries.

Waiting for the shops to reopen after their noon closing, Juno sat down and unfolded her newspaper. Communiqué #3, printed in full, contained nothing new; it seemed almost to be a playback, with the same turgid phraseology as the first two communiqués. Although it concentrated its heaviest fire on the presence on Italian soil of "hellish, terroristic" American germ warfare missiles, it also touched base on a handful of other familiar left-wing targets: the unemployment problem, inflation, corruption in high places, the contradictions of the capitalist system, the perfidy of the Church, the brutality of the police, the plight of youth, the fascist conspiracy at work with the tacit approval of the government, the duplicity of the established trade unions, the NATO Alliance, the bloodsucking rich. . . .

Not until the end did it refer to Michael and Joe Bering: the CIA pig Bering and his piglet Sultan would soon undergo trial before a people's tribunal for the crimes of colonialism, warmongering, and moral piracy.

The accompanying story—written in the freewheeling style of Italian journalism, a blend of hard news, think piece, and editorial comment—speculated that, although no mention of ransom had yet been made, the release of the prisoners would be conditional on the removal of the germ warfare missiles the terrorists claimed were emplaced in Italy, and both the Italian and American governments denied existed. The terrorists understood that the matter was frozen there, deadlocked; they also knew that an antimissile stance was popular with the public. Hence, they would extract all the public relations juice from the issue that they could, escalating their threats against the lives of their captives, until, finally, when nothing more could be gained, they would show their toughness by—

But Juno couldn't read to the conclusion of the sentence. She folded the paper decisively and stood up. She shut her eyes for a moment, then opened them and shook her head vigorously, as though to clear it of the unthinkable words she had refused to read.

It was about time for the shops to be reopening. She folded the paper into quarters and said to the young mother of the sleeping child, "Would you mind if I slipped this under his head?"

The young woman said, "It doesn't matter. Go ahead, if you want to."

Juno knelt beside the child, lifted gently, and slid the paper beneath his head. "He'll be more comfortable."

The young woman shrugged. The child slept on, its brow still furrowed.

Below the Steps, on the Piazza di Spagna, tourists were busy photographing each other. A *gelati* vendor was doing a thriving business. A group of inattentive British schoolboys was being lectured to in front of number 26, where Keats had died. Four nuns were entering Babbington's English Tearoom, where just about nobody spoke English.

She waited for a lull in the rushing traffic and dashed across. The Via Condotti lay ahead, a long straight street that was a compendium of international stores: Rosenthal, Ginori, Pucci, Gucci, Bucellati, Bulgari. . . . The prices on the articles in the windows were breathtaking, but she had to have clothing. Besides, she wasn't going to disgrace Michael in front of the terrorists by looking like a *shlepper!*

And then it occurred to her, all jokes aside, that a similar thought might have crossed her mother's mind as she chose her wardrobe, twenty-five years ago, for *her* rescue mission. . . .

Six

At the age of twenty, Juno had been torn between quitting college and dying—nothing so sordid as suicide, understand, but a gradual ebbing away of her life force until, a songless Violetta, she slipped off into nothingness while all about her people wept.

Her mother, who phoned her once a week, flushed out the undertones of despair in her voice and demanded to know if she was sick, or, if not sick, something worse. Juno denied that anything was wrong, but her mother, a skilled diagnostician in the pathology of distress, putting her trust in the resonances of "a mother's heart," knew better. She hung up, packed a grip, and, no plane being available until midmorning of the following day, took a taxi to the bus station at midnight. *Midnight*, mind you, which was an hour past her normal bedtime.

She rode a bus all night, in the company of pale young women with wan infants bound for distant army camps to join their husbands; men who drank from bottles encased in paperbags and glowered silently; an assortment of people as insubstantial as ghosts in the haze of the bus's night lights. At three o'clock in the morning, the bus pulled in for a fifteen minute pause at a grimy station in an anonymous small town. She used a ladies' room that wasn't fit for a pig, I tell you, and sipped coffee at an unsanitary lunch counter rank with the smell of frying meat. A drunk on the next stool fell asleep with his head on her shoulder.

But she bore these discomforts, this immersion in an alien world, with fortitude and never wavered in her determination to perform her duty. Her daughter was in trouble, deep trouble, and, although she had denied it—she could deny it until her head fell off—desperately needed the loving comfort and sagacious advice that only a mother could give her.

In the morning, Juno was pulled out of her first class—dropping out or dying to one side, she couldn't afford another cut in Phil. 204—and instructed to go to the office of the dean of women. Her mother was waiting there, hollow-eyed from her night-long ordeal, her smart traveling suit disheveled, her eyes dark pools of sympathy and concern, her arms extended in an invitation to enter the nest. Stunned by her mother's presence, angered by it, embarrassed by it and, finally, overwhelmed by it, Juno ran into those comforting arms. They rocked each other and shed copious tears while the dean of women looked on, shaken by the primitive emotion of the scene, the loudness of the wails, the unrestrained artlessness of this commonplace reenactment of the *pietà*.

It was only later, after her mother had napped, refreshed herself, met her roommate (in a whisper: "Such a pretty *shiksa*, but all skin and bones, if I was her mother I would see to it she ate") and sat down for lunch in an off-campus rendezvous, that Juno realized that she hadn't the faintest idea of what the trouble was, but had simply divined a crisis from the sound of her daughter's voice on the telephone.

"So tell me all about it, Blanche, and maybe I can help you. What is the problem?"

Except for the members of her family, nobody had called her Blanche since her sophomore year in high school, when an art teacher, penetrating the disguise of her self-conscious klutziness, had said that her figure and bearing were Junoesque. The name had stuck. From then on she had been Juno, and now Blanche sounded strange to her.

"For every problem," her mother said, "there is an answer. *Every* problem."

Juno had already found an answer, worked out her salvation in the long torturous sleepless night: she would neither drop out of school nor die a lingering death, but simply go on, sadder and wiser. It had struck her, somewhere around five o'clock in the morning, that, however painful it might be, her affair with Professor John Avery, with its woeful aftermath, was entirely predictable and banal. Banality was the foe of high drama; therefore she would do nothing drastic.

She had given up her virginity to an inveterate womanizer (the modulation for that unflattering word was Byronic, which is how Profesor Avery, of the chemistry department, was known on the campus). He was slender, pale, wavy-haired, poetic, with, as the impressionable girls about campus put it, "burning eyes that look down deep into your soul and lay it bare." *Lay* was the operative word. Not to mention *bare*. An hour after he had turned his burning eyes on her in chemistry lab, they were in a motel room where he was undressing her with exquisite technique. She had given herself to him wholeheartedly, wantonly. She had been madly in love with him, wildly infatuated, she would die for him, live for him, do anything he asked her to. And she was still desperately in love when, after a month, he had tired of her, as he had of so many others, and taken up with another girl (at the same motel) who had succumbed to the burning eyes and the poetic look. She had written him letters, telephoned him night and day, lain in wait for him, wrecked herself against the adamancy of his indifference and, at last, swallowing the bitter pill of wisdom, admitted to herself that she had never been loved, merely used.

In the face of a baffling silence, Juno's mother fell back to a prepared position: "From the time you were a little child you were always stubborn. It's time you grew out of it."

"I don't want to talk about it, Mother."

"But stubborn as you are, I can be just as stubborn. You ought to know your mother—she never gives up."

"Mother, I appreciate your coming here, but it was totally unnecessary. I'm perfectly capable of taking care of myself."

"Unnecessary? When I knew my child was suffering?"

"Eat your sandwich. I'm not going to discuss anything with you. And if you don't stop questioning me, I'm going to walk out of here."

"You're too high-strung for your own good. All right, I'll respect your wishes. But can I ask you one question?"

"No, Mother."

"Not even one little question? After I traveled all night to get here? There were *cockroaches* on the bus, they shouldn't allow food."

"No, mother."

"Just one little question, and after that I'll leave you alone. Are you pregnant?"

"No, thank God."

"Thank God is right. You want to know something? I knew in my heart it was man trouble."

Juno said nothing, but masticated the cardboard they had mistakenly given her in place of a sandwich.

"So," her mother said, "I have just one question to ask you."

"You've already asked two."

"My question is—and I hope you answer it truthfully. Believe me, no matter what, I won't censure you. My only purpose is to help."

"You can't help," Juno said, in a renewal of her earlier mood of romantic hopelessness. "Nobody can help."

"What I want to know—did you sleep with this boy?"

"He's not a boy, he's a grown man."

Her mother brushed the irrelevancy aside. "Believe me, Blanche, the secret will die with me. I won't under any circumstances repeat it to your father. My solemn oath."

Wearily, because she knew her mother would never give up and, perhaps, because she owed her a debt for that all-night bus trip, she said, "Yes, Mother, I slept with him."

Her mother shut her eyes for a moment, and rocked back and forth. Rolling with the punch, Juno thought. But then her mother smiled and produced a surprise.

"I'll tell you a secret I never before told to *anybody*. You think I was a virgin on my wedding night? Not by a long shot. Your father and I, we had an affair for six months before we got married. So what do you think of that?"

"Well, I don't intend to marry anybody."

"I'm going to ask you just one more time, and you can change your story if you want to. Are you pregnant?"

Her suffering, compounded by the humiliation of having made an absolute fool of herself, had had a curiously salutary side effect on Juno. It had burned away the last remnants of her baby fat, brought up the bone in her face, sculptured it, so that, as the saying had it, she "came into her beauty." She became a candidate for Homecoming Queen, although, in the event, she lost out to a little beauty from Oklahoma with beguiling dimples and a hundredworth of pizzazz.

"Pearl Harbor," her mother had once said, rolling the words out portentously, "was like the end of the world, and nobody ever forgot exactly what they were doing at that time for the rest of their lives. It was a Sunday afternoon, and I was listening to the broadcast of the Philharmonic. They were playing the Brahms Fourth Symphony, and they interrupted it: FLASH! Pearl Harbor attacked! Ever since, the Brahms Fourth means one thing: Pearl Harbor. I ran into the bedroom and I grabbed you out of your bed."

"Why did you do that, Mother?"

Her mother had looked at her as though she had lost her senses. "You didn't let a peep out of you. You were such a good baby, never cranky."

The announcement of Michael's kidnapping had been Juno's Pearl

Harbor, and as long as she lived she would never forget exactly what she had been doing at that moment, ordinary as the details were. She could reconstruct the moment as if it were frozen in a photograph. ... Saturday, coming up to one o'clock, the radio turned on in the kitchen. She was preparing a salad for lunch, slicing radishes into the bowl, Jerry at the table blowing his nose into a pink tissue (he had a slight cold), the chime for the news, the announcer saying, as she popped a sliver of radish into her mouth (bitter vetch!), "This just in. From Milan, Italy. Two American businessmen have been abducted by the left-wing terrorist group Forze Scarlatte, or Scarlet Forces, an offshoot of the notorious Red Brigades. The two, who have been accused in a communiqué received by Italian police earlier today as being quote agents of the infamous CIA unquote, have been named as Joseph Bering and Michael Surton. ..."

Identifying Michael as a CIA agent was only slightly more absurd than characterizing him as a businessman. Poor dear Michael, if a name had to be put to him at all it would be "lover." Lover—that was why he was in Italy at all, following that girl round like a faithful dog—that Adriana, with whom he was so sufferingly in love. But what right had she, Juno, to be critical of the madness of love?

It hadn't put her off so much as a split second when they had botched Michael's name—"Surton" for "Sultan." The instant they had mentioned Joe Bering's name she had known at once what was coming. With the unswallowed sliver of radish burning her tongue she had blacked out.... No, not really blacked out, but been suffused by such an overwhelming wave of blind terror that she hadn't heard a word of the rest of the bulletin. Not that there was much more, simply a statement from the Italian government that the matter was viewed with the utmost gravity and that full measures were being taken.

She remembered dropping the knife into the sink with a clatter, and walking out of the kitchen, past Jerry, who was half out of his chair, the tissue arrested against his nose, pallor beginning to spread, and rage, if she knew her Jerry, just an instant away. He was a doer, a man of action, a man who couldn't sit still. She had never known, nor ever would, why she had ignored him and gone directly into the bedroom. Somewhere in her subconscious, perhaps, she blamed him for having involved Michael with Bering in the first instance, though to do so was insanely unfair; because of his infatuation with Adriana, Michael would have been in Italy under any circumstances, whether working for Bering or not.

The next day a newspaper, elaborating untruthfully, wrote that she had walked into the bedroom and immediately begun to pack a valise.

Later, some other papers and a television station had repeated this version of events, though it was absolutely untrue. She had gone to the bedroom because she had wanted to be alone with her tears—it was as simple as that. But it *was* true—never mind the nonsense about the valise—that she had already made up her mind to go to Italy.

And so, as she was compelled to admit (to herself, at any rate), there was a straight line leading from her great-grandmother, who had lived on Hester Street and worn a babushka, to her grandmother, who prided herself on being a Yankee, to her mother, a college woman (three years at Hunter before she got married and quit), subscriber to the Met and the Philharmonic, faultlessly tasteful dresser...and yet her mother, however many arias of Verdi, Donizetti, and Bellini she could identify and even credibly hum, her mother had dowsed out a tremor in her daughter's voice over six hundred miles of telephone wire and, counting no cost, ridden in a jouncing bus through the alien American hinterland to administer the medicine of mother love. And she, Juno, who had been so embarrassed and mortified at her mother's turning up in the office of that cool understated dean of women, and hated her—yes, hated—for being a stereotype of the Jewish mother, hadn't she, Juno, behaved exactly as her great-grandmother would have, and her grand-mother would have, and as her mother *had*, and as her own daughter, Sharon, inevitably would when she had her own children...?

But, for all of that—as even one of the newspapers, playing on the Jewish mother theme, had acknowledged—it had been a *gentile* mother, during the hostage crisis in Iran, who had defied the authorities by going to Tehran to see her captive son. All mothers, the article had gone on to say, Judy O'Grady and Colonel Moskowitz's lady, were sisters under the skin.

Dating from the Saturday when the news had first broken—was it possible that that lifetime was a mere two weeks?—Juno had learned to mistrust the media, beginning with that first afternoon, when the television people had turned up. She had still been in a state of shock, and so had Jerry, or she would never have let them in. They had some-how, speedily, using sources that were probably better than the gov-ernment's, ascertained that Michael—Sultan, not Surton as first report-ed—was the son of the well-known furniture manufacturer and de-signer Jerry Sultan, and here they were, overrunning the apartment with cameras, wires, lights, microphones; and here was the well-known reporter who was even better looking (but much shorter) than he looked on camera.

Before they knew it, she and Jerry were sitting side by side on the sofa. The well-known reporter asked if she wanted to spruce up a bit, refresh her makeup, and Jerry, at least, had had the presence of mind to snarl no thanks, that they would come as they were. The bright lights went on, and the reporter started asking questions. Jerry, for the most part, sat there grimly silent, and she had carried the ball. Boy, had she carried the ball, including breaking into tears, which certainly must have warmed the cockles of the network's heart. After some warm-up questions, the reporter deftly, casually, said, "Is your son Michael a CIA agent?"

She glared at him before blurting out, "Of course not, it's ridiculous!"

"How can you be so sure?" the reporter said softly. "If he *was* CIA, he certainly wouldn't tell you so, would he?"

"Well then," she said, "if he wouldn't tell me, how could I possibly answer your question?"

The reporter smiled. "Then how *do* you account for his being in Italy?"

She felt a slight tremor from Jerry, but he didn't say anything; he looked drawn, pale, and he was staring at the tips of his shoes. She knew he was still undergoing guilt pangs, even though she had earlier convinced him, or thought she had, that he was to accept no blame for what was truly an accident. A little over a year ago, he had taken Michael with him to a furniture fair in Bologna. There the accident had happened: Michael met Adriana, who was then a premed student at the University of Bologna. Could Jerry blame himself for the spontaneous, incandescent passion that had engulfed the two of them?

Michael had stayed on in Bologna after Jerry left. When he wrote, it was to say that he had entered the university, where he would take courses in political science.

A few months later, Jerry had gone to Rome on business, and flown up to Bologna. He found Michael hanging out in one of the student cafés under an arcade on the Via dell'Arte.

They had had what Jerry described as "a pretty good argument." Michael wouldn't hear of coming home, nor would he accept any money from Jerry; they had that kind of touchy relationship. Then Michael had absently combed his hair with his hands, which until then had been hidden beneath the table. "Like raw meat," Jerry had told her, his eyes reflecting horror and pity. "Cracked, split, in a few places the skin entirely gone and the flesh exposed. . . ."

Michael was supporting himself—his tuition at the university as well as his living expenses—by working as a dishwasher in a *trattoria*. "Okay," Jerry had said, "at least let me pay for a doctor so you can get those hands fixed up." Although his hands must have been causing him agony, Michael refused the offer of help. What could a doctor do, he wanted to know, that the next night's immersion in suds and abrasives wouldn't undo?

Jerry brought up the hands again after he had met the girl, Adriana.

"She has a lovely delicate skin," he said. "How can she bear having you touch her with those hands?" But almost before the words were out of his mouth he knew the answer Michael would give. "She thinks they're beautiful, she says they're hands that have made their own way in the world." Jerry had known his case was hopeless.

He had tried to satisfy Juno's curiosity about the girl, but he was no great hand at description. She was pretty, he guessed, fine blondish-brown hair, tall and slender, poised—

"Yes, but what's she *like?*" Juno had asked, seeking a clue to the special quality that had entranced Michael.

"I'm trying to tell you. She has class. A very serious type, she didn't smile once while we were talking. Good manners, intelligent, speaks English well, though she and Michael seem to do most of their talking in Italian..."

When Jerry next returned to Italy, Michael had dropped out of school and was about to move to Padua. Adriana had completed her premed courses and had been admitted to the Medical School at the University of Padua. Michael was vague about his own plans, but he would find some kind of work in Padua. Washing dishes? Yes, if that was all he could get, he would wash dishes.

At that point, Jerry had taken the train to Milan to see Joe Bering. They had first met a dozen years ago, and hit it off very well. They kept running into each other at the Principe in Milan, the Ritz or George V in Paris, the Savoy in London, the Alphonse XIII in Madrid. They were kindred spirits, what an earlier generation called sports, meaning that they liked to live well and were free with a dollar. On the occasions when they ran into each other they would dine at the best restaurants and do the town together. When Jerry had broached the idea of Bering's hiring Michael as a combination interpreter, assistant, and gofer, Bering had been enthusiastic. If Michael caught on to the business, then eventually, when Bering decided to retire, since he had no son of his own, why, Mike might even take it over.

When he brought the proposition to Michael, Jerry had been prepared to do a selling job. He could sell almost anything to anybody else, so why not to Michael? He braced himself for fireworks, imagining immediate hot refusal, but in the event, Michael had been quite reasonable. Cradling his flayed hands delicately in each other (God, how they must have hurt, Jerry thought), he had simply said that he would like time to think it over.

"It's a great opportunity, Mike. Interesting work, travel, living in the best hotels, learning a trade, and a damn lucrative one, I might add..."

"Dad, do me a favor, please, don't *pitch* this thing. I said I'd think it over. Let's just leave it at that."

"Okay." Jerry said. Rich living, money—those things didn't cut much ice with Michael. "Okay. How much time will you need?"

"I'll let you know tomorrow."

The next day, when Michael said yes, Jerry's delight had been somewhat tempered by his certainty that the decision had been made by Adriana; the girl had a firm grip on Mike's balls. Telling Juno about it, he had said, "You know why she told him to take it? Because she couldn't stand looking at those horrible hands anymore." Juno told him he was being unfair—that if the girl loved him she would have done what she thought was best for Michael. Jerry hadn't been all that sure, but the thing that really mattered to him was that at last, maybe, Michael was about to become a *mensch*. This filled him with jubilation.

In the television interview, of course, none of this came out. Answering the reporter's question about what Michael was doing in Italy, Juno merely said, "He works there, in the import-export business."

The reporter, eliciting from Juno the fact that she intended to go to Italy, remarked that the authorities took a dim view of amateurs mixing in and might attempt to deter her from leaving.

Bridling, Juno said, "Is that so? Well, I'd just like to see somebody try to stop me!"

The reporter shrewdly ended the interview right there.

Everyone in the world saw the telecast that evening—relatives, acquaintances, and, of course, Fernald, who immediately flew up from Washington. He didn't reach their house until nearly nine, and by then the phone had rung dozens of times. Juno was uncharacteristically short with most of the callers—who gave her performance a rave review—except for her mother and Sharon. Her mother cried a lot—Michael was, after all, her darling *aynekul*—cursed the terrorists, and offered various bits of advice, all of which Juno accepted, and none of which she would carry out.

Sharon's call turned out to be a surprise. To begin with, instead of sounding bored, as usual, she was animated, even euphoric; instead of criticizing Juno for being an archtypical Jewish mother, she professed to be delighted with the "bold, feminist fuck-you directness" of her answer to the reporter.

"Well, darling, I just said what I felt."

"If I didn't know better, I might have guessed that somebody had been raising your consciousness. Whatever—you came out with a gorgeous *gut* response. It was beautiful."

"All right. I'm wonderful. But isn't it time you had something to say about Michael?"

"Michael?"

"How badly you feel about him, how worried you are, how much you're hoping and praying—"

"What do you *mean*—" Sharon began in her familiar affronted voice, and then she stopped and let out a heartfelt wail followed by a freshet of tears.

Juno, too, burst into tears, and for five minutes they did little but weep. Juno got control of herself first. She told Sharon to go wash her face, and maybe take a hot shower and a couple of aspirins. . . .

Sharon stopped her tears with a convulsive laugh. "And have a good bowel movement? You forgot the bowel movement, Mother."

She had never—at least since Sharon went off to college—monitored her bowel movements, but she didn't bother denying it. The conversation ended with much good feeling, although at the end Sharon reverted to militancy: "Sock it to them, Mother!"

In a way, the phone calls were a blessing, because they kept her and Jerry apart. He had been flatly opposed to the idea of her going off to Italy. It was pointless, dangerous, the terrorists would never let her see Michael, she should let the proper authorities handle the matter. . . . She had felt outraged by his attitude, betrayed, and with an uncharacteristic burst of temper had rushed off to the bedroom and locked the door. Jerry pounded on the door and threatened to break it down, but after hitting it a few thumps with his fist, went to make phone calls—God knew to whom: his lawyer, a police official he knew, an army officer who was the relative of a friend, low-level people in the Department of Commerce in Washington. She knew Jerry—the *macher*, the doer, the man of action, who could never sit still and do nothing. . . . And what did he accomplish? *Bobkes*, Zayde would have said: beans, nothing.

Fernald, the man who called himself Fernald. She and Jerry, silent and avoiding each other's eyes at the table, were eating a hastily improvised omelet, with the phone off the hook, when the door chimes rang. Jerry opened the door, and there he was, Fernald, presenting his credentials for inspection. It was these credentials, the ID with the great seal of the United States on it, that had impressed the doorman and gotten him by without being announced. Jerry invited him in.

He was disarming. He told her with candor—it was like letting her in on affairs of state, which might have been its flattering purpose— that he had heard her on the TV and considered her declaration of purpose, and its air of challenge, so alarming that he had left his dinner untouched, rushed to the airport—

"Could I make you something? Would you like an omelet?"

No, but he wouldn't mind a cup of tea. She put up the kettle and fixed a plate of cookies, and brought everything back to the living room on a tray. Jerry was sounding off, his face flushed, his finger wagging at Fernald. At her appearance he fell silent. She placed the tray on the side table beside Fernald's chair.

"I forgot to ask whether you took cream or lemon. I brought both."

Fernald thanked her and complimented her on the teacup and saucer, delicate, almost transparent Royal Worcester. She sat down on a loveseat facing him. He sipped the tea, taking neither lemon nor cream. No sugar, either.

"Mrs. Sultan," he said, "I'll try to get to the point quickly."

"Try the cookies," Juno said. "Those spice ones are delicious."

"Juno, please," Jerry said.

Fernald took a tiny bite of the spice cookie. "Delicious. The purpose of my visit, it should come as no surprise—"

"Eat the whole thing," Juno said, "there are plenty more."

"Juno, stop that and let him talk," Jerry said.

She said to Fernald, "You're wasting your time. I'm sorry you missed your dinner on my account, but nothing you can possibly say will change my mind."

"Juno," Jerry said, "let the man speak. You don't even know what he's going to say."

Of course she did; not word for word, maybe, but the substance. Why couldn't Jerry see it?

"It's not like her to be discourteous," Jerry said to Fernald, who was now looking from one to the other of them and munching on a cookie. Jerry turned to Juno. "I know you're upset, darling, but this man, a representative of our government, is just doing his duty. It's wrong to be angry with him."

Fernald said, "She's not angry with *me*, Mr. Sultan."

"With *me*? How can she be angry with *me*? That's ridiculous."

She was angry with both of them. With Fernald because he was messing in something that wasn't any of his business. With Jerry because his attitude struck her as verging on being disloyal.

Fernald said, "Mr. Sultan, would you allow me to speak to your wife alone?"

Jerry flushed, but said quietly enough, "I'm as involved in this as my wife is. Michael happens to be my son, too."

Juno said, "Go into the bedroom, Jerry."

"It might make things easier," Fernald said.

Jerry glared at both of them. Juno turned away from him. "Your tea is getting cold, Mr. Fernald."

Jerry pointed his finger at her. His flush had turned darker. "I want you to stop the comedy act—" He broke off abruptly, with a look of surprise, and grimaced.

"Try to calm down," Juno said. "And why are you making faces?"

Jerry pushed his chair back and got to his feet. He was still grimacing, massaging his stomach with the palm of his hand. "Cramp. Will you excuse me for a second, Mr. Fernald?"

He started away from the table. Juno said, "Where are you going?"

"I'm going to the bathroom, for God's sake. Okay?"

"Want me to help?"

Bent slightly forward, as if to accommodate his pain, Jerry made a hopeless gesture to Fernald. "In this household, everything is a big deal." He said to Juno, "I appreciate it, but I'm old enough to go to the bathroom by myself."

He crossed the room, slightly stooped. But he didn't neglect to slam the bedroom door. Fernald was bent discreetly over his teacup. He was a slender man with a narrow face marked by lines and wrinkles that made him appear older than he probably was. He looked sensitive and intelligent, and his wrinkles were appealing: you had to respect a man who worried so much, presumably about his country.

She mistrusted him completely.

He said, "I'm sorry, I didn't mean to precipitate—"

"It's all right. A quarrel between us is never fatal, we always make up."

"May I explain our position to you?" He didn't wait for a reply but went on. "To begin with, you must understand that we are quite as anxious as you are to secure the release of your son. And of Mr. Bering."

Could he truly believe that he—the government he represented—could possibly be as concerned as the captive's own mother? If so, he was a fool. If not, a liar. He waited for her to respond, and seemed discomfited when she remained silent.

"I would hope that you might accept that premise, Mrs. Sultan."

She said calmly, "If that's what your premise is, Mr. Fernald, you might as well save your breath."

"I beg your pardon?"

"Do you have a child, Mr. Fernald?"

"I have two daughters."

"Two lovely girls. If I told you that I was quite as anxious about your daughters as you are—I believe *quite* was the word you used—would you believe me?"

Fernald's smile managed to be both wintry and rueful at the same time. "If I thought you could be more helpful with my daughters—"

"Yes. Excuse me. This is the first time the question of competence has come up. Before it was anxiety—who cared more."

He bowed his head in acknowledgment. "You're right, of course. The issue is which of us is more capable of helping your son."

"Can I give you more tea?"

"No, thank you. Mrs. Sultan, the branch of government I represent is highly skilled in handling these matters. I assure you that we will bend every effort—have already begun to do so, in fact—to secure the safe release of Michael and Mr. Bering from the terrorists."

"I believe you."

"Thank you. May I then ask you to reconsider your decision to go to Italy?"

"What does one thing have to do with the other?"

"There is a long answer to that." Fernald's smile was downright winsome. "The short answer is that you might be a hindrance, might unwittingly obstruct our efforts."

"I'll be quiet as a mouse. You won't even know I'm there."

Fernald said, "It's not a joking matter, Mrs. Sultan."

"No. And I apologize. But you haven't really convinced me that I'll be in the way. Do you remember the woman who flew to Iran to see her son? The government objected to her going. But she went anyway, and she saw her son, which did both the woman and her son a lot of good, and unless you want to put the blame on that woman, I'll remind you that it took you people four hundred and forty-four days to get those poor hostages released."

"The woman was there early on. Clearly, her presence didn't help either."

"It helped *her*—she saw her son—and it helped *him*, believe me, it helped him to see his mother."

Fernald bowed his head and smiled his winsome smile. "I must look a villain, standing in the way of mother love."

"You're arguing your case, that's all. But I'll tell you again—you're wasting your breath."

Fernald picked up his empty teacup, looked into it, and set it down again. Juno cocked her ear to the bedroom. Not a sound. Jerry was in there brooding. The real battle, she knew, would begin after Fernald left.

She said, "I don't want you to think I'm being rude, but my mind is made up. Michael needs me. That's my priority. I'll be glad to give you some more tea, but there's nothing you can possibly say that will change my mind. *Nothing*."

"Do you think there's even a remote chance that you can get to see him, given the nature of his captors?"

"I can try—and that's all that you can do, too. And at worst, I'll be in Italy, I'll be three thousand miles nearer to my son."

He studied her for a moment. "You really mean to go."

She nodded. Why should he sound surprised? "Yes, Mr. Fernald, I certainly do."

"In that case, it's my duty, now, to inform you that we will not *allow* you to go."

"Ah. What took you so long getting around to that point? Maybe the tea and cookies softened you up?"

Fernald might have smiled at that a minute ago. But now he had shifted gears: charm was out and he was operating from power. "You can make it easy or hard—it's entirely up to you but, by one means or another, we will interdict you."

For all his smoothness, for all his appealing face and good manners, Juno thought, these were Fernald's true colors; and *interdict*, that ugly official word, was his native language. He was here to stop her one way or another—when reason failed he turned to the exercise of power; if that failed he would try coercion; and if coercion failed, she was sure, he would resort to force. She tried to think of him as hateful, but couldn't do so. He was following his own star, his duty, as she was following hers.

She said, "I hope it won't bore you to be reminded that we live in a democracy, and that I'm a citizen in good standing. Mr. Fernald, you can't stop me."

"I can. For one, we can lift your passport."

"On what grounds?"

"Anything we want." He shrugged. "That your actions are inimical to the interests of the U.S. government, that you're subversive...*anything*."

"Don't make me laugh. The press would tear you to pieces."

Fernald stood up. "Will you reconsider, Mrs. Sultan?"

She shook her head.

"I know when to quit." His smile was rueful; he had fallen back on charm again, and she could not help liking him. "I do understand your position, even sympathize with it, in a way. Nevertheless..." He let the word hang, an unstated threat.

"Don't feel too bad about your feelings," Juno said. "If you do, just think about your daughters."

"Thank you for the tea, Mrs. Sultan."

At the door she said, "You've thought twice about trying to lift my passport, but you have other ways—am I right, Mr. Fernald?"

"Please say good-bye to Mr. Sultan for me."

When the door closed behind him she took the tea things into the kitchen and then she went to the bedroom. The room was dark. Jerry was standing at the window, his shoulders slumped, his whole body sagging. Time to make up, she thought, by now they were both ready. She switched on the light. He turned toward her, and at that precise moment his hand flew up to his chest and he began to gasp, hyperventilate. As she ran toward him he staggered, and before she could reach him he collapsed, striking the edge of the bed, bouncing off it and falling to the floor with a crash.

Seven

At quarter of eight, restored by a nap, refreshed by a shower and head wash with the jasmine-scented *schiuma* the hotel provided for the bath, Juno dressed in the beige skirt, emerald-green silk blouse, and navy jacket she had bought—along with other purchases, including a valise—on the Via Condotti. She would be at least a half hour early. The Forze Scarlatte letter had stipulated that she was to arrive at the Via Veneto at eight thirty. Sometime in the next two hours she would be contacted. For all the abstruse windy language of the letter, it was precise about details. When she got to the Via Veneto she was to take a seat at Carpano and order a drink. If she was not contacted by nine thirty, she was to make a circuit of the Via Veneto from the Pincian Gate to the Excelsior, recross the street to the starting point, and begin the circuit over again. If by ten thirty she still had not been contacted, she was to return to her hotel, and another, later attempt would be made. The person who contacted her would be holding the missing portion of the picture of Michael.

When she left the hotel, she walked slowly up the Via Sistina, with its sidewalk so narrow that two people abreast could barely manage to squeeze by each other. It was already dark; the street was meagerly lit only by the occasional night light in a store window. Traffic barreled down the street with abandon. Once, when a motorcycle roared by, she remembered the warnings she had heard about the *scippatori*, the cyclists that swooped down on pedestrians and snatched their bags on the run. She took the standard precaution of shifting her new leather purse to the side away from the curb. The cyclist went by harmlessly.

She turned into the Via Francesco Crespi, and then went straight on to the Via Veneto. She killed a few minutes browsing at the huge newsstand at the corner before going on. The Via Veneto was not as crowded as it had been years ago, when she had first visited Rome; the Piazza Navona was now the "in" place. But it still had its share of people turning out for a drink at the sidewalk cafés or for a stroll—practicing the art of the Via Veneto, which was to see and be seen.

By dawdling in front of shop windows, she managed to reach Carpano only five minutes early. She took a seat beneath the green awning spread above the sidewalk. A dozen people or so occupied the tables with their lemon-colored cloths. And three-quarters of them appeared to be tourists, the rest Italian; none showed more than a normal interest in her. She ordered a vodka and tonic and, as an afterthought, a chicken sandwich; she hadn't eaten since lunch. The waiter brought her order. A tiny feather clung to the plate. Okay, Carpano, it's real chicken.

Her seat was in the front row facing the sidewalk, with an unobstructed view. In the next hour she exchanged glances with many passersby, but none made any overt sign of recognition. At nine thirty, with a feeling of disappointment and the first gnawing sense of anxiety, she paid her bill, got up, and walked slowly toward the Pincian Gate.

"Hello, my baby."

She stopped dead, and waited for him to come up from behind her. He was seventeen—maybe less. Glossy black hair, long and thick, slender arching Roman nose, tawny skin, large lustrous eyes with sweeping lashes. Wearing a pink silk blouse and skintight shiny leather jeans.

"What says you, baby?"

She walked on, stunned. Granted, it was Rome, but still, this child . . .

He fell in step beside her. "You are much beautiful, lady."

Lady, all right, that's an improvement over baby. Eyes straight ahead, she quickened her pace. What would the people watching from the tables think? Who cared what they thought. Besides, since it was Rome they might be mildly amused, but no more.

With a trace of annoyance the boy said, "Why you don't say nothing? Don't speak no English? *Est-ce que vous êtes francaise? Oder Deutsch?*"

And then it occurred to her that, outlandish as it might seem, this creature might be her contact.

"Yes I speak English."

"Ah, *molto bene.* So pray tell me—you wish to have sex with a pretty boy?"

"That's not what I'm interested in."

"Not interested, you say?" He put a look of incredulity on his face. "How is this possible, lady?"

They made the turn at the Pincian Gate, where a large marble slab was inscribed with the names of the young men of the Ludovisan quarter who had fallen in the 1914–1918 war. She said to the boy, "Look—do you have something for me?"

His eyes brightened. "To be sure, my lady. Have large equipment."

She made a sound that was part exasperation and part despair, and turned away from the boy.

"Much recommended for durable, lady. Guarantee four, five, seven times the night."

Some courier, Juno thought. He was exactly what he seemed, a young stud who made his living from pleasing foreign ladies of a certain age. "Go away, please."

She found a break in the flow of traffic and hurried across the street. The boy followed. "Maybe you like tender? I can be your little boy."

"If you were my little boy I'd keep you home at night. I'd make you do your homework and stay out of trouble."

"You do not like me, lady? I am not pretty?"

She walked on, ignoring him.

"Is possible. But maybe you like my friend?" He glanced back over his shoulder and gave a short whistle. A thin blond boy trotted up. "I present Paolo. From up north, fine blond fellow. You like?"

They ranged themselves on either side of her. It was no longer funny, they were a liability: whoever her contact was would be hampered by the presence of the two boys. She quickened her pace.

"You like *two* boys, lady? Two for one, same price."

She hurried on toward Doney's tables, magenta cloths under a blue canopy. The boys came closer, hemming her in. She stopped short. "All right, that's enough. If you don't go away, I'm going to call the police."

The boys looked at each other in astonishment. She knew what they were thinking: It was one thing not to play by the rules of the game, but to flout them flagrantly by invoking the police . . . Yet, as she walked on, they continued to flank her closely. She stopped again.

"Will you please get lost?"

She had raised her voice, and attracted an audience among the people at Doney's tables. She took a step forward, and the boys, perhaps deciding to punish her, blocked her path, grinning at each other.

A man rose from a table, bowed to her, and said, "Permit me, signora."

He faced the two boys and spoke to them in a low voice. There was a response from the boys. The man took out his billfold. The boys stepped out of the way. Juno moved on quickly. When she looked back, the man and the boys were walking toward the Pincian Gate. The man had an arm around the waist of each boy. Well, it was Rome, wasn't it?

She walked by the Excelsior: a constant stream of people going up or down the steps leading to the entrance; off to the side, a half dozen young men with cameras, paparazzi, watching the entrance, hoping for some target of opportunity.

Crossing the street again, Juno felt her cheeks burning. She had let herself become flustered by the boys and made herself conspicuous. Would the Forze Scarlatte courier, if he had been watching, think that she was a fool, and not to be trusted? She reached the curb, and began the second lap of the circuit. It was five minutes of ten.

She went past the newsstand, past a men's store where Jerry had admired, but not bought, a striped shirt that cost a hundred and twenty-five dollars; past what seemed like two dozen shoe stores; past Rizzoli, the bookstore; past Carpano... but not quite past Carpano without incident. A man seated at a table watched her approach, gave her a lewd wink, languidly unfolded himself from his chair, and caught up with her. He was a different type from the two boys, older, in his thirties. He was wearing a silk shirt open halfway down his torso, a medallion dangling from a thin gold chain in the thicket of a hairy chest, designer jeans, Gucci shoes. His face was handsome in a bony, tough, taut-skinned way; his eyes were hooded, sexy, slightly sinister; his hair was blow-dried in an artfully careless plume that dropped over his forehead.

He was half a pace behind her when she reached the Pincian Gate and crossed the street. He caught up with her as she strode toward Doney.

He leaned toward her intimately. "The signora wishes to be shown Rome by one who is well acquainted with the Rome a tourist never sees?"

His English was very good; his hand rested lightly on her arm.

"No. Go away. I don't have any need for a *cicisbeo*."

His brows arched in surprise. "You know this word—*cicisbeo*?"

"I know one when I see one."

A *cicisbeo* was a gigolo who, in centuries past and particularly in Venice, would dance attendance on upper-class ladies, often with the acquiescence of the ladies' husbands.

Approaching the block-long canopy of Doney with the man, the *cicisbeo*, at her side, she thought, I'm putting on quite a show, I'm going to have the people at the tables rolling in the aisles. She hurried on. The man put his hand on her wrist, not lightly, but with enough pressure to detain her.

"Signora."

They were almost to the entrance of the Excelsior. She pulled her wrist free. "I'm not going to tell you this again. Go away or I'll..." Or I'll what? Scream? Punch him in the nose? "Just go away, please."

"Let us walk on, Signora," he said in a quiet voice, "and I'll show you a certain picture."

But before she could respond there was an eruption of blinding lights, of shouting voices. It left her stunned, disoriented, and it was several long moments before she realized that she was the center of an antic mob of paparazzi, jostling each other for position, aiming their cameras and popping off their flashes, screaming at her to smile, to stick out her chest....

She covered her face and turned her back to the flashes. She looked for the *cicisbeo*. He was nowhere in sight. The flashes and the yelling went on for another while, then stopped abruptly. The paparazzi had left her and were pelting back toward the hotel, where a tall man in evening dress was coming down the steps. She recognized Marcello Mastroianni. Unnoticed now, she ran to the corner and crossed the street. It was quarter past ten. Uncertain of what to do now, she went back to Carpano and sat down. Nobody came, nobody spoke to her. At ten thirty she knew that it was over for the night, but she lingered another half hour. Then she paid her bill and walked back to the Via Ludovisi. Across the street the paparazzi were still clustered below the steps of the Excelsior.

She turned to her right and walked back to her hotel.

Between Orlandi's phone call, which waked her, and his appearance at her apartment, Giuseppina had had time only to wash her face and apply a touch of lipstick. She hesitated between a woolen robe and a more coquettish silk one and finally chose the wool. It would be stupid to think he was coming for anything but business reasons.

His dark eyes were apologetic when she opened the door to him.

"I'm sorry, Pina, it's a great imposition."

"Yes, yes. As the English say, it's the policeman's lot. Come in, Alfredo."

It was the first time he had been in her apartment in five years. The thought must have occured to him, too; uncharacteristically, he seemed ill at ease.

"Please sit down, Alfredo. Will you drink something?"

He shook his head. "We picked up the courier, Pina."

"Wonderful. How did it happen?"

"Quite simple—I wish everything was this easy. Once we found out where she was staying, we staked out a plainclothes detail at her hotel.

They were tailing her when she went out this evening. She walked up to the Via Veneto, sat down, had a sandwich, a drink, kept looking around her—it was very obvious she was expecting a rendezvous. We had half a dozen men on the street. After an hour she got up and walked."

"Left the Via Veneto?"

"Circumambulated. Two little pimps tried to pick her up."

"The couriers? Rather clever."

"So we thought. One of our men intercepted them and offered to pay them for sex. They went with him willingly enough—men, women, all the same to these little shits. Our cop got them into a police van and gave them a working over, but they turned out to be exactly what they seemed—punks working the tourist trade. Our man kicked their behinds and turned them loose."

"I know at least two of our boys who would have used them first."

Orlandi didn't smile at her joke. "She was nervous, hard to blame her, I suppose. Kept looking at her watch. Started walking again, and soon there was another pickup attempt."

"It was bound to happen. She's very attractive."

"This one was older, and very convincing, but he picked the wrong place to make his delivery—in front of the Excelsior. The paparazzi recognized her—you know how good those devils are—and flashes started to go off. The courier got scared. He ran off before he could make the delivery. We picked him up and ran him down to the Questura. Success."

"He's a Forzista?"

"No question about it."

"He admitted it?"

"Not yet. He's a tough one. This is no *irregolare*, but a hardened Forzista. Granted, we don't have his name on any list, but he's the real thing. Works at the Ministry of Transportation."

Giuseppina made a face. "That's the hotbed."

"Other agencies as well. I sometimes think half the government is made up of Brigate Rosse, Prima Linea, and Forze Scarlatte."

She nodded. "The fascists would be in the civil service too, if they were smart enough to pass the tests."

"The courier's name is Giancarlo Benevista—mean anything to you?" She shook her head. "I doubt that he knows where the two Americans are being held—they're smarter than that, usually—but if he does, we'll wring it out of him. We've just started his workout."

He could have told her all this in the morning. She said, "You haven't gotten to the good part yet, right, Alfredo?"

Orlandi smiled. "We took something from him." He took an envelope from his pocket. "Pina, how would you like to play the part of a Forzista?"

She held her hand out for the envelope. It was a plain white one; across its face somebody had typed: SIGNORA SULTAN.

Orlandi said "Inside the envelope you'll find a note from the FS to the Signora Sultan, some railroad tickets, and a photograph—to be exact, *half* a photograph."

"Ah," she said. "Perfect. My credentials as a Forzista."

He stood up. "I must get back to the Questura. Can you go at once?"

"Yes."

"Wear the black dress, of course."

"Of course. You must come again, Alfredo."

Diebold sat in shadow on the parapet at the top of the Spanish Steps, with a clear view of the hotel entrance. He had been in place since ten o'clock, after learning where the subject was staying. A phone call established that she was not in, so he sat patiently and awaited her return. She showed up a little after eleven. She came out of the darkness of the street, and when she moved into the hotel entrance, her hair bright in the glow, the gossiping taxi drivers at their ranks fell silent and watched.

Diebold had no idea of where she had been, what mischief she might have done, or how long she had been gone; no point mooning over what was irreversible. She was here now, and she would be covered henceforth—by himself until midnight and by a two-man relief team afterwards. Although he was convinced that she would stay put for the night, it was typical of Diebold that he never relaxed his vigilance, never took his eyes from the hotel entrance.

And so it was that he registered the arrival of the woman in black the moment she got out of the taxi.

Coming out of the elevator, seeing her seated in a corner of the lobby in the same black dress, Juno found it impossible to believe that anything had changed. But as she came closer, she realized that only the dress was the same and everything else was different. The woman's legs were crossed (good, shapely legs), she was smoking a cigarette, but, above all, her eyes were confident, the tilt of her head was poised.

"Please sit down, Signora Sultan." There were two armchairs with a marble-topped table between them.

Her use of English was no longer a surprise, of course. When she had called up on the house phone a few minutes before, she had begun in Italian, and then switched to English. Juno sat down.

"You are surprised, of course, signora. I am sorry to have misled you, but it was necessary for security reasons."

"It's about Michael?" Juno said.

"Yes. I am here to help you, signora."

"Who are you? What is your name?"

"You understand, there must be no names. But you may call me Giuseppina, if you wish."

"Michael is all right? He's well?"

"Yes." Giuseppina leaned forward to put out her cigarette. The lobby was empty except for a man in the concierge's booth, and a porter standing nearby. "I am here to give you something."

"You are with the Forz—"

"Please, signora. Suffice it to say that I am a courier."

Suffice it to say, Juno thought; she had learned her English in school, she had read in English literature. "How do I know who you are?"

A couple entered the lobby and picked up their room key, then moved to the elevator. "A photograph, yes?"

Juno's heartbeat accelerated. "Why didn't you contact me on the Via Veneto, instead of the *cicisbeo?* Or on the airplane? We were sitting side by side for seven hours...."

"Do not question our methods. We are, we must be, very security conscious." Her voice had turned harsh, her great eyes were steely.

"I suspected you on the plane, I don't know why.... You look quite different now, of course. But you still don't look like a terrorist."

The woman smiled. "You know what a terrorist looks like? A big beard, perhaps, or if a woman a thin mouth and cruel eyes?"

The couple at the elevator entered the car and the door slid shut.

"You may open your purse now, and place it on the floor. I will place an envelope in the purse. Then I will leave, and you may return to your room. *Capisce?*"

"Yes, *capisco.*"

The woman's hand moved quickly below the coffee table, and then she stood up. *"Buona notte, signora."*

Juno touched the woman's sleeve. "Will I be seeing Michael soon? Can you tell me that?"

"I can say nothing more." The woman started to move away, then paused. "Not to worry signora. *Buona fortuna!"*

Juno picked up her bag, closed it, and went to the elevator.

* * *

The woman in black was in the hotel less than ten minutes. She looked contemplatively at the taxi ranks, then decided to walk. Diebold gave her a substantial start before slipping off the parapet and following. He kept close to the building line, maintaining his distance. But when the pavement became hard-packed dirt, absorbing the sound of his footsteps, he closed in, timing himself so that he would overtake her as she came abreast of the tall wooden doors of an old apartment house. A long final step brought him to her heels. He whipped his left arm around her waist, and clapped his right hand over her mouth. He lifted her off her feet and, holding her tightly against his body, pushed against the doors. Momentum carried him inside. He kicked the doors shut behind him. He was in a vestibule, a covered passageway that led out to a small courtyard, with a semicircle of shuttered windows above, and an entrance to the building over to the left.

The woman was struggling, kicking backwards sharply with her heels, punishing his shins. He set her down with a jolt, and in the same movement turned her facing him. She went suddenly limp. He concentrated on keeping her erect, and so he never saw her hand starting toward him, and it was a lucky ray of light through an imperfectly closed shutter that saved him. It glinted off the blade, and although it came too late for him to block or deflect the knife, he turned away from it intuitively, so that the blade didn't plunge into his stomach, as it was meant to; instead, it penetrated his side, just above his belt. He felt the point glance off a rib.

She was withdrawing the knife for a second stab, but his hand had found her wrist, circled it, and he actually helped her withdraw the blade, so that, when it came out of his flesh, he was in control of it. He ground the bones of her wrist and heard her gasp, but she fought him. He was ready for her when she tried to knee him in the groin; he turned and took it on his thigh. At the same time he wrenched the knife from her grasp, and, as the nails of her other hand raked down across his cheek, pushed it into her in a short, hard, punching movement.

Her breath expelled against his hand. She staggered and sagged against him. He held her up, but he knew she was dead. By training and by instinct he had gone for the kill, and slipped the knife between her fourth and fifth ribs, and now he would not be able to interrogate her. He lowered her to the ground softly. Above, the shuttered windows remained closed. He picked up the woman's bag, pushed the door, and went out into the street. His jacket was stained—it was a glossy black in the darkness—with his own blood and perhaps some of the woman's. He knew that his wound was deep, but there wasn't much pain.

He walked back down the street toward the taxi ranks. One of the drivers held a door open for him. He gave the driver the name of a street that crossed the Via Boncompagni, two blocks away from the safe house. The ride took less than five minutes. He paid the fare and got out, holding the woman's bag pressed against his wound. He tipped the driver generously to make up for his finding his seat bloody later on. In a niche between two buildings he went through the bag. After reading her police ID he closed the bag. He tossed it in an alley on his way to the safe house. He felt inconvenienced by the blood that ran into his shoe and slightly nauseated, but he had no trouble making it to the safe house.

Juno stood at the window and looked out at the white sweep of the Spanish Steps. There were still people lounging there. At the top, near the parapet, three small boys were engaged in horseplay, wrestling, pretending to punch each other, falling down stagily. What were boys of that age doing out so late? One of them leaped up on the balustrade, struck a heroic pose, and began to sing.

"*E lucevan le stelle ed olezzava la terra....*"

Cavaradossi's lovely aria at the end of *Tosca*, clear and haunting in a boyish treble. The other two boys listened for a moment, and then they pulled the singer from the balustrade and all three resumed their roughhouse play. They ran off across the Piazza and out of her view. Their cries disappeared, and there was no sound but the hum of the traffic going by the Piazza di Spagna at the foot of the Steps.

She returned to the desk and sat down. She smoothed out the pieces of Michael's picture—her own and the half that the woman, Giuseppina, had given her. They fit together perfectly. On the other half there was nothing revealing, it was mostly shadows of indeterminate shape. She looked longingly at Michael, then put the two halves of the picture into the envelope Giuseppina had given her. It contained a first-class railway ticket for Milan, and a supplementary seat reservation on a TEE train leaving from Roma Terminii at ten thirty tomorrow morning.

The note, written in English, was very short: "*Take this train to Milan. We will get in touch. Long live the people of Italy!*"

She tucked the envelope into her bag, zipped the bag up carefully, and went back to the window. To her right, above and beyond the bell towers of the Trinità dei Monti, the Roman sky was bright with stars.

E lucevan le stelle: the stars brightly shining. Somewhere in Italy, beneath these same stars, was Michael. And tomorrow she would be heading north, closer to him, closer to her son. Sleep well, Michael.

* * *

Fernald, preparing to leave for the day, had one arm in the sleeve of his topcoat. Locksley's secretary came in. "He wishes to see you, please."

By setting an example, Locksley had people saying "wishes" instead of "wants" and "please" for everything. Fernald hurried along the corridor after the secretary, who let him into the inner office. Locksley glanced up and pointed his pipe at the extension phone, which sat on a free-form glass-topped coffee table, austerely bare except for a Lalique ashtray. Fernald picked up the phone; it would be Diebold. Six o'clock here, midnight in Europe.

Locksley said into the phone, "Fernald's on now, thanks for waiting, old man."

"We're not used to this kind of excitement, you know. I'd heard rumors about him, but I wasn't prepared for...I hardly know where to begin."

Fernald recognized the aggrieved voice. Not Diebold, after all, but Potter, the Rome embassy's political officer and the Agency Chief of Station. At this hour he was undoubtedly phoning from the safe house off the Via Boncompagni.

Locksley said, with a touch of sharpness, "Wouldn't it be appropriate to begin at the beginning?"

He hadn't said "please," Fernald noted. Locksley didn't take kindly to criticism of Group Nine, even if it was only faintly implied. He thought of Group as being under constant beleaguerment by the more orthodox components of the Agency and was quick to take offense. Potter obviously caught the drift; his own voice, when he continued, was controlled, neutral.

"Very well, sir." He paused, as though trying to determine precisely where the beginning might be found. "To begin, Mackey is in the hospital."

"In hospital, you say?"

"He was knocked down by an electrified baggage wagon at the airport. He suffered a fractured skull. And some minor facial abrasions."

"I take it you have seen him?"

"Yes. His condition is satisfactory, but he's definitely *hors de combat.*"

Fernald couldn't remember the last time, if ever, he had heard the phrase *hors de combat* spoken aloud. He said to Potter, "Where was Diebold when the accident happened?"

"Right beside Mackey. In fact, he tried to pull him out of harm's way, but he was a fraction too late."

Fernald's mouth twitched in a sour smile, and he thought, no, not too late at all, but perfectly timed, right on the button.

Locksley said, "Are we sure it was an accident?"

Paranoia, Fernald thought; normal, natural, healthy paranoia, it's the way we are. But Locksley was off base, he was thinking Russian when he should have been thinking Diebold.

"The driver of the wagon said it was, though of course he would hardly admit to being at fault. He claimed Mackey walked right into his path."

And Mackey would back up the driver's version, Fernald thought. His pride wouldn't allow him to admit that Diebold had sandbagged him. When his broken head healed, he would try to even up the score. Make a mental note, Fernald thought: keep those two apart.

"... could have the driver checked out, of course." But Potter's tone suggested that it was a waste of time.

"Damned inconvenient," Locksley said. He added plaintively, "He'll want a case officer, but we're stretched to the absolute limit."

"I'll see what I can come up with," Fernald said. And if Diebold knocked off another one, which he was perfectly capable of doing?

"And then, of course," Potter said—and Fernald detected a note of suppressed glee in his voice—"he lost the woman."

"He lost her, Diebold *lost* her? How the devil did that happen?"

"He lost her while he was tending to Mackey after the accident."

"What a bloody balls-up!"

"But we recouped," Potter said, and now his voice was undeniably smug; the desk man showing his value. "We traced her to her hotel through her registration card—we've got a helpful asset in the *polizia*—and she's under tight surveillance."

"What time did you find out about the hotel?" Fernald said.

"About nine thirty this evening."

"Then she was on the loose after Diebold misplaced her, from approximately one o'clock on. Where is she now?"

"In her room, and we've got two men posted. It wasn't *our* doing that she slipped away at the airport."

"Why do you say *slipped?*" Locksley said. "Do you suspect that Diebold was blown?"

"I don't know, sir. Slipped was just, well, an innocent verb."

Locksley said, "Where is Diebold now?"

"He's in one of the bedrooms."

"Would you put him on, please?"

"I'm afraid I can't," Potter said. "The doctor is still working on him."

"Working on *what?* Is he ill?"

"On his wound. I'm afraid he was stabbed. And some superficial scratches on his face."

Locksley was silent. Fernald said, "Who stabbed him and how bad is the wound?"

"A mugger, he says," Potter said, with an unmistakable emphasis on "says." "It's a three-inch-deep puncture wound, according to the doctor. It caromed off a rib which slowed up the thrust, and it hasn't harmed anything vital."

There's nothing vital to be harmed, Fernald thought, it's all the impermeable rock-hard attitude of the fanatic, which is different from flesh and blood.

He was silent as the phone call ran its course. Locksley: Is the nature of Diebold's wound such that he can carry on? Potter: He calls it a scratch. Locksley: I wish to be certain that there is no police involvement. Potter: Not to the best of my knowledge at this time. Locksley: You understand, of course, that this mission has engaged the personal interest of the DCI himself, and that the fullest cooperation is expected . . .

Locksley hung up and lit his pipe. "Well, there *are* muggers in Rome, you know."

Fernald nodded gravely. "And those electrified baggage carts do dash around Fiumicino with Italianate abandon."

"I'm afraid," Locksley said, "that Diebold is ideal for the operation, and that being the case, I'm inclined to overlook a few little irregularities."

Irregularities—plural. So Locksley must also have accepted that Diebold had pushed Mackey into the path of the baggage cart. "We know what happened to Diebold," he said, "but we forgot to ask what happened to the other fellow, the stabber."

"I didn't forget, I thought it wise to skip it."

"You know," Fernald said, getting up, "Diebold is at least fifty percent pure psychopath."

"Oh, more than that." Locksley smiled through a nimbus of tobacco smoke. "But he's *our* psychopath, isn't he?"

Eight

Vicenza, which lies roughly midway between Verona and Padua, calls itself the Palladian City. It is the birthplace of the great sixteenth-century architect Andrea Palladio (although there are some who claim he was born in Padua), and it is graced by many of his finest buildings. Vicenza attracts only a modest number of tourists, mainly those with an interest in the handsome public buildings and villas designed by Palladio, and young architectural students who are brought in by the busload, and are often to be seen sitting in front of the Palazzo della Ragione, the Museo Civico, or the Teatro Olimpico, making painstaking drawings in their sketch pads.

Looking southward from the Viale Roma, the main street leading from the railroad station to the center, there are hills with a few houses visible, gleaming white in the sun; many more are hidden in the folds or by the shrubbery. One large house, styled in the Palladian manner, was built fifty years ago by a wine merchant named Bertoni. At his death, his family moved to Trentino, and in the ensuing ten years the house had been rented out. Because of its size and its state of disrepair it attracted groups—students, or, according to the neighbors, "hippies." Its classical facade was discolored, its pillars flaking, its interior decaying, its yard overrun with weeds. The neighbors would have liked to see it torn down and replaced, but the merchant's widow refused to sell it, less out of sentiment than shrewd expectation that continuing inflation would boost its price each succeeding year. She was content to hold on to it, and let it molder, as long as she could rent it out and defray the annual tax bill with the proceeds.

* * *

Gildo, the Sicilian, spotted the three cars far below on the Viale Roma. At three o'clock in the morning, more than two cars in Vicenza constituted a traffic jam; and if they moved in stately order, their lights equidistant from each other, in military precision, the dumb shits, you knew they were *polizia* or *carabinieri*.

He was watching from a window in the once grand sitting room of the Bertoni house, whose peeling ceiling occasionally sent down a gentle rain of old paint. He sat on a wooden kitchen chair drawn up to the window, which looked directly down on the city. The Viale Roma was clearly marked out by a straight line of streetlights like strung beads. The darkness inside the room was relieved only by a faint glow from the dial of a portable radio turned to an all-night program of rock and roll music, mostly performed by famous English and American groups. The volume was turned up high, not only to help keep him awake, but because he liked it that way. And if the sound disturbed the sleep of the others in the bedrooms upstairs, the thought didn't trouble him. It was his job to keep awake on his watch, and as for the others, *me ne frego*—I don't give a shit.

Below, the line of cars disappeared. He waited patiently and then began to pick up their lights, which became visible at intervals as they wound upward on the road that climbed into the hills. The lights were evenly spaced, as though they were performing a parade ground drill. *Carabinieri*, he guessed, with their fondness for the military tradition. *Polizia*, on the other hand, would try coming up the hill with their lights off, and you could count on their running off the road. Either way, he thought, his square teeth gleaming, they were hopeless.

When the procession of lights was about halfway up the hill, Gildo turned off the radio and climbed the steps to the dark silent bedrooms.

Michael replayed the death of the chauffeur, as he did almost every night in his sleep: the spouting of blood, the backward flop, the eyes wide open in surprise and disbelief, already dulling down to the sightlessness of death. He had not actually seen the shooting; this version had created itself in his dreams, and it never changed. His limbs twitched and he woke. He opened and shut his eyes rapidly in the dark, blinking away the lingering vividness of the dream. Beside him, Adriana slept soundlessly. Her face was smooth and relaxed, the intensity of her waking mode damped down, banked. Her honey-colored hair was spread out on the pillow; the blankets were bunched at her waist, exposing the creaminess of her breasts, the pale rose of her nipples.

He had believed at first, with no basis other than that he loved her, that she would share his indignation at the brutal killing of the chauffeur.

"It was necessary," Adriana had said. "If he had no scruples about selling Bering to us, he would have none about selling us to someone else."

"That's an assumption, a paranoia, and no reason to kill a man."

"He was not a man, he was a merchant, a trader in people."

"He was a man, he looked like Primo Carnera, an Italian fighter—"

"I have heard of Primo Carnera, please don't instruct me."

"—and he had a wife, most likely, and children. You might have killed the father of four, five children."

"Bourgeois sentimentality," she said. Her lip curled in scorn, and to his dismay Michael found that even the curled lip was beautiful. "You find it hard to unlearn your past, Michael. Sometimes, often, I despair for you."

"Because I hate cruel, needless killing?"

"Because you see it as cruel and needless when it is merely necessary. You have no understanding of what one must do to serve the cause."

"Everything—right? No line drawn anywhere—right?"

"Exactly. What is necessary, however cruel it might seem, is by definition good. The cause creates its own moral standards. Nothing supersedes the cause, nothing matters but the cause. I am prepared to die for it. You are not, or you would understand everything."

She had spoken the simple truth: she was ready to die. And her mere willingness, no less the chance that she could be given the opportunity to do so, broke his heart. He tried to kiss her, but she held him off.

"Don't do that," he said. "Don't keep me from loving you."

"Don't try to keep me from loving the cause. As for you, please don't deny it, it is only me you love. You are not interested in the cause without me."

He had attempted to deny it, expounded his distaste for the government, his hatred of the powerful, of reactionary authority; stated his fierce belief in equality, the rights of man, the needs of the poor, the priority of freedom for all. . . . But even as he spoke he knew that he would never think of killing anyone for his beliefs. And he knew that Adriana knew it, too.

She said, "All meaningless, failing your willingness to kill for it and die for it yourself."

"I would die for *you*."

Her lip curled again. "Thank you. But such a death is without value. You are incurably bourgeois."

She was not attacking his background but a state of mind. She herself came from an old family of Veneto *nobili*. Her father was a distinguished gynecologist, head of a department at the University of Bologna; a brother was the youngest member of the present government's cabinet; another brother was a judge; she herself was a promising medical student. Yet, in her view, she had overcome the severe handicaps of her background and transformed herself into a revolutionary. Why couldn't he do the same? Well, maybe because he lacked the certainties provided by a lineage that could trace itself back to the Venice of the doges. The farthest he could trace his own family was to Zayde, and most of that by hearsay; the rest petered out in the unrecorded history of the czar's *shtetls*.

Until the bloody death of the chauffeur, he had never let himself think about the realities of terrorism. A bomb goes off, and the toll is two dead and twenty injured. The numbers were impersonal, they had no names or human features or blood to let. But the killing of Primo Carnera had brought the realities home to him. Two dead was a stenographer torn apart, a messenger boy splashed against a white wall; twenty injured was bleeding, screaming, pain, and panic. Reports of terrorist attacks never included the redness, the sound effects. . . .

He had tried to tell her all that, and something else as well. "What you don't see is that you're killing your own constituency, the stenographer and the messenger are the very people you're trying to make a better world for."

It had been a bitter, irreconcilable argument, ending up in controlled violence: poking at each other, pinching, slapping. . . . But as always, they patched up the quarrel at night. The bed was off limits to argument. But they both knew that the gulf between them was widening and before long would be unbridgeable.

The door opened and a light pierced the darkness. Michael sat upright, his heart thumping.

"Don't get excited, lover, it's just me."

Michael recognized the headlong Sicilian dialect. The flashlight moved closer to the bed, and in its back-glow he could make out Gildo's heavy features.

"What do you want?"

"We're about to have visitors," Gildo said. "Get your ass out of bed."

"The police?"

"*Carabinieri,* probably. They'll be here in about ten minutes."

Michael slipped out of bed, reached for his pants, and drew them on over his nakedness. It was cold in the room. He was shivering. He pulled a sweater on over his head. When he reached under his pillow for the Beretta, Adriana stirred. Gildo focused the flashlight on her breasts.

"What the hell do you think you're doing?" Michael yelled.

"Smaller than I like them, but nice," Gildo said. He swung the light back to Michael. "You have work to do. Get going."

"What about the others?"

"Don't rush me. I want to enjoy the scenery a little more."

The light swung back to Adriana's breasts. She drew the blanket up to her neck.

"Wake the others up," Michael said.

Gildo laughed and sat down on the edge of the bed.

"Get off that bed, you—"

"Michael! Don't let him get your goat." Adriana looked at Gildo with contempt. "Nothing to worry about. I don't like apes."

Gildo laughed again and got up. "Pleasant dreams, *duchessa.*" Michael waited until he started toward the door and then followed him out.

Michael ran up the steps to the third floor. In the central hall he jumped for a handle set in the ceiling, and pulled it downward. A section of the ceiling opened, folded down to the floor and became a narrow ladder staircase. Michael pushed the Beretta into his belt. He climbed the ladder to an attic and waited for the counterweighted ladder to swing shut. Bending far forward to clear his head of the low overhead rafters, he scrambled across the floor planks in a kind of four-pointed ape walk. At the far wall of the house, he probed with his fingers for a spring hidden behind a large square of black-covered insulation batting. He pressed the spring and supported the batting, framed on the inside with heavy wood, when it opened downward. He boosted himself into the opening and pulled the disguised door closed behind him. On the outside it would again appear to be a seamless section of insulation.

It was Federico, with his training as an architect, who had discovered the secret room. His eye had been struck by what he described as "an apparent spatial anomaly" in the construction of the roof and the placement of a chimney. He had climbed to the roof, done some arcane measurements, and then gone into the attic crawl space and found the secret room. Although he deplored the "vulgarity" of the imitation Palladian style of the house, he gave its architect high marks for his cleverness in designing a hideaway that was virtually undetectable. Nobody could imagine why the wine merchant had had the room built. The first time they entered it they found an old newspaper on a rocker, bearing the date June 17, 1932. That might have been the last time anyone had been in the room.

"That you, Mike?"

Michael could see that Bering was sitting up in bed.

"Yes. Keep your voice down."

He inched forward until he came to the area represented by the false chimney, where he could straighten up to his full height. He pulled the rocker up beside Bering's bed and sat down.

"Is it morning?" Bering said.

"No. We're going to have some visitors."

"Police?"

"Or *carabinieri*. Makes no difference."

"This is the third time," Bering said. He sounded almost gleeful. "I think they're on to you."

"Don't get your hopes up. When the police came the first time, it was because the kidnapping was new, and Rome was putting on the pressure. They hassled us because we're all young, not because they suspected anything."

"Then why did the *carabinieri* come?"

"Because they do everything the police do, and vice versa. They're each afraid the other one might steal a march."

"Sooner or later if they come back often enough, they might tumble to something."

Bering was waving his hand for emphasis. His splinted finger stood out stiffly.

"Is the finger all right?" Michael said.

"Fine. Today she put on a lighter splint and a fresh bandage. I'll say this for her—she has a gentle touch. She must be a nurse or something—right?"

Michael didn't say anything. He wondered if the *carabinieri* had arrived yet. Not that he would be able to hear them. The room was so well soundproofed that only a very loud noise could be heard through its walls.

"Day or so and the splint can come off," Bering said. "Seems to know her stuff, though I don't care an awful lot for her bedside manner. . . . What would happen if next time I tried pulling that mask off her face?"

"Don't try it."

"No real point to it—except to see if she's pretty, and I could find out easier by asking you. Is she pretty?" Bering grinned slyly. "Dumb question. I can't see you getting involved in this stuff for an ugly girl."

"Look," Michael said, "I asked you to lay off that crap. I believe in what I'm doing, so don't keep trying to make me out a simple cunt-crazy goon."

Bering yawned and said, "I'm hungry."

"After the dinner you put away? Well, we're not about to let you raid the icebox."

Bering licked his lips. "The food is one thing I don't have any complaint about. You know what I figured out? From the kind of food, one of you is a southerner. Right?"

"Why don't you try getting back to sleep," Michael said.

"And miss the fun when they bust in here and rescue me?"

"Not a chance. But if they get lucky..."

"Yeah, I know, you'd have to kill me."

"Don't delude yourself that we wouldn't."

"What do you mean by 'we'? The others, yeah, I'm sure they would grease me, including the girl. But you—I know your family, I know your background..."

"Don't test me."

"Are you packing the gun?"

Michael thought of drawing the gun and displaying it, but it seemed childish. "Yes, I'm packing it."

"Suppose I started to holler, would they hear me?"

"I'm not sure. Just don't try it."

"But suppose I did. Would you shoot me?"

"Without a second's hesitation."

"I tell you, I don't think it's all that easy to pull the trigger on a fellow human being. I think you might freeze. Maybe if you pulled it off once it would get easier to do afterwards. But the first time, going against the whole grain of your upbringing—"

"Where'd you learn all that psychological stuff—do they teach it to you in the CIA?"

"CIA," Bering said, sighing. "It's okay for your friends to believe that, or say it whether they believe or not, because it suits their purpose. But Mike, for God's sake, you know better, don't you?"

"You don't give us credit for any kind of truth, you think we're totally amoral."

"Them, yes, but not you. I honestly don't think you could shoot me, and that's my considered opinion."

"Until it's more than just an opinion, don't try making any noise."

"Suppose, one day, when you're relaxed, I thought about this, you know, suppose I rushed you, you know, overpowered you..." Bering paused, his head cocked, as if weighing the proposition. "Fat chance. Never. Take on a young muscular guy like you? Sure, I outweigh you, but it's all blubber. In fact I've put on more weight since the kidnap."

"You've got yourself to blame for it. We take you down to the cellar four times a week for exercise, but you stand around doing nothing."

Michael held up his palm for silence and listened. The sound was faint, no more than a distant scratching, but he was sure they were in the crawl space. He slipped out of the rocker and sat down on the bed. Bering's face was turned toward him, huge and white and moonlike in the darkness. He put the muzzle of the Beretta gently against Bering's forehead.

"Don't do *anything*," he said in a conversational tone. "We've been through this twice before, right? All you have to do is sit here quietly. If you don't..."

"You'll shoot?"

Michael nodded and increased the pressure on Bering's forehead. He could hear them now. The sound was muffled, but he was sure they were rapping walls, thumping here and there with a gun butt. It didn't matter; they could rap all night and not know there was a room behind the slope of chimney and roof wall.

They sat in the dark listening to each other's breathing, and Michael didn't move even when he was sure they were gone. In the darkness, breathing in each other's breath, they shared an extraordinary intimacy; they were fellow conspirators in the cause of silence.

So that when, finally, the trapdoor opened inward and they could see Federico's face reflected in the back glow of his flashlight, they broke away with a start, like lovers whose guilty sins had been discovered.

"They've gone," Federico said in Italian. "You can come down now, Michael. Tell the CIA jackal to go back to sleep."

Bering chuckled. "You can skip the translation, Mike, I'm beginning to catch on to some of the language—especially about the *Chee Ee-greque Ah sciacallo.*"

"Good night," Michael said.

"Good night, Mike." Bering turned toward Federico. "You too, chief."

Nine

On a Saturday morning in early August of 1980, two bombs, containing TNT activated by a simple timing device, exploded in the second-class waiting room of the railroad station in Bologna. The explosion occurred at the height of the August exodus from the city. Ten thousand people jammed the station on that day.

The bomb left a huge crater in the waiting room and blew away one entire side of the building. Eighty-five people were killed, more than two hundred were wounded.

Shortly after the blast, an anonymous caller claimed responsibility in the name of the neofascist Organization Armed Revolutionary Nuclei (N.A.R.). The motive—according to the police—was revenge for the arrest and indictment of four right-wing terrorists for the 1974 bombing of a train near Bologna that had left twelve people dead. The N.A.R. was also responsible for the 1969 bombing of a bank in Milan that had killed sixteen and injured ninety; and dozens of other attacks, most notably the killing in 1980 of a Roman judge, Mario Amato, who had been investigating their activities.

The Bolognese, a sophisticated, somewhat complacent people, had been terribly shaken by the wanton slaughter at the railroad station. At a memorial service for the victims in the cathedral of San Petronio, nearly a quarter of a million people had crowded into the Piazza Maggiore to pay tribute to the "Martyrs of Bologna."

One of the onlookers had been Beppo Di Lorenzo, who had watched the proceedings with barely contained pride and excitement. It was

Beppo who had placed the two suitcases packed with explosives in the waiting room. At the time, he was sixteen years old.

Now, a few streets from his room in the working-class Zucca district, as he crossed the Via Matteotti bridge spanning the deep cut where the trains ran, he glanced to his right at the reconstructed station, and as always felt a thrill of accomplishment. Dare he hope that the urgent early morning call from the *comandante* of his squadron of the N.A.R. meant another bombing, perhaps even the railroad station again? How such a feat would shake up the Communist bastards who ran the city!

He walked with a spring in his step, buoyed up by expectation. From the arcades of the Via dell'Independenza he cut diagonally across the Piazza Maggiore. The steps of the cathedral were already strewn with a dozen addicts, dazed from their morning fix. He struck off to his left, toward the Via Massimi D'Ageglia, where the *comandante* had his apartment, daringly and contemptuously close by the Questura.

The *comandante* was dressed in the black shirt, trousers, and boots of the N.A.R., which of course, they could not wear in the open, though one day, Beppo did not doubt, that uniform would be honored and feared by all the people of Italy. He saluted the *comandante* smartly, his outstretched hand steady as a rock.

"At ease, Di Lorenzo," the *comandante* said. "Have some coffee."

Beppo stood until the *comandante* finished pouring the coffee and had himself sat down. The *comandante* was a man of nearly fifty, and for this reason, as well as his rank, was in Beppo's eyes very much a man of respect.

"Have you seen this rag this morning?"

The *comandante* held the belief that all of the newspapers of Italy, regardless of whether they were openly left-wing or not, even the professedly conservative ones, practiced "lily-livered liberalism," and hence were either covertly or by default supportive of the left.

"Look at the picture on the first page."

The photograph showed a woman who appeared wide-eyed and startled, perhaps by the flash of the cameras. Beppo read the caption underneath the picture, which stated that the lady was the mother of one of the two Americans who had been captured by the Forze Scarlatte.

"Could you recognize this woman if you saw her again?" the *comandante* said.

Beppo studied the picture closely. "Yes, *comandante*."

"She is here in Italy to try to persuade the FS to allow her to visit her son."

"They would never allow it. It's foolish."

"We'll see. Consider this: that if they permitted it, it would cause them to look less barbaric than they in fact are."

"You know they will do this, *comandante?*"

"Given their cleverness and lack of scruple, it is a possibility. The police, of course, will hope that she might lead them—whether by prearrangement or unknowingly—to the hideout of the FS. Do you follow me?"

Beppo said, with a confidence he did not feel, "Certainly."

"Well, I'm not sure you do. Listen to me carefully. First, assume that the FS has decided to bring the woman and her son together. Next, assume the opposite—that they will not allow it. Finally, assume that something dreadful happens to the woman. Then in either case—you see it?—the FS would be dishonored, in the first hypothesis because they were not capable of protecting her, in the second because they had acted cruelly to prevent her from seeing her son."

The *comandante* paused. Beppo said, "It's rather complicated."

"You'll get the picture, don't worry. Now—the matter of the police. Since it is their duty to protect her, they too would be dishonored."

"Ah," Beppo said. "Now I see. Both the police and the FS disgraced at one blow. *Perfetto.* Then you wish me to leave for Rome?"

"No. As you can see from the paper, she's blown in Rome. With all that attention, nothing can happen there. I'm convinced she'll have to come north. When she does, we'll find her, and then you will kill her."

"Thank you, *comandante.* I am honored to be chosen. But—" Beppo hesitated. "Just this one person?"

The *comandante* smiled grimly. "Sorry to disappoint you. But this can be more important to us than killing a dozen people of no consequence."

"I understand the importance of it," Beppo said. "I'll kill her."

"Fine. Have some more coffee."

"She's as good as dead, *comandante,* you have my word for it."

The *comandante* shook the pot. "I'll make some fresh coffee."

"Set your mind at ease," Beppo said. "I'll kill her."

Gray, one of the two watchers at the Hassler, phoned Diebold from Roma Terminii. He reported that the subject had boarded a TEE train, carriage 8, seat 34, destination Milan, arrival time 4:34. The train would depart in fifteen minutes.

"The train makes stops, doesn't it?" Diebold said. "How can you be sure her destination is Milan?"

"The train has a baggage car. I took a look at the tag on her valise when it was taken aboard."

"See if you can get a ticket for the train. I'll fly up to Milan. Look for me at the station there."

"All right. I'd better hurry if I'm to make the train."

Diebold phoned Potter, the Chief of Station, and asked him to book a seat on a plane for Milan, on or about one o'clock. He would stop by on his way to the airport to pick up the ticket. Potter said it wasn't necessary to inconvenience himself, he would send it to the safe house by messenger. Diebold smiled grimly. Head of Station didn't want to see any more of him than he had to. Violence made him uncomfortable.

"I'd appreciate your sending over your camouflage man," Diebold said.

"I'll phone him right away. And the doctor. Can I have the doctor come over again to look at your wound?"

"I looked at it myself, it checks out fine. Just the camouflage man, please."

He had examined the wound first thing in the morning. It had been neatly stitched and it appeared to be clean. It hurt somewhat in certain positions, but not too badly. He had a high pain threshold, which was to say he didn't let pain bother him. The loss of blood had made him giddy the night before, but he felt fine now. The facial scratches had seeped a little blood onto his pillow but they were superficial. More important, they made him conspicuous. But the camouflage man would take care of that.

He went into the spare room and rooted through the well-stocked closets and dressers for suits, linens, and shirts. He stowed them into a Valpac, and then sat down with a copy of *Foreign Affairs* to wait for the tickets and the camouflage man.

He read through two articles before the camouflage man appeared. They were both highbrow bullshit.

The train pulled out of Roma Terminii on time. It was a TEE, one of an international fleet of crack trains: de luxe, well appointed, air-conditioned, fast, silent. There was a middle-aged couple in Juno's compartment. They spoke French to each other and ignored her completely. The reservation card posted outside the compartment indicated that another couple were due to board in Florence.

She balanced copies of the European editions of *Time* and *Newsweek* on her knee. When she had bought them at the newsstand in the station concourse she had discovered her picture on the front page of four newspapers. The photoflash had made her face depthless, flat, but nevertheless it was identifiable as Juno Sultan's. She had been self-conscious walking through the terminal, but no one had appeared to recognize her. And as far as the self-absorbed couple in the compartment was concerned, she was nonexistent.

A white-jacketed steward came through the train with reservation cards for the two sittings of the dining car. With some regret she declined the card; TEE food was traditionally good and the service wonderfully well organized. But she didn't want to expose herself to being recognized in the crowded dining car. The French couple reserved for the first sitting.

A half hour later the steward came through the car again, ringing a little bell. The French couple got up, bowed stiffly to her, and went off to the dining car. Juno put her magazines on an empty seat, let her head rest against the coolness of the window, and dozed. She dreamed of the first day she had brought Michael to nursery school. When she called for him, later, she had been told that, disputing possession of some toy with a little girl, he had kicked her in the shins and made her cry.

"Oh, Michael," she whispered as she woke, "that wasn't a very nice thing to do, not a bit nice."

On his way to a late breakfast at a small café off the Piazza Cavour, Strawberry had bought a newspaper. There was a picture of the subject on the front page. He read Italian well enough to decipher the caption: the lady had been photographed last night on the Via Veneto. How she had continued to fool him was still a puzzle, but now, with her whereabouts known, perhaps he could get back into the game and redeem himself.

He was still smarting from yesterday's conversation with Grigoriev, who had abandoned his customary suavity for open and brutal threats, but had stopped short of ordering him back to the States or, worse, to Moscow. If he ever got back on the woman's trail, Strawberry thought, he would not lose her this time; in fact, if she were so much as to try to make a fool of him again, it would go very badly for her. Good-natured he was, yes, but he must not be trifled with.

He decided to have his breakfast before phoning his control in Milan. It was three o'clock in the morning in the U.S., not the most advantageous hour to ring Grigoriev's telephone bell. Waiting for his breakfast order to be filled, Strawberry thought pleasurably of his adventure of the last night. His control, who had listened in on his savage lacing from Grigoriev, had urged him to solace himself by enjoying some of the amenities of the city and recommended an excellent restaurant in the neighborhood of the Brera Museum. After a refreshing sleep, Strawberry had bathed and changed his clothing and taken a taxi to the restaurant, where, as luck would have it, he had been seated next to a table of four black American girls with whom he had struck up a conversation. They were tall, slender, vivacious, and dressed in clothing so flamboyant (riotous colors, daring necklines, turbans, theatrical accessories) that it might have been construed as an offense against the state in Moscow. (Joke). The four were high-fashion models who traveled from one major European city to another, modeling the creations of noted designers at fairs and exhibits.

Of the four, one spoke fluent Italian, two were reasonably proficient, and the fourth knew only ghetto English. They had invited him to join their table, and amid much laughter and good cheer, Strawberry put Grigoriev out of mind. After dinner they had gone to a disco. In the end, one of them—she had the rather odd name of Sweets Charity—took him back to her hotel room. She had taken him for an American and most flatteringly referred to him as "cowboy." Quite amusing that, approaching climax, she would scream, "Ride 'em, cowboy!"

His eggs arrived. He asked for more coffee, more rolls, and began to eat with great appetite.

At this moment, the menace of Colonel Grigoriev seemed remote.

The *agenti* met by prearrangement forty-five minutes after departure time on the platform between the fourth and fifth cars of the train. They had boarded separately and occupied seats in different cars. They were both clean shaven and dressed in business suits. Normally, as detectives of the anticrime squad, they would go for a week or more without shaving and wear unwashed denim jeans stiff with grime, torn shirts, soiled windbreakers, all of which would, they hoped, make them indistinguishable from the *teppisti*, the hoods, who were their quarry.

The fat one, who was in his mid twenties, with a pink complexion that made him look even younger, said, "Tomasso, you look very high class, like a bank robber."

"And you, Vito, you remind me of a high-born, very rich young man I put the collar on in Syracuse, who used little boys and then killed them."

"It's nice of you to say so. I wish you'd tell that to my girl. She complains I go around looking like a beggar."

Tomasso, the older one, had deep creases in his face and hectic eyes that made him look tubercular, which he had been in his youth but had outgrown. He said, "You checked the lady out?"

Vito nodded. "She's prettier than her picture. You?"

"I saw her. Also, I asked her if she liked fat cops who looked like rich boy-fuckers. She said if she ever met one she would tear his balls off."

"I've never been on a TEE before," Vito said. "Such luxury. Did you take a ticket for the dining car?"

"Second sitting. You?"

"First sitting. I hear the food is delicious, true Bolognese. I hope we can put in an expense account."

"We'll put them in, all right. The question is, will they honor them."

Vito looked worried. He husbanded his modest earnings and lived in the *caserma*, the barracks, to save money. When his girl's father died (which he hope would not be too long; the poor old fellow suffered a great deal), she would be free to leave home, and once she found a job they would get married. If he was not reimbursed for the expensive lunch it would be a setback.

"Maybe I shouldn't take a chance. Tear up the ticket?"

Tomasso waved his hand airily. "Live it up for once. It'll give you something to tell your grandchildren."

The steward came through the cars ringing his bell. "First sitting, signori."

"Go ahead," Tomasso said after the steward had moved on. "Eat."

"You'll watch her?"

"No need. The train doesn't stop until Florence. Go have your expensive lunch."

"Bolognese—everything is cream sauces, like the French. But they say it's wonderful."

"Eat. *Buon appetito!*"

Gray had been lucky. A cancellation showed up on the computer in the nick of time, and he was able to board the train just before the doors closed, running hard and with his freshly purchased ticket clutched in his fist. His reservation was in the compartment adjoining the subject's.

He took his seat, stumbling over feet, apologizing breathlessly, still winded from his run. Then he realized that he needed to urinate—it was a chronic problem in surveillance work—but since he didn't want to start stepping on feet so soon again, he held his water. Finally, when it became agonizing, he got up, apologizing profusely, and banged knees to the corridor. The nearest men's room was in the next car. On the platform between cars, two men, who had been speaking animatedly, fell silent. A fat young one and another with a thick, heavily lined skin. Cops. He smelled it from the stiff way they wore their clothing, the cop shoes, the suspicious looks they gave him, which were not personal but generic.

Okay, cops, he thought, addressing the urinal with a sigh of relief.

It didn't necessarily mean they had anything to do with the subject, but neither did it mean they didn't. In any case, it was none of his affair. It might complicate things for Diebold when he met the train in Milan, but that was Diebold's lookout. Let Diebold worry about it. From what he had heard about Diebold—Double-Oh-Seven, they called him—he had a roughshod way of solving problems. The thought startled him. Would he wax a couple of cops if they got in his way?

He wondered, as he started back, whether the cops had looked that easy to take, but when he opened the door between the cars both men were gone and the platform was empty.

At one o'clock, just before he was due to leave his office in the American consulate for lunch, Graham Lutz, the CIA Station Chief in Milan, accepted a call from Sweets Charity. She came on the phone jabbering fluently in Italian, although she knew full well that his knowledge of the language was rudimentary.

He said, "Okay, you've had your fun, now please speak English."

"Yes sir," Sweets said. "I had a Russian last night—I thought you might be interested."

"Had?"

"Fucked, man."

"Yes, well, we don't pay for that."

"He was pretending to be American."

"Oh?"

"Not bad at it, either, but not good enough to fool a smart American nigger. Fucked like a Russian, you know? Good stamina but no finesse. They don't think of the lady's pleasure too much."

"Just lay off that smart talk, will you, and get to the point?"

"Yes sir. What happened, we went to a disco, and he seemed like a swinging dick—understand?—so I took him back to my room. Seemed pretty hip, like I say, so I was surprised when he told me to turn off the lights while he undressed. Later, I turned the light back on, and he got flustered and pulled the sheet up under his chin and made me turn it off. Got dressed in the dark, too, before he left."

"I haven't got all day," Lutz said. "Are we getting to the point?"

"Sure am, honey. Before he managed to get that sheet up, I saw he had a lot of birthmarks on his neck. Those little strawberry dots?"

"Ah," Lutz said. "Ah. Can you give me a description of him?"

"I thought you'd like it," Sweets said. "I can describe him by looks and by feel. Which you want?"

"Stop fucking around," Lutz said.

"Tee-rrific," Sweets said with a squeal of joy, "You learning to talk English."

Orlandi's Alitalia plane landed at Linate Airport in Milan in the customary morning fog. He took the airport bus to the terminal in the Viale Sturzo, and from there a taxi to the Questura Centrale on the Via Fatebenefratelli. As always, he felt comfortable in Milan; he had grown up here. Yet he understood that it was, and always would be, second to Rome. It had its great history, its culture, even its wickedness, but essentially it was a business city with businesslike people, and Rome was truly the heart of the country, the keeper of the soul of Italy, the direct descendant of imperial Rome.

Three policemen stood at the entrance to the Questura, wearing their Beretta P-38's slung low on their hips, cowboy style. It was getting to be an epidemic. Even the slovenly bank guards wore them that way. Everybody was John Wayne.

As he paid the taxi fare, Orlandi saw the three cops eyeing him, trying to decide whether he was important or not from his clothing and demeanor. His suit was a Briony and it won the day. That or his limp— it was well-known that he had been kneecapped. The three cops drew themselves up to attention and gave him a sweeping salute.

Trusting to their judgment, they would have let him walk in without showing his identification. That wouldn't do, so he said, "I am Orlandi of the Rome Questura."

Of course, of course. Would he enter, please? More salutes as he passed between the high walls into the courtyard, which was badly in need of sweeping. Three cars and two motorcycles were parked in the road. He entered the building and, after identifying himself to another cop, was led through the corridor to the ground floor office of Antonio Bassano, the *vice questore* (Political). Bassano, who was short, dark, with a bustling air, got up from his desk to greet him.

"Ah, *dottore,* welcome to Milan."

"*Dottore,*" Orlandi said, shaking hands, "good to see you again."

Bassano seated him, then went back behind his desk. "Good flight, *dottore?*" Bassano said.

"The usual. The stewardesses get to look more American by the day. What's becoming of our country, *dottore?*"

But what could become of Italy that hadn't been taking place for countless centuries? Take the *"dottore,"* for example. What kind of country was it where policemen of high position preferred being called by the honorific their university degree conferred upon them rather than by their resounding and impressive police titles? Italy, of course, where culture counted for more than authority.

"Coca-Cola is a subtle poison," Bassano said, smiling. "In any event, welcome to Milan. We're delighted to have you here."

They were, of course, anything but delighted. His presence carried with it the implication that Milan could not be entrusted with an important case without intervention from Rome, much as Milan had earlier usurped command of the operation from the police of Verona. The Milanese police were jealous of their prerogatives with respect to Rome, and there was much to be said for their point of view. They had a great deal of experience dealing with the likes of the Brigate Rosse and the Forze Scarlatte, and they had an excellent *antiterrorismo* force. So, he thought, there would be jealousies to contend with, not to mention that the *carabinieri* would have their own claim to involvement. Ah, well, that was Italy.

He said, "Did you know Giuseppina Cavalera?"

"Pina? Yes, of course," Bassano said.

"She was killed last night."

"Christ!"

"With her own knife. She carried a stiletto, and she was very good with it. The person who killed her was better."

"The bastards. *Terroristi*, of course?"

"We're not sure. The investigation has just begun."

"Family? Children?"

Orlandi shook his head. "An ex-husband, that's all." And a fair quota of ex-lovers, including Dottore Alfredo Orlandi. "Did you see the newspapers this morning?"

"The American woman? Yes."

Orlandi told the *vice questore* about the capture of the terrorist Benevista on the Via Veneto, and the delivery of the note from the Forze Scarlatte to Mrs. Sultan. "She's on her way to Milan."

"Perfect. We'll have her right under our eyes."

Orlandi said, "She'll be under the eyes of anyone who bothers to look at a newspaper. Including the CIA, if I'm not mistaken."

"Shit," Bassano said. "Those bastards have been around here for days, waving their dollars around like an exhibitionist waves his prick. They think because some Brigate Rosse people sold out in the Dozier case that it's common practice. I've tried explaining to them that the weak sisters were shaken out in the Dozier affair, but they think everybody is for sale if the stakes are high enough. Maybe they're right—who knows?" He sighed. "CIA—they think we're shit."

"The one I have in mind," Orlandi said, "was trailing the lady. We'll try to keep an eye out for him."

"You know what he looks like?"

"He looks like a CIA agent."

Locksley came into Fernald's office carrying a sheet of the pale blue paper that Group Nine used for translations in clear of encoded cables.

"Rocket from Lutz in Milan," Locksley said. "Strawberry is there."

Fernald raised a brow. "We don't know what Strawberry looks like."

"We do now. One of Lutz's assets slept with him last night. She spotted the birthmarks and gave Lutz quite a decent description."

"Good work. But I wonder why Strawberry is in Milan."

"Exactly. It could be coincidence, of course, but we don't put much stock in coincidence, do we?"

"Has Diebold been informed yet?"

Locksley shook his head. "Lutz is playing it safe. He handed us the ball. Your opinion?"

"It would certainly deprive Diebold of an edge not to know." He paused. "Yes, I see the point—it would act as a red flag to Diebold. He might not *forget* about the operation, but the priority might blur while he planned to dispose of Strawberry."

"Absolutely. He'd see Strawberry as big game."

"Do we want Strawberry terminated?"

"No sense to it. It could start a gangland war. They'd feel obliged to kill one of ours, and then we'd have to do one of theirs. . . . But Strawberry's presence does pose a threat to the extrication operation, doesn't it?"

Fernald nodded. "But if he's there in Milan specifically for that reason, the Russians wouldn't simply fold their operation because we terminated Strawberry. They'd put somebody else in, somebody we might not have any book on."

"Right. It's comforting to know whom one's dealing with. On the other hand . . ."

"We've got to tell him."

"We've got to tell him," Locksley said. "But he must be instructed forcefully not to take any offensive action on Strawberry."

"Do you want Lutz to tell him?"

"He won't pay any attention to Lutz. In fact, it might work wrong way about, make him go right out gunning for Strawberry."

"Which puts it up to me?"

"I'm afraid so, old man."

"I'll tell him the next time I talk to him."

"He'll listen to you. Direct order, and all that?"

"Um," Fernald said.

*   *   *

From the upper regions of Latium, Rome's province, the train crossed into Tuscany, regarded by many foreigners and all Tuscans as the most beautiful part of Italy, where the purest Italian was spoken, where the most beautiful city (Florence) was located, where the history, culture, cuisine, and character of the people were unsurpassed anywhere in the world. Juno had heard the same claims advanced, of course, by the citizens of Venice, Bologna, Rome, Parma, Cervino, Cortina d'Ampezzo, and many other cities, including those of the least-favored areas of Calabria and Sicily.

Few with even a remote claim to objectivity would have denied that the northern part of the province was one of the most graceful and harmonious landscapes of any in Italy. The soft greens of the valleys darkened as the land rose up into the moderate heights of the enveloping Apennines. Under a blue sky above the fertile earth there were no harsh outlines. Vineyards passed by in endless rows; dusty, silvery-green olive trees covered the gentle slopes of hills, with cypresses higher up. From time to time the train passed by red carpets of poppies, crowding up almost to the railroad right of way.

"Biglietti, per piacere."

Juno looked up. The conductor was braced in the doorway of the compartment. He was young and handsome, and he wore his powder-blue uniform with Sam Browne belt, his leather pouch and elegantly shaped visored cap, with the dash of a hussar. She handed him her pale green first-class *biglietto di viaggo* and the gray *posti assegnati* card. He frowned at them magisterially, shuffled them, snapped at them with his punch, and then handed them back to her with a murmured, *"Grazie, signora."* He punched the tickets of the French couple, who had returned from lunch somnolent and seemed barely awake, with an air of disdain. Another *"grazie,"* and he withdrew, sliding the compartment door shut behind him.

Juno put the tickets in her bag after a moment of hesitation. Through the window, she saw a cluster of new buildings, tract homes, each identical with the next. At home they would not be worthy of comment; here, in this ancient landscape, they were intrusive, alien. Above, on the crest of the slanted hills, a line of pines stood in marching order.

Why had she hesitated before putting the tickets in her bag? Fleetingly, they had felt not quite right. But she had seen the conductor punch them and return them. She dug the tickets out of her bag. Between the *biglietto di viaggio* and the *posti assegnati* something had been inserted: a sheet of notepaper cut to the same size as the tickets. It was the slight extra thickness that had seemed odd. There was a message typed on it, single spaced, both sides of the paper. She read: *Signora, noi delle Forze Scarlatte* ... We of the Scarlet Forces ...

The conductor was one of them. He had known where she would be sitting, of course: the tickets had been provided by the Forze Scarlatte themselves. The French couple were stirring. She slid open the compartment door and went along the corridor to the ladies' room. Inside, she locked the door and, translating slowly and with care, read the note through.

Ten

Michael sat in a dilapidated armchair and watched Bering make a halfhearted attempt to do push-ups on the soiled carpet that covered a portion of the cement floor.

The cellar compartment had once been a storage bin for coal. Although it had been thoroughly scrubbed, it still retained stubborn sooty stains, and there was an invisible and perhaps illusory dusting of coal in the air. The carpet, which many years ago had been a brilliant Chinese red, was now dulled down to a gritty gray.

Bering abandoned his pretense after a few attempts that barely cleared his belly from the floor. He fell flat and made comic swimming motions with his arms and legs.

"Look," Michael said, "it's you who's being hurt. Whether you like it or not, you have to exercise to keep healthy."

"I don't believe in exertion."

With an exasperated air, Michael got up. He stripped his T-shirt off. "Come on, I'll do it with you."

He lowered himself to the carpet with athletic grace, and began to do push-ups, his tanned powerful torso rising and falling with controlled ease. Bering rolled onto his side and watched.

"Terrific," Bering said. "I mean it. You've got the body for it."

Michael did a dozen more push-ups, accelerating his pace, then hopped to a squatting position. His torso was gleaming with sweat.

He said, "You could have some kind of a body, too, if you exercised." But it sounded unconvincing even to himself. "Well, anyway, a better one than you've got now."

"I really don't want a body." Bering thought for a moment. "What I really want is a cigar."

Michael shook his head. "We're all nonsmokers and we don't want your smoke poisoning the environment."

"Maybe I don't understand," Bering said. "But how come you care so much about the environment and so little about the life of a chauffeur?"

Michael glared at him, then said, "Come on, get off your ass and do something. Get healthy!"

"What's the sense of it if I'm going to be killed? You think I'll feel better if my corpse has terrific muscle tone?"

"You're not going to be hurt—how often do I have to tell you. I made them promise that, and they agreed. Whatever else you may think of them, they keep their word."

"But suppose they changed their minds. Suppose the girl said, 'Never mind what we promised, let's kill Bering.'"

"That's ridiculous," Michael said. "Come on, do a couple of push-ups."

"It scares me because you'll do anything that girl tells you to do. You believe in the girl, not in anything she or the rest of them believe in."

"You're wrong. I believe deeply in everything they believe in. Like them, I want those filthy germ warfare missiles out of Italy, and I'll go to any lengths to get it done."

"Including killing me, if the girl says so. I'm scared of that."

"Look," Michael said, "I'm getting tired of denying it. Anyway, why didn't you think about the risks *before* you joined the CIA?"

Bering sat up. "Tell the truth, Mike. Do I look like CIA?"

"How do I know what they look like? Maybe they all look like you."

"The truth is you haven't got the slightest idea if I am or not. Maybe your friends believe it, but you, maybe you *hope* I am, because it would justify selling me out, but you honestly don't *know*."

"Assuming you were CIA, could I get a straight answer out of you?"

"Would it matter? For the sake of argument, let's assume I could prove I'm not, which I'm not, but how do you prove it? But if I *could* prove it, do you think your friends would just apologize, brush off my clothes, and turn me free?"

"If it could be proved, yes, absolutely, they would set you free."

"And in that case, what about you?"

"Me? What about me?"

"Give it a little thought," Bering said. "If they let me go, they can't turn you loose as well because they know I'll spill the beans. But if they killed you, it wouldn't matter if I spilled the beans."

"Or," Michael said, "I'd simply go underground."

"You think they're that simple? You think they'd risk your endangering them, after you'd been blown?"

"Blown. That's not a businessman's word, it's a CIA word."

"You can read it in four out of every five spy novels. Think about it, Mike. Either they kill me and turn you loose, or they let me go and kill you, or they kill both of us, which is what I'm betting on. I know you can't imagine them doing anything to you, because the girl wouldn't allow it. But ask yourself: Who does she love more—you or the cause?"

Michael was silent, his face blank and unrevealing. But he was thinking about it, Bering thought, and if he exercises his brain instead of his body, and if he's honest with himself... And suddenly, because he thought that, behind his blank face, Mike was getting there, suddenly he felt sorry for the boy.

"Hey, I feel like exercise." Bering braced himself on the soiled rug. "Let's see who can do the most push-ups."

Adriana whipped her tiny *cinquecento* down the steep roads furiously, riding her brakes, squealing them through the curves. She was late for her first class. She continued to press the little car on the A4 *autostrada*, racing the 30 kilometers from Vicenza eastward to Padua well over the speed limit. In Padua, she parked a long street away from the Via Febbraio, where, at Number Eight, the university had begun to function in the year 1222.

If that date was a sore point with some Padovanesi, who resented that Bologna, founded almost a century earlier, was the oldest university in Europe, they could console themselves with the thought that their medical school was established before any other, including Bologna's. She knew the spiel by heart: "Where the Englishman Harvey was a student and mapped the path of the circulation of the blood... where Di Fallopia lent his name to a woman's oviduct... where the little fat Galileo taught, where Copernicus was a student, where Oliver Goldsmith learned his medicine...." She had been skeptical about Goldsmith, the English poet, and had looked him up in the encyclopedia. Sure enough, he had learned his medicine—not overly well—in Edinburgh and Leyden.

The *professore* interrupted his lecture when she slipped into the room, gave her a deep ironic bow, and thanked her for coming. With an irony of her own that eluded him, she apologized at exaggerated length. The *professore* began a long rambling story about the first woman graduate of the university in 1668, and concluded by saying that, like herself, the lady was a member of the Venetian *nobili*, and, perhaps because of her social standing, had also felt free to come late to her classes.

"If it will please you to take your seat now, signorina, we may proceed with our discussion of the pancreas."

At noon, Adriana went off with a fellow student for a coffee and pastry at Pedrocchi, where, later, buses would unload tourists who would line up for coffee at "the famous neoclassic café where medical students have gone for over four centuries." Her companion, a young Pisan woman who had no politics and apparently no interests other than medicine, unfolded a newspaper. On the front page was a picture of Michael's mother.

Adriana drank her coffee and ate her pastry calmly, then asked the Pisan to inform the *professori* of her afternoon classes that she was suffering severe menstrual cramps and had returned home. She bought a newspaper on the way to her car and drove back to Vicenza at top speed. The town was vibrating to a sustained diapason of automobile horns. It was a *manifestazione* of local students to protest the high cost of textbooks. Her lip curling with disdain for the timid stupidity of such a demonstration (after an hour of steady horn-blowing the students would end up with nothing to show for their efforts but drained batteries), she began to push the *cinquecento* up the winding hill road to the fake Palladian house.

Adriana was guided to the huge kitchen of the house by the clash of angry voices, with Michael's predominating. Federico, Carlo, young Giorgio, and Michael were seated at the round table. Gildo stood at the vast old black stove, stirring a saucepan simmering with an aromatic sauce.

As she entered, Michael was shouting, his face dark and congested, his Italian thick with rage, almost incomprehensible. In the center of the table lay a newspaper, with the picture of Mrs. Sultan showing above its fold.

Federico, waiting for Michael to draw a breath, said, "I told him everything, Adriana."

Putting her hand on the paper, Adriana said, "We have a problem."

Michael snorted. "You bet your sweet ass we do," he said in English.

"Speak Italian, please."

"*Certamente,*" Michael said. "Was this your idea, whore?"

"Thank you for your courtesy. As for your question, no, it arose out of a discussion after the appearance of your mother on American television. The decision to activate the idea was arrived at democratically by all of us."

"All those present. I wasn't invited."

"We knew you would have dissented."

Gildo laughed.

"Your logic is insane," Michael said. "Even Gildo knows it."

"I'm laughing at the sauce, is all. Making a sauce for pasta without garlic—that's what's insane."

Adriana said, "I'd like to speak to Michael alone, please. Afterward we can take up the implications of this picture."

"The implications are self-evident," Carlo said. "We have to abandon the idea, unless we want a regiment of police trailing her right into our parlor."

"It is a matter for discussion," Adriana said coldly. "Michael, will you come upstairs with me?"

"You idiotic whore, this democratic decision you excluded me from was about my mother. My own mother. But you never had a mother, did you? Just a whore, which is no mother at all. Whore daughter of a whore."

In an odd way, she thought, as Federico, in his most magisterial tones, sought to convince Michael that insult was not a reasonable means of discourse, in an odd way, she was pleased by Michael's display of temper. He was too often moony, lovesick. But now there was force in him that was exciting, sexual; his heightened color even made him handsomer.

"Shove your reasonable discourse up your ass," Michael said to Federico.

Adriana said, "Michael, come upstairs with me."

"How about me? I'll go upstairs with you," Gildo said. "You could use a little Sicilian pepperoni."

Michael wheeled on him. "Shut up, you stupid bastard," he said in English.

"Shaddap," Gildo said. "That much English I know." He burst into laughter. "Are you trying to stifle free and open discussion?"

Federico said, "This is tiresome. Are we terrorist revolutionaries or are we not?"

"Shove your revolution up your ass," Michael said.

Adriana said, "You do have cause for complaint, *caro*. But I believe it can be talked out. I cut my afternoon classes—which I can hardly afford to do—because of it. Won't you allow me to talk to you?"

"I begin to question that we are serious people," Federico said.

"Come, Michael." Adriana moved toward the door. "Nothing is ever lost by an exchange of thoughts."

Michael stared around the table, as if looking for a challenge, then pushed his chair back and got up. Adriana held out her hand to him.

"Here's where he gets to vote at last," Gildo said. "With his dick."

Adriana felt Michael tense. Gently, she drew him out of the room.

When they started up the steps she put her arm around him. There was a moment of awkwardness in the bedroom. It contained only the bed and a battered old dresser; there was no place to sit but the bed. Adriana sat down. Michael remained standing. She patted the bed beside her. He shook his head.

"It won't compromise you," she said. She moved to the foot of the bed. "You can sit at the other end."

"I'll stay where I am."

"As you wish. I hope you will try to be reasonable. Did Federico tell you that it was you yourself who first put the thought in our heads to bring your mother to Italy?"

He stared at her.

"When our television showed the clip of your mother's appearance on American television you were embarrassed, but also, in a way, you were proud of her. You said, trying to make a joke of it, 'She's a very determined lady. Thank God she can't get here or she would turn Italy upside down.' Do you remember?"

"What of it?"

"You also said, 'She's a Jewish mother, there's nothing like it in the entire world.' Well, there is—any other mother."

"Barring your own, that patrician whore—"

"Even she. Once, when I was a teen-age girl—"

"Tell me your reminiscences some other time. Get on with the bullshit."

Adriana's lips tightened, but she spoke with control. "Everybody's mother, there was the key. Knowing how Italians revere motherhood, the family, we saw that permitting a reunion between your mother and you would win us enormous sympathy. At the same time, if we could effect such a meeting under the difficult circumstances, it would be sticking our finger in the eye of the CIA, and our own police. It would be bold, defiant, show our superiority. In short, a perfect stroke of propaganda."

"My mother is not a vehicle for propaganda."

"At the same time, if you would look at it intelligently, it is a very fair quid pro quo, it would grant to your mother the fondest wish of her heart—to be allowed to see her beloved son. Such an emotion embarrasses you?"

"Coming from you it makes me laugh. You're as sentimental as a trolley car."

"Admit it, Michael, you're angry because we excluded you when we made our decision."

"I would have hoped that you—never mind the others—that *you* would have been sensitive to my feelings."

"You should have learned by now that where personal feelings conflict with the cause, they must be ruthlessly swept aside."

"The fucking cause overrides everything—truth, loyalty, trust, every-thing."

"Exactly. And until you understand that, you understand nothing."

Michael sat down on the edge of the bed. "Do you love me?"

"Why must you ask me this question?" She looked away from him for a moment. "Yes, I love you, Michael. It troubles me. Before I met you I would not have believed that I could love outside—" She smiled wanly. "Outside the faith. Also, I know that the reason you are with us is not conviction but because you love me."

"Star-crossed, that's what we are."

"Star-crossed?"

"Shakespeare. *Romeo and Juliet.*"

"I don't believe in those two idiots."

"They're poetry," Michael said. "It's poetry you don't believe in."

She took his hand and pressed his palm to her lips. "When you are near me like this I believe in you and in nothing else." She drew his head down toward her. "Come to bed with me, *caro.*" The muscles of his neck tightened, resisting her pressure. "As for your mother, perhaps it is true that we are using her. But she will see you, and that will make her happy, and then she can return home."

She locked her hands behind his neck, and lifted herself up until their faces almost met. For a moment they glared at each other like adver-saries, but it didn't last. She released her hold on him and fell back to the bed. She opened her arms to him. He made a half turn on the bed and lowered himself on top of her.

When they returned to the kitchen the discussion began: was it fea-sible to go on as planned, now that Mrs. Sultan's presence in Italy was so widely known, or should their plan be aborted.

Gildo's pot of water began to boil; he fed his pasta in by the handful, a homemade spaghetti from a shop in Bologna.

Michael sat with his head bent and said nothing. The stilted language of their polemical style bored him to the point of nausea: "It is necessary to see this matter in the light of..." "Let us not fall into the fatal errors of the orthodox so-called Marxists..." "We must not forget the lesson of..."

Adriana argued skillfully and coolly for pursuing their plan, this same Adriana who a few minutes ago had heaved and threshed beneath him, crying out his name, proclaiming in a voice hoarse with passion that he was her godhead, her only possessor....

Gildo interrupted an exchange between Adriana and Carlo with the announcement that the pasta was ready, that he would have to serve it now or it would be mush. He turned to Michael: "You want to take the CIA bastard his lunch?"

Michael, glad for the diversion, helped Gildo fix a tray with a heaping dish of spaghetti *alla puttanesca* and a large tumbler full of red wine.

"Michael," Adriana said, "do you wish us to wait until you return?"

"Not necessary." Michael carried the tray out of the kitchen. Behind him, the discussion was already in full cry again.

Upstairs, balancing the tray carefully, he climbed the attic ladder into the crawl space and duck walked to the secret room. He placed the tray on the floor of the room and then boosted himself in.

"Lunch," he said.

Bering was lying in bed, looking up at the low ceiling. He said listlessly, "I'm not really hungry."

Michael carried the tray to the taboret beside the bed. "It's a long time until dinner."

Bering sat up. He sniffed at the spaghetti. "It smells good."

"I'll pick up the tray in about a half hour." Michael started toward the trapdoor, then turned around to Bering. "I'm going to try to get you out of here."

Bering stopped chewing. His mouth hung open. "You serious, Mike?"

"I said so, didn't I?"

Bering took a sip of wine. "You change your mind about these people?"

"I'll get you out, that's all you have to know. You want to go, don't you?"

"Hell, yes." But the hope in his eyes was dampened by uncertainty. "Are you sure you can do it?"

"I can do it."

"I don't see how."

"You don't have to. I'll handle it."

"Jesus, Mike, don't leave me hanging this way. *When?*"

"Tomorrow morning. Everybody will be out. Tomorrow."

He went out and replaced and locked the panel of batting. In the kitchen, the discussion seemed over. Everyone was eating. Michael fixed himself a plate of spaghetti.

Adriana said, "Unless you wish to speak to the subject, Michael, we're ready to vote."

"Nothing to say," Michael said. "What we call in my country a conflict of interests."

Adriana shrugged. "Here is the position—that we'll proceed as planned if the following conditions are met: First, naturally, that your mother is aboard the train, that Benevista passed her the tickets last night. Second, that Rizzo, the conductor, was able to slip her the note of instructions. He will phone us when the train arrives at Florence and tell us whether all is well or not. We will observe her arrival at Milan station, proceeding on the assumption that she has almost certainly been under surveillance. Finally, accepting that there is a fair degree of risk involved, we will, nevertheless, plan on keeping our rendezvous tonight."

Caution would have argued against their going ahead, Michael thought, yet it was the very riskiness of the situation that attracted them. Their cause to one side, they were reckless people who throve on excitement, on danger. Despite the lengthening of the odds—perhaps because of it—they couldn't pass up the opportunity, as Adriana had put it, of sticking their finger in the eye of the authorities.

Federico said, "We are agreed. Shall we now put the issue to a vote?"

"But if you're all agreed," Michael said, "why vote?"

"The principle of democratic centralism requires it," Federico said. "All in favor?"

Federico counted the raised hands. "Five in favor. Michael?"

"Abstain."

"Five pro, zero anti, one abstention. The point is carried."

"You're not eating, Michael," Adriana said.

"How can you eat a spaghetti *alla puttanesca* without garlic?"

"Bravo," Gildo said. "The boy is a Sicilian at heart."

As soon as Michael's head and shoulders appeared in the opening, Bering said, "There's something I have to tell you, Mike."

His plate and glass were empty. Michael said, "I'm here for the tray. No time for talking."

"I work for the CIA."

Michael said, "Jesus," explosively, and stared at Bering.

"Just occasionally, and at a low level. I don't want you to get the idea that I'm a big-time spy. Mostly I act as a courier."

"Why in hell are you telling me this, for God's sake!"

"CIA has a lousy rep," Bering said, "but I think they do some good work. So why shouldn't I help them out? I don't accept any pay for it, you know, not even my expenses." He grinned. "Surprised, Mike?"

"Surprised, yes," Michael said. "Surprised that you told."

"Not sure myself, why I blabbed. Pride, maybe—I didn't want your help under false pretense. If you change your mind it's okay, I understand."

"No," Michael said. "It doesn't make any difference."

"Way I figured," Bering said, grinning. "After all these years of knocking around, I became a pretty good judge of human nature." His grin turned sly. "How do you know I won't blow the whistle on you after you help me get away?"

"It doesn't matter to me."

"You're coming with me, aren't you?"

Michael picked up the tray and started toward the trapdoor. "I don't know."

"For chrissake, Mike, they'll kill you like they killed that chauffeur."

Michael opened the trapdoor.

"Look," Bering said, "don't worry about me talking. I won't say a word. Not that I feel I owe you, even for getting me out. After all, you sold me out in the first place. But in my book you're essentially a decent kid who got screwed up—"

Michael pushed the panel in place, cutting Bering off. He locked it and began to duck walk across the attic floor.

Eleven

Vito, the fat young *agente*, pushed the door open while the train was still in motion and hopped out. The train stopped. He walked forward to the baggage car and stood a little distance away, watching. Porters were already clustered, waiting with their carts. The first of the passengers appeared, holding their receipts up to the two *facchini* in the baggage car. In another moment he saw the lady. Old Tomasso was a few paces behind her on the platform. When the lady lined up at the baggage car, Tomasso angled over to join Vito.

"So far so good," Vito said.

"If she goes down the steps to the taxi ranks, our work is over," Tomasso said. "But if she goes to the elevator with the porter, we must get on the elevator with her. Never mind what the porters say, just get on the elevator."

"Why should the porters say anything?"

"It's a freight elevator exclusively for the use of the porters. Can you imagine them having to trundle their carts up or down all those steps?"

"But if it's only for the porters, how can someone who is not a porter get on?"

Tomasso gave him a pitying glance. "You have a lot to learn."

They watched the lady hand her baggage check up to the *facchino*. A moment later she received her bag. They saw her look at the mob scene of passengers importuning the porters, shake her head, and then, carrying her bag, move along the platform.

"Let's go," Vito said.

"Give her a start," Tomasso said. "Without a porter we can eliminate the elevator."

Keeping a respectable distance behind her, they followed the lady out into the huge busy upper concourse of the Milan station, lined with shops and travel agencies, tourist and railroad bureaus.

"Some station," Vito said. "A cathedral. It makes Roma Terminii look like a whistle stop."

"By now," Tomasso said, "the *agenti* from the Milan Questura should have picked her up. But we'll follow anyway, to make sure."

The lady started down the long sweep of steps to the street level, and they followed. Vito checked the crowds flowing down the steps, and tried to pick out someone who looked like a plainclothes cop. Of course, if they were any good, they wouldn't look like cops. There they were! One was just a few steps below them, another was fiddling with a newspaper at the bottom of the stairs. Well, maybe they weren't that bad, after all. A cop could always smell out another cop.

On the main level, the lady picked her way through the crowd toward the street exits.

"Did you spot them?" Tomasso said.

"Sure. The one in the tweed jacket, English cut, and the tall student-looking one with the beard."

"Not bad," Tomasso said.

The lady was approaching the exit beneath the TASSI sign when suddenly two men sprang out in front of her. A flash bulb went off, then another and a third. The man in the tweed jacket, English cut, and the bearded one who looked like a student, leaped forward.

"Should we do anything?" Vito said.

"It's not in our brief to chase paparazzi. Nor dignified."

One of the paparazzi ran off into the crowd; the second one paused for another picture, but before he could shoot, the cop in the tweed jacket jumped him, whirled him to the floor, and wrested his camera away. The lady, after a moment's hesitation, went briskly through the exit. The cop in the tweed jacket opened up the camera, tore out the film, dropped the camera, and ran toward the exit.

"Not bad," Tomasso said. "But the one with the beard has lost the other paparazzo—see?"

Vito followed his pointing finger. The bearded cop stood in the midst of the jostling crowd with his hands on his hips, looking baffled. Then he suddenly darted off to his right. The crowd parted before his rush, then closed again.

"Maybe we should have helped," Vito said.

"Never volunteer, nothing good ever comes of it. Those two cops would probably have taken us for *terroristi*—"

"In these clothes? Never."

"—and shot us full of holes."

"Look," Vito said.

The bearded cop was returning, smiling grimly, trailing an open roll of curling film behind him. He dropped the film to the floor and headed toward the taxi exit.

"Pretty good," Tomasso said. "Well, youngster, our work is done. The ball is on the feet of the Milanese cops now."

"You call it work? That high-class train, that wonderful lunch? What do we do now?"

"We go to the Questura Centrale and report to Dottore Orlandi. He'll probably tell us to stay the night and go back to Rome in the morning."

"Will he send us to a hotel?"

"I doubt it. They'll dig up a couple of beds in the *caserma.*"

"The *caserma!* That stinks. Can we at least take a taxi to the Questura?"

"If you want to risk your own money. Milan is full of buses and trams."

"Do you think there's a chance they'll send us back on another TEE train?"

"You're spoiled. We'll go back on a *diretto,* two hundred and twenty eight stops between here and Rome. Second-class carriages."

"Second-class? That's an outrage."

Tomasso laughed.

Juno's taxi driver was fatalistically calm in the madness of Milan's rush hour traffic until a very large Mercedes limousine cut him off and forced him to stamp on his brakes and come to an abrupt jolting stop.

"*Mafioso,*" he yelled, shaking his fist. "Why don't you stay where you belong, in Sicily with the other animals."

He trembled with indignation. He was undoubtedly right about where the Mercedes came from, Juno thought—he could tell from the lettered prefix on the license plate—but *mafioso* was pure guesswork. North against south, it was like a national infection.

She was no longer shaken by the appearance of the paparazzi at the station, but angry and dismayed. Now, just as in Rome, her picture would appear in tomorrow's papers. Still, since her rendezvous was to take place this evening, perhaps it didn't matter. She felt a surge of renewed hope: it was entirely possible that tonight, at last, she might actually be seeing Michael.

Her driver, now that his equilibrium had been knocked out of kilter, was taking affront at everything: the creeping traffic, which made a snail seem like a whippet; the pedestrians who were trying to make him an accomplice in their suicide; the thousands of imbeciles who chose the busiest time of the day to go for a pleasure spin; the fools who changed lanes every ten seconds without warning (which was exactly what he himself was doing).

The traffic on the broad, boulevardlike Via V. Pisani eased up, and her taxi turned onto the spacious Piazzale della Repubblica, with its high rises and luxury hotels. The driver swung into the ramp leading to the entrance of the Hotel Principe di Savoia. "I have many times driven great screen stars to this hotel. Charles Bronson, Sophia, the Lord Olivier. Were you perhaps one time a screen star, signora?"

A first-class compliment, Juno thought, tempered only by the tense of the verb. A porter ran out of the hotel and picked up her bag while she paid the taxi fare. She looked about her cautiously before following the porter inside.

Diebold said, "She'll be going to the Principe di Savoia or the Palace."

"She's not going *anywhere*," the driver said, "and neither are we."

The car was a sporty Porsche and the driver was a handsome young Ivy League type whose nominal job at the Milan consulate had something to do with tennis, so far as Diebold was able to figure it out. He was a complainer; he regarded the present traffic jam as a major affliction.

It had been simple enough for Diebold to pick up the subject at the station, and follow her through the milling crowd. Gray was a few feet behind her. He made a tiny gesture of dismissal, and Gray veered off. He had been close to the taxi exit when the flap with the paparazzi occurred. The two men who chased them down had plainclothes cop written all over them. All right, so the police were on her trail, as they had been in Rome. He thought of the woman in black. She had almost wiped him out, but almost wasn't good enough.

There was hardly a time when you didn't have competition, he thought. You simply had to take it as it came.

The subject's taxi broke free of the traffic jam, and they followed it up the ramp to the entrance of the Principe di Savoia.

"That's it," the driver said. "The Principe. We go home now?"

"No. Go beyond the entrance and pull up and wait."

"What for?"

Diebold didn't answer.

"Surely we're not going to surveil her? My impression was we'd just spot her for the watchers."

"Keep your motor running and don't talk so much."

The driver sulked. He was never going to be any good, Diebold thought, absolutely no patience. Not that it required much; she was out again in about five minutes, followed by a porter carrying her bag. The doorman signaled for a taxi.

"Be damned," the driver said. "How could you know?"

Diebold had guessed that since she had succeeded with that simple trick of misdirection with the airlines, she might try it again with hotels. The naiveté of an amateur.

The Porsche trailed her to a hotel just off the Piazza Cavour. This time Diebold was sure that she would stay put, but he made the driver wait for a half hour anyway, just to be certain.

"Hungry or not," Juno's mother had said to her when she was a child, "you have to eat if you want to be strong."

So Juno went to the hotel's restaurant and looked at the menu with glazed eyes. The maître d'hôtel, perhaps thinking that she couldn't read Italian, offered to help her order. She thanked him, and presently a waiter brought her *tortellini in brodo,* the pasta is homemade, signora, *delicioso;* and afterwards a veal Milanese, three large thin slices that filled the plate, and *polenta,* the Lombardian specialty. "When you start to eat," her mother had said with confidence, "you'll find you'll *develop* an appetite." But her appetite failed to develop. She ate a third of the *tortellini,* a quarter of the veal, and a bite or two of the *polenta.* The maître came over with a worried look. She assured him that the food was wonderful, but that she was suffering from a headache.

What else—tell him that she was so excited at the prospect of seeing Michael that she had all she could do to swallow a single mouthful?

The maître offered to call a doctor for her, but she said that she would be all right, that when she got a bit of fresh air she would be fine. To assure him that she was not terminal she ordered an *espresso.*

She left the hotel at nine o'clock. The lobby was jumping with a noisy, animated, youthful crowd. They were stylish, vivacious, intense young designers, in Milan to present their clothes at a big show at the fairgrounds. A young man winked at her as she walked by, held up a wash drawing of a bikini, and said, "It could be for you, signora, you would stop hearts on the beach, true?" She pleased him by saying she would take a dozen, and as she went by she heard him telling his companions what the witty signora had said to him. A show of friendship, of good nature, tickled Italians immoderately. Well, there were many worse ways to be.

When she refused a taxi and said she would walk, the doorman expressed concern: the streets were unsafe, signora, congested with *terroristi, scippatori* (he made the sound of a motorcycle and mimed a snatching of her bag), and *cattivi ragazzi,* wicked boys bent on mischief.

She said that she was bound for the *centro storico* and knew the safe streets.

Actually, the Via Manzoni, right off the Piazza Cavour, led in a straight line directly to the Piazza Scala. To be sure it was dark—Italians didn't waste energy on lighting up the outdoors—but there were many other strollers as well as auto traffic and trolley cars. Most of the shops were closed, but their windows were artfully lit, showing smartly displayed and expensive merchandise.

She paused at a shop that sold objets d'art and vertu; its green baize background drape made its window a fair reflecting surface. So far as she could tell, nobody seemed to be following her. The window contained an elaborate jade fish enscrolled with gemstones. It was beautiful, but she knew it would be sinfully expensive. Still nothing suspicious in the glass. She moved on.

Across the street, she recognized the Poldi-Pezzoli Museum, its exterior unassuming, even dowdy, giving no clue to the riches inside. She remembered taking Jerry there once. He had spent a half hour unmoving in front of Pollaiuolo's lovely blond *Young Woman.* "This is good-bye," Jerry said. "I'm going to divorce you and marry her."

She smiled at the memory and then was suddenly conscience-stricken. She was treating Jerry cruelly. Tomorrow she would phone him—not from the hotel but a post office, so she couldn't be traced. And, of course, by then she might already have seen Michael, so it would no longer matter that his phone was bugged. She walked past the taxi ranks in the Piazza Scala. It was still over an hour to her rendezvous, but already her heart was thumping painfully.

The radio crackled and then a very loud voice said, "Rabito here, *dottore.*"

Orlandi turned down the volume. "Yes?"

The office they had put aside for his use at the Questura was bare except for a four-year-old poster advertising the Venice Biennale. The desk was scarred oak, government issue, and the chairs were all maimed; the swivel chair behind the desk would turn only to the right. The office was on the ground floor, down the hall from the *vice questore* (Political), directly beneath the ops room, with its consoles and computers, its battery of television cameras focused on highway entrances, airports, the central station. . . . Occasionally there was a thumping sound on the ceiling above him, as if, Orlandi thought, someone was venting his anger at a recalcitrant computer with a kick.

Rabito said, "She left the hotel on foot a few minutes ago, now walking along the Via Manzoni."

"Alone?"

"Yes. Sometimes she glances over her shoulder, sometimes looks into windows, to see if she's being followed. I'm half a block behind her, Stefano is front-tailing, and Volpe is on the other side of the street. Parillo in the car is lying back a block or so, and tying up traffic. You hear the horns, *dottore?*"

"All right," Orlandi said. "Make sure you don't lose her."

"Not a chance," Rabito said. "It's easy work. Her height, you know, and that beautiful hair, *rosso tiziano*. She's a fine-looking lady, *dottore.*"

"No suspicious characters?"

"Nothing. So far, everything is clean."

"Thank you," Orlandi said. "Over and out."

Built in the shape of a cross, the Galleria was a resplendent lay cathedral, with fine shops and cafés at ground level, commercial offices occupying space behind its rising interior facade. There was marble underfoot and a handsome curved leaded-glass ceiling forming the highest soaring reaches of its roof.

Juno entered the Galleria from the Piazza Scala and paused, goggling at its lighthearted immensity as if coming upon it for the first time. *Si comporta come una turista.* Act like a tourist. The letter was in her purse, but she knew its brief contents by heart. *Noi, della Forze Scarlatte*—We of the Scarlet Forces. From this opening it went on in the by-now familiar stilted and pretentious style that put her in mind of children incongruously dressed up in their parents' clothing and putting on adult airs. But if they were children, she thought, they were children whose games ended in death and destruction.

Si comporta come una turista. She had come early—it was still an hour to the rendezvous, so she would have plenty of time to perfect her act. *We of the Forze Scarlatte are now ready, in the harmonious spirit of humane behavior, to bring the devoted mother together with her son. Do as follows: go to the Galleria and play the tourist...*

She moved on, stopped at the Rizzoli bookstore, and looked at the titles of the books in the window; paused again at a shop selling women's wear; gazed upward again at the grand sweep of the gallery. She took note of the tobacco shop, but no more than fleetingly, without special interest. At the intersection of the four arms of the Galleria, groups of people stood chatting; others were snapping pictures.

The outdoor tables at Biffi, which ran from the Duomo entrance almost half the length of the Galleria, were crowded with people drinking or eating the café's light snack specialties. But unlike the diners on the Via Veneto they didn't appear to be there solely to stare and be stared at.

A difference between sober Milan and a Rome drunk on its own reputation?

She went on into the huge Piazza Duomo. Under the arcade, people were buying newspapers; small intense groups of men were talking politics, loud, argumentative, making sweeping gestures, sometimes shouting, more often laughing derisively. Italians took their politics, or at least their arguments about politics, seriously. There were groups congregated in various parts of the immense piazza, and many strollers, crossing and recrossing the multicolored tile of the pavement.

Juno turned to face the great Duomo, bone white in the moonlight, a vast sand-dripping that was part Gothic, part rococo. She had heard Italians scoff at the cathedral, at its mélange of styles, at the two-thousand-odd statues studding the facade, at its outsize Madonnina; and then, with a shrug that concealed pride, adding, "But it works, of course." They might have said the same thing of the paradox of Italy itself—it worked.

There were people sitting on the steps of the Duomo, mostly youngsters, many with portable radios tuned to rock stations. The strollers threw soft inky slow-moving shadows. At the distant far end of the piazza, across the street, red, yellow and blue neon signs flashed garishly.

A man sidled up. Showing his teeth in a gleaming smile, rolling his eyes, he said in English, "Would the signora care for companionship?"

"No spik English," she said, and walked back toward the Galleria.

"Rabito here, *dottore*. The subject is now seated at Biffi."

"Alone?"

"Yes. She is having a drink. A co-*ka*, I believe."

"The others are in place?"

"We have her covered like a blanket. A few minutes ago, in the piazza, a male approached her."

"Yes?"

"He spoke to her. She said something and left. I saw the whole thing. I was no more than six feet away. He was trying to pick her up."

"You're sure of that?"

"Afterwards, he tried to pick up another lady."

"How long has she been at Biffi?"

"About ten minutes."

"I'll come there directly."

"Yourself?" Rabito said. "Aren't we doing well?"

"You're doing exceptionally well. I appreciate it."

"Grazie, dottore."

* * *

A man who was trying to thread his way to an empty table lost his balance and jogged her elbow lightly.

"*Scusi, signora.*"

"*Prego.*"

He said with a smile, "You are English, madame?"

"American."

He smiled again and went on to a seat at a nearby table. She wanted to look at her watch but suppressed the urge and sipped her Coke. She had been stealing glances at her watch every few minutes. It wouldn't do, it was a giveaway.

You will go to the tobacco shop at precisely 2235 hours and you will buy a package of cigarettes...

Almost without being aware of it, she looked at her watch, then glanced around her guiltily to see if she had been detected. The man who had jostled her elbow was ordering a drink. She suddenly had the feeling that she had seen him before. She studied him as he was speaking to the waiter. About fifty, olive skin, a thin, slightly curved nose, black hair, a slender man in a very good suit (Jerry had taught her to recognize fine tailoring). He finished with the waiter; quickly, she averted her gaze.

She held her left hand beneath the level of the table and looked at her watch. Twenty-five past ten.

...enter the tobacco shop and buy a packet of cigarettes. You will leave the store, move slightly away from the entrance, and remove a cigarette. You will search in your bag as if for a match. A passerby will give you a light, and then offer you his box of matches. You will accept them...

Like a word on the tip of one's tongue, she was tantalized by the face of the man who had jostled her elbow. She *had* seen him. Where? She studied him over the rim of her empty glass. Familiar, yes...He must have become aware of her scrutiny. He met her eyes briefly, then turned away.

Ten thirty-one, her watch read. How long would it take to reach the tobacco shop? Fifteen, twenty, at most thirty seconds. Patience, Juno. She felt in her purse for a few coins to leave the waiter. She took another look at the man at the nearby table. He was sipping coffee and reading a newspaper. It was thirty-three minutes past ten when she pushed her chair back and got up. She would be there too soon. At the central intersection of the Galleria she paused and gazed upward at the leaded skylights. Now it was time. She walked to the tobacco shop, stood aside to let a man come out, then entered.

"A package of cigarettes, please."

"Yes?" The young man behind the counter frowned. "Which kind, signora?"

She didn't smoke, never had, she didn't know one cigarette from another. She saw a placard with a cowboy on it. "Marlboro."

She gave the young man a 5,000-lire note, accepted change, and went out of the store.

Diebold had spotted two, possibly three people in the Galleria who were surveilling the subject. He was pretty certain they were cops; he had seen one of them using a radio. He thought that he and Gray were a lot less visible, but when you were working a circumscribed area like this, with only two men, you'd have to be pretty lucky not to be detected.

There had been two occasions when he had thought she had linked up with her contact, but they had both turned out to be false alarms. The first had been in the Piazza Duomo, when a man had come up and spoken to her. But it was just a simple try at a pickup, and she had brushed him off and gone back into the Galleria. The second time was when a man nudged her elbow at the café, but there had been no communication between them that he could spot. Of course, given that this was Italy, you could argue that it was suspicious that this second man *hadn't* tried to pick her up.

When she got up from her table at a little past ten thirty, he was standing near the restaurant, Savini, just inside one of the arms of the Galleria, and he had a good view of her possible path toward the Scala end, where he could see Gray leafing through postcards at the souvenir stand near the entrance.

When she turned into the tobacco shop he was alerted. She had been in the nonsmoking section of the plane, and he hadn't seen her at any time with a cigarette. He checked out the elbow jostler. He hadn't moved; he was sipping his drink and reading his newspaper. At the far end of the Galleria Gray was looking toward him. Two of the cops, including the one with the radio hooked to his belt and making a bulge under his jacket, were strolling toward the tobacco shop.

She came out of the shop with a pack of cigarettes, which she began to open. If Diebold needed any further evidence that she was not a smoker, her awkwardness would have ratified his judgment. She took a cigarette from the pack, put it into her mouth, and began to fumble through her bag. And fumbled. And fumbled. A minute went by, and by now it was clear to him, and of course to the cops, that the linkup had gone sour. She stood there for possibly five minutes, with the look of bafflement on her face changing to dejection. And finally she gave up and began to walk slowly toward the Piazza Scala exit.

Gray would pick her up there; and so, presumably, would the cops. And so would he himself, in good order. But he was convinced that the evening was over.

Shortly before they were due to go off the A4 at the Vicenza exit Giorgio said, "Do you want to hear a coincidence? I just looked at my watch. It's ten thirty-five, to the dot."

"I can't deny it's a coincidence," Carlo said, "but it's a rather meaningless one."

"What I'm trying to put across," Giorgio said, "is that at this very moment she is at the tobacco shop, following our instructions. But nothing happens, since we're not there, the matchbox that was to have been given her destroyed. . . ."

Giorgio must have realized he was floundering. His face was pale and melancholy in the reflection of light from the dashboard. More than ever he looked like a choir boy; actually, he had in fact been intended for the priesthood until he had been diverted to another faith.

"All I'm trying to say," Giorgio went on, "is that it's a pity all our planning has gone down the drain. I mean, it's too bad, isn't it?"

"It's neither good nor bad," Carlo said, "but a simple fact. And facts have objective meaning only, not qualitative ones."

Carlo recognized that he was out of sorts to be picking on poor Giorgio. It was no fun doing a round trip of 450 kilometers in Adriana's rattletrap *cinquecento* only to come up empty. Not that there had been a choice once he and Giorgio had witnessed the scene at Milan station: paparazzi, police, everyone, you might have thought invitations had been sent out to attend the lady's arrival. Obviously, it would have been madness to proceed, so they burned the matchbox, and then went off to have a drink or two until it was time to make the prearranged call at seven o'clock.

Federico had answered the phone. *"Pronto."*

"I'm sorry," Carlo said, "but I won't be able to deliver the *Germania* of Tacitus, as I had hoped to do."

"But it was supposed to arrive today."

"It arrived on schedule, that's not the problem."

"If it arrived, I don't see why I can't have it," Federico said testily.

"Well," Carlo said, "the point is that you're not the only one who wants that particular volume, you know."

"Are you telling me others know it has arrived?"

"I'm afraid so."

Federico was silent.

Carlo said, "I assure you that if I dared try to send it to you I would be putting myself right out of business."

"All right," Federico said in a surly voice, and hung up.

Telling Giorgio about the call, Carlo had said, "I swear, from his tone you'd have thought it was all our fault. We didn't create the situation, you know, we merely reported it."

"It's a reflection of his disappointment," Giorgio said. "After all, he couldn't *see* what was going on at the station. When we spell it out for him..."

But when they reached the fake Palladian house, Federico was out. There had been a hot alert signal (a certain wrong number call on the phone), and he had hurried down into town to check it out.

Rabito stood stiffly in front of the desk in Orlandi's borrowed office in the Questura. Overhead, the ceiling vibrations were muted; the computers and consoles were not overworked at this hour of the night.

Orlandi said, "Go back to what he did after the subject left the Galleria."

"He walked about a bit, looking in this window or that, and then he went outside into the Piazza Duomo. Took a look at the Duomo, counted some stars in the sky, then bought the American paper, *Tribune*, and went back into the Galleria. By then everyone else—Stefano, Volpe, Parillo—had gone off to follow the subject, and you yourself had left as well, *dottore*. He took a seat at Biffi and ordered a drink. Scotch whiskey, ice, and water. If he made no attempt to follow her or to see where she went, then perhaps he is not what you believe him to be?"

But he would have had confederates, Orlandi thought, he would have had backup. While he enjoyed his drink in the Galleria, his backup would have been tailing her.

"To me," Rabito said with an air of apology, "he didn't look like a CIA agent. He seemed to be a well-dressed American civilian of the prosperous class."

"That's what they look like," Orlandi said, and his words seemed an echo. Hadn't poor Pina, describing the man who had asked about the Sultan woman at Fiumicino airport, said more or less the same thing? "In any event," he went on, "eventually he did a disappearing act?"

"My humble apologies, *dottore*. One moment I had him clearly in sight, and the next he was gone. But I did not feel he had given me the slip, merely that I was too relaxed and lost him."

"Don't take it to heart, Rabito, you're a good policeman. And you may be perfectly right about his innocence."

But Orlandi didn't think so. The man had a pretty good act, and perhaps he would have paid no attention to him if Pina hadn't been weighing so heavily on his mind. Early in the evening he had heard from Rome, reporting that Pina had left her mark on the killer: there was skin and blood under her fingernails; and there were different blood types on the knife, one of them Pina's, the other unknown. Two bloods. Had she stabbed her assailant before being killed with her own weapon? Perhaps because his mind had been so full of Pina, he had immediately become suspicious of the American when he spotted him in the Galleria.

It was all conjecture of the most trivial kind, he had absolutely nothing concrete to go on. But however baseless his suspicions might be, he could not put them aside. He had learned to rely on his instincts in the absence of facts. Occasionally, he thought wryly, they turned out to be correct.

Rabito asked if there was anything else required of him.

"No. I think we'll call it a night."

Federico parked in the Piazzale Stazione and then walked along the Viale Roma, which was bordered on both sides of the street by the broad lawns of the Campo Marzo. On the lawn to the right, hovering low to the ground, there were two flashlights, separated from each other by perhaps ten or fifteen meters.

There should have been only one flashlight. Federico stopped on the pavement, uncertain. Then a blocky crouching figure behind the nearer of the two lights whistled softly. In the backlighting he could see that it was Picciano. Federico went across the lawn to him. The second light started to move toward them.

"What the hell is going on?" Federico said.

"It's all right," Picciano said. "It's only my daughter."

"It gave me a start, but really, it's quite good. Disarming."

Picciano shrugged. "She enjoys picking mushrooms." The girl came up to them, a bright-eyed slender child of ten or eleven. Picciano said to her, "Try back there, Silvia, over toward the trees, it's a good place for them."

The girl trotted off with her pail, the flashlight bobbing as she ran. Mushrooms grew in the park, and poor people were often seen harvesting the lawn for their stewpots.

Federico said, "Well, what is it?"

"He said you're to call him, at the Rome number. He said it's urgent. Okay?"

Federico thanked him. He went back to the pavement and started toward the station. Behind him, the two flashlights were still visible. He went into the station and took one of the phone booths. He gave the operator the Rome number and then dropped *gettoni* into the box, until there were enough of them and the operator connected him. The informant was an *irregolare* who held a minor post in the Ministry of Justice.

"Last night on the Via Veneto, Benevista was taken into custody. They brought him to Regina Coeli, where he's being held on an open charge.

"A short while ago I saw him being led through the corridors. He was banged up—lips puffy, bloodied, one eye swollen shut. As he passed by he gave me a wink with his good eye. You know Benevista, he's iron, he eats up pain. They'll never break him by punching him around. But once they understand that, they'll start in with the real treatment, wires and the rest of it. Even a Benevista, with all his courage, could crack. So the question is this: does Benevista know where you are?"

"Yes," Frederico said. "I'll hang up now."

Fernald was signing the day's dictation when Diebold's call came through. He dismissed his secretary and took the call.

Diebold said, "The subject had a rendezvous at the Galleria that went sour. She returned to her hotel, and that's where she is now."

"How did it go wrong?"

In short precise sentences, Diebold described what had taken place at the Galleria. "No way I can guess whether wires got crossed or the terrorists caught on that the setup was booby-trapped."

When he told Locksley about it, Fernald thought, he would say "twigged," he would beat him to the punch with the British slang word. He said to Diebold, "Were you twigged?"

"I don't think so. But there was plenty of competition around."

Fernald said, "Forgot to ask—how are your wounds?"

Diebold grunted, and Fernald thought, He's embarrassed for me, making a fuss about something as ordinary as being stabbed and almost having your eye scratched out.

He said, "Describe the competition."

"Two or three of them were pretty surely Italian plainclothes cops. There was another one..." Diebold trailed off uncertainly.

"A Marlboro man?"

"What?"

"Sorry. Go on, please."

Diebold told about a man who had jogged the subject's elbow at Biffi. He had been watching, and if there had been any kind of exchange, he was sure he would have spotted it. Tables were close together, accidental and innocent jogging was not unusual.

"What did the man look like?"

"Italian. About fifty, good-looking, expensively dressed, a little—what do you call it?—effete."

Not Strawberry. Fernald said, "We know that the Russians are on to her."

"Is that right?"

With no more inflection or interest, Fernald thought, than you would display if someone told you it would be cloudy tomorrow. "So they may have guessed how important Bering is."

"Is he important?"

Fernald let Diebold's indifference nettle him. He said sharply, "Would we have mounted an extrication operation if he wasn't?"

"I don't analyze these things," Diebold said, "I just do them."

And that was it, truly. Diebold was a soldier in the trenches. He made no presumptions, simply did what he was told to do. "Why he's important doesn't matter to you?"

"It doesn't matter."

"Not that you need the incentive," Fernald said, "but I'd like to fill you in. There was some heavy corruption going on during the cruise missile negotiations. Bering was the bagman for a part of it. What he knows could bring the Italian government down. That's not in our interests."

"The Ivans know about this?"

"They've probably guessed he's our asset, and they can see the advantage of squeezing him to see what comes out. We don't think Bering could stand up under their kind of pressure for two minutes. You understand his importance now?"

"Yes sir. Is that all?"

"No, it isn't all. You'll recall that I mentioned a Marlboro man?"

"Is it some kind of code?"

"It's a very rough thumbnail description of Strawberry. You know who Strawberry is, of course?"

"Certainly. I wasn't aware we knew what he looked like."

Fernald said, "Through one of our assets we have a description of him for the first time. Tall and rangy, about six two or three, about a hundred and eighty-five, blond, cancel that, make it wheat-colored, hair. Like one of those cowboys in the Marlboro cigarette ads. Speaks American very well, but if you listen hard enough you can hear a faint trace of accent, and he makes little mistakes in slang. He's in Milan."

"Is that right?"

Behind the casual words Fernald could sense a quickening of interest, even a form of pleasure. "Watch out for him, but understand that we have no interest in seeing him terminated."

"Am I to understand that he's off limits in all circumstances?"

Bastard, Fernald thought, you know I don't mean that. "You'll protect the integrity of the operation, it goes without saying. But you're not to go gunning for Strawberry. Stress *not*. Do you understand that?"

"Yes sir."

"Be sure you do."

"By the way," Diebold said, "it occurs to me, the Russians to one side, that the terrorists might try to squeeze Bering."

"It's not their style. They kill without qualms, but to date we don't know any instance of their using torture. You have it straight about Strawberry? You know what our wishes in the matter are?"

"Sure," Diebold said. "Anything else?"

Just try to make a strenuous effort not to kill anybody, there's a good fellow. "No, nothing else," Fernald said. "Good night."

"Any time you're in trouble," Zayde would say, "go straight to the only people you can trust. *Mishpocha*."

Who was to say that Zayde's primitive, tribal wisdom was wrong? And so, slumped on her bed in confusion and despair after returning from the Galleria, Juno picked up the phone and gave the operator Jerry's hospital number. When you want to cry, seek out the shoulder of *mishpocha*, family. Besides, she owed Jerry a phone call.

"You can hang up the phone," the operator said. "I will ring when the call is consummated."

"I don't mind holding on."

"As the signora wishes."

She heard a series of cabalistic and, presumably, transatlantic clicks and murmurings. It was nearly midnight, six in the evening in New York. She knew the call would be monitored, but what secrets could she possibly give away by reporting her failure?

In a surprisingly short time, the operator said, "The call is completed. Proceed, please."

Jerry's voice said, "Hello." The connection was clear, noiseless.

"Jerry? It's me."

"And high time, believe me. Where are you?"

"Italy. I thought you'd know by now."

"Of course I know. Your picture was all over the papers. You're in Rome, right?"

"Milan. How are you feeling?"

"You're in Milan now? At the Principe di Savoia?"

"No. Do you think I called to discuss hotels? You haven't said how you're feeling."

"I feel wonderful. I'm trying to get out of here, but you know doctors, it goes against their ethics to give you a straight answer. We always stay at the Principe. How come you didn't go there?"

"Have you had your dinner yet?"

"I just finished. Dinner at five thirty!" He paused, and then, his voice trembling, said, "How are you, darling? God, you can't imagine how worried I've been about you."

"I'm fine, Jerry, I'm—"

The sudden wail of despair that led the way for a great burst of tears must have taken Jerry by surprise, but she had been feeling a scalding hotness building up behind her eyelids for moments now, eroding her unnatural calm, working toward a climax. . . .

Bawling. What she was doing was bawling, a loud, undignified, heart-solacing demonstration of uninhibited weeping. She heard Jerry's dismayed voice in the background, pleading with her, entreating, but she bawled on. The end came of itself, as if some physiological thermostat had signaled "enough already!" There was a grand climactic wail, followed by snuffling, a sobbing intake of breath, a shudder, and then it was over. She felt worn, content, at peace.

Jerry was babbling frantically. She waited for a pause and then said in a muted voice, "Jerry, do you love me?"

"What an insulting question! Don't you know by now that I love you like crazy?"

"Thank you, Jerry. Thank you, darling."

"Thank you. She thanks me. Are you going to cry again?"

She thought his question over. "No, I'm fine now." She cleared her throat—at transatlantic prices!—and was pleased when her voice emerged steady, unblurred by weepiness. "I want to apologize for sneaking away without letting you know. But you know why it was necessary."

"You mean the CIA?" His tone was a mixture of reproach and playfulness. "How do you know they're not listening in right this second?"

She was sure they were, but it didn't matter. "Last night," she said, "I was *this* close to seeing Michael."

Quickly, sparing of details, she told him what had taken place at the Galleria.

When she finished he was silent for a moment, his breathing regular. "Why didn't they contact you?"

"I don't know. Unless—"

"The CIA was watching them?"

"Don't laugh. It's possible."

He sighed. "What will you do now?"

"I don't know. I hope they'll try to get in touch with me again. But I won't give up. At least here, I'm *near* Michael."

"You're just going to hang around waiting for something to happen?"

"Maybe I'll think of something." She waited for Jerry to speak, then said, "If you need me, darling, if you want me to come home..."

"Me? I'm in great shape. Look, Juno—I want you to do what you have to do. Okay?"

"Yes. Thank you, Jerry."

"He's my son, too, isn't he? Just take care. If you let anything happen to you, I'll break every bone in your body."

To forestall another spate of tears—this time of gratitude—Juno said good-bye and hung up. But however warmed and solaced she might be, she was unable to fall asleep; the events of the evening kept playing themselves back like an unwelcome rerun of a movie she was forced to sit through again against her will. Why had the Forze Scarlatte, after all their carefully planned arrangements, failed to contact her? It could only be that she was being watched, and they were aware of it.

She had seen a number of people more than once, but there was nothing suspicious in that: people strolled back and forth in the Galleria as they might on a favorite boulevard. The only person she had taken any note of was the man who had jogged her elbow at Biffi. He had seemed familiar to her, and now, more than ever, she was certain that she had seen him before.

Concentrating, she tried to project his image on the ceiling, as if on a screen. Black hair and soft dark eyes, olive skin—a Renaissance face... and the answer to the puzzle eased itself into her mind. Yes, she had seen the man at Biffi before, not once but many times, on the street, in shops, on buses. These people were, after all, excepting their dress, no different in appearance from their ancestors, many of whom had modeled for the paintings of the great Renaissance masters. Yes, she had seen the man at Biffi before, in the guise of a cleric, a mourner, a courtier, tucked away in the corner of a masterpiece by Raphael, Mantegna, Titian, Bellini....

So much for those particular suspicions. She smiled into the darkness of the room, and presently she slept.

Twelve

Bering entered the kitchen, then stopped abruptly when he caught sight of Adriana; she was filling a syringe from a small vial. He let out a roar and charged back through the door. He butted Michael out of the way and got a few paces into the hall before Gildo tackled him around the hips and slowed him down. Bering plowed forward a few feet, dragging Gildo with him. Then Giorgio and Carlo joined in. Bering continued to buck and flail, and he bloodied Giorgio's mouth with a wide swing of his arm.

Adriana looked up, frowning. Michael did nothing. He stood out of the way and watched, surprised, even pleased, at Bering's clumsy show of strength. Finally, Gildo put an end to the struggle. He clamped a powerful forearm around Bering's neck in a headlock and bulldogged him to the floor. Then the three of them found an arm or a leg and hauled him back into the kitchen. He continued to thresh wildly for a moment, his face congested, his eyes bulging, and then, suddenly, the fight went out of him, whether because he had exhausted himself or simply realized the hopelessness of the situation, Michael couldn't tell.

He lay still, his chest heaving, and offered no resistance when Adriana, kneeling beside him, rolled up his sleeve and swabbed his arm. His eyes rolled, found Michael, and stared in reproach.

A few minutes earlier, when Michael had gone up to the secret room and waked him, Bering had been calm, drowsy, and displayed no apprehension at being told to get dressed.

"Something going on every night," Bering had said yawning. "What's the idea?"

"We're moving."

Bering looked more alert. "What time is it?"

"Two thirty."

"Where are we going?"

"Venice."

"How come?"

"It's not safe here any longer."

"Pretty sudden, isn't it? At two thirty in the morning?"

But they had always known that when a move became necessary it would be a rush job. For once, after Federico's return from his phone call to Rome, there was no parliamentary discussion, no dialectical arguments. Federico had stated the proposition flatly.

"We can't take a chance, we can't bank even on Benevista's courage. We're moving to the backup house."

It was only when he was finishing dressing that Bering had given Michael an anxious look. "You're not kidding me, are you, Mike? I mean, this isn't..." His voice faltered. "Are they going to kill me?"

"No. All we're going to do is move you."

Bering nodded, but his eyes remained wary. "What about your helping me to escape? This changes things, right?"

"Just the plans, not the intentions. One way or another, I'm committed to getting you out."

Climbing through the trapdoor, making his way along the attic crawl space by the glow of Michael's flashlight, Bering had been calm, even chipper. But the moment he saw Adriana loading the syringe, he had leaped all the way to the conclusion that he was about to die.

Now, lying on his back, his arms and legs pinned to the kitchen linoleum, he said, "Mike, are you going to let them do this to me?"

"It won't hurt you. It'll put you to sleep, that's all."

"Sure. But am I going to wake up?"

"Let him go," Adriana said. "He's not going to struggle any more or he'll have a heart attack." She held the syringe up vertically and produced a bubble of liquid at its tip. "This is a barbiturate. You'll go to sleep, and later you'll wake up. When we're ready for something more drastic we'll let you know. Fair enough?"

"Mike?" Bering said.

"It's the truth."

Her brow furrowed in concentration, Adriana slid the tip of the needle into the vein in the crook of Bering's elbow.

*   *   *

The blue-and-white car of the *polizia stradale*, the highway police, appeared in Adriana's rearview mirror just after they had passed the Padua exit of the A4 *autostrada*.

She turned to Federico, who sat beside her in the front seat of the van. "Police. About a hundred meters behind us."

"Damn," Federico said. "Can you outrun them?"

"Not in this tub."

"Is he trying to overtake us?"

She checked the mirror. "No. He's just hanging back there."

Someone was rapping at the window that separated the cab from the body of the van. It was Gildo, pointing to the back of the van and yelling.

Federico, nodding his head, yelled, "Yes, we know it. Just sit tight."

The trip to Venice was audacious, but the danger lay ahead, once they crossed the causeway, so it was ironic, Adriana thought, that they should experience trouble on the comparatively simple run on the highway. Not that any of it could be considered without hazard, in view of the vigilance of the police. She was glad Michael was not with them, for more than one reason.

Michael had been elected to drive Adriana's *cinquecento*, which they couldn't leave behind in Vicenza. He had left ten minutes earlier than the van, after helping them carry Bering out of the house. Bering was swathed in blankets, and the five of them, all except Adriana, had staggered under the burden of his inert weight. They had put him into the back of the van at five minutes before three. There was a chill in the air and it was dark; the moon was hidden by clouds, which was all to the good, especially for the tricky part of the operation in Venice.

"Are they still back there?" Federico said.

"Yes. It's this goddamn van."

The police associated vans with young people and drugs, and often stopped them for a search. She checked the mirror. The police car was still there, maintaining its distance. She drove evenly, resisting the urge to speed up, which would have been pointless. It might have been different if she had been driving her mother's Maserati. She had cut her driving teeth on that car.

"They're in the outside lane now," Adriana said.

The *autostrada*, at this hour, was almost deserted. Now and then a car had passed them in the fast lane, but traffic would be very light until, an hour or so from now, the trucks began to roll.

"They're moving up on us."

Someone was rapping on the cab window. This time it was Carlo. Federico yelled, "Yes, we know, we're not asleep." He said to Adriana,

"Just go on as you are, do nothing differently, maybe they'll pass us by."

But almost before he had finished speaking they heard the wail of a siren, and the blue-and-white came up beside them. The cop in the passenger's seat was waving his gloved hand toward the shoulder of the road. Adriana drove on. The cop gestured more emphatically.

"Well," Adriana said, "what shall I do?"

"Do you have a choice?"

"Of sorts. I can try to ram him."

Federico shook his head. "Pull over."

She slowed the car and edged off onto the shoulder. The police car fell back and then pulled in behind them. Carlo's face was at the window, very pale. Federico put his fingers to his lips and waved him away. Adriana braked to a stop.

"And now?" Adriana said.

Federico shrugged. "Be charming."

She rolled her window down, and, in the sideview mirror, watched the two cops get out. They strolled slowly along the shoulder, with their hands at their holsters, fingering the butts of their P38's. One of the cops came up to the window; the second stood back. His gun was halfway out of its holster.

"*Buona sera, signorina.*" The first cop bent to the window.

"*Buona sera,*" Adriana said, smiling. The cop was young, with flaming red hair. "Did I do anything wrong?"

"Not at all," the cop said politely. "May I see your documents, please?"

"Certainly," Adriana said. "Oh dear, I'm sure I wasn't speeding."

She felt in her bag for her wallet and handed it to the cop, then put her hand back in the bag, searching for the butt of her Beretta.

The cop said, "May I have yours as well, signore?"

"What for?" Federico said. "I'm not driving."

"Nevertheless, I would like to see your papers."

"It's not logical," Federico said. "If I were driving—"

"Oh, Federico, darling," Adriana said, "don't be such a stickler. If he wants your papers, show them to him. I'm sure he has a good reason for asking."

Federico sighed and reached into his breast pocket. The second cop tensed and drew his gun. Federico leaned across Adriana to hand the red-haired cop his license.

"Thank you," the cop said.

"It's silly to make a fuss over it," Adriana said.

"I just don't like to be hassled," Federico said.

The red-haired cop studied both licenses, then handed them back.

Adriana smiled. "I'm sure everything is in order. May we go on now?"

"Would you mind telling me where you're going at this hour?" the cop said.

"To Trieste. To visit my grandmother in the hospital."

"Do you expect they'll allow you into the hospital at this hour?"

"Oh, yes. She's dying, you see. The hospital phoned a short while ago. In fact, there's some question whether or not we'll make it in time. Poor thing, she's had a stroke, and is already in a coma, but I want to be there anyway, she's so old and alone, and I'm sure that even though she's unconscious she'll somehow sense my presence."

"I'm sorry," the red-haired cop said. "Naturally we won't want to hold you up in these circumstances."

"Oh, thank you, *grazie mille*—"

"So if you'll just allow us..." He nodded to the second cop, who moved toward the rear of the van. "If you'll just allow us to check the back of the van, then you can go on to Trieste."

"There's nothing there, it's empty," Adriana said.

"See," Federico said, "they're hassling us. Just because we drive a van and we're young."

The second cop called out from the rear. "It's locked."

"May I have the key, please?" the red-haired cop said.

"We lock it because we park in the streets, and the spare tire is in there."

"I understand. May I have the key please, signorina?"

"Certainly," Adriana said.

"Have you got a search warrant?" Federico said.

"Federico, you're being absurd." Adriana removed the keys from the ignition ."It's the yellow one," she said, handing the keys to the cop.

"Thank you. Please remain in the car."

Both cops moved on to the rear of the van. She and Federico sat very still, looking straight ahead through the windshield. Adriana heard, or thought she heard, the key being inserted in the lock, but then such subtleties were overwhelmed in the crash of gunfire. It seemed to go on for a very long time—the bang of pistol shots, the roaring of Gildo's *lupara*. When it stopped, leaving a profound silence in its wake, she and Federico jumped out of the car. The cops were sprawled on the verge of the road. One of them had had his face shot off, obliterated. The other, the red-haired one was alive. He was moaning, and his legs were twitching.

Gildo, Giorgio, and Carlo were in the doorway, still crouched, still in shooting position. Carlo looked ill; Giorgio seemed dazed; Gildo was smiling.

"Finish him off." Federico pointed to the red-haired cop.

Giorgio jumped down, bent over the red-haired cop, and fired. A splinter of bone jumped out of the cop's head. He lay still. Adriana looked the length of the highway in both directions. It was empty, but she thought she heard the distant hum of a motor.

"Back in the van," Federico said. "Let's go."

"The keys," Adriana said.

She found them clutched in the right hand of the red-haired cop. She bent quickly and retrieved them; there was a single drop of bright blood on the ignition key. The red-haired cop's hat had flown off. Blood was spreading on his head, dying his hair a darker red.

Adriana ran around to the front seat, put the key into the ignition slot, and started the engine. Federico jumped in beside her.

"Never mind the speed limit," he said. "Who's to stop you now?"

Adriana stepped down on the accelerator. The van's engine whined and picked up speed. Suddenly, to their left, in the fast lane, a car sped by. Adriana jerked the van sharply to the right. The wheels rode the shoulder for a moment before she straightened out on the road again.

"What do you call that?"Federico said. "Are you nervous?"

"Do you think they saw the bodies?"

"I doubt it. They probably saw the blue-and-white, but that's all. Would you like me to drive?"

"I'm fine."

"Keep the car straight, please. They were only cops."

"Yes."

"We've killed cops before, you may remember."

"I know."

"Well?"

She took her hand off the wheel to make a slight gesture. "There's a difference, you know, between executing policemen as an act of political choice, and bumping them off on the roadside the way addicts do. I do not regard myself in the least as a killer, but as an instrumentality for dispensing justice to the lackeys of the oppressor."

"Well and good. Would it have soothed your fine-tuned sense of propriety, then, if instead we had allowed ourselves to be captured?"

She shook her head and drove in silence for a moment. Then, shuddering, she said, "Did you see that piece of bone fly up when Giorgio did the *colpo di grazie?*"

"An irrelevance. You're going soft, Adriana. It's Michael and those pathetic humanistic ideas of his. It's good you're finished with him."

She said coldly, "You are our leader, I accept that I must take our political line and strategy from you. But when it comes to personal affairs, to the interaction of two people of the opposite sex, you're absolutely hopeless. Please don't undertake to advise me."

Federico said, "I have only one concern—the cause. If your attachment to him is still such that it will intefere with your duty, perhaps this is the time to say so."

She turned toward him, her face pale and furious. "I'll compare my dedication to anybody's, including yours."

"Keep your eyes on the road. . . . There's the sign for the Mestre exit, half a kilometer."

Adriana eased the van off the ramp and paid the toll into the hand of a sleepy attendant. She turned into the Ponte della Libertà, the causeway over the Laguna that separated the industrial grime and squalor of Mestre from the otherworldly fantasy of Venice, La Serenissima. She crossed the bridge over the Canale Santa Chiara and slowed down.

"What if he's not there?"

"Shut up," Federico said. "He'll be there."

Then she spotted Gianni, or, rather, his wagon, the large pushcart from which, during the day, he sold cheap gloves in the outdoor market on the Rialto Bridge. The cart was a cumbersome necessity: they couldn't very well carry an unconscious man out in the open; in Venice, even at this time of the morning, there was always a possibility that people might be wandering about.

She pulled up beside the pushcart. Federico was already out of the van, and she could hear the others jumping down from the rear. Gianni gave her a wink as he peeled the soiled, weatherbeaten canvas from the cart. The others came into sight with Bering. Federico and Giorgio were holding his feet, Carlo and Gildo his arms. Bering's head was lolling. When they stretched him out in the cart they discovered that it was a few centimeters too short for his length, so they carefully bent his knees. Gianni replaced the canvas and tucked in its edges.

Federico slapped the side of the van. "Get going."

As she started to roll, she saw them begin to trundle the cart on the long haul to the Fondamenta della Croce, where the scow was to meet them. She drove straight ahead to where the upcast of lights from the Piazzale Roma was truncated by the lowering black sky.

The Piazzale Roma was land's end for motor vehicles, a large square lined with car rental and livery services, travel bureaus, souvenir shops, and quick food places, all serving the modern, multistoried parking garage and open-air lot crowded with cars, trucks, and a vast number of tour buses.

After parking the *cinquecento*, Michael ambled through a dark narrow street, hardly more than an aisle between the ancient tenements that loomed above it on both sides. The alley ended at the Fondamenta della

Croce, the embankment on the Canale Santa Croce, where it flowed in from the Laguna and just before it made a sweeping curve that merged it with the Grand Canal.

The waters were lapping softly against the concrete of the deserted *fondamenta*. The canal, a bustling waterway during the day, was deserted. Peering toward the Grand Canal, Michael could see no sign of the scow. But Giuseppe was reliable; he would show up. "Don't be nervous," Federico had said. "Just find a doorway and wait. We'll be there, and so will Giuseppe."

The doorway he picked was deeply recessed and odorous; he felt broken tiles under his feet. Across the canal a light went on in a building, and although its glow was barely visible behind the ubiquitous shutters, he shrank back into the doorway. The light went out. Michael looked at his watch, but it was too dark for him to read. He thought he smelled the deep bitter aroma of coffee, but it wasn't likely; the building above him seemed heavy with sleep.

He looked out over the vista of dark water and black shuttered houses, and tried to pick out the place, perhaps a half mile to the north and east of here, where the Ghetto lay moldering in its ageless decay. He thought of the first time he had seen the Ghetto. He had been thirteen, and he hadn't wanted to go; he had been balky and sullen about his father's insistence. Jerry Sultan had regarded it as a duty, a form of pilgrimage.

"I want you to realize what it was like to be a Jew many years ago. Then maybe you'll understand how good you've got it now."

If Jerry had deliberately set about to choose a self-defeating approach, one better designed to stir up the antagonism of a boy who had already begun to challenge his father's assumptions, he could hardly have done better. But, ironically, where Jerry Sultan had failed, the Ghetto itself had succeeded. Michael had been profoundly moved by the pitiable crumbling buildings, huddled together in the partnership of common misery, by the palpable stink of poverty, by the five ancient synagogues, by the worn pavements which he could visualize being trodden by generations of garbardined Jews. And, of course, by the mutely eloquent plaque listing the names of those who had been "taken by the Germans" to the concentration camps.

But finally it was something beyond the squalor and poverty, beyond history and fact, something mysterious and undefinable that had called out to him from an even more ancient past and resounded in his blood. Suddenly, his outward indifference had been ruptured by a burst of tears. Jerry had been tender, soothing, and secretly self-congratulatory at having opened his son's eyes to the somber colors of his heritage.

*   *   *

Michael heard a grinding sound of wheels, and presently he saw the bulky cart appear from the mouth of an alley. He jumped at the sound of a voice.

"As soon as Adriana comes from the parking lot we'll signal the boat. Sorry for the delay. Unavoidable."

Federico melted away, and, Michael assumed, found a doorway of his own, as the others must already have done. On the embankment, close to the water, Gianni had stopped wheeling his cart.

Federico's mention of Adriana brought forth a resurgence of Michael's resentment at their encounter earlier in the evening. It had taken place after the meeting in which it had been determined that it had now become too risky to continue their efforts to bring him and his mother together, and that the plan would be abandoned permanently.

Adriana had said to him, "Well, you must be happy, now that we are no longer using your mother, as you put it."

"How can I be? You're still using her, maybe even more cruelly than before. You raise her hopes, drag her across the ocean, and then suddenly leave her high and dry."

"You're singing a different song now. Does the little boy miss his mother?"

They had barely spoken after that. And yet, now, with a recurring sense of helplessness, his feelings for her swept away his bitterness. He visualized her walking swiftly through the alley with that proud gait of hers, silken-haired, luminous-eyed, and he knew he was without defenses where Adriana was concerned. They were an impossible couple, with no compatibility but the unfathomable mystery of love. It had always amused him to compare her social background with his own. She was the daughter of a family that had first acquired power and status in Venice seven or eight hundred years ago. His own family? So far as he knew, it connected only to Zayde, his great-grandfather, whom he had known only briefly—a jolly, somewhat smelly old man—before his death. Beyond that it didn't exist, except where it might remain in the dim memories of a few survivors, if any, of a *shtetl* in Lithuania from which Zayde had emigrated with his wife, the *bubbe* who had died before Michael was born.

He had once taken Adriana down to the Ghetto, hoping she might see it through his eyes. Her reaction had been predictable.

"All the dispossessed, wherever they are, whoever they are, are in the same boat as the Jews. Does it matter what religion you are if the blood is sucked out of you by the rulers of the world? A slave is a slave no matter what God—what false god—he might in his ignorance worship."

He hadn't attempted to breach that ideological wall. Instead, he had told her solemnly that long ago, perhaps four or five centuries—what was a hundred years more or less?—her noble family, fallen on hard times, had come to the Ghetto, vivid with arrogance and pride, and pawned some of their possessions—majolica, fine chairs, perhaps even a Titian portrait of the head of the family—at the shop of one of *his* forebears, a cringing, obsequious Jew in shiny gabardine, wearing the prescribed red cap on his bony skull, rubbing his hands together, making a very sharp deal with the impoverished *nobili* . . .

"Your ancestors were Italian?" she had said sharply. "You never told me this. Can it be true?"

No, only spiritual ancestors, with whom he had made sharp and memorable contact by walking the streets, sensing the life in the brick and mortar, feeling the rhythm of long dead hearts.

He saw a shadow emerge from the alley, and he recognized it as Adriana. Someone called out to her in a whisper, and she disappeared from his view. He saw Federico move toward the water's edge, and direct three quick beams of light from his flashlight across the canal. Then he joined Gianni beside the cart.

"Michael."

Adriana glided into the doorway and into his arms. She pressed the length of her body against him meltingly, and he felt the thrust of her breasts, the length of her thighs. "Hold me, *caro*, hold me tightly, Michael."

He felt the moist warmth of her breath against his cheek. "Are you all right?"

"Yes. Hold me."

He heard the rachitic chug of a boat on the canal, coming closer. The scow loomed up, closing in on the embankment, and now, from nowhere, the others were appearing—Giorgio, slight as a boy, Carlo, Gildo with his *lupara* looped over his shoulder.

Adriana gave a little cry, almost a sob. "This is lovely, Michael. This is how you must always remember me."

"Always."

"Now, at this moment, I love you completely, nothing else exists." And then, with a grave, profound sadness, she said, "It will not always be so."

He felt the flutter of her heartbeat. "It will," he whispered. "It will, *cara*."

She parted his lips with her fingers and kissed him.

"Thank you, *caro*," she said. "Now we must go."

She slipped away and started toward the embankment; he followed. The scow had edged alongside, bobbing, and Carlo and Giorgio were down on their knees, trying to steady it. The motor was quieter now, idling, but still it chugged its uneven sound out into the quiet of the Venetian night.

Six of them, including Adriana and Gianni, but with the exception of Giuseppe, who stood on the scow and watched, struggled with the weight of the cart. It was hard work, but, lacking a second cart to meet them at their destination, they had no choice. Grunting and heaving, they succeeded in lifting the cart over the gunwales of the scow and dropping it heavily on the deck, which was covered with pipes, wrenches, clamps, and the assorted ironmongery of Giuseppe's trade as a plumber. They jumped into the scow and, half lifting, half shoving, pushed the cart into the shed in the center of the deck. Then they crowded into the shed, which gave off a stink of oil and grease and rust. There was no room inside for Michael. The scow was already pulling away from the shore.

"Never mind," Giuseppe said over his shoulder, "one of you can stay out here."

Michael went forward to join Giuseppe, a youngish man with a fierce, hook-nosed profile. The scow was picking up speed, heading toward the bend where the Canale Santa Croce flowed into the Grand Canal. After the turn they passed the railroad station. A garbage scow, heavily laden, giving off a sweet odor of putrefaction, swept by them in the other direction. Ahead, Michael saw a sleek *motoscafo* coming toward them.

"*Carabinieri*," Giuseppe said. "A patrol. Bow your head to them like a polite little gentleman, full of respect."

There were three *carabinieri*, in tan uniforms with shiny black holsters. One steered the *motoscafo*, the other two stood in the stern. Between these two, a small Italian flag fluttered over their wake.

As they came abreast, Giuseppe bowed his head slightly, and Michael did the same. The *carabinieri* paid no attention to them, but swept on-ward in dignified silence.

"Pigs," Giuseppe said.

Michael looked back. The *motoscafo* was moving on its deliberate way, the *carabinieri* were as unmoving as statues. Giuseppe took the scow into a sharp left turn into the Canale di Cannaregio and veered toward the right bank, lined with stores and low buildings. He passed under a bridge, brought the scow in to the *fondamenta*, cut his engine and stopped.

Federico put his head cautiously out of the shed. "Here?"

"Here," Giuseppe said. "Start unloading."

Bracing themselves on the deck, they tugged the canvas-covered cart out of the shed. Then they had to lift again, staggering under the weight of the cart and the sway of the scow. They dropped the cart on the concrete embankment; its wheels were no more than an inch away from the edge.

Panting, Federico said, "*Grazie, camerata.*"

"All in a day's work," Giuseppe said. "*Ciao.*"

They didn't turn to watch the scow pull away, but put their shoulders to the cart, turning it toward the narrow mouth of an alley.

"Easy does it," Federico said. "We're almost there. All together, please."

They rolled the cart through the alley into the old Ghetto, and stopped in front of the scarred wooden door of a house with peeling facade and unpainted shutters discolored by weather and the ages. Federico knocked at the door, which opened at once. They stripped the canvas away from the cart, lifted Bering out, and carried him into a dark entry.

A flashlight blinked on and then off, and in its brief flicker Michael could see a narrow hallway flush with a long flight of stairs hemmed in by walls on both sides. There was no room to maneuver, and they jostled each other, bending and straining, before they got Bering lined up with the stairs. They labored upward, colliding with each other. Near the top, someone lost his grip on Bering's legs, and they dragged him up the remaining steps.

The flashlight went on again, blindingly, moving from one to another of them. It settled on Michael. He lifted his hand to shield his eyes from the glare. Against the wall, an elongated shadow appeared, reaching upward to an apex, then descending in a swoop. Michael felt a heavy thud against the back of his head, tasted blood, and went spinning down into a spiral of blackness, at the bottom of which he no longer felt anything.

Thirteen

Juno left the hotel at nine o'clock in the morning. She wandered through the city for more than five hours, and at four, when she returned, the concierge, smiling and bowing, said, "Ah, signora, a letter has come for you. *Eccola!*"

It was a plain white envelope with her name printed upon it. She knew that it was from the Forze Scarlatte.

She had started off without any destination, walking briskly, taking pleasure in the length and sureness of her stride. She had always been able to take sustenance in the sheer exuberance of exercise. But when she turned into the Via Manzoni, she was forced to moderate her pace; the street was crowded with people on their way to their offices and shops. She paused to admire the jade fish she had seen in the window the previous night, and then, on impulse, turned in to the shop. The man who greeted her in the hushed, faintly perfumed interior invited her to sit in one of three amrchairs placed before a low counter.

"Tell me, signora, how I may give myself the pleasure of helping you?"

In English it would have sounded egregious and florid, but in Italian it was merely standardly gracious. She told him that she had been admiring the jade fish.

"Thank you. It is my own favoite piece. It was made, perhaps a thousand years ago, for a Japanese samurai family. The craftsmanship is..." He touched his fingers to his lips and blew a kiss. "Stupendous. It has been in my own family for two hundred years."

She asked him its price.

"It is twenty thousand dollars American."

She shook her head. "It's far out of my price range."

"Nevertheless, because you admire it, you shall see it on the counter."

She protested, but he wouldn't hear of it. It pleased him when someone else shared his deep appreciation of the fish. He reached into the window and carefully lifted it out.

"Would your husband perhaps care to see it?"

"My husband?"

He nodded toward the window. "I see him waiting outside for you. Many husbands, not interested as their wives are, do this—"

She got up, mumbling an apology, and went out of the shop. But she saw nobody who seemed to be watching. He must have seen her start for the door and melted into the throng of passersby. She stood for a moment in frustration, then resumed walking toward the *centro storico*. Her first thought was that her "husband" must have been from the Forze Scarlatte, but then why would he disappear? And if he *wasn't* the FS, then who was he?

She turned into the Piazza Scala, past the dowdy facade of the old opera house that contained no suggestion of the red and gold splendor of the interior, circled around the stern government building patrolled by two tall, handsome, preening *carabinieri* in ceremonial rig, and went into the Galleria. It was busier than last night, now that the shops were all open, and figures could be seen above, moving against the windows of the offices; a man with a Vandyke beard and a homburg hat looked down from one of the narrow balconies, stroking his beard.

She paused in front of the tobacco shop, with a sense of loss, then moved on. She remembered the package of cigarettes she had bought the night before, and looked around for a receptacle to throw them in. A girl was ambling toward her with a cigarette in her mouth. Why waste them?

"Excuse me," Juno said. "Would you like to have these?"

The girl frowned and looked her over. "You wish to sell them, signora?"

"No, no. I bought them last night, but . . . I've decided to stop smoking, so I want to give them to someone."

The girl studied her for another moment and seemed satisfied that she was not being made the victim of some swindle. "Well, why not?" She smiled and took the cigarettes. "Thank you, signora, and good luck with your not smoking."

Juno had moved on only a few paces when she heard a scuffling sound and an outcry of indignation. Behind her, the girl she had given the cigarettes was struggling in the grasp of two men who were dangling their wallets in front of her. A small crowd had already gathered, and more kept coming as the girl said loudly, "So you're the damn police! What has that got to do with me, you idiots?"

The policemen, discomforted by the attention they were attracting, tried to calm her down.

"The cigarettes?" The girl was shouting now, trying to shake off their hands. "You want the damn cigarettes, take them!" and she threw the package against the chest of one of the cops. She addressed the growing crowd. "All over Milan," she said contemptuously, "citizens are being mugged, having their bags snatched, being shot at, stabbed, garroted, pushed under cars, raped, and what is our wonderful police force doing? I'll tell you what they're doing—they're harassing innocent young women. It's enough to make you puke!"

The crowd burst into laughter. The two cops were now red-faced. One of them bent close to the girl and whispered something.

"No, I never saw her before in my life. Of course I don't know who she is. Do you think I ask for the pedigree of a woman who gives me a pack of cigarettes? Go catch a terrorist, you fool!"

The crowd applauded wildly. The cops were whispering to each other. Then one of them took out a notebook and asked the girl something.

"Name? Address? Telephone number?" She appealed to the crowd with her arms out, her eyes turned upward. "You see? This is how these idiots try to get girls." The crowd tittered. "They stop somebody on a pretext, extort a phone number. . . . Well, I tell you, if one of these hooligans dares call me, he'll get such an earful that he'll wish he was back in his mother's womb."

"All right," the cop said, deeply flushed. "All right, you can go. But we're confiscating the cigarettes."

"I hope you choke on them!"

She fixed the two cops with a final outraged glare and strode off toward the Scala end of the Galleria. The crowd cheered and yelled *"Brava!"* Juno went on toward the Duomo, relieved that it hadn't been necessary to intercede on the girl's behalf; in that case, the cops would surely have thought the girl was somehow involved. It was probably one of those cops, tailing her from the hotel, who was the "husband" outside the shop on the Via Manzoni; and he, or one like him, whose presence in the Galleria last night had warned off the Forze Scarlatte from keeping the rendezvous.

If she had been asked, later, to describe her itinerary that day, Juno would have been able to do so only roughly. What she remembered best was a small apartment building in a working-class quarter. The shape of the building, its stained facade, even the accumulation of wind-blown newspapers at its base, brought back memories of the tenement Zayde had lived in before he had moved in with his son's family.

The person she remembered best from her childhood was Zayde. He was at home during the day, while both her mother and father were out. Her father had just opened his own furniture store, working punishingly long hours to try to make a go of it. Her mother taught an afternoon session in a kindergarten, so she was in Zayde's care much of the time. He had just retired, which wasn't any great change, since he hadn't worked much in the past ten years or so. He had been a lithographer in the old country and found work in New York, but lithography was a dying trade, so retirement merely signaled that he had given up looking for a job.

She had never known how old Zayde was. All he would ever tell her was that he was as old as the hills, or, his favorite response: "Old enough to know better." Zayde was a wisecracker, a kibitzer, a kidder. His jokes weren't all that funny—she remembered her parents wincing when he pulled them—but they laid *her* in the aisle. And he had a hoard of Yiddishisms that never failed to delight her: *Hock mir nit kayn chainik,* which meant "don't bother me," but translated literally as "don't chop me a teakettle." *Shvehr zu zein a Yid,* which meant "tough to be a Jew," and wasn't all that funny. But her favorite, invoked for almost anything unpleasant, from a rise in the rent through the wrong candidate becoming president to a bad head cold, was *Ah klug tzu Columbus,* a curse on Columbus, who, by discovering America, was undeniably to blame for everything.

Zayde adored her; she was his first and only grandchild. In her turn, she found the cigar-smelling old man loving, tender, indulgent and, in his simplicity, a perfect companion for a child. His last years were plagued by various illnesses, although the burden was lightened by the proprietary joy he took in seeing his son become a success: enlarge his original store, open a second in a shopping center in New Jersey, a third on Long Island, with advertisements in the papers and on television. Television!

In truth, much of the credit for her father's accomplishment belonged to Jerry Sultan. Jerry had begun as a commercial artist with a knack for glamorizing furniture in wash and line drawings. Juno's father was his best client. In those days Jerry had been—it must be admitted—a rather brash young man with confidence to burn. He had met Juno one summer when she was working in her father's office, and at once set his cap for her. He was open, extroverted, cheerful, and deeply in love with her. He was also, in his stocky, barrel-chested, very masculine way, most attractive. Among his other qualities, she liked him because he was in all ways so different from the poetical professor of her college days.

A year after they were married, and shortly before Michael was born, her father invited Jerry to join his firm. Jerry, as expected, was a dynamo, but his style was too headlong and daring for her father's comfort. There were disagreements, quarrels, and Jerry pulled out to start his own business. Eventually, however, he and her father came together again, as full partners. Zayde died. A year later her father retired, and a few months afterwards suffered a fatal heart attack. Her mother remained in Florida, where she lived in comfort, *kvetched* about her health in a weekly telephone call, and missed her two *ayniklach*, Michael and Sharon.

On his own, Jerry gave his audacity free rein. He began to design his own furniture, which he produced in a modest way and introduced to the public through his stores. Then he took a big plunge—sold the stores, and with the proceeds bought a furniture plant in North Carolina. He also undertook the first of his trips to Europe where, as he put it, "I stole ideas and later sold them back with variations." He had become prosperous, but not rich; a certain lack of respect for money saw to that, as well as a tendency to gamble on the boldness of his vision.

And so the Jerry Sultans were happy and fortunate people, up to the point where Michael had been kidnapped by terrorists and Jerry had been betrayed by an uncooperative heart.

Ah klug tzu Columbus.

When the concierge gave her the letter on her return to the hotel, she was so excited that she forgot to take her room key and had to be called back. She went up in the elevator, ran down the hallway to her room, and tore open the envelope.

Going to the hotel itself had been a bold and clever stroke, but it posed a hazard that Beppo Di Lorenzo had not foreseen: it was so warm and comfortable, after the damp chill of the outdoors, that he was in danger of falling asleep. To do so—not even to mention that he might thus lose his quarry—would be to display extreme lack of physical and moral manliness.

Beppo had promised the *comandante* that he would kill the lady today. If one reckoned the day as ending at midnight, he had seven hours remaining to complete his mission. But he must remain alert at all times. The chair he had chosen commanded an unobstructed view of the elevators; he could not fail to see the lady entering or leaving the hotel. He allowed himself an inner smile at the thought that, if she had some way of knowing she was being stalked by Beppo Di Lorenzo, the hero of the bombing of the Bologna station, she would be too terrorized to do either one.

When he found his eyes fluttering, despite his resolve, he moved from his soft overstuffed chair to another with a high carved back and an unpadded wooden seat. Here his view of the elevators was oblique but sufficiently unobstructed so that her entry or departure would not escape him. Let Communists, Socialists, and liberals sleep; Beppo Di Lorenzo would never close his eyes. If a fascist could not be strong, cope with discomfort and hardship, he was not worthy of the name.

He had received a phone call from the *comandante* at twelve thirty and been instructed to report at once. This time there had been no coffee. He had stood at attention while the *comandante* spoke.

"You will be interested to know that Signora Sultan arrived in Milan yesterday evening."

"Just as you predicted, *comandante!*"

The *comandante* allowed himself a grim smile. "At ease, Di Lorenzo. By a stroke of luck we also know her hotel. The taxi driver who took her there happens to be the father of an N.A.R. *squadrista* in Milan."

"The driver is to be commended."

"Perhaps," the *comandante* said with a shrug. "He merely mentioned it to his son as a bit of gossip. The son called me no more than twenty minutes ago."

"You wish me to undertake the mission?"

"Yes. I wish you to go to Milan and liquidate the lady."

Beppo snapped to attention and jerked his arm upward in salute. "Then I will kill her as you order me—today."

The *comandante* had embraced him. He had then returned to his rooms, where he had changed into corduroy trousers and a midlength leather coat, covering a holster he had designed himself; it held both a .22 revolver loaded with explosive bullets and a six-inch blade which slipped into a sheath stitched to its front. It was one fifteen when he straddled his motorcycle and set out for Milan, some 200 kilometers to the north-west.

He hadn't been on his way five minutes before the frigid wind, blowing head on from the north, made him wish he had worn a sweater. His fingers were icy in their thin leather gloves, and the flimsy silk scarf at his throat would better have been replaced by a woolen one. By the time he reached the outskirts of Milan he was half frozen. In the city itself the cold was less biting, but his teeth were still chattering. He stopped at a service station to relieve himself, then threaded his way through traffic to the lady's hotel.

There, for the first time, he realized how difficult it was to do surveillance without making himself conspicuous. It was an entirely different operation from the affair of the Bologna station, where he had simply walked in, parked his suitcases under a waiting room bench, and then walked out. He discovered a small sandwich shop partway down the street which permitted him a partial view of the hotel entrance. He warmed himself up with coffee and some food, but it was not the kind of place where people lingered; he must not be seen as hanging around. When he left the café he window-gazed in the shops across from the hotel, but his position again exposed him to curiosity, and with the approach of evening it was turning colder; his teeth were chattering constantly now. Then he got his grand idea. He had noticed that a stream of people kept going into the hotel, many carrying brief-cases. It was clear that some kind of meeting was going on. So, if the lobby was crowded, he thought, then nobody would notice him. He crossed the street and boldly entered the hotel.

The doorman murmured "*Buona sera,*" and touched the peak of his cap. Beppo walked up a few steps to the lobby and saw that it was indeed crowded with people drinking, smoking, conversing with each other, or reading newspapers. He settled down to watch and wait. At one point, worried that the concierge was eyeing him, he flagged down a passing barman and ordered a cocktail. It was brought to him on a tray along with a dish of potato chips. The drink and the potato chips restored his confidence and also allayed the suspicions of the concierge, who no longer looked his way.

When someone left a newspaper on a nearby chair, Beppo picked it up. He was hardly interested in the contemptible lies of the subsidized press, but reading the paper, or pretending to, was a natural thing to be doing. Besides, concentrating on the columns of type might help counteract the drowsiness his drink had induced, and help him remain alert.

And yet he must have nodded, because he was aware of his head jerking upright. It was at that moment, as luck would have it, that the lady came out of the elevator, large as life, and passed directly by his chair. He did not move. She had no coat, so she would not be leaving the hotel.

He watched her pick her way through the crowd toward the bar. It was six o'clock—still six hours before he had to redeem his pledge to the *comandante*. In that time an opportunity was sure to present itself, and when it did he would strike.

Signora: With regret we inform you that we are totally and irrevocably with-drawing from any further attempt to bring you together with your son, the CIA terrorist Michael Sultan. Much as we would wish to honor your maternal desires, it is no longer feasible. Return to your own country. The important work of the People's Tribunal may no longer be endangered by sentiment, but must now pursue its inexorable course.—The People's Tribunal of the Forze Scarlatte

A copy of the picture of Michael was enclosed.

The phone rang, and so Juno did not know whether, having read the letter, she would have wept or raged.

A calm, courteous voice said in English, "Forgive the intrusion, signora. May I introduce myself? Doctor Alfredo Orlandi, of the police."

"Yes?"

He might have taken the flatness of her tone as mistrust. "Perhaps it would be best if you phoned me here at the Questura? So that there may be no misunderstanding?"

"Do you have news of Michael?"

"I am sorry that I do not. But it concerns your son, of course."

"Oh, I see."

He picked up the disappointment in her voice. "I believe that we might be of help to each other, signora."

"I don't see how."

"Perhaps if we meet and speak together," he said patiently, "then we should see how."

If the Forze Scarlatte were out of the picture, she thought, then she was totally adrift and helpless. For the first time she felt a sense of dependence, a need for a sympathetic ally. The police might be that ally, if only professionally.

"Very well. Please give me your name again."

"Alfredo Orlandi. The telephone number is—"

"Thank you, I'll look up the phone number myself."

"Ah yes, of course. You are very wise, signora."

But it was less wisdom than experience of a second hand sort: she had seen a movie in which the villain had given a woman a number purporting to be police headquarters but which was, instead, his own. She found the police number in the directory and dialed it.

"Questura Centrale. *Pronto.*"

She asked for Dr. Orlandi. A click, and he came on the phone. "Thank you, signora. Would it be convenient for you to take a drink with me at the bar of your hotel at six o'clock?"

"Yes."

It would give her ample time to take a nap, get dressed, and, if that was the way her emotions led, to weep a little.

She recognized him at once. He rose from a small table in a corner of the bar and came forward to meet her.

"Alfredo Orlandi, Signora Sultan, good evening." He smiled ruefully. "But I see you remember me from last night at Biffi."

"Good evening. It's safe to assume you weren't there by accident?"

"Please sit down, signora." He held her chair for her, then, moving with a slight awkwardness, circled to the other seat. "The only accident was when I stupidly nudged your elbow. I think my men might have had a good laugh at that."

"Your men? There were more than one?"

"Regrettably, yes." He signaled to the barman. "And not only *my* men. Others, perhaps, as well."

No wonder the Forze Scarlatte had failed to contact her; the Galleria must have been jammed to the walls with people who were watching her. Who were the others? How had everyone known where she would be?

The barman stood above them, smiling. Orlandi asked if she liked sherry, and she nodded. "I have a weakness for that English favorite. Otherwise, everything Italian."

She watched him as he spoke to the barman. He was wearing a tan suit with a thin vertical green line. His black hair was touched with gray, and worn long. In profile, even more than straight on, he reminded her of that Renaissance face in the corner of a picture. His gesturing fingers were long, agile, manicured, buffed. He didn't look like a policeman, but then, of course, this was Italy. She remembered the detective sergeant who had run the self-defense class; not much style, but if she were attacked by a mugger, he was the man she would want to come to her rescue.

The barman went off. Orlandi said, "I appreciate your consenting to see me, signora."

"How did you know I would be at the Galleria last night?"

"We followed you from your hotel." He made a deprecating gesture.

"How many were you?"

"Three men. I am sorry, signora, but we felt it was necessary. No, four, if we count myself. I came directly to the Galleria from the Questura, and, of course, made a fool of myself."

"You said there were others, apart from your men. Who were they?"

"Since I can only guess, perhaps I should not try to say."

"And what was the reason for all that attention?"

"Ah, signora..." His smile was gently reproachful. He waited until the barman, with a flourish, placed their drinks in front of them on small red napkins. "Shall I be candid with you?" He raised his glass. "Or should I better say, shall we be candid with each other?"

She took a sip of her wine. "We must certainly do our best, Dr. Orlandi."

"Good. I shall start by telling you that I have come up from Rome to oversee the effort to find the terrorists who have kidnapped your son and Signor Bering."

"Thank you. And in return I will tell you that I am here in Italy hoping to see my son."

"Next, I will tell you that my men and I were at the Galleria last night because we expected the FS to contact you there."

"What made you think so?"

"Signora, so far neither of us has gone beyond stating what is obvious. Now I hope to prove my intention to be open and frank with you." He lifted his glass and set it down again untasted. "Giuseppina Cavalera—does that name mean anything to you?"

"Did she call herself Pina?"

"To her friends, yes. Perhaps she regarded you as her friend."

"How did you know about her?"

He held out a plate of peanuts. She shook her head. He replaced the plate on the table. It's all very studied, she thought, an actor's punctuation, a trick to heighten suspense. "Two nights ago, signora, in Rome, in a hallway near your hotel, perhaps a few minutes after she left you, Giuseppina Cavalera was stabbed to death."

She had braced herself for a revelation—he had telegraphed it with his little act with the peanuts—but her shock was complete. The image of the helpless peasant woman on the plane rose up before her, and her eyes welled uncontrollably with tears. She picked up the red napkin from her lap and covered her face with it.

"Signora Sultan, forgive me."

She dabbed at her eyes before lowering the napkin. Across the table Orlandi was leaning forward, distressed. She remembered the woman's huge eyes glowing with thanks for the gift of the earphones. It was a performance, of course, but it remained with her, as though this was the real Giuseppina, and not the cool competent lady with the fine legs who had given her instructions in the lobby of the Hassler.

"I should not have been so brutal," Orlandi said. *"Mi dispiace,* signora."

Juno folded the red napkin carefully. "Who killed her—the police?"

"Pina Cavalera was herself a policewoman. She worked in my division."

She stared at him in bewilderment. He nodded his head slowly. She said, "I'm terribly sorry about Signora Cavalera. I feel I am responsible in some way."

"She was my good friend," Orlandi said. "I appreciate your feeling, but you have no blame for it. She took risks, she knew what she was doing." His voice took on an edge. "I would like to catch who did it."

"You have no idea who might have killed her?"

Orlandi might have hesitated for a moment—she couldn't be sure—then said, "None, as yet."

"I realize now that she was only pretending to be from the Forze Scarlatte, and I think I understand why. But how did she come to be in possession of the letter?"

Orlandi looked around him. The bar was crowded and the barman and his assistant were working frantically to fill orders. Overall, there was a bright cheerful hubbub; the entire lower floor of the hotel was noisy with chatter and laughter.

With a trace of a smile, Orlandi said, "Normally we don't reveal how our tricks are done, signora, but in this instance—well, I have made a compact with you, have I not?"

"You owe me an explanation because you have involved me," Juno said. "And that's a polite word. Fooled me, used me. Isn't that so, Dr. Orlandi?"

"Yes." He nodded. "Yes. In extenuation, I tell you that we did so only in the hope that it would help you to find your son."

"Our interests are not the same. You want to capture the terrorists, I simply want to see my son. Without asking, you intruded yourself into my affairs."

"But surely you see that our paths are parallel?"

He wasn't all that different from Fernald, barring the threats—and that might come in time, as well. Both of them, under the guise of justifying themselves to her, sought to make her an ally in pursuit of their own interests. If anything, Orlandi was the worse of the two; he had used her as a cat's-paw. She finished her drink, and he caught the bartender's eye and ordered two fresh ones.

"You are angry with me," Orlandi said, "and I cannot deny that you have the right to be."

His dark eyes were filled with compassion—or at least they seemed to be. He was handsome and suave, she thought, and he would know very well how to deal with women; already, she was regretting the harshness of the tone she had been taking with him.

"Do I have the right—as you say—to use you? I think not. But is it my *duty* to do so? There the line is not so clearly drawn. To sympathize with my motives you would need a firsthand appreciation of the havoc terrorists have created in my country. Not only the Forze Scarlatte, the Brigate Rosse, and other organizations of the left, but the lunatics of the extreme right as well. They have killed many innocent people—a bomb, and often a gun as well, cannot make judgments, cannot evaluate, cannot separate the innocent from the 'guilty.' Yet the deaths, the maimings, even these do not define the full extent of the matter."

He picked up his drink, but set it down untasted. His agitation seemed genuine, but how could she be sure he was not again creating a theatrical effect?

"Although there are, in terms of numbers, no more than a handful of terrorists, their presence is pervasive. People fear them because of the way they strike—audaciously, unexpectedly, without conscience, and always with cold cruelty. No one knows when they will strike next, or where or how, and this is why they are powerful, why they generate terror. People, ordinary people, are aware of the unpredictability of their attacks, and they know when they are in this public place or that, a market, a piazza, a park, that simply to be passing by means they might become victims. Then consider this—that terrorism breeds mistrust of the government because we are unable to prevent it from taking place. And each success of the terrorists makes them seem omnipotent. I do not want to go too far, but it must be said—terrorism has begun to change the character of Italians, and that is perhaps the worst consequence of all."

His ardor and eloquence had ruffled the surface of his urbanity, and now she could not doubt his sincerity; he had turned open and vulnerable. This was the underside of the coin of Italian character, she thought, a melancholy, a sense of the tragic beneath the surface of style, wit, and gaiety.

"So I have now explained my motivation," he said quietly. "It is to do everything in my power to lift this burden from my country and my people. This is both the duty of my office and the urging of my heart. I am the son of Italy, but it is also my son, my daughter, and I act as a parent, even as you do on behalf of your son. *Non è vero?*"

If she couldn't fail to be moved by his eloquence, she was nevertheless aware that he had dealt with her complaint about being used by belittling it with odious comparison: what was a personal *kvetch* against the anguish of an entire nation? The fine Italian hand!

He sipped his drink and watched her over its rim with what her mother would surely have described as "very fine eyes."

She said, "Dr. Orlandi, you haven't told me your reason for coming to see me."

His smile seemed calculated now, the courtier's display of charm. "I wish that it was merely for the pleasure of sitting across a table from a beautiful lady. But no. I am here to plead for your help."

She shook her head. "I'm no longer in a position to help you. You're too late."

She reached into her handbag and took out the envelope from the Forze Scarlatte. She held it out to him.

"Ah yes, the letter. But I have already read the letter, signora."

* * *

When the lady came striding out of the bar Beppo straightened up alertly in his chair. Her face was flushed, from which Beppo judged that there might have been a lover's quarrel. He had previously glanced inside the bar and seen her with a man. He had taken the measure of this man, who was neither young nor physically imposing, and concluded that he would not be a formidable obstacle, if it came to that.

As the lady went by, he directed his eyes ahead of her (leading her, as he had been taught to do when aiming a rifle at a moving target), wondering if she would continue through the lobby to the street. It was nearly seven thirty, and the evening rush was over; there would be few cars and even fewer pedestrians on the dark street. He could follow and make short work of her, with the knife. But she stopped at the elevators. In that case he would take the lift himself, and observe where she went. Then, after a few minutes, he would knock at her door and say that he was a bellboy with a message. When she opened the door . . .

The elevator arrived. He rose and started toward it, but the man she had been sitting with brushed by him and addressed her. The lady stepped away from the elevator, and moved back a few paces. Beppo returned to his chair.

The lady and the man were speaking together in a low tone. She seemed aloof and the man was pleading with her, that much was clear from his expression and his gestures, palms out and upward. Occasionally a word came to him, but they were speaking English, which he couldn't understand. The woman listened somberly, with a touch of obstinacy, though he thought that, as the man went on, she seemed to be softening. The man must have sensed it; he appeared to be pleading his cause with increased ardor. Beppo's lip curled with scorn. With women you didn't stoop to begging, you simply let them have a good one in the mouth.

At one point the man turned and gave Beppo a look. Beppo returned the glance casually, but after that avoided looking at them directly, instead just allowing his eyes to brush on them occasionally, as if by accident. Thus, he was somewhat taken by surprise to see that the man was smiling, and that the woman returned his smile. They spoke briefly, and, then, unexpectedly, she entered the elevator. Caught unawares, he could not have followed her without jumping toward the closing door, and that would have given him away.

Her companion slipped his topcoat on but did not leave. Beppo ventured the guess that he had persuaded the woman to have dinner with him, in which case she would have gone to her room for a coat. And presently his judgment was verified when she appeared again. She joined the man and together they went down the steps to the exit. Would they walk? If so, he would kill her—and the man as well, if necessary—before they had gone halfway up the street.

But when he trailed after them he saw them get into a taxi that had just discharged a passenger. Beppo moved swiftly. They were still settling themselves in the taxi when he slipped out and ran foward to where he had parked his motorcycle. He was already astride the bike when the taxi went by. He kicked his starter and took off after them. Still more than four hours to midnight, he thought, as he followed the red taillights of the taxi. One way or another, before his deadline, he was confident that he would redeem his pledge to the *comandante*.

Fourteen

The restaurant was medium-sized, softly lit, with the inevitable snowy white covers and freshly cut flowers on the tables. The maître greeted Orlandi effusively and led them to their table with flourishes. Orlandi accepted the attention graciously.

Juno said, "From the red-carpet treatment, you must be a favored patron."

"I've been here only once before, perhaps six months ago. But if he wants to pretend that I am a highly valued patron, then I shall pretend to believe him. Very insincere, very Italian, but no harm in it."

"An exercise in style."

"Ah," Orlandi said, giving her an admiring glance. "You understand the Italian character. Style is a national mania, and too often we sacrifice substance to it. It is a part of our larger problem, which is that we know very well how to live today and yesterday, but not tomorrow. We are improvident, we are the grasshoppers of the world community."

She thought of telling him that he could run down Italy in her presence only at his peril, but decided it was too arch, or, worse, intimate. He had become relaxed and bouyant enough, without any need of extra encouragement. So she merely said, "*Viva Italia.*"

"*Viva Italia,*" Orlandi said.

"*Viva Italia.*" The maître was beside their table again. "May I be of service?"

Orlandi said, "Will you permit me to order for you?"

She weighed the offer for male chauvinism and found it not guilty. After all, it was his turf, he knew the territory, so why not?

"Thank you. That would be nice."

A half hour ago, she thought, she would have snorted with disbelief at the notion that she would be dining with Orlandi. Yet here she was, in the warm murmurous ambience of a restaurant, watching a lively transaction taking place over the selection of her dinner. She had, after all, walked out on him in the bar, hadn't she?

Interestingly enough, she had kept her emotions under control when he had revealed that he had read the letter from the FS. Instead of expressing outrage at this latest invasion of her privacy—did they have that concept here in Italy?—she had stared coldly at him across the table and addressed herself to the paradox that had struck her.

"Since you have read my mail, and know the terrorists have washed their hands of me, why are you here? Isn't it clear that I'm of no use to you now?"

He shook his head slightly. "I am not entirely sure of that, signora." He paused until another outburst of laughter from the bar had subsided. "Remember that we are dealing with intelligent, clever, subtle people. Suppose they banked on our intercepting their letter, wishing us to *believe* they had no more interest in you?"

"You're saying that they do intend to bring me to Michael?" She felt a flush of hope, of excitement.

Orlandi spread his hands. "It is purely a supposition. But, anticipating that it might possibly come about, I am here to ask you to cooperate with us." He spread his hands again. "We have so little to go on, signora, that we grasp at any straw."

But if she grasped at that same straw, she thought, then Orlandi and his police would be a liability, a rat the terrorists would be sure to smell out again, as they had at the Galleria. However moving he had been about the blighting effect of terrorism on the Italian spirit, he still intended to use her as a counter in his game.

She had picked up her bag, slid out from under the table and said, "Thank you for the drink, Dr. Orlandi. *Buona sera.*"

His mouth had fallen open, and she thought with some satisfaction, as she swept out of the bar, that for once she had taken someone else by surprise. But she had not expected him to follow her.

"You are angry with me, signora, and how can I blame you? If you would allow me to make amends..."

Making amends meant taking her to dinner, which struck her as pure *chutzpah*. She couldn't recall his specific arguments now, except that he kept promising to turn over a new leaf, to take her into his confidence, "to lay all the cards on the table," to explain everything. None of it moved her. What it was, finally, was the strangely affecting sight of him as he had dragged across the lobby on his injured leg, threading his way through the noisy—and able-bodied—young crowd. Was that a reason to have dinner with someone? Maybe it was something simpler than that: she needed a respite from her loneliness, she needed someone to order her dinner for her.

The maître was bowing himself away from the table, and Orlandi, smiling at her across the table, said, "What are you thinking, signora?"

A *soldo* for my thoughts? Watch yourself, Juno, don't get carried away because of a romantic limp. Rather severely she said, "Cards on the table. Can we get down to business?"

"At once, signora, of course."

A waiter arrived with a bottle of wine and one of *acqua minerale*. They watched as he unscrewed the cork from the wine and decanted a little in Orlandi's glass. Orlandi tasted it and nodded. The waiter filled the glasses and departed.

"Wine from the Friuli region," Orlandi said.

"Yes," Juno said. "It might be best if you began with Giuseppina. How did she come to be in the next seat on the plane, and how did she get the Forze Scarlatte note?"

"As to the second," Orlandi said, "we found the courier who slipped the note to you at Bloomingdale, and learned you would fly to Rome and not Milan. As for Pina's place in the airplane, we corrupted a woman at the airline, and she made the arrangement."

"And you knew what was in the note, and about the rendezvous on the Via Veneto."

"We didn't know what was in the note. But it was not hard to find out your hotel, and from there our agents followed you. Next you ask, How did Pina have the letter containing your ticket for the train to Milan? Do you recall a man on the Via Veneto who accosted you near the Excelsior?"

"Yes. The *cicisbeo!*"

Orlandi smiled. "He was not what he seemed. Actually, he was—" He broke off abruptly. "Ah, and here is our waiter."

They were served smoked trout with a small portion of *risotto*, the famous Milanese saffron-tinted rice. As they ate the fish, Orlandi told her where the trout came from, and something of the method of its preparation. He might have been stalling, to be sure, but he gave the impression that he was too tactful to complicate her enjoyment of the food with irrelevant chatter.

"There are many, you know," Orlandi said, "who claim that Italian cuisine is superior to the French, that anything Italian is superior to everything else. These many, of course, are all Italians."

"I think you're maneuvering me into the position of defending Italy and the Italians," she said. "Very well. Is there another country where so much beauty has been created and survived? The Renaissance—you know how my husband put it? He said, 'With the whole population producing art, how could anybody have gotten a pair of pants pressed?'"

And why, she wondered, as Orlandi laughed aloud, why had it been necessary to bring in Jerry? Was it to remind Orlandi that she was a married woman—a tactic in the art of womanly self-defense?

A waiter removed their empty fish plates, and served them *costoletta di vitello alla Milanese* with *polenta* and fresh asparagus.

"When in Milan, do as the Milanesi," Orlandi said. "The man who accosted you on the Via Veneto, whom you call the *cicisbeo*, was named Benevista, and was a member of the FS. Apparently, just as he was about to deliver the message, he was frightened off by the paparazzi who took your picture. My men were observing. They followed him and found the railroad ticket and letter of instructions in his possession. They took it from him and gave it to me. I asked Pina Cavalera to pretend to be of the FS, she did so, and gave you the tickets in your hotel lobby. Afterwards, she was murdered."

A couple went by toward the front of the restaurant. The man stopped abruptly and came back to their table. He was middle-aged, silvery-haired, with an ample body filling out a handsomely tailored dark suit. His companion was a frosted blonde.

"*Scusi.*"

"Yes?" Orlandi said.

"Ever since you came into the restaurant," the man said, "I have been admiring your lady's hair. *Tiziano.* The most perfect titian color I have ever seen. Didn't I say that, Ada?"

His companion, who had remained a few feet away, nodded icily.

"Ada claims—she is in the business, she is a prominent *parruchiere*—that it is a wig. I say not. Signora, I know this is an imposition..."

"Worse than that," Orlandi said. "It is rude."

"See, you fat fool," the woman said. "Now he will take you outside and beat you up."

Blushing, Juno said, "It's my own hair."

"Aha," the man said triumphantly. "Signora, permit me to thank you, you are a beautiful woman. Excuse me. *Buona sera.*"

The man bowed and joined the scowling woman who said, "Fat fool," and they moved on.

Orlandi, shrugging, said, "Do not be embarrassed. It is the way we are. Everything out, everything on the table. He meant no harm."

"Would you have beaten him up?"

"For telling the truth? Never."

Well, Juno, what do you expect? You ask a foolish question, you get a flirtatious response.

* * *

The motorcyclist went by the restaurant at a crawl, which was in itself a giveaway; motorcyclists thrived mindlessly on speed. And then, of course, he had to turn his head sharply and stare at the restaurant before moving on at a faster clip into the darkness of the street.

Strawberry, watching from the parked car, said, "You saw him?"

The driver, whose name was Dmitri, said, "Excuse me, Comrade?"

"A watcher on a motorcycle," Strawberry said. "And none too bright, either. He might just as well wear a sign saying, 'Doing surveillance work.'"

"I did not notice him. I must be more alert from now on, Comrade."

Strawberry sighed and wondered where they had dug Dmitri up. A very earnest fellow, no doubt a dedicated Party member, but not *kulturny*. No imagination, and no sense of humor, either. All in all, it was going to be a boring night, especially considering what his original plans had been. He sighed again.

"I beg your pardon, Comrade," the driver said.

And if I farted, Strawberry wondered, would he try to figure out the Marxist-Leninist interpretation? Well, best to relax; the poor fellow might be understandably nervous at working with the famous Strawberry.

"Hear that?" Strawberry said. "Hear his engine? Watch." The sound of the cycle became louder, and then the cyclist went by, but not without slowing down and glancing at the restaurant entrance. "See? He's even dumber than I thought. Twice as dumb. If he comes again, you can change that to three times."

"In your opinion, Comrade," Dmitri said, "he is an agent of the CIA?"

"That character, that kid? The CIA employs only gentlemen who wear three-button suits. They never ride on motorcycles. It's more their style to sit in the restaurant and fill up their bellies with good food and wine while they surveil. More likely he's an Italian cop. They enjoy dressing up like hoodlums."

They waited, but the cyclist didn't appear a third time. He had probably pulled his bike into a doorway or alley. Yes, probably an Italian cop, and that was no great thing to worry about. Strawberry thought wistfully that if it had not been for the conversation with Grigoriev, he would at this very moment be taking dinner with the black girl, after which they would return to her hotel and make the bedsprings sing. But once he had spoken to Grigoriev, of course, there was no question of shirking his duty. There had been no time to tell the girl he could not keep their date. She would be disappointed, naturally; she would have been counting—as she put it—on his fucking her brains out.

Strawberry slid down on the seat. It would be a couple of hours before the lady finished her dinner. No need to remain alert all that time. Surely Dmitri could be trusted to watch a doorway?

"Be as watchful as a lynx, Dmitri. I shall be thinking with my eyes closed."

"Don't worry," Dmitri said. "I'll be very vigilant."

But sleep did not come; the memory of his conversation with Grigoriev kept intruding.

"Ah," Grigoriev had begun. "You are here. How nice. I'm not disturbing you, Strawberry?"

Grigoriev had sent a cable instructing him to be in the office of the Chief of Station to receive a telephone call at seven o'clock. "I have been waiting eagerly for your call, Comrade Colonel."

"I'm well aware of your devotion to duty," Grigoriev said. "First, I want to congratulate you on anticipating the subject's destination."

There was no trace of irony in Grigoriev's voice, but Strawberry knew better than to take it at face value. He said warily, "Anticipating, Comrade?"

"Brilliant of you to fly directly to Milan, knowing that that was her true destination. I will have to inform Moscow Center of your cleverness."

Now Grigoriev's voice was dripping with the familiar sarcasm. Strawberry said nothing. The tip on the lady, including the name of her hotel, had been given to the Chief of Station by an Italian newspaperman, a comrade.

Grigoriev dropped his bantering tone and turned grim. "I would advise you to take this matter very seriously. We now have information that leads us to believe the lady is working for the CIA."

"That is incredible," Strawberry said.

"Really? Why is it incredible, my dear Strawberry? Please enlighten me."

Grigoriev was baiting a trap for him, of course, but he had already sprung it with his remark, so he had might as well go on. "It was my understanding that the CIA opposed her going, and in fact had her under house arrest, but that she escaped them. Is that not correct, Colonel?"

"Do you know the name Diebold?"

"Of course. The one they call Double-Oh-Seven."

"Would it surprise you to learn that Diebold flew to Rome on the same plane as the lady? And that we must assume he is presently in Milan?"

"Can this be so?"

"The CIA was clever, for once. They conspired with the lady to pretend she was their prisoner, then arranged for her to escape. How else would Diebold be on the plane with her?"

"I admit I am surprised that this woman is CIA."

"Member or tool, it doesn't matter. Her mission is to lead them to the agent Bering. But we are counting on you to get to Bering first, Strawberry, and bring him out."

"You may count on me, Comrade Colonel. About this Diebold—"

"We're running a computer search on him, you'll have our findings soon. Meanwhile, be especially alert."

Strawberry had wasted no time after the conversation with Grigoriev. Although it amused him to play the clown, he was at heart a most serious person. He had reached the subject's hotel in time to see her leave in a taxi. Dmitri had tailed her adeptly, and here they were.

"Excuse me, Comrade," the driver said. "If you are hungry—"

"Do you believe I could possibly think of my own comfort when the fate of the whole world might hinge on the success of our mission?"

The driver apologized abjectly. Such an ass, Strawberry thought. What was the sense of making a joke if you were to be taken literally?

"However, if you wish to eat something, you may do so. There is ample time."

The driver protested. He understood now, having been instructed by Strawberry's words, how to place duty above everything. In the circumstances, although he admitted to being hungry, food could taste only like cardboard.

And a lousy toady to boot, Strawberry thought. "Go, Dmitri. Socialist man, too, needs fueling."

"Thank you," Dmitri said. "May I bring something back for you, perhaps a sandwich?"

"It hardly matters. But if you wish . . ."

"Everything out," Orlandi said, making an expansive gesture with his arms. "We embrace you with our openness. And yet, when we appear to be most outgoing, it is then, often, that we are concealing something. The man who asked about your hair . . . a buffoon, yes, but something else as well. He admired you, yes, but he was undoubtedly evening up some score with his lady. She knew it, of course."

He ordered them *espresso* and a liqueur. The restaurant was full; it was noiser than before and there was louder and more frequent laughter. Late diners, Juno thought, who had had more time to stoke up on alcohol.

"May I smoke, signora?"

She nodded.

"You notice I don't offer you one," Orlandi said with a smile. "We could tell from the way you opened the package of cigarettes in the Galleria last night that you did not smoke."

She watched him light a match and incline his head to touch his cigarette to the flame. She said, "I suppose you also saw me give the cigarettes away this morning?"

"Not I, but my men. They seized the girl, they thought you were passing her a message, but of course she was innocent." He puffed a cloud of smoke toward the ceiling. "By the way, we're still unsure of how you received instructions for the rendezvous at the Galleria."

From his offhand air, she guessed that the answer was important to him. Well, why not, what did she owe the terrorists? His eyes glittered when she told him about the conductor, but he merely nodded casually.

She said, "I have a question, Doctor. How did you know about the note that was left for me at the hotel this afternoon?"

"The concierge. But you must not blame him for betraying you. We left him no choice. As for who delivered it, one of our agents ran out into the street after the messenger."

"You caught him?"

"A nine-year-old boy on his way home from school. Somebody gave him a thousand-lira note—that was clever, it was enough money for a boy like that—and asked him to deliver the envelope. The boy described the person as 'a tall man.' "

"That's all you know—that he was a tall man?"

"Even that is worthless. To someone the size of this boy"—he lifted his palm a short distance above the edge of the table—"any adult would be tall."

Their *espresso* and liqueur arrived. Orlandi lifted his glass in salute. His eyes looked across at her with an intimacy that took her by surprise. But it would be rude not to respond, or to withhold a smile. Since when did she need a censor? She raised her glass. Then the maître loomed up at the table and, in a tone containing both an apology and a sense of importance, announced that there was a telephone call for Dottore Orlandi.

Orlandi's expression was bland, lightly regretful, as he excused himself. "A nuisance, a bore. *Un momento,* signora."

But as he followed the maître toward the front, there was an urgency in his step that rendered his limp barely noticeable.

Whatever Sweets Charity might have thought a man would look like who proposed to hide under her bed or someplace—it turned out to be in the bathtub, behind the opaque shower curtain—it certainly wasn't the gentleman (she construed the word as an epithet) who had arrived a little after seven thirty.

She greeted him in the cultivated voice she reserved for her dealings with educated Europeans: "Good evening, Mr. Stark. Do come in."

He gave her a perfunctory sidelong glance and began to pace off the room, stalking it with the speed and single-mindedness of a predatory animal. He paused now and then to make mental measurements: distances from the door, from the bathroom, between one piece of furniture and another. He opened the armoire, pushed aside her clothes, and swept his hand through it from corner to corner. He crossed to the window, opened the drapes, drew them shut again. He brushed by her and examined the locks on the door.

During all of this he had not given her a second glance, although she was buck-assed naked. Before his arrival she had bathed, put a little touch of perfume here and there, but not gotten dressed. So far as this cat was concerned, she was invisible.

You're ready for the old lady's home, baby.

When he returned from the door she arched her body strategically, shooting out the old breastworks, but he loped by as if she didn't exist, charged into the bathroom, and slammed the door shut.

Ah, that explains it, Sweets thought, poor fellow's been caught short. Moment he's taken care of natural functions he'll start reacting like a human being to the prospect of five foot ten inches of prime black ass. Never been known to fail before, had it?

But when he came out of the bathroom he said, "Put your clothes on."

She cocked her head to study him: narrow nose, thin lips, flat cheeks, Mr. WASP Square, vice-president of the bank, prematurely graying hair, Brooksy topcoat. . . . But the eyes were smoky and the color of an ice cube.

"I'm not sure I heard you correctly. You are asking me to put my clothes on?"

He took a step toward her. "Get dressed. Be quick about it."

"If that's what you want, okay. Promise to shut your eyes and not peek?"

Not so funny, Sweets, she thought, as he stepped forward again; and you might as well admit this coldass bugger has got you scared shitless. She turned away from his fixed, furious eyes, and sidled past him, giving him lots of room. She picked up a pair of silk panties and stepped into them. He was surveying the room again, tabulating its contents, of which she was not one.

Bastard! Standing there in that proper gray topcoat, every button buttoned, nose up in the air. No-good cockless anti-semite—Shit! I mean racist honky Kluxer. She put her head through a pale blue blouse with glittering gold threads.

"Imbaratti," she said. "Ain't it gorgeous? Six hundred dollars retail. He let me keep it." She was chattering to keep her nerve up and avoiding looking at him. Crossing to the armoire, she plucked out a long black velvet skirt. "Di Freddi. He didn't give it to me, cheapo faggot, I pinched it." She stepped into the skirt and cinched it with a broad belt with a gold scarab-shaped clasp. "There. I'm decent. You want me to put on my shoes, or is bare-footy okay?"

He faced her. "What did Mr. Lutz tell you?"

"What he told me and what I do has some variation—you know? I'm not his slave, I'm an independent contractor, you might say."

The gray eyes swung around and focused on her like a pair of matched gun barrels. He hadn't changed position, and yet those eyes moved in on her like a zoom lens. Her own eyes sought out a resting place on the wall beyond his shoulder.

"He told me I was to do what you asked." She found the courage to vent her indignation. "He didn't say he was sending Simon Legree. I'd like to know what you're up to. I don't want any trouble. I'm a highly respected model, and my reputation is, you might say, unbesmirched."

He said, "When he arrives, I want you to order dinner sent up to the room."

"We were planning on going out."

"Do as I say."

"Suppose he doesn't want to eat here?"

"Persuade him to stay. Take your clothes off again. Or his. But it won't come to that. Nobody turns down that kind of offer."

"Except maybe you." She blinked. "Okay, doc, you got it."

"Don't say it that way. Say 'Yes, Mr. Stark,' and sound as if you mean it."

She was swept by a new wave of indignation. "Yes, Mr. Stark. Where do you come on with that shit? It isn't even your right name."

"Who told you that?"

She had asked Graham Lutz for the name of her visitor, and he had had to fish for it, so she had known it was a phony.

He said, "Answer my question."

He was tensed up. She said quickly, "Nobody told me that."

"I thought not. Tell me what you're to do."

"Order dinner and let nature take its course. What I'd appreciate knowing—what are *you* going to do?"

"No questions."

She flared up. "Look, I'm not any goddamn automaton. I got a right to know."

He glided forward, the upper part of his body still. He stopped, and raised his arm. She shied away, lifting her hands to shield her face. But he was only pointing his finger.

"You talk too much. Shut up."

She wanted to snap back at him, but his finger, an inch or two from her face, was as menacing as a club.

"I'm going in there now." He jerked his head toward the bathroom. "Follow your instructions."

He turned away and walked into the bathroom and shut the door. Somebody's going to get hurt, Sweets thought, and I just hope it's not me. She sat down at her dressing table and began to brush her hair. At eight o'clock she started to feel very nervous. At eight thirty she allowed herself to hope that he wasn't coming. At nine thirty she went into the marble bathroom. He must have been hidden by the opaque black-and-red-striped shower curtain. There was no sound, but she knew he was there; he couldn't be anyplace else.

She said, "I've been stood up. Okay?"

There was no answer, and she began to wonder if the sonofabitch hadn't disappeared into thin air. Then, quietly from behind the curtain, he said, "Get back into the other room."

She started to protest. The curtains parted. He stared at her with a cold static fury, and she fell silent. Without another word she turned and went out of the bathroom. She sprawled out on the sofa, shivering. She covered herself with two of the back cushions and fell asleep. Later she sensed rather than heard him. She opened her eyes and saw him crossing the room toward the door. It was ten thirty. He left without a word, without looking at her.

After the door clicked shut behind him she said, "Thank God."

Juno watched him return from the front of the restaurant. His step was slower now, his limp more pronounced. He made a gesture of apology and sat down. He took a sip of his cooling *espresso* and set it down with a gesture of distaste.

"Benevista—whom you call the *cicisbeo*—he decided to talk this evening."

His voice was casual, almost bored, but there was a certain grim satisfaction to the set of his face. Decided—there was a twist to the verb when he mouthed it. The phrase third degree popped into her head.

But that was probably outmoded. Brainwashing was the current modulation. Had brainwashing "decided" him? She watched Orlandi's face as he went on.

"He gave us the location of the hideout where your son and Signor Bering were being held."

She drew in her breath sharply and stared across the table at him.

"A house in Vicenza. A half hour ago a detachment of *polizia* burst into the house. It was empty. Our birds had flown. I am sorry."

She tried to visualize the scene: a military force, bristling with rifles, shotguns, machine guns—nervous men with itchy trigger fingers.

"This was my telephone call," Orlandi said. "As for Benevista, after he peeped, as he was led back to his cell, he broke away and threw himself over a railing. He is dead." He shrugged. "No more from the *cicisbeo.*"

She wondered why he would kill himself *after* he had talked, but her mind balked at pursuing the thought. Instead, she envisioned the house in Vicenza, surrounded by the invading force, bursting forth at a signal, screaming in rage and fear, guns blazing. If the terrorists had been inside, with Michael... Like terrorist bullets, the police bullets could not discriminate between friend and foe either.

With apparent irrelevance, Orlandi said, "I have been to the United States four, perhaps five, times for conferences on international terrorist activities, in Washington, New York, San Francisco. Inevitably, in a speech, a report, an informal conversation, I hear the phrase 'Back to square one.' A good idiom, denoting at the same time a setback but also a determination to succeed. So, signora, we are back to square one."

She said, "How many policemen were at the house in Vicenza?"

He seemed puzzled for a moment, but then a flicker in his eyes showed that he understood. "Remember, signora, we rescued General Dozier in Padua, and he was not hurt."

But she recalled that when the police had invaded the apartment in Padua, one of the Red Brigades people had had a gun to Dozier's head. An infinitesimal flexing of a finger and he would have been dead.

"With hostages," Orlandi said quietly, "a certain danger is always present in a rescue attempt." His hand moved across the table and touched hers for a brief moment. "And yet if we do not try, they face even more certain death."

That was the naked thought she had never permitted herself to accept, and she could not do so now. She stared at him with resentment, even anger. He didn't seem to notice; he was tasting his cold *espresso* again.

"The question, of course," Orlandi said, "is where to go from here.

Back to square one, *non è vero?* Sometimes we have dossiers on the terrorists, on the makeup of the various cells, we search for specific people. But this is a hard case because we have not been able to fix the identity of any of the kidnappers."

But they must have tried to squeeze such information from the *cicisbeo,* from Benevista. He had given away the hiding place, and having accomplished that much they would surely have tried to get him to name his colleagues. Perhaps Benevista had been able to gauge the limits of his own resistance to pressure, and seen a leap to the concrete below as his only honorable option.

Orlandi said, "Naturally, we will make a thorough search in Vicenza, and perhaps we will be lucky and find some clues to where they have gone."

"How did they know the police would raid the house?"

"We can only guess. A possibility is that somehow they learned that Benevista was in our hands, and on the chance that he would talk they decamped."

"If you knew the raid was to take place, what was the point of coming to see me and asking for my cooperation?"

"A feeling, a policeman's instinct, perhaps, that it would fail. I learned of it only a short time before I left the Questura for your hotel. In any event, in case something unhappy took place..."

His unfinished sentence hung in the air between them, ratifying her worst fears about the possible consequences of a police raid.

She said only, "Thank you for your considerateness."

"Signora, you must know that I feel concern for your predicament. You are a courageous woman, and your sentiments for your son move me." He signaled for a check. "And now, signora, I must return to the Questura. But I would like to ask you again, should the FS try to contact you, will you confide in me?"

She thought of the machine guns, the ring of firepower, the vulnerability of Michael's flesh.... She said, "I can't promise that, Dr. Orlandi."

"But I hope you will take it under consideration?" He didn't press any further. He attended to the check. "Now I will ask them for a taxi and let you off at your hotel."

Orlandi stopped at the front desk to order a taxi. She went on through the door and up the steps to street level. She waited for him in the pool of light outside the restaurant. The racket of a motorcycle engine broke the silence. The cyclist loomed up out of the darkness. Then he turned sharply to his left, jumped the curb onto the sidewalk, and bore down upon her.

* * *

After more than two hours, Strawberry was ready to defect. Ha-ha, a joke, Colonel Grigoriev, but I'd like to see you in my place, locked up in a car with this peasant of a driver whose silences were as offensive as his speech, throwing off odors of sweat, mortadella, and stale tobacco. Try that out for yourself, Comrade Colonel, and see if you don't entertain counterrevolutionary thoughts!

His chin was tucked down into his chest, his eyes closed, but he felt too rebellious to drowse. More than two hours in which he could have—how many times?—ridden a gallop on top of that cheerful black girl. For this kind of work, Colonel, I am overqualified, underemployed, suffocated, and getting a sore ass into the bargain.

"She has come out, Comrade," Dmitri said.

He heard the motorcycle start up in the darkness, and when it roared into view he shouted, "Blasted motherfucking," and felt for the door handle. But he couldn't locate it, and knew that even if he had, there wasn't time. The black shape of the cyclist was leaning forward, gripping the handlebar with one hand, the other holding something out in front of him—a knife or a gun, he couldn't tell. He saw the woman turn toward the cyclist, and he yelled into the echoing interior of the car, "Back down the stairs..."

She seemed transfixed as the cyclist jumped the curb and swooped down at her. Strawberry kept urging her to move, to get back down the stairs, fall down them, anything, but of course she couldn't hear him, and he knew she was a dead woman, a goner. He groaned, because in some maliciously labyrinthine way that he couldn't forsee, Grigoriev would hold him at fault for her death....

The figure appearing at the top of the steps—it was her dinner companion—jerked his head around to the racket of the motorcycle, and in the same movement ran head on toward it. The cyclist's mouth was wide open, as if he was screaming or gasping for breath. Strawberry saw the woman's companion turn aside, just as the cycle was on him, and in the next moment everything went flying: the cyclist tumbled backward off the back of his bike, landing flat on his back and head, and the cycle itself went roaring by the woman, who fell to her knees. The bike carried on briefly, then went wild. The front wheel twisted back on itself and the bike skidded and ran off the sidewalk. It hit a parked car, caromed off with a clang of metal, struck a second and then a third car, did a caracole, and then fell flat in the center of the street, sliding, its wheels spinning, pieces of it dropping off and skittering away.

"Let's get away from here," Strawberry shouted.

Dmitri started the car and pulled out of the parking space. As they passed the restaurant Strawberry saw people running up the steps, one of them with a napkin tucked under his chin. The cyclist was lying on his back, with blood dribbling from his head. The lady's companion was helping her to her feet. Strawberry took a good look at him through the window. He didn't look very impressive, not very tall, not much meat on him, either, and a slight limp, too. But anyone with the reflexes and the balls to pull that trick of his, leaping to one side and shooting his arm out, catching the cyclist under the throat, clotheslining him, chopping him off the bike, and right under a gun, too—he was, as the Italians said, a man of respect.

Strawberry had seen the cyclist bounce at least four times, mostly on his head, like a basketball being dribbled. His helmet had been ripped away with the impact of the outstretched hand. If he lived, which didn't seem likely, he would have one hell of a headache.

He said to the driver, "Do you know where the Piazza della Repubblica is?" Dmitri nodded. "Drop me off there. I have further socialist business to attend to."

Sweets Charity was picking over the remains of her room service meal when the cowboy arrived. Who else would rap at the door with a shave-and-a-haircut tattoo? Nervy sonofabitch, she thought, sipping her coffee, stands me up and then barges in at eleven o'clock—a mere three hours late, and expects me to be available.

He knocked again, a bit louder this time. Stupid bohunk didn't realize she had his life right in her hands. All she had to do was telephone. Life? Jesus, yes! What else did Mr. Stark have in mind—dance him a waltz? He was pounding on the door with his fist now, and hollering out her name. Dumb asshole was going to wake up the whole floor. I'm quality folks here, can't have that kind of shit going down. The knock changed: it became a steady tom-tom beat. He was still singing out he. name.

Shit.

She got up and opened the door. He swept in, grinning. "Lafayettes, we are here."

He grabbed at her. She fended him off, backpedaling, and said, "Few minutes late, aren't you cowboy?"

"Unavoidably detained, baby. Better late than never?"

"No. Never is better. You squarehead, you think you can stand me up like some cheap hustler and then show up when it suits your purpose, the front of your pants straining at the leash? Boolsheet." She ducked by him and opened the door. "Vamoose, cowboy."

Laughing, he slammed the door shut, wheeled around, and lifted her off her feet. He carried her kicking across the room, tossed her on the bed, and flopped down on top of her.

"Says what?" he roared into her ear.

"Let me up, you fucking rapist." She struggled vainly against his weight.

"Says what?"

I should start screaming, she thought, or better, knee him in the crotch. I hate a man who takes me for granted, and he's not all that terrific, either. But I won't, because of Mr. Stark, and that's the only reason. This is one in your face, you stinking dead-eye monkey.

"Says what?" He was shimmying on top of her, using his knee to pry her legs apart. "Says what?"

She threw her arms around his neck and her legs over his hips. "Ride 'em, cowboy!"

Diebold was playing solitaire when Gray phoned and told him about the incident outside the restaurant.

Gray said, "The man she was having dinner with was Orlandi—the cop in the Dozier case."

"Did you see it happen?"

"Heard it. I came running out of the restaurant as soon as I heard the crash."

"Where did the woman go afterwards?"

"Orlandi sent her home in a police car. She went up to her room."

"Did he say anything to her?"

"He apologized for his brutality."

Diebold grunted. "Any idea who the cyclist is?"

"No. He was young and Italian. And nearly dead."

"The hotel is covered?"

"Yes. Have you seen Strawberry yet?"

"No. I'm not particularly looking for him, you know."

Fifteen

Michael awoke to the odor of fermentation, wondering if he had gotten drunk and passed out. He was lying on his back on a cot. A light dangling above him hurt his eyes. He shut his lids and became aware of pain at the back of his head. His hair was matted and wet, sore to the touch. His head was throbbing. He opened his eyes and brought his hand to the front. There were two of them, two right hands, both smeared with blood. He levered himself up on his elbows. He felt his eyes cross. He let himself down to the bed again.

A voice said, "Welcome to the club."

He turned toward the sound of the voice, moving slowly, not daring to risk raising his head. Bering—sitting on another cot a few feet away. Two Berings. He wondered if he had a fractured skull.

He said, "Why are we?" He had meant to say "where," but "why" was to the point too, maybe more so.

Bering leaned toward him, speaking slowly, his voice slurred. "I just woke up myself. My throat's dry. We're in some kind of cellar."

"Do you smell a booze smell?"

Bering nodded. "It must have been a wine cellar. I can see bins, and some broken bottles on the floor. You're bleeding, Mike."

Michael remembered a bright light, a shadow poised to strike, and the taste of blood. He said, "How long have we been here?"

"Who're you asking? They stuck a needle in me, remember? Your girl friend. Who hit you?"

The light was covered by an open shade with tan burn marks on it. Michael said, "Can you help me get up?"

"I don't know. I haven't tried to get up myself. I'm woozy. My throat is so dry I can hardly swallow."

"I'd like to get up," Michael said. "See if you can help me."

"Say please."

"What?"

"Well, you're not giving orders anymore, are you?" Bering said mildly. "I mean, you're just another CIA pig now, aren't you?"

Michael tried to nod his head. "I don't blame you for feeling like that. I really can't blame you, can I?"

"Ah well," Bering said, "I shouldn't gloat. I'm sorry for what I said. What happened to you? I mean *why*, why are you down here?"

Michael recalled the fierceness of Adriana's embrace in the doorway when they were waiting for the plumber's scow to arrive. It was her good-bye, her apology for the blow that would knock him unconscious, for whatever else they would do to him now. He felt moisture on his eyelashes.

"They double-crossed you," Bering said. His voice was raspy. "If you can figure out why they shot the chauffeur you can figure out . . . Oh, hell." He was silent for a moment. "Where the hell are we?"

"Venice."

Bering shook his head. "Can't be Venice. There are no cellars in Venice, at least none I ever heard of."

He was right, Michael thought, it was impossible to build a cellar below ground because the whole city was built on marshes. But people would have wanted wine cellars, which this certainly was, or had been. He remembered the hemmed-in entry hall and stairway.

"It's Venice all right," he said, "and it's a cellar, but it's built on the ground floor, with the living quarters above."

"Beautiful Venice." Bering laughed: a dessicated croak. "I'll help you get up."

Bering heaved himself up on his legs, throwing a vast ungainly shadow on the rough cement wall behind him. When he moved across the space between the cots the shadow on the wall shrank, moved down the wall, and disappeared. Bering stood above him, foreshortened. Two Berings.

"Slowly," Michael said. "Bring me up easy. Please."

Bering sat down. The cot bowed under his weight. He put his arm behind Michael's back and lifted. His breathing was a series of grunts, the noises a fat man made when he exerted himself.

"There's blood all over the back of your collar," Bering said. "Ugh, it's tacky."

Michael was sitting up. His head was spinning and he felt sick. He held tight to Bering's arm for support.

"Any better?" Bering said. "I think the problem is dryness, no water. Maybe I can find a bottle of wine. You know, it may have been overlooked or something?"

Michael said, "I want to see if I can stand up. Can you give me a hand?"

"Maybe you ought to wait a while and I'll try to find a bottle of wine?"

Bering's face came into view, round and very pale. Michael said, "You don't look all that good. Go back to your cot and lie down awhile."

"I'd be fine if I had something to pour down my throat."

There was a sudden flood of light above them. A door had opened at the top of a flight of stairs. Michael saw a figure in the doorway, not quite a silhouette but black against the back lighting. He knew it was Adriana. There was a second figure slightly behind her.

"May I come down to clean you up a bit?"

Her voice was cool, uninflected. Michael said nothing. Beside him he heard Bering's breathing.

"Michael? I'd like to tend your wound."

"You come near me," Michael said, "and I'll break your neck."

The second figure came forward, tall and thin. Michael recognized it as Ugo, the rawboned former soccer player whose broken knees had invalided him out of the game.

"Would that help your wound?" A tremor in her voice betrayed her matter-of-factness.

Bering said, "Listen, we need water. I'm so thirsty I can't speak."

"Behind the steps," Adriana said, "you'll find a toilet and a washbasin. The water is potable." She turned to Ugo, who handed her a tray. "Michael, I'll leave this on the top of the steps. An antiseptic, swabs, absorbent cotton. Bering can help you."

"What time is it?" Bering said.

"*Basta,*" Ugo said.

"It's seven o'clock," Adriana said. "We'll bring you breakfast presently." She started to turn away, then paused. "Michael, you must try to understand."

"I do," Michael said. "Oh, I understand all right. I understand that you're a miserable cunt."

She turned away and the door closed. The stairs remained only as an afterimage on Michael's moist eyes.

Orlandi was waked at seven thirty by the telephone. The caller was one of the *agenti* from the detail watching Mrs. Sultan's hotel.

"I'm phoning from the Stazione Centrale," the *agente* said. "The signora has bought a ticket for Padua on the eight o'clock train."

"Padua? What the devil for?"

Orlandi was in a temper. He had been in bed approximately three hours. He had waited for the ambulance to arrive at the restaurant for the cyclist, followed it in a police car to the *pronto soccorso,* and then accompanied the stretcher into the emergency room itself. The emergency room doctor had cleared an operating room and called in a surgical team. Orlandi trailed the stretcher and took a seat on a hard wooden bench outside the surgery after exacting a promise that he would be allowed to see the patient at the first opportunity. He chain-smoked until the surgeon finally appeared, his mask around his neck, pulling off his bloody rubber gloves.

"Can I see him now?"

"Why not?" The surgeon waved toward the operating room, and followed Orlandi through the door. A team of nurses was busy cleaning up. The cyclist was lying on the table. The top of his skull was laid open and folded back, like an awry hairpiece.

"What the hell is this?" Orlandi said.

"*È morto,*" the doctor said. "But since you were so intent on seeing him, I have obliged."

"Your grandmother is a whore," Orlandi said, "and you are her pimp."

He left the hospital and returned to the Questura. Papers in the boy's pockets had identified him as Beppo Di Lorenzo, who lived in the Zucca district of Bologna. He was twenty years old. An inquiry had already been telephoned to the Bologna Questura. It might take some time; their computer was down. It was almost two thirty when Bologna telephoned. Di Lorenzo was a known member of the neofascist N.A.R. Beyond having been arrested once and charged with rioting during a right-wing demonstration—charge dismissed—his crime sheet was clean.

"N.A.R.! How in hell can those fools possibly figure in this? Why should they want to kill the lady? It's senseless."

"A fascist is a fascist," the Bologna official said. "They have Mussolini where their brains should be."

Orlandi said to the *agente* on the telephone: "Did the lady have baggage?"

"Yes. A valise."

Orlandi sighed. "You will be on the train?"

"To be sure, dottore."

"Thank you. Keep in close touch with me, please."

The door at the top of the steps opened and Giorgio appeared, carrying a large tray.

"Breakfast," he said. Ugo stood behind him watchfully; he was holding Gildo's *lupara*. "I will put it down here on the landing. After we leave you may come up and get it."

"Hi, Georgie," Bering said. "They making a waiter out of you?"

"When you have finished, leave the tray on the steps. We will collect it in a half hour."

Michael lay on his cot, looking upward past the dangling light at the shadowed ceiling.

"Man signs up to throw bombs and exciting stuff like that, and they turn him into a flunky." Bering laughed. "Don't get mad, Giorgio, I'm just joking."

Giorgio said, "We'll see how you joke when we put the gun to your head. That's when we'll see exactly how funny you are."

Ugo said something in a sharp undertone. Giorgio went out. Ugo slammed the door shut. The cellar darkened and seemed colder.

"I'll go get the grub," Bering said. "I could eat, you know."

The tray contained two pots of coffee, a basketful of fresh rolls, butter, and little pots of preserves. Michael drank some coffee but offered Bering his share of the rolls.

"The only thing I can't complain about," Bering said, "is the food. What do you think they'll do now, Mike?"

Michael shrugged.

"I know what you're thinking," Bering said. "You're thinking that your girl has betrayed you and you don't give a damn what happens. Life isn't worth living, right? Well, let me tell you something—no matter what, life is worth living."

Michael was silent, brooding.

Bering carried the tray to the steps and set it down. When he came back, he said, "It can always be worse than it is. At least we have a toilet here. At the other place, I hated having to shit in that can. No matter how tight I made the cover, I could always smell it."

"I'd like to sleep, please," Michael said, shutting his eyes.

He touched his head tentatively. There was a big bump at the back, but Bering had said, after cleaning the wound, that it seemed superficial. His double vision had cleared. Bering started to lie down on his cot, but sat up when the door at the top of the stairs opened. Federico was standing in the doorway. As before, Ugo, holding the shotgun, stood beside him.

"*Buon giorno*," Federico said.

Bering said, "Hello, leader."

"Is Michael asleep?" Federico enunciated in his correct, pedantic English. "If so, please awaken him, I wish him to hear what I have to say."

Michael said, "Tell him his bullshit sounds better when I can't hear it."

"You may listen or not, as it pleases you," Federico said. "I will speak anyway."

"What I'd like to know," Bering said, "is why you did this to Michael. Me, I understand, I'm a CIA blood sucker, but why Michael?"

"We have no obligation to explain, but since you are both dull-witted, I will extend myself. So far as Michael is concerned, his fate was to have been the same as that of the chauffeur. He was to have died on the road because, like the chauffeur, he was a liability."

"Oh, boy," Bering said. "You've got some terrific friends, Mike."

"But Adriana, out of sentiment, persuaded us to spare him. I agreed against my better judgment, although in my mind I accepted it as a delay of sentence rather than a reprieve. When Michael's mother announced her intention of coming to Italy, we quickly saw the opportunity for good propaganda in the press. Although risks were present, the situation appealed to us. But then the odds against success became too great, and in addition we were losing some of our people. We canceled the project, and with Signora Sultan out of the picture, Michael reverted to the status of a liability. So now you must both stand trial together."

"No," Bering said, "it's not fair. Let Michael go."

"Michael does not believe in our beliefs. He gave them lip service, but only because he was Adriana's lover. Sooner or later he would betray us."

"You've got it wrong," Bering said. "Mike wouldn't turn you in. He's an honorable kid."

"All of this that I have told has, after free democratic discussion, been ratified by unanimous agreement of all of us."

"Well, it's nice to know nobody's just being railroaded," Bering said.

Federico drew himself up. "I hereby serve solemn notice upon you that later today you will both stand trial before a people's tribunal of the Forze Scarlatte."

Michael spoke for the first time. "In that case, I'd better send my clothes out to the cleaners."

"There will be no need for that," Federico said, "since the presence of neither one of you will be permitted at the trial."

Bering said, "You're kidding."

Michael laughed.

"Is there anything either of you wishes to say?"

"Yes," Michael said. "Kindly convey my fraternal greetings to Comrade Adriana."

* * *

Padua was a compact city. It was less than a five-minute walk to the university on the Via VIII Febbraio. Past the iron gate barring entry to the main courtyard, Juno turned the corner to the Via Antenore, where there was a direct entry into the Medical School. The old stone walls of the building were overlaid with a crazy quilt of posters, most of them inflammatory, calling variously for expulsion of American terrorist missiles, for defiance of the Church, for deportation of blacks who deprived Italian workers of bread by accepting jobs at slave wages. A dozen blood-red graffiti read, *Morte ai tiranni fascisti*.

It was five minutes of twelve; a few students were already straggling out of the building. Juno stood at the curb and watched the door. It occurred to her to wonder if, while she watched, someone was watching the watcher. Earlier, when the train started sliding out of the shed in Milan station, she had seen a tall rangy man, long legs flying, sprinting down the platform. She didn't know whether he had caught the train or not, and certainly had no reason to be suspicious. But after the events of last night she had begun to mistrust reason: someone, for no conceivable motive, had tried to kill her.

If she had been asked to justify the single compulsion that had caused her to leave Milan abruptly, she would have been hard pressed to name it. Thinking about it on the train, motives had lined up like a squad of awkward soldiers, each out of step with the next. High on the list was pure terror: the memory of that monstrous figure in black bearing down on her with an extended gun, a visitant from the miasma of nightmare. And, as in a nightmare, she had been helpless, frozen in horror, and if not for Orlandi she would surely have been killed.

Which led to the next soldier in line: Orlandi. She was still astonished by her reaction when, after saving her from the cyclist, he had put an arm around her to comfort her. Neither shattered nerves nor gratitude and relief could fully account for her abandonment. She had pressed against him, burrowing her whole body into him, with a sexuality she had demonstrated for no man since she had married Jerry. Even now, despite her embarrassment with her performance, she felt a wanton shiver of erotic pleasure.

Danger, Juno, danger!

But, finally, everything else to the side, the moving force was the certainty—despite Orlandi's reservations—that the Forze Scarlatte meant what they had said in their letter: they were washing their hands of her. If she had not questioned them when they said they would bring her together with Michael, she could not logically question the opposite.

And so she decided to seek out Adriana, to find comfort—and to give comfort—in the only other person in Italy with whom, in love for

Michael, she had a community of interests. It would not be easy. Outside of a given name and a fair memory of the girl's looks in the picture Jerry had shown her, her only clue was that Adriana attended the University of Padua Medical School.

And so she waited and watched at the door on the Via Antinore during the lunchtime break in classes.

By twelve thirty the flow of students had slowed to a trickle. There might have been another exit, but since she couldn't cover more than one at a time, and this seemed to be the main one, she decided to stay where she was. No one paid any attention to her, although it had crossed her mind that someone might have followed her from Milan—for example, her suspicion of the long-legged man sprinting after the train. And, she thought with a shiver, if there was another assassin lurking, she presented an easy stationary target.

By ten minutes past two, the last straggling student appeared to have returned. She lingered another quarter of an hour before giving up.

She strolled into the Piazza delle Erbe, the ancient market place. She sat in the sun at a small café and ate a prosciutto sandwich and drank a small bitter coffee, then returned to the university and took up her post again. She spent a fruitless hour watching the door before calling it quits and walking back along the Via Garibaldi to her hotel. The concierge gave her a chit with her key. It was a message from Orlandi, asking her to return his call. She walked toward the elevator with a quickening pulse. But when she got to her room she tore the chit to bits methodically.

Late in the afternoon Orlandi took a call from Regina Coeli in Rome. "We snatched your conductor right off the train in Roma Terminii and brought him here. A fine fellow, handsome as a tenor and wearing a uniform cap crushed carefully to look like an airman's."

Orlandi said, "You checked out the identification through the Ministery of Transportation? I don't have to tell you it's a hotbed of sympathizers. Are you positive you've got the right man?"

"Name of Rizzo. He's the right man, all right. Looks like a hussar— or did I say airman?—but very little guts. We know he's the right man because he owned up to it, told us flat out that he handed the note to the signora on the train."

"He admitted that?"

"With hardly any persuasion. You know how these handsome ones are—we gave him a fat lip and right away he started worrying about his face."

"Vittorio, come on, get to the point."

"I'm getting there, Alfredo. I thought I would save a little wear and tear on our boys, so I waved a fat wad of lire under his pretty nose and said, 'Tell us where they're hiding out and you can have this and no questions asked.' Greedy bastard began to salivate, but he swore he had no idea where they were, and I believe him. He damn near broke into tears, he was itching so hard to get his hands on the money. He said that he had been paid to deliver the note and I believe that too. He's no Benevista, take my word. I even gave him a bit of leeway, so that he could jump over the railing if he wanted to, like Benevista. Never entered his mind. He doesn't know anything helpful, I'd bet my pension on it."

"*Buffone*," Orlandi said.

"I can squeeze him a bit more, Alfredo, but there's no juice there, I can tell."

"I'll take your word for it. No point in rough stuff for its own sake."

"Wouldn't be any fun to it, anyway, he has absolutely no backbone. Would you believe it—one rap in the mouth, not very hard either, a love tap, and he went and pissed his pants?"

Sixteen

On her second day in Padua, inadvertently, accidentally, Juno found her.

The day had been drizzly and cold from the start, and she had varied her stand in front of the university entrance by moving about from time to time to warm up; but never more than a few paces. At two, wet and chilled, she'd given up and crossed the street to Pedrocchi. She had ordered a coffee and pastry, then turned to drape her coat over the back of her chair, and there was Adriana at the next table. She recognized her immediately and without question. She was talking to another young woman; then she raised her eyes, which, after a moment of uncertainty, widened and stared.

"You're Adriana," Juno said. "Do you know who I am?"

"How could I not? Your picture has been often in the newspapers. Why are you in Padua?"

She wasn't quite beautiful, Juno thought, she was too solemn for that, but with her almost-blond hair and brown eyes, and a pale skin now slightly flushed, she was striking.

"I came here looking for you," Juno said.

Adriana's companion was a delicate, tiny young woman with pale blond, finely spun hair. In Italian, Adriana said, "This is Signora Sultan, the mother of Michael. Signora, my friend Francesca."

Juno and Francesca exchanged smiles.

Frowning, Adriana said, "How did you think to look for me in Padua?"

"I knew from Michael's letters that you had entered the Medical School."

"Ah yes, now I understand. For how many days?"

"I started yesterday." Juno laughed self-consciously; Adriana's directness was disconcerting. "It's a miracle that I should have sat down next to you in Pedrocchi."

"I am here almost every day," Adriana said. "Will you join us here at our table, signora?"

"Thank you, I'd like to very much."

Francesca excused herself, saying she had a class. Juno's waiter brought her coffee and pastry. Except for a fleeting smile at the departing Francesca, Adriana's expression had not changed; it was serious, reserved, unsmiling. Juno offered to share her pastry.

Adriana shook her head impatiently. "Please tell me, signora, why you were looking for me?"

Maybe it was unrealistic, Juno thought, to have expected the emotional meeting she had hoped for: an embrace, a meeting of compassionate eyes, perhaps even a mingling of tears. But surely asking her to explain her motive was carrying coolness too far.

She said, "I thought you would understand without an explanation."

For an instant Adriana seemed to have taken offense; but she said softly, "I am sorry. But you must understand, signora, that we are different. Our generation, where our emotions are concerned, we practice the art of concealment."

Why? Juno thought. What's to gain therefrom but ulcers? Since when did a little honest emotion hurt anybody? But she said simply, "I suppose it's different for mothers."

"For some mothers," Adriana said, and momentarily Juno thought she caught a glimpse of some torment, some hidden pain. Then it was gone. "For lovers it is different."

"Lovers have been known to die for love, to die *of* love."

"They are fools," Adriana said. "I am sorry, signora, that I am not what you expected. You do not find me *simpatico?*"

Juno said politely, "You're very attractive."

"Thank you. But in other respects I do not please you. Perhaps, even, you wonder how Michael might have loved me?"

"Such judgments are beyond my scope. If I know anything at all about people, it's that who will love whom is entirely unpredictable."

"Exactly. Or for what reason." For the first time, Adriana seemed to approve of something. She looked at her watch. "Signora Sultan, you must excuse me. I have a class to attend."

Please don't go yet. Please!

Adriana began to gather up her things. "I am sorry, signora, that it did not turn out as you had hoped." She signaled to the waiter. "Perhaps it will comfort you to know that Michael spoke of you often. He is very fond of his mother."

"You do love him, Adriana?"

"Yes."

"And you worry about him—about what might happen to him?"

Adriana handed her check to the waiter. "Yes. Perhaps you would not think so, perhaps Michael might not. But yes, I do love him, yes, yes." She held out her hand. "Now I must go."

Juno stood and took her hand. They were the same height, and their eyes met on a level. Adriana tried to withdraw her hand. Juno held it tightly.

"Signora?"

"Please, Adriana, tell me..." She felt tears start in her eyes. "Before the kidnapping you were with Michael, you saw him. Don't you see my need?"

She was crying out for a sharing, for a partnership of grief, but Adriana's eyes were unrelenting. Slowly, Juno withdrew her hand.

"I can tell you that he was happy, that he looked well." Adriana was impatient, but Juno sensed that she was at least trying. "Yes, in his great black beard he looked exceptionally well. Very strong, very manful. Yes, signora, what is it?"

Juno forced a smile, almost lost it, then somehow broadened it into a foolish grin.

"Yes?" Adriana said, frowning.

"I was just thinking to myself—who would want to hide a gorgeous face like that behind a beard?"

Adriana gave her an uncomprehending look. "Good-bye, signora."

"Just a silly joke," Juno said, half to herself, as she watched Adriana's slim, elegant figure moving through the tables to the door. "Just a simpleminded little Jewish-mother joke."

She sat down heavily in her chair. Outside, Adriana, with her intent, straight-ahead look, was going past the window. After a moment a man went by. Juno recognized him: he was the tall man she had seen running after the train on the platform in Milan station.

Strawberry followed the girl smoothly through the wet streets. She was dressed in thin, well-worn jeans and a short gabardine coat; she was slender and tall but by no means as slender and tall as Sweets Charity. She moved with long strides and held her head proudly, taking no account of the steady drizzle that flattened her long hair to her shoulders and darkened it as well.

His own blond hair was soaked, and he wore his collar turned up to keep the rain from running down his neck. Why hadn't Grigoriev, who knew everything, to hear him talk, thought to warn him about the icy rain in sunny Italy? He made a mental note to buy a hat as soon as he could, probably at Standa, where he had acquired his jacket this morning, real buckskin more or less, with fringes on the sleeves. Hey-hey, wild west.

Outside Pedrocchi he had instructed Dmitri to watch the lady while he took off after the girl. Although Dmitri would never win the Order of Lenin for brains, he was dogged and he obeyed orders. Yesterday morning, he had tailed the lady to the Milan station, and bought two tickets on the same train (second class; no capitalist pretensions, old Dmitri). Strawberry, freshly returned from the arms, and other parts, of Sweets Charity, had taken Dmitri's call in the bath. He had thrown his clothes on, rushed to the station, and arrived just as the train was pulling out. He had pelted down the platform after it, but to no avail. But Dmitri was aboard, and he had followed the lady to her hotel. Later, Strawberry had driven up to Padua on the *autostrada*.

In choosing to follow the girl, he had been acting partially on an instinct that told him the girl was more important at this point in time—ah, how he loved that idiom introduced by the main players in the Watergate comedy—but also because it had been very boring watching the Sultan woman outside the university. She had been clever, however, in pretending that her meeting with the girl in Pedrocchi was accidental.

Two streets distant from where he had started after the girl the chase ended. He saw her present her ticket to the parking attendant and then hurry into a tiny Fiat among the diagonally parked cars. As she backed out, he noted from the prefix letters of her license plate that the car was registered in Bologna; but the numbers were mud-spattered and he could read only two or three of the digits. After the Fiat had scooted off he approached the attendant, an old fellow wearing a peaked cap with a white canvas top, and, around a yellow slicker, secured by a belt, a pouch containing his parking slips and money.

In his slow labored Italian he said, "That girl who just drove off—do you know what her name is?"

"How would I know what her name is? She comes every day, she parks, she pays for her ticket, she leaves."

"When does she come?"

"I told you, every day, Monday through Friday. She doesn't ask my name, why should I ask hers? This isn't a social hall, it's a parking place."

"What time of day does she come, and when does she leave?"

"What am I, a clock tower? What do you want to know for, anyway."
Strawberry winked lewdly. *"Amore,* old fellow—you understand?"
The attendant shrugged. "She comes in the morning and she leaves
in the afternoon. She's a student at the university. The rest you'll have
to do yourself. What am I—a matchmaker?"

"I appreciate your help, little father." Strawberry handed the attendant a 5,000-lire note. "You have advanced the cause of a lovelorn heart."

"What's the money for? You didn't park here."

"It's because I like you. Buy yourself a fine bottle of wine."

The attendant's face glowered. "I am forbidden to drink wine.
My liver. Can you imagine the agony of an Italian who can't drink
wine?"

"Then buy some bread."

"What is bread without wine? Excuse me, I see someone trying to get
into an empty space, if I don't watch these characters they'll try to rob
me blind. Thanks for the five thousand, anyway."

When Juno returned to her hotel, the concierge gave her a chit: Orlandi
had phoned again. She crumpled it, carried it to her room, and threw
it in the wastebasket. Then she put in a call to Jerry. Waiting for the
call to be completed, she reached into the wastebasket, salvaged the
message, straightened out the slip of paper, crumpled it again, and
threw it back in the wastebasket.

Jerry's voice, starting off subdued, brightened.

"How are you feeling, Jerry?"

"I'm fine. They tell me I might get out of here one of these days.
Which could mean anything. The next doctor who says to me, 'You
know, Mr. Sultan, these things take time,' I'm going to punch him out."

"Well, you've got to be careful. Do they let you walk around?"

"Practically as much as I want. I swear I feel as if I could play a fast
game of handball."

"Is there a public phone booth on your floor?"

"There's one down the hall a way, but...oh, you're still worrying
about the CIA?"

"I want you to go to the public phone booth now, copy down the number,
and then come back and tell me what it is."

"Juno, you're nuts. Oh, all right..."

She heard him put the phone down. Waiting, she looked at the wastebasket. No, she wasn't about to return Orlandi's call, now or ever. She
wanted to see him, and that was a prime reason not to. If you dreamt
about the tone of a man's skin, the angle of his eyelashes—run in the

opposite direction as fast as you can. She was no longer a gawky moon-calf of a girl, but a levelheaded, respectable, *faithful* woman of a certain age who loved her husband. . . .

Jerry was back on the phone. "Are you wearing your trenchcoat with the turned-up collar? Here's the number."

She jotted it down on her bedside pad. "Go back to the booth again and wait for my call." She hung up and gave the operator the new number. The call went through in ten minutes, and Jerry answered. "Can you talk without being overheard?"

"Sure. Who's listening?"

"Don't repeat anything I say. I'm in Padua."

"Pad—? I mean, what are you doing in that place?"

"Listen to me, carefully, and try not to interrupt. Two days ago, in Milan, I got a note from the terrorists saying they were backing out— they weren't going to let me see Michael. So I went to Padua, to try to find Adriana."

"Michael's girl friend? What for?"

"Don't repeat anything, especially names. It seemed important to talk to someone who had been with Michael before he was kidnapped. In case, you know . . . in case I never saw him again. . . ."

"Stop that. I don't want you to entertain thoughts like that."

"Yes. All right. All I had to go on was that she was a medical student at the university, and I had an idea of what she looked like. . . ."

"Juno, for God's sake, you're losing your grip. How could you hope to locate someone with so little to go on?"

"I found her, Jerry."

"You did?" Jerry chortled. "Juno, you take the cake."

"You remember the picture the Forze Scarlatta sent to the newspapers after the kidnapping? Michael was clean shaven, wasn't he?"

"Yes."

"But in the picture they sent me with their letter he had a beard. Remember you said his beard was as heavy as yours?"

"Of course I remember. So?"

"So the last time Adriana could have seen him he was clean shaven, right?"

"Juno, will you get to the point?"

"Jerry, when I asked her to tell me about Michael she mentioned his beard, her exact words were that he looked very manful in his beard."

She paused, listening to Jerry's breathing quicken.

"Which means," she said, "that she has seen him since he disappeared. Which means . . ."

"I know what it means," Jerry said. "Yeah, I sure as hell know what it means." He let out a bitter little laugh. "Boy, that kid sure knows how to pick them, doesn't he?"

"The question is," she said patiently, "the question is, what should I do about it?"

"For God's sake, Juno, get in touch with the authorities, right away."

"What authorities?"

"The American consulate. Who else? There's one in Milan in the Piazza dell Repubblica."

"Why not the Italian authorities?"

"No, for God's sake. You know Italians, great singers and all, but what do they know about policework?"

She remembered the speed and violence of Orlandi's attack on the motorcyclist. "Don't be so sure of that. Besides, they know the territory. What can the American consulate do—sever relations with Italy?"

"They have resources."

"You mean the CIA?"

"Yes, the CIA. They get a lousy press, but they're vastly underrated."

"No CIA, Jerry. That's final."

"Are you going to hold your grudge against them forever?"

"Yes. Forever."

And then, as Jerry railed at her, urged her to take her information to the consulate, it struck her with the force of a revelation that, if the CIA were thorough and resourceful enough to bug Jerry's room as well as his phone, wouldn't they be thorough and resourceful enough to anticipate that she might call on a public phone and bug that, too?

"Juno, for God's sake, where are you? Are you listening to a word I'm saying?"

"Get well, Jerry. I'll call you."

But she could be dead wrong about it, she thought as she hung up. They couldn't think of *everything*, could they?

Locksley's desk was covered with swatches of cloth. He looked up when Fernald entered and said, "My tailor sent these along, thinking to tempt me."

Fernald eyed the array of tweeds, worsteds, Glen Urquhart plaids, shetlands. "They're very handsome."

"I don't need any new clothing, but that's the best time to buy, wouldn't you say?"

One of Locksley's epigrams, which sounded wonderful until you began to parse them for sense. "Oh, absolutely," Fernald said.

"Which would you choose for a hacking jacket?"

"I like the hairy ones, myself."

"I'm eliminating the Irish tweed," Locksley said. "It has some appeal but it's, well, a bit *Irish*, don't you think?"

"We have something from the hospital listening post."

"Yes?"

"It might change the entire nature of the game."

"Ah," Locksley said. He gathered up his swatches, stacking them neatly and placing the pile on a corner of his desk. "Tell me."

"The lady has received a note from the Forze Scarlatte telling her that they're cutting her off, they won't let her see her son."

"Any reason given?"

"Too risky with all the watchers around."

"They're not just putting that about as disinformation?"

"I don't think so. That's our kind of thinking. They're more direct." He noted a slight tinge of pink on Locksley's cheekbones, and added, "They haven't the capacity for our kind of subtlety."

"If you're right, it removes Mrs. Sultan from our plate?"

"Seems so," Fernald said. "But I'd still keep a watch on her as a precaution. She's a very determined lady. And not without some resourcefulness of her own, as we've learned."

"She showed some wit at the beginning," Locksley said, "but since then she's been fairly simple to read."

"There's a bit more," Fernald said casually. "She has identified a member of the gang who are holding Bering and her son."

"Come now," Locksley said, looking at Fernald as if for signs of humor. "Damn it all, how did she do that?"

"Accident, more or less."

Fernald told him about Adriana's slip.

"It's a tiny thing, but barring any other explanation, we must accept that this Adriana is one of the Forze Scarlatte."

"You've turned it this way and that, of course, to see if there are any holes in the theory?"

"This way and that. She absolutely couldn't have known about the beard unless she had seen Michael Sultan since his capture."

Locksley picked up a swatch of material and held it close to inspect the weave. Its color was an almost perfect match for his mustache. He put the swatch down with elaborate care.

"Perhaps I should have asked earlier," he said. "What sort of check did we run on Bering's and the boy's associations after the kidnap?"

"Fairly thorough on Bering..." Fernald trailed off.

"Nothing at all on the boy?"

"Some, but evidently not enough. We focused on his months in Bering's employ. We should have gone back farther. As you know, we're critically shorthanded.... Yes, it's slipshod work."

"The Italian police didn't turn up the girl, either, if it's any comfort to you."

"They probably leaned too heavily on their computer and came up empty. Shoe-leather investigation takes a lot of time and effort, but it's sensitive to things the computer misses." He grimaced. "No, it's no comfort."

"Yes, well, don't feel too badly. After all, Bering is the principal and the boy just an innocent bystander." Locksley's brows arched upward. "That's all he is, isn't he?"

Fernald felt himself flush. "The thought never occurred to me."

"Any particular reason it should have?"

"None. Except that it violates the axiom that everyone is suspect from birth to death. I'm very sorry."

"Never mind. At this point it's academic. Let's push on. What do you predict Mrs. Sultan will do with her information?"

"I'm afraid she doesn't like us."

"Who does?" Locksley's lips quirked, but not quite enough to constitute a smile.

Fernald said, "She'll give it to the Italians eventually. Not that she trusts them either, but she owes a debt to Alfredo Orlandi."

Locksley nodded. "Saved her life, so she's eternally grateful. How do we stand with Orlandi?"

"As you suggested yourself, how do we stand with anyone?"

"What are his politics?"

"So far as we know, nil."

"Is he buyable?"

"Not on his record. We tempted him rather grossly when we were spending on the Dozier thing, but he wouldn't touch it."

"Not political, not corruptible—what the devil *does* the man believe in?"

"Duty."

"Oh dear. The worst sort. So we can't reasonably expect him to turn Bering over to us without a debriefing, assuming he can rescue him?"

Fernald shook his head and said gloomily, "Bering can name three ministers who took our money."

"Is the fall of the government as important as we've been led to believe?"

"Hard to tell. Italian governments are a revolving door, but we favor this one. Then there's the rest of it. If Bering is persuaded to talk he might name his cutouts, and there's no telling where the thing would stop. And that brings us back to where we started."

"Extrication. Yes. How can we circumvent Orlandi?"

Fernald remained silent, thinking, aware of Locksley's growing impatience. Then he said slowly, "Maybe not try to get around him, but instead join him."

"I don't follow you, old man."

"Give him our information about the girl, Adriana."

"But he'll be getting it from Mrs. Sultan."

"Give it to him, anyway. He'll be impressed by our generosity and the sincerity of our wanting to cooperate."

"Ah," Locksley said. "It does have a certain subtlety. The message bearer will be Diebold, of course?"

"Yes."

"Good-oh," Locksley said.

After her call to Jerry, Juno delved into the wastebasket and rescued the chit with Orlandi's phone number. She lifted the phone, then replaced it. But she remained beside the phone, waiting for a suitable time to elapse, like, she thought, a widow who wished to avoid criticism for marrying again too soon.

But that was nonsense! Whatever her ambiguous feelings about Orlandi might be, the call was strictly business. She picked up the phone and gave the operator the number of the Questura in Milan. She was connected to Orlandi's office. An unfamiliar voice told her that Dottore Orlandi was not there.

"Can you tell me when he is expected back?"

"Will you be so good as to say who you are, signora?"

She hesitated, as if simply giving her name was an indiscretion. But wouldn't withholding it smack even more of something clandestine? Juno, my dear Juno, you're like a girl on her first date. I know, I know, and I wish I wouldn't be thrilled by it.

"This is Signora Sultan."

"Ah, signora, yes. Is there some way I may assist you?"

"Thank you, but I must speak to Dottore Orlandi."

"Of course. But Dottore Orlandi is in Vicenza and will not return until late tonight."

"Can you reach him?"

"I do not think so. He may perhaps phone sometime during the evening. If so, I will be happy to give him your message."

Good, then tell him I have a crush on him, and the idea makes me *tsitterdik*. Surely you know what *tsitterdik* means, everybody does.

"Thank you. Would you kindly ask him to phone me?"

She showered and dressed for dinner, leaving the bathroom door open in case the phone rang. She ordered dinner from room service, and afterwards turned on the television and watched western movies. At eleven she went to bed. She felt as if she had been stood up.

Oh, Michael, Michael darling, your mother likes a cop, but never fear, it's just a harmless little middle-aged silliness. You remain the first priority, Michael, the only priority, and everything else is *mishegahss*, nonsense.

He'll call in the morning and I'll be all business. Good night, Michael. Good night, Jerry. Good night, Alfredo.

Michael awoke restored from a short deep sleep. The wound on his head was sore to the touch but no longer throbbed. Bering was asleep on his cot, snoring, his broad face peaceful, almost angelic in repose. Michael rolled off his bed and began to do push-ups. He continued until he broke a sweat, then jogged in place. Afterwards, he wrapped himself in a blanket—the dampness was penetrating—and began to explore the cellar.

It was an unbroken cube of solid concrete except for the far wall, where a metal gate was set into the wall. Behind the gate, far enough back to allow clearance when the gate was opened, there was a heavy wooden door. The gate was made up of a grid of horizontal and vertical bars, six inches apart. It was emplaced in a heavy metal frame sunk into the concrete. There were no hinges visible, which meant that they were on the far side, probably unreachable. Three modern unpickable locks, top, bottom, and center, were embedded flush in the right-hand vertical of the metal frame, undoubtedly fixed to dead bolts. Michael tried shaking the gate. It didn't budge. The metal was old, but except for a surface pitting, it appeared solid and impregnable.

It seemed a hopeless proposition, but later he would examine it more closely. Bering was watching him. He moved on to the toilet cubicle. The plumbing was sealed into the concrete. He went back to the wine racks. They consisted of wooden bins in two sections separated by an aisle. The smell of ancient fermentation was pervasive. There were shards of glass and broken bottles on the floor, a scattering of discolored corks, several bottles in the shelves. He was examining one when Bering spoke behind him.

"Nothing in them, Mike, empty."

Bering was on his feet, shivering.

"Put a blanket on," Michael said. "I've been checking out our prison. It doesn't look hopeful."

Bering lumbered toward him, awkward in his wrapping of blanket. "We look like a couple of wild Indians." He let out a whoop and did a clownish parody of a war dance. "That's how us Injuns got our exercise."

Michael looked at him with wonderment and a degree of admiration. Bering wasn't stupid, he knew the predicament he was in, and yet he somehow found the resources for gaiety.

Bering drew one of the bottles out of the bin. "Barolo. That's a beautiful wine." He turned serious. "I guess I'll never taste it again, right?"

They both wheeled around to a flood of light. Federico was standing at the top of the steps. This time Gildo was beside him, smoothing the barrel of his *lupara* lovingly with his hand.

Federico said, "Will you come forward to the bottom of the steps, please?"

"Go fuck yourself," Michael said conversationally.

Bering shook his head. "Not worth the trouble, Mike. After all, what's he asking us to do? Just walk a couple of feet."

He tapped Michael's arm, and after a moment Michael shrugged. Together, clutching their blankets around them, they walked to the steps. Federico was holding a sheet of paper in his hand.

"I wish to read a statement to you," Federico said. "It is in English. It is short." He cleared his throat. "The Revolutionary People's Tribunal of the Forze Scarlatte, sitting in solemn plenary session, has deliberated the cases of Joseph Bering and Michael Sultan. Both Bering and Sultan, members of the imperialist-terrorist CIA, have been found guilty of capital crimes against the people of Italy. This verdict is unanimous. The sentence, also unanimous, is death. The sentence will be executed in seventy-two hours. End of statement. Do you wish to say anything?"

"Yes," Michael said. "Shit on your Revolutionary People's Tribunal."

"I have something to say too," Bering said. "I want to express my appreciation to the court for a fair and speedy trial, especially the speedy part." There was a grin breaking through the mask of his solemnity. "And I want to tell you that we intend to appeal the verdict all the way up to the Supreme Court, if necessary."

Michael burst out laughing. He clasped Bering awkwardly in his arms and hugged him.

Seventeen

The guide met the first tour group of the morning downstairs in the marble-floored entry hall. They were about a dozen American *vecchi*—senior citizens, as they called themselves. He had led many such groups through the tour, and never ceased to wonder that retired people could afford to travel. Italy's own *pensionati* were lucky if they could scrape up enough for an occasional bus excursion into the countryside.

Speaking slowly so that all might understand his English, he introduced himself with his standard opening. "Welcome to the Medical School of the University of Padua, the oldest medical school in the world. I am Guido. Guido the guide, yes?" The group chuckled. Americans were very polite; they never failed to laugh at his little joke.

He led them upstairs to the anteroom, with its pale frescoes on the wall and its indifferent paintings of all the *rettori* of the school since 1861. When they were assembled in a circle, he pointed out the different colored hats of the students in the fresco—red for medical, white for agricultural, etc.

"Medical School founded around the year thirteen hundred, the oldest in Europe. Formerly a palace owned by a family named Casarini. Dr. Harvey was a student here, also Copernicus, also Vesalius, father of anatomy, also many others. We will now go into the Aula Magna, the Great Hall, built at the end of fifteenth century, used for the most important events."

He opened one of the great wooden doors. There were the usual awed exclamations as the tour entered the vast paneled room, dominated by the dais with its chairs of brilliant red and gleaming golden backs and arms.

"Here the Pope sat"—pointing to a thronelike chair on the dais—
"when he came to Padua in December 1981, for the celebration of the
seven hundred and fiftieth anniversary of San Antonio, whose great
cathedral you have already, perhaps, visited." He swept his arm toward
the walls. "You will see here pictures of the *nobili*, the great families of
Italy. The colored plaques—there are over three thousand of them—
represent the escutcheons of these families. We will now move on to
the Aula di Medicina, the Hall of Medicine."

In the connecting room he paused before the ancient wooden pulpit.
One of the *vecchi* said that it looked like an old wagon.

"Galileo Galilei taught at the university for eighteen years. This is his
pulpit. Yes, the ramp leading up makes it appear to be a wagon. It was
built for Galileo, because he was a little fellow and very fat, so that he
could climb up and be seen when he lectured to the students."

In the Aula di Medicina there were more oohs and aahs for the polished elegance of the chairs, the imposing severity of the room.

"Here at these chairs, behind the long table, sit the *professori*, each
with a microphone before him, and there facing them are the students
when they take the examination for their medical degree. On the wall
behind me you will find the skulls of the great *professori* who donated
their bodies to the school for anatomical study."

He turned and led the way, then stopped so abruptly that several of
the old ones collided with him. There, in the eye socket of one of the
skulls, was a rolled sheaf of paper, sticking out like a misplaced horn.

"Irregular," the guide said in dismay. "This is most disrespectful."
He hurried forward to pluck the sheaf of paper from the eye socket.

Orlandi slept late on a cot in a room that had hastily been fixed up
for him at the Questura in Vicenza. At nine o'clock, as he was shaving,
he was told about a note that had been found sticking out of the breast
pocket of a vagrant who had been—and still was, at last report—sleeping off an alcoholic stupor in the bus terminal in Treviso. A police
stenographer had taken down the contents of the note over the telephone and transcribed it.

It was headed Communiqué Number 4, and, stripped of some of its
ideological garbage, it said that the arrogant and adamant refusal of the
so-called government to remove the deadly bacterial missiles from Italian
soil—indeed, even to acknowledge their presence, which was an open
secret—had led to the promised trial of the CIA pig Bering and his piglet
Sultan. The verdict: guilty. The sentence: death. The sentence to be
carried out in seventy-two hours, thus meting out revolutionary justice
to those epigones of the United States and its pitiful Italian vassal. This

decree is irrevocable unless, in the interim, the filthy inhuman missiles are summarily removed. Death to the running dogs of capitalistic imperialism! Long live the Forze Scarlatte, savior of the enslaved Italian people!

In the course of the next hour or two, Orlandi was to learn that the identical letter had turned up in the lady's toilet of Harry's Bar on the piazzetta in Venice; in the eye socket of a skull in the medical school at Padua; taped to the underside of "Juliet's balcony" in Verona; on the windshield of a car in a used car lot in the outskirts of Milan.

It was all according to standard terrorist procedure. And if it followed form, Orlandi thought drily, a fifth and perhaps even a sixth letter would have been hidden so well that it wouldn't be found for another week.

A secretary in the Milan Questura phoned to give him messages that had accumulated in his absence. Two of them were of particular interest to him: one from the chief of police in Rome, another from the Signora Sultan. He phoned Rome first, and briefly discussed the note that had been found in Treviso.

"Yes, well," the chief said, "the government will tell them to stuff it, you know that. The government has said there are no germ missiles here, and even if there were, they would refuse to remove them. The FS know that, of course. They're out to get some publicity, and then, of course, they'll kill their hostages."

Orlandi was silent. He didn't know himself whether or not there were truly germ missiles emplaced in Italy, nor did he consider it worth more than a moment of idle speculation. It wasn't his place to make either policy or moral judgments, merely to catch terrorists if he could.

"Did you find anything out there in Vicenza?" the chief said.

"Very little. You know how people are where terrorists are concerned. They'd like to help, of course, but, after all, they saw nothing, heard nothing. The landlady? She got her rent money promptly in the mail, in cash, and that's all she cared about. The occupants of the house owned a van—color and license plate unnoted, of course—and one of them was a girl or woman who drove a *cinquecento*. What color was the *cinquecento*? Gray, or blue, or white. The girl or woman? Well, she was always going down the hill so fast it was impossible to tell. But her hair was long, short, black, blond, or red. As for the shopkeepers, nil. They doubtless did their marketing elsewhere than in Vicenza."

"And the fascists?"

"We rousted them in Bologna and took them in. They're a scurvy, stupid lot. The interrogation is still in progress, but it seems a dead end. The attack on the Signora Sultan seems absolutely pointless."

"By the way," the chief said, "I congratulate you on your role in that affair. You can still be a roughneck when you have to be, eh, Alfredo?"

"No great deal. I killed a twenty-year-old."

"You saved the lady's life. By the way, Alfredo, I'm sending somebody up from Milan to see you."

"Yes?"

"An American. A journalist."

Orlandi said with feigned innocence, "He wants to interview me?"

The chief sighed. "They do keep up their silly pretenses, don't they? Well, look, the fellow claims to have some important information."

"Must it be delivered in person? There are telephones, you know. Or even the mails—a journalist should know how to write a persuasive letter."

"The request, I should tell you, came from very high up. It can't be ignored."

"Damn!"

"He claims to have very important information. He wants to bargain for it."

"Why didn't he bargain with *you*? Why didn't he give *you* that information?"

"It's you who must pay the price, so I'm leaving it in your lap. Not that you have any choice, of course, given the weight behind this. What he's asking is to be allowed to work in concert with you. It seems a modest request."

"Do I need a whole regiment of CIA spooks cluttering up my operation?"

"No, no, just one of them, two at the most."

"The number that appeals to me is zero."

The chief sighed. "He'll get in touch with you, Alfredo. You're going back to Milan, I presume?"

"No. I've decided to stay up here in the Veneto. I'm convinced they're here somewhere within arm's length. I can feel it in my bones."

"One of their notes was left in Milan, wasn't it?"

"This is their territory."

"All right. You'll make your headquarters there in Vicenza?"

"No, I'm moving on to Padua in a few hours. The American can phone me at the Questura there."

"Why Padua?"

"No reason, one place is as good as the other, I just like the town better."

"As you wish. I'll have Mr. Stark get in touch with you there."

Next, Orlandi phoned the Signora Sultan. She was not in. He left word that he was coming to Padua and would call again when he arrived.

* * *

A bit after noon, with her back turned, using the window of a store across the street as a reflecting glass, Juno saw Adriana come out of the Via Antenore exit of the Medical School and walk briskly to the Via VIII Febbraio. She waited until Adriana had turned the corner, then followed. It was not difficult to keep her in sight even on the crowded street; the girl's erect bearing and light flowing hair, lifted by the wind, made her a conspicuous target. Opposite Pedrocchi, Adriana crossed the street and turned left at the corner. Juno plunged into the traffic, heedless of the tooting horns, and made it safely to the other side.

Now, on a narrower street, progress was slower. Juno fell back slightly. Watching the girl's springy hair rise and fall, her proud youthful stride, she found it incredible that she was a terrorist. Yet she knew that young women like Adriana—well educated, of upper-class families—abounded in the extremist left organizations, and could be as fanatic and trigger happy as their male counterparts. How Michael could ever have become involved with her was a mystery; it was even more of one that Adriana, with her doubtlessly obsessive radical views, could have become interested in Michael, whose politics, at least as far as he had ever expressed them at home, were nonexistent. Did you ever hear of sexual attraction, Juno?

Adriana stopped. Juno sidled toward the shelter of a building wall. She saw Adriana speak to a parking attendant, then unlock a car and get into it. She backed out abruptly, halting traffic, then came back in Juno's direction. Juno tried to make out the license number, but wasn't quick enough. While she was still looking after Adriana's car, another car, a BMW, passed directly by her. The man in the passenger's seat, wearing a fringed cowboy jacket and a Stetson hat, was the man she had seen on the train platform in Milan, and again, yesterday, passing the window of Pedrocchi.

Adriana's car turned left at the corner. The car with the two men turned in the same direction.

"At home," Strawberry said, "if anyone drove a car like these Italians drive, we would have him beheaded."

"Comrade!" Dmitri said, and then, "You are making a joke, of course?"

Bad enough a dunce, Strawberry thought, but in addition a literal-minded one. "Not a joke, merely an exaggeration, to make a point that Soviet drivers are the best drivers in the world."

"Yes, of course, I agree," Dmitri said. "After all, driving is my specialty. Soviet drivers are the best in the world, and I am the best of the Soviet drivers."

"Drive cleverly—make sure she doesn't know we're on her tail."

"She does not know, or else she would not be going on such a direct course."

The girl's car was perhaps a block ahead of them; it was difficult to keep in sight among the numerous other tiny Fiats on the broad street. To make it worse the car was—what?—the color of dust. It crossed the Adige River, which practically encircled the city; it was no more than a narrow stream at this point. At a green *autostrada* sign it made a turn toward the east.

"A question, please, Comrade?" Dmitri said. He was a disciplined driver; he never took his eyes from the road.

"If you wish," Strawberry said.

"The girl is of the radical fascist right wing?"

"Hardly. She is undoubtedly a counterrevolutionary infantile leftist, a disruptionist Maoist-deviationist. If the opportunity arises we will punish her in a special way."

"Ah," Dmitri said.

"Yes. Turn by comradely turn, we will fuck her until she is dead."

Dmitri turned pale, then a faint, sickly smile twitched at his lips. "You are joking, Comrade."

"Of course I am joking. The personal hygiene of Maoist women, as everyone knows, is deplorable, and sleeping with one inevitably leads to a social disease. She is about to turn into the ramp for the A-4 *autostrada*, Comrade, look alive."

"Although she did not signal," Dmitri said, "I knew she would do so. It is my instinct as a driver."

There were two cars between them and the girl at the toll station, where they picked up their ticket. Past the toll booth Dmitri kept the same two-car-length distance behind her. Traffic was moderate, and the girl was driving well within the speed limit.

"Ahead," Strawberry said, "is the exit one would take to Venice. Venice-Mestre, it is called. Keep your eyes open."

"Venice I have heard of, of course," Dmitri said, "but I do not know Mestre."

"An industrial city, as squalid as Venice is beautiful, separated from each other by a causeway over the water. Ah, she is signaling a right turn, getting off. She will be going to Venice."

"Not to Mestre?"

"Nobody goes to Mestre. Everybody goes to Venice."

Dmitri loitered on the exit ramp to allow a distance between him and the Fiat.

215

"Don't let her see us now," Strawberry said. "Lay back. Once she gets on the causeway there's no place else to go but Venice, and only so far. There's a place where all cars must stop, beyond that there's only water."

But when they reached the entrance to the causeway, the girl's car was nowhere in sight. Then Strawberry spotted her, going off into the drab sooty streets of Mestre. Dmitri turned sharply to follow her, but she had disappeared in the traffic.

After a half hour of frantic turning through this street or that, by pure guess, they admitted that they had lost her.

"Well, Comrade," Dmitri said, bringing the BMW to a stop, "we won't be fucking the young woman to death, at least not today."

Strawberry said sharply, "Bad enough you've lost her. Must you make jokes about it as well?"

"I am sorry for the joke, Comrade," Dmitri said, "but I was under the impression *we* had lost her."

"Was I driving?" Strawberry said. "She's a clever bitch. Well, never mind, tomorrow is another day."

Orlandi was quite sure that Stark recognized him from the stakeout at the Galleria, just as he recognized Stark; but neither of them revealed anything. An even match, Orlandi thought, between professionals.

He said, "I am pleased to meet you, Signor Stark. I'm sorry for the state of this office."

The Questura in Padua had been hard pressed for space, and had installed him in a room where old files were stored. They had cleared out some of the files and brought in a battered desk and a couple of chairs. Doubtless a form of pique on the part of the *questore*, who would resent the arrival of a man from a higher headquarters as a usurpation of his own authority. Never mind; he was not proud in such matters, although as a practical matter he would insist on more light. The only illumination in the room was a gooseneck lamp they had placed on the desk.

"I didn't expect you here quite so soon," Orlandi said. "Will you sit down, please? I apologize for the condition of the chair."

"I took off from Milan by car as soon as I heard you would see me here."

He was wearing the same tailored topcoat and snapbrim hat he had worn at the Galleria. His voice was flat, colorless; his face was in shadow. Was he the man who had spoken to Pina at Fiumicino Airport? He felt an urge to tilt the gooseneck lamp so that it shone on the man's face, but it was much too obvious, too amateurish. One took some pride in playing by the rules.

"Well then," he said pleasantly, "you are a journalist, Mr. Stark?"

The square, well-tailored shoulders lifted in a slight shrug. "If you wish."

"If *I* wish?" Interesting, Orlandi thought, the man had no use for the protocol of the CIA. "And your name—since we are more or less laying our cards on the table—what is your name, Mr. Stark?"

The man frowned, as if at an unseemly joke, which, Orlandi admitted, it was. He said, "I assume, Mr. Orlandi, that your chief has told you that I want to work with you on the kidnapping?"

"Just you, yourself, Mr. Stark?"

"And my colleague, a Mr. Gray."

Orlandi nodded. "I told my chief I would try to accommodate you. Somewhat reluctantly, if I am to be frank."

"He told you, also, that I have some important information?"

"Yes. A quid pro quo. You give me the information, I allow you to work with us."

"In addition to the information, we're prepared to sweeten the pot with a respectable amount of money."

"The pot? Ah, yes, a poker term. As to the money, signore, it is not always as persuasive as your people seem to think."

"The money is thoroughly discretionary. There's no need on my part, or anyone else's, to account for any of it."

"Sorry," Orlandi said. "I don't play poker."

Diebold shrugged. "We feel the need for direct involvement in the affair. Bering is an American citizen, and we pride ourselves on protecting our own."

"And young Sultan?"

"Oh, him too."

The casualness was deliberate and it was calculatedly revealing, Orlandi thought. In all but so many words, Stark was admitting that Bering was a CIA agent. And it was clear that the offer of money was in the nature of a ransom for Bering's person, payable to the Italian government, or its representative, if they were able to rescue him.

"And your valuable information?"

"Yes, well, first let me tell you that we know Mrs. Sultan is no longer in the game, that the Forze Scarlatte has pulled back from its offer."

"That is your information?"

"No. That's a freebie."

Orlandi didn't say anything. Nor did Diebold. He simply peered out from his shadows, smiling with hardly any show of teeth. It was not, to Orlandi's tastes, the most attractive of smiles. The silence prolonged itself as they faced each other across the desk, and then Diebold's smile widened a fraction and he spoke.

"We can identify one of the terrorists. Her name is Adriana, last name unknown. She is a student at the Medical School here in Padua."

Orlandi had been unable to conceal his look of surprise. Diebold was no longer smiling.

"This Adriana," he said, "if you misunderstood me, is one of the kidnappers of Bering. And the boy."

"Well then," Orlandi said, "this is indeed a valuable piece of information. If it is true. May I ask how you acquired it?"

"Sorry," Diebold said.

"Of course. You journalists must protect your sources," Orlandi said gravely. "In addition to her given name, do you have a helpful description of the young woman? She is young, I assume, since she is a student?"

Diebold reached into his pocket and brought out a wire photo. He handed it across the desk. It was a narrow sliver of picture, showing a young woman seated at an outdoor table; she was squinting against the sun. The light had flattened out her features, but the picture was wholly adequate to identify her. At the edge of the picture, where it had been cut away, there was a portion of a strong bare arm, a man's arm.

"May I keep this?" Orlandi said.

"Yes."

"I think, with this picture, as well as her name, that we may have some success identifying her through the university. Thank you, Mr. Stark. One further point. Before I go upsetting the university authorities, I would appreciate—without your revealing your sources, to be sure— if you could give me some corroboration for your information."

"Sure. You can check it out with Mrs. Sultan." Diebold stood up; his head and shoulders disappeared in the shadows of the upper reaches of the room. "Mr. Gray and I will take a hotel room here in Padua. I'll let you know where we'll be."

"I understood you, signore—Mrs. Sultan knows this girl?"

"Yes."

Orlandi's face was impassive as he stood up. "I'll see you out, signore."

They wound their way through the old halls. At the door, Orlandi held out his hand. In the light, he saw the man's face clearly for the first time. It was an unremarkable face except for the eyes, which were an unusual shade of gray.

"I see you have hurt yourself," Orlandi said. He ran his hand down his own face, from the eye to the chin. "An accident?"

The man said nothing. His gray eyes were depthless, as if, Orlandi thought, they had the faculty of closing themselves off from the brain. He was a man who understood the uses of silence.

"I look forward to working with you," Orlandi said, smiling pleasantly. "I'm sure it will be mutually beneficial, and it may be interesting for you to see how we operate here in Italy. You have been in Padua before?"

Diebold shook his head.

"But you know Italy, of course. Surely you have seen Rome?"

"Yes."

"Of course. It has changed somewhat, but it is still Rome. You have been there recently?"

"I go there a lot."

They shook hands, and the man left. Orlandi watched him for a moment as he moved off down the street, the image of a conservative American businessman. Those had been long healing scratches on his face, and skin had been found under Pina's fingernails. It probably meant nothing. But why had he gone to the trouble of covering up the scratches with facial makeup?

"The chef," Orlandi said, "is a native of Venice, and so it is feasible, even advisable, to order the Fegato alla Veneziano. The smoked salmon is excellent and I recommend it for our first course. I dined here often when I was working on the case of General Dozier."

They were sitting in the bar of her hotel and later would have dinner in the adjoining restaurant. When he had phoned her on his arrival in Padua, her emotions had flopped dizzily between despair and elation. Given that she had fled him in self-defense, could she keep from flinging herself at him again? She had failed the first test by accepting his dinner invitation. Well, it would give her a chance to test her resolve and discipline. Well, it would, wouldn't it? As for his having taken a room at the same hotel, she would be a fool to read anything into it. There weren't all that many hotels in Padua, and he had said, almost as if to prove the innocence of his motives, that the hotel's restaurant was the best in town.

When their drinks arrived she expressed her surprise that he had come to Padua.

"I wished to be closer to what I consider to be the main arena of the action. And I wished to be near you, signora."

She blushed, surprised at a frontal attack that seemed foreign to his style.

He went on: "By now you have read a newspaper, with the latest communiqué, as they call it, of the Forze Scarlatte?"

"In the *Corriere della sera*. Do they mean what they say, that in seventy-two hours..." Her voice faltered, and she fell silent.

"It is because of that, signora, knowing you to be alone, that I wished to be here to give you courage and support."

Why should his explanation have left her with a feeling of disappointment? "I appreciate your thoughtfulness, Dr. Orlandi."

"It is a blow, I know. Suddenly there is a date set. But terrorists are not famous for keeping their word. Sometimes they make propaganda, to stir up the animals, as you say."

"But sometimes they mean what they say?"

He turned to look at the bar, where a group of Scandinavians were chattering. She took note of his profile, that delicate Renaissance profile.

"It would be a disservice to mislead you. Sometimes they keep their word. In this case, we cannot tell....I have several things to tell you, signora. First, about the motorcyclist in Milan."

"I haven't thanked you enough for saving my life. And for your bravery."

"I did what was necessary." He sipped his drink. "The cyclist was a neofascist from Bologna. We cannot imagine his motive in attacking you. In any case, he is dead."

"I'm sorry. I know he tried to kill me, but...I can't abide violence."

"That I was the instrument of his death, I don't enjoy that. But I am a policeman, it was necessary."

His shrug was a rebuke, denying any need to defend himself. And of course he was right. It was necessary. She had moved into another world, and she was finding it difficult to live by its parameters.

"As for Vicenza," Orlandi said, "we have come up empty-handed. A few petty details, mostly inaccurate, and nothing more. I am sorry."

"I have something of my own to tell you." She leaned across the table toward him and said in a hushed voice, "I know who one of the terrorists is. One of the ones who are holding Michael."

"Yes?"

She drew back. "You don't seem very surprised."

He made a noncommittal gesture. She hesitated in the face of his seeming indifference, then took a breath and told him about Adriana and how she had given herself away with mention of Michael's beard.

"It is slight evidence to go on," he said when she paused, "a few facial hairs more or less."

"Yes," she said, "I'll admit that it would have been more helpful if she just came out with it and confessed. I can't deny that that would have been neater, Dr. Orlandi."

He smiled.

"Have I said something funny?"

"Forgive me. I was reminded of the many American films I have seen in which a character says, 'You know, you're beautiful when you get angry.' The joke, of course, if that she is beautiful whether she is angry or not."

It was an arrant compliment, but it struck her in the circumstances as being unfeelingly flippant. She said, "I'm glad that I have amused you."

"Please, signora, I have been insensitive. Forgive me. I take the matter of the girl seriously, but as a policeman I proceed with caution, I look for harder evidence than a chance remark which might turn out to be innocent."

"But there was absolutely no way she could have known about Michael's beard unless she had seen him since his capture—none."

"Very well. Accepting your view for the moment, did the girl realize her mistake?"

She shook her head, and told him about how she had attempted to cover her own shock with her Jewish-mother joke. "She showed no sign of it."

He smiled. "That was resourceful of you, signora."

"I've learned a thing or two these past few weeks," she said grimly. "Besides, it's true."

"He is a fortunate boy to have such a devoted mother. You know Adriana's last name, of course?"

She shook her head.

"You can describe her?"

"Yes. But I can do better than that. Tomorrow I can point her out to you."

"If she is what you say she is, you realize that by watching her you are putting yourself in danger?"

"If I had had a car today, I'd have gone after her. I followed her to her parking place."

"Yes? And did you notice what kind of car she drives?"

"A Fiat. One of the little ones, a *cinquecento*. It's a light gray in color, and badly in need of a wash. I wasn't able to read the license plate. Oh, and the cowboy and another man followed her in a car."

"A cowboy?"

"He was wearing western-style clothing, a fringed jacket, and a big hat, and he has a kind of rawboned, square-jawed cowboy face." She told him about seeing the man in the Milan station, and again outside of Pedrocchi. "Seeing him in the car was the third time."

"A cowboy. By this you mean he is an American?"

"He looks American, but I don't know."

They had finished their drinks. Orlandi paid the bar bill and they walked through to the restaurant. After he had ordered dinner he said, "Have you told anyone of your suspicions about the girl?"

"No. Oh...yes. Yesterday afternoon. I spoke to my husband. I told him about it."

"Only him?"

She told him her fears about his room at the hospital being bugged by the CIA. "But I had him call me from a pay phone. Surely that was safe."

"And your phone at the hotel?"

She covered her mouth with her hand. "Could they do that—here in Italy? And how would they even know that I had come to Padua?"

"I knew you had gone to Padua. And here is our smoked salmon."

Juno said, "I guess I'm not as clever as I thought I was."

"Look, signora, here is what I propose to do. First, find out exactly who this young woman is. Find out who her friends are, her politics, her habits..." He broke off. "You are shaking your head."

"You're talking in terms of days when all we have is hours."

"Yes, that is so. Then I will take her in and try to squeeze information out of her."

"And if you can't? If she's made of very strong stuff, as I suspect that she is, if she isn't squeezable—then what? In that case you'll have used up your first and only lead to the terrorists. If you gamble on the girl talking and fail, then there's nothing left."

"It is conceivable."

"Another point. If the FS find out you have the girl, then they'll surely kill Michael. *Could* they find out?"

"It is not impossible." He opened his palms outward. "We must work with what we have, and there is risk in it. What else can we do, signora?"

"We can follow her ourselves."

"*We*, signora?"

"You and I. Unless you object to it for some reason, in which case, Dr. Orlandi, I'll do it all by myself."

Orlandi's brows arched upward, but he said nothing. He reached in his wallet and handed something across the table to her. "Is that Adriana?"

She looked at the snapshot. "Yes! Jerry, my husband, shot it in Bologna. How did you get it?"

He said, "Do you know a man named Stark?"

"I don't think so. No."

"About six feet tall, graying hair, gray eyes, Anglo-Saxon, dressed in business clothing, gray coat and hat, perhaps some marks—resembling scratch marks—on his face."

"I don't know him. Who is he?"

"Let us say for the moment, until he proves himself innocent"—his lips quirked in a smile—"that he is of the CIA."

"If he's the one who gave you the picture, then he's CIA. Our apartment is empty. I wouldn't put it beyond them to have ransacked it."

"Perhaps." But he didn't look convinced.

She picked up the picture and studied it closely. "That arm! That's my Michael's arm!"

With a loud wail, she burst into tears.

They strolled up the Corso Garibaldi, which, like so many Italian thoroughfares, changed its name in midstream—in this case to the Corso del Popolo, as it neared the railroad station in the northern part of the city.

After her tears in the dining room she had felt in need of fresh air, or so she told herself, and he had offered to accompany her. The night air was damp and chilly, but she felt her spirits recovering. The lovely little park that adjoined the Scrovegni Chapel seemed idyllic in the moonlight.

"As in New York, one avoids such places at night, alas," Orlandi said. "It becomes a marketplace after the sun has set."

"You mean for drugs?"

He told her that Padua, along with Verona and Milan, was a thriving drug center of northern Italy. "We have adopted all of your worst American characteristics, I am sorry to say. A higher standard of living—that we have not imitated."

His limp seemed to be painful. At times, as they walked, he tried to conceal a grimace. She suggested turning back.

"It will work itself out. I've learned all its little idiosyncracies in the past several years. I was shot by the Brigate Rosse, a kneecap job."

"I'm sorry."

"They are devils. They could just as easily have killed me, of course, but the kneecap is their trademark. They understand the Latin temperament. Some of us would rather be killed than suffer the humiliation of being crippled. Foolish. But that is our romantic weakness."

The station was ahead, deserted except for a few people visible in the waiting room. Two taxi drivers were conversing beside their cabs, and there were several buses parked with their engines idling. They turned at the station, and headed back on the Corso del Popolo. He asked a polite question about Jerry. She told him about his heart attack, and how he made his living, and there seemed nothing further to say.

"You have other children?"

She told him about Sharon, and then, as an afterthought, about her mother. He said that he had been in Florida ten years earlier for a seminar, when he had been a drug enforcement officer.

"Did you like it?"

"Very warm. I prefer our own Italian Riviera. But then, I am prejudiced."

She thought of her mother trying to get up a bridge game at Rapallo, say, and suppressed a giggle. She asked him if he had children. Not—take note, Juno—if he was married.

"I have a son and a daughter. The girl is a university student, the boy teaches in Calabria. I would not have chosen that place for him to pursue his career..." He smiled wrily. "But he is very socially minded, he is devoted to helping those who have not had his advantages."

He sounds perfect for Sharon, my budding social worker, she thought. Maybe I can make a *shidach?*

"And your wife?" Well, it was a natural question, wasn't it?

"Divorced, ten years ago. We have divorce here in Italy now, you know, in certain circumstances."

So he's not married. But you are, Juno, you definitely are.

They turned in to the hotel. He asked her if she wanted a nightcap. She shook her head. They went up in the tiny elevator. When they got out, he walked her to her room.

"Good night."

"Good night, signora." He bent and kissed her hand.

She turned away suddenly and unlocked her door and went into her room. It was an ungracious departure, but she knew that if she hadn't been so abrupt she would have invited him in.

It took her a long time to fall asleep. She thought of Michael, and of Jerry, and of her mother, and of Zayde, long dead. And she thought of Alfredo Orlandi, with the Renaissance profile, whom she wanted very much.

Eighteen

Juno woke in the dark from an explicitly erotic dream in which, with Alfredo Orlandi as her partner, she performed a series of sexual acts that, in cold daylight, struck her as being anatomically impossible or, at the very least, superhuman. The dream lingered on into waking, producing a blush, less because of its abandonment than because she had thoroughly enjoyed it.

Take a cold shower, Juno.

As she was finishing her coffee in the hotel dining room, a short swarthy man came over to her table. He introduced himself as detective Rabito, and said he had been sent by Dottore Orlandi to confer with the signora. She invited him to share breakfast with her. His face lit up and he sat down, apologizing for his appearance. He was wearing a black leather jacket, worn jeans, and hush puppy shoes, and he needed a shave. She had the feeling that she had seen him before.

"I have driven up from Milano this morning, signora. Much traffic. I made it in three hours, exactly."

His Italian was very rapid, his consonants eccentric. Sensing that she was having some difficulty understanding him, he made an effort to slow down.

"I have seen you before, signora." He grinned. "At the Galleria in Milan. Of course you did not see me. I was under cover."

He had been one of a number of people she had thought—or fancied—might be watching her that night. "Has Dr. Orlandi given you any message for me?" Was it necessary for her to look so strenuously unconcerned when she mentioned his name? After all, Rabito didn't know her dream.

"Yes. It is this. I am to be the driver of our mission today. He wishes me to tell you that. I do not know what the mission is to be. I am sure he will tell me in time. Also, he wishes me to inform you that this morning he will go to the university to make inquiries about the signorina in question. He did not tell me who this signorina is. Undoubtedly he will tell me in good time, as well. Finally, signora, he requests you to phone him at the Questura at eleven thirty."

She phoned Orlandi at exactly eleven thirty; there was a tremor in her voice when she said good morning.

He sounded official and busy—so much for romance. There was a babble of voices in the background. He told her that a visit to the university had produced little of interest. Adriana Ferrari, twenty-two, youngest member of an old, aristocratic Venetian family. Home address given as her mother's home (a *palazzo* on the Grand Canal, he knew the house); investigation in process to see if she actually lived there. Had her premed work at Bologna, now a first-year student at the Medical School here, good student, very bright, proposes to become a surgeon. No known political associations, mild left leanings but no record of activism.

"If she is a member of the Forze Scarlatte," he said, "she has concealed it cleverly. This was, of course, by its nature, a quick and superficial investigation. Can you be at the Via Antenore entrance in fifteen minutes? You will see me there, but we will not acknowledge each other's presence. Rabito will be nearby in an unmarked car. We will see what happens."

She dressed warmly, with two sweaters under her coat. She spotted Orlandi when he rounded the corner briskly from the Via VIII Febbraio. He was wearing a powder blue topcoat with a navy collar, and a gray Borsalino hat. He passed by her without a glance. His limp was barely noticeable, perhaps, she thought, because he knew it made him conspicuous and was making an effort, however painful it might be, to conceal or minimize it.

She didn't see him a second time until five past one. By then, the exodus of students for lunch had dwindled to nothing. As he passed, he said without turning, "Follow me, signora."

She followed him, a half block to the rear, into the Piazza delle Erbe. He threaded his way between the carts, whose owners, bundled up in heavy coats, scarves, and woolen caps, were stamping their feet to keep warm. At the far end of the square he stopped and waited for her to join him.

He said, "Surveillance is cold work, *non è vero?*"

"It's very stupid of me," she said, "not to have mentioned the other exit. She used it the day I met her in Pedrocchi."

"We know about it. Rabito is parked near there. She is not in Ped-rocchi. Are you hungry, signora? Perhaps a sandwich or a plate of soup?"

She shook her head. "The students will be returning. I don't want to take the chance of missing her."

"Another detective is in place. He'll know where to find me."

"Yes. But suppose she comes *out*."

"Then the other detective and Rabito will follow her."

The door of the restaurant opened, and a man came out; so did the inviting smell of food. There was a piece of pasta sticking to the man's chin. She was chilled from her vigil on the Via Antenore. What would Orlandi say if she did a few fast laps around the Piazza delle Erbe to get her circulation stirring?

She said, "Yes, but neither one of them is Michael's mother. I must go back now, Dr. Orlandi."

He sensed her resolve and didn't try to dissuade her. "Very well. Afterwards—I am a beast to sit in a warm place and eat while you are out in the cold—afterwards I will come by. Then there is business to attend to at the Questura, but always I will be only a minute or two away."

She walked back to the Via Antenore. The detective standing near the corner gave himself away with a start of surprise when he saw her. His dress was almost identical to Rabito's—a "hood" outfit, including the week-old beard. She told him that she was going to take up her post again and that he could relieve Rabito if he wanted to. He stayed for a moment or two, then left.

It struck her that Orlandi was far from being committed to the prop-osition that Adriana was a member of the Forze Scarlatte, and even less so that she would lead them to the hideout. Otherwise, he would cer-tainly have mounted a more elaborate operation than this one, consisting of himself and Rabito and the fill-in detective. It was hard to escape the conclusion that—for whatever flattering reason—he was indulging her.

Forty minutes after she had left him in front of the restaurant he came down the street, walking briskly. He didn't look at her, but she under-stood that she was to follow him. When she turned the far corner he was waiting for her.

"Nothing?"

She shook her head. If there had been a bit of pasta on *his* chin, she thought, she would have killed him.

He handed her a paper bag. "I shall go back to the Questura now. If she comes out, you know where to find Rabito. I will be in radio touch with him. *Ciao*."

She went back, found a doorway that allowed her a not-too-distant view of the exit, and opened the bag. It contained a prosciutto sandwich and a pear. She had eaten the sandwich and begun on the pear when she noticed a tiny figure in a red raincoat pausing at the entrance. She recognized Francesca, the little blond girl she had met at Pedrocchi with Adriana. The girl looked at her, hesitated, then crossed the street.

"Signora? I am Francesca, Adriana's classmate."

"Yes. *Buon giorno.*"

"I saw you standing, and thought perhaps you are waiting to see Adriana?"

Being spotted was the last thing she had wanted, but a denial would simply make her seem foolish. She nodded.

"But Adriana is not here."

"She has no classes today?"

"She has only evening lectures, tonight. From seven until ten. If you wish to see her, that is the time to come."

She thanked the girl and smiled and then said casually, "Will you be seeing Adriana any time today?"

"I am sorry, but I am finished today at four o'clock. But if you come here before seven, you will be sure to catch her."

"Fine. Thank you for telling me."

Juno watched her cross the street, her fine blond hair lying back over the collar of her raincoat, and go through the door. She walked back to the hotel and went up to her room. She picked up the phone, but put it down again. Orlandi had intimated that it might be bugged. She returned to the lobby, and called him from one of the accommodation booths.

Orlandi bent the gooseneck lamp so that its beam focused on the back of the chair facing his desk. He waited for Stark at the door, shook hands, and waved him to the chair.

"I hope you are comfortable here in Padua," Orlandi said.

"Yes."

"It is not a city noted for its cuisine, but there are one or two passable restaurants—"

"I haven't heard from you since yesterday." Diebold leaned forward and pushed the lamp downward. "Do you mind?"

"Of course. A stupid lamp they have given me here. I have been busy and there is little to report. I intended phoning you later in the day if you did not come in."

"Have you checked up on this girl?"

"Certainly, but cautiously, you understand, not to tip our hand. But you realize that any kind of meaningful investigation takes time."

"What have you turned up?"

"Her name, her family background. Little of significance."

"You asked Mrs. Sultan about her?"

"She confirms your suspicions. She also wonders where you got the picture you gave me."

Diebold stared across the desk and said nothing.

"She thinks somebody in New York ransacked her apartment for it."

"Until a short while ago she was staked out in front of the Medical School."

Orlandi raised his brows. "Is that so?"

"I saw you there, too."

"I happened by, saw her, and invited her to take lunch with me. She declined."

"I'd like to be kept in the picture. Saves wear and tear, hanging around in the cold."

"I didn't feel it was necessary to bore you with these dull preliminaries."

Diebold took his hat off. His hair was carefully combed, with wings at the side brushed back over his ears. "I don't mind being bored."

"Yes, well, as you guessed, we hope that by following the girl she might lead us to where the FS are hiding." He smiled apologetically. "It is Mrs. Sultan's idea. It strikes me as far too simple, but..." He shrugged. "In a desert of leads it is at least a possibility."

"Instead of playing hide and seek, why not grab the girl and beat some truth out of her?"

"I thought of that. But Mrs. Sultan pointed out that if we used force with the girl and it failed, then we would have squandered our lead. It makes some sense."

"I'd like to have a shot at her. I'll guarantee she'll sing."

"I can't allow that, Mr. Stark."

"You don't believe in persuasion?"

"This is an Italian police matter. We don't let out our work to private contractors."

"It's your show, of course." The gray eyes were veiled. "That leaves following the girl. Am I invited?"

"So far, I regard any action we're taking now as purely exploratory. I'm not totally convinced—apologies to you and Mrs. Sultan—that the girl really means anything."

"Then why are you doing it?"

"Because it pleases me to do so," Orlandi said coldly. "If we turn up information leading to a raid, you will be a part of it, as I promised."

"I think you're indulging the lady, more or less," Diebold said.

Orlandi, controlling a rush of anger, said, "More, you might say, protecting her. If I don't cooperate she will go off and follow the girl herself, and that, of course, is very dangerous."

"Fucking amateurs," Diebold said. "Can't you restrain her?"

Orlandi smiled. "She is a lady of some determination. But perhaps you already know that?"

"Let's see if I have it right." Diebold made little effort to conceal his contempt. "You're going to trail the girl and hope she leads you to the hideout?"

"That is the idea."

"When is this taking place?"

"Whenever she shows up. Today, I hope."

"And if she leads you to the hideout?"

"Then I will plan an attacking raid in force. And then, Mr. Stark, you will be a part of the operation."

Diebold rose and put on his hat.

"I'll see you out," Orlandi said, coming around his desk.

"You know what I think, Orlandi? I think you've got a losing proposition, any angle you look at it."

Orlandi said pleasantly, "That is your considered opinion as a journalist, Mr. Stark?"

"Shit on that," Diebold said. "I can find my way out, don't bother."

Orlandi bowed his head slightly. "I see your facial wounds are healing nicely. Good afternoon."

Diebold said nothing, not even good-bye. He simply turned and went out.

When Fernald found out about Jerry Sultan, Locksley had already left. He was lunching in Georgetown with the DCI himself. Fernald might have rung him at the restaurant, but Locksley wouldn't take it kindly. He had lunch with the Director about twice a year and regarded it as a gala occasion. He had shown himself off to Fernald before leaving: he was wearing a double-breasted blazer with vermeil buttons, a Household Guards (if Fernald had it straight) tie, Black Watch plaid trousers, and a three-hundred-dollar pipe that had just arrived by mail from London.

Locksley got back near three o'clock, flushed with the auspiciousness of the occasion and, doubtless, an after-lunch brandy or two. Fernald gave him a few minutes to settle in, then went along the hall to his office.

"Nice lunch?" Fernald said.

"Jolly good. They do the best mutton this side of the Atlantic. You must give it a go sometime."

"Sultan has skipped," Fernald said.

"Skipped?"

"Left the hospital. Put his street clothes on under his bathrobe, got rid of the robe in a john on the main floor, rolled down his pants, and walked out."

"Where were our watchers?"

"Just one, we didn't think any more was needed. Sultan skipped when the watcher went for coffee."

Locksley sighed. "What's his health like?"

"He's all right. He'd have been ready for release a week ago if we hadn't wanted to keep him there."

"Where is he?"

"On the way to Italy."

"What the devil for?"

"Well, it's his wife and son, you know."

"You're sure that's where he's gone?"

"I checked his apartment and his office. I checked the airlines out of JFK and found him. He left for Milan on a TWA flight at eleven this morning."

"Can we intercept him at the Milan airport?"

"It could be pretty messy. He'll raise hell if we try anything."

"He'll go to Padua, of course, and likely play bull in a china shop. I don't think Diebold is going to be pleased."

"I think I'd best go over myself."

"Diebold will like that even less."

"I have a feeling, given one thing or another, that the situation calls for a wiser head."

"Is that you, old man?"

Fernald grimaced. "I'm not all that sure, in the abstract. Wiser—or at least saner—than Diebold, yes."

"It's a long time since you've been in the field."

"I'm not overflowing with joy at the prospect, but Uncle Sam needs me. There's an Alitalia plane leaving for Milan at six, arriving at nine tomorrow morning. Sultan will be getting in well after midnight and might not be able to get transport until the morning, so maybe I'll catch up with him."

"Good. Can I have my secretary make arrangements for your tickets?"

"Thanks. I'll put Ellie on it. She knows my preferences."

Ellie had already made arrangements a few hours ago. What would he have done if Locksley had said no?

"Godspeed," Locksley said.

Nineteen

Rabito, with a slight turn of his head toward the backseat, said, "She just turned the corner, dottore."

Juno peered cautiously past Rabito through the windshield. Adriana was striding along briskly, her coat open and sailing behind her.

"Ten past ten," Orlandi said. "Your little blond friend was correct."

He had been skeptical about Francesca's information, even suspicious. True, her meeting with Juno outside the school might have been accidental, but she might also have been deliberately misinforming them.

"It could pin us down here for three hours while she's off doing mischief elsewhere. Not a bad joke, that."

But Adriana had arrived a few minutes before seven and hurried into the Med School. Juno had shown Orlandi the girl's parking place and pointed out her dusty *cinquecento*. Rabito parked some distance along the street, with a view of both the *cinquecento* and the corner she would have to round to return to her car. Juno had insisted on sharing the watch with Rabito, and by now she was numb with inactivity and boredom.

Orlandi, who had arrived a half hour earlier from the Questura, had been sympathetic. "Waiting, signora, is the curse of policework. But it is also the very heart and backbone."

Not to mention backside, Juno thought.

He sat beside her in the rear of the car, though "beside" overstated the matter. They sat apart, at opposite ends of the seat. Yet in spite of that, or perhaps because of it, there was a tension present that was palpable, erotic. In the front seat, Rabito might have been their chaperone. Twenty years ago, she thought, she would by now have sighed theatrically and folded into Orlandi's arms. And who could say, if Rabito wasn't there, that she wouldn't have done it now?

Adriana gave no sign of concern that she might be under surveillance or had any need to be wary. Rabito was speaking softly into his radio transmitter.

Adriana stopped at her car, unlocked it, and got in. An instant later her headlights went on, illuminating the fierce political graffiti on a wall. The sound of the *cinquecento*'s four-cylinder engine was noisy but steady. She backed out of the parking space, her brake lights glowing red, then shot off noisily down the street.

They didn't move. Rabito, with his eyes following the red taillights of the girl's car, was jabbering on the radio. Their engine was not even on. She leaned through the darkness toward Orlandi.

"Soon, signora," he said calmly.

When the girl's taillights whipped around a corner Juno began to fidget. Rabito was still talking on the radio, Orlandi was sunk quietly in his seat.

"We're going to lose her," Juno said urgently.

Orlandi spoke to Rabito, who started his engine, turned on his lights, and backed out.

"Another of our cars is behind her," Orlandi said. "He is directing us in his tracks by radio. Later, so that she does not suspect she is being followed, this first car, which is baby blue in color, will drop off. Another car, which is off-white, will take its place. Since we will be guided by radio, we can follow her without being seen. We cannot have an infinite number of cars, so eventually we will take the first place, and then we will see how good Rabito is."

All the same, Juno thought, she wished Rabito would step on it, and at least turn the same corner the girl had taken ages ago. Nor would it be amiss if Orlandi abandoned his supercool air and showed a little anxiety. Why should she be the only person in the car to be *tsitterdik*?

"We're anchorman in a daisy chain," Strawberry said. "It's ridiculous."

"What is anchorman?" Dmitri said. "What is daisy chain?"

"A daisy chain is an intertwining of daisies. An anchorman is the fellow on the American television news who sits at a desk and talks a lot."

"We're making a left turn," Dmitri said. His large hands were graceful on the steering wheel of the BMW. "Everybody. Dark blue car in front of us, then light gray, then light blue, then the girl..."

"It's a waste of time," Strawberry said. "If she leads us somewhere we're at the end of the line, we'll have to wait our turn. Is it too much to expect that we could have been given some backup? You ask for help, and they start spouting figures and budgets at you. What are we, GUM, or are we the KGB? I told Grigoriev this, and he said, 'Strawberry, shortage of funds to run government agencies properly is a worldwide problem. We are all tightening our belts and learning to make do with less. I expect that you and Dmitri will compensate by working that much harder, since you are both top of the line—'."

"Is that so, Comrade? The colonel said you and I were top of the line?"

"He was really speaking about me, but graciously included you as well."

"But if he said so, he must have meant it about me being top of the line too."

"Dmitri, you're in danger of developing your own cult of personality, like Stalin, like Krushchev. You know what happened to those two."

"Oh no, no, never, I am a modest person."

"She's heading eastward," Strawberry said, "toward Venice. I have a bold idea, Comrade, a top-of-the-line idea."

"Ah, top-of-the-line."

"We know where she went last night—A4 to Venice-Mestre, right?"

"Yes. And that's where we lost her."

"I didn't ask you that. She's heading toward the A4, and I am betting she will take it to the Venice-Mestre exit. So...pay attention now...let us anticipate. Instead of trailing at the end of a long line like shit coming out of an asshole, why, Comrade, let's just run ahead of everybody, including the girl, take the A4, get off at Venice-Mestre, and wait past the toll booth for her to show up."

"But the others will also show up, won't they, Comrade?"

Strawberry nodded. "The only sensible thing, in view of the crowd following this girl, would be to go home and go to bed. But Colonel Grigoriev wants us to put in extra hours, whether they're productive or not. So, Dmitri, can you leave this line and find a quicker way to the A4?"

"Certainly. A top-of-the-line driver always knows the territory. But are we sure of where she intends to go, Comrade Strawberry?"

"We are sure of nothing in this world. Except, of course, taken for granted, the eventual triumph of worldwide Marxist-Leninist thought under the wise leadership of the Soviet Union."

"But if we are wrong, Comrade?"

"In that case we'll go home and go to sleep."

"But, Comrade..."

"If the girl doesn't show up on the A4 then we will have lost the trail. That's the truth. Isn't it?"

"In one way it may be the truth, but in another way—"

"Truth is indivisible. Let's not have decadent sophistry from you. Don't try to befuddle my honest Soviet brains."

"Comrade, that is not my intention, I assure you."

"There is the A4. Take it, Dmitri. This way, at least, we avoid the risk of giving ourselves away. We may not catch anything, but at least nobody will know we were fishing."

Diebold said, "We're the filling in a sandwich."

"I thought so," Gray said. "Light blue in front, dark blue behind?"

"I spotted another one a while ago, well back. Being guided by radio."

"Either that," Gray said, "or *we're* guiding him."

"Radio," Diebold said humorlessly. "Orlandi probably knows we're in the chase. Which way are we headed?"

"Generally easterly direction, I think. The girl doesn't seem to be trying any tricks. Easterly, toward Venice. Treviso, Portogruaro, and Trieste at the end of the line, though that seems too much of a daily commute for the girl."

Diebold watched as Gray, following the red taillights ahead of him loosely, not crowding them, made a right turn, stayed straight for several blocks and then turned to his left. They were on the outskirts of Padua now, in an industrialized zone, amid plants and factories sequestered in darkness behind steel mesh fences.

Gray said, "By the way, did you spot the BMW cruising by when we were waiting for the girl to show up? It flashed by us twice more."

"Saw it," Diebold said. "It's Strawberry. Not the driver, the other one, big fellow."

"Ah," Gray said. "I've been wondering about him. I thought he might have gotten lost."

"No. He's in the game, back there somewhere. He's right in the game with us."

It didn't concern him that there was competition from a top Soviet agent, Gray thought. Just the opposite, he relished it. He was doubtless daydreaming about killing him. Well, that was the way Diebold was, by all accounts.

Gray patted the steering wheel. "Pretty good car. Nobody ever gives the Italians enough credit for making big-ticket items. This one is a good piece of iron."

"He knows I don't trust him," Diebold said. "Orlandi, I mean. So he probably expected me to be on his tail tonight. Open mutual mistrust—there are worse ways to have an understanding."

"She's bypassing the A-4," Gray said. He took note of a northward jog in the route. "Maybe she's headed for Treviso now, that direction. Note the SS sign? Stands for Strada Statali, state road."

"The light blue," Diebold said. "He's about to drop off. There he goes."

"And an off-white or some such, is coming from behind us into the left lane," Gray said. He held his speed steady as the other car overtook them and then slid smoothly into the right lane. "Look at the acceleration. Car looks like a wreck, but there's a very sharp motor there."

"What are you carrying?" Diebold said.

"The usual. Snub-nose .38."

"That's all?"

"It's enough to shoot somebody."

"It's okay when you're in tight, and very good then, too. But at a distance all it can do is scare somebody with its noise, it can't hit anything."

Gray had learned the secret of getting along with Diebold. Don't argue with him. If you see a disagreement looming, change the subject. "Did you know, by the way, that the pistol was an Italian invention? The name comes from the town of Pistoia in Tuscany."

"Drop back a bit. There isn't anything the police can do about our tailing him, but let's keep up appearances, please."

"Going off the state road up ahead," Gray said. "I hope it's not too far to go. Country roads are very tough. There's usually just two of you then, so you're exposed."

Gray eased off the state road and made the right turn where the other lights had turned. The road was empty.

"Don't lose them," Diebold said.

Gray accelerated. "They're up ahead someplace. Over the brow of that hill we should be picking up their lights."

They sped up the hill. Past the crest, the road ran in a straight line.

"Well?" Diebold said.

"They must be up there." Gray sounded shaken. "Maybe they're running without lights." He switched his motor off and rolled the window down. "I can hear something in the distance."

"Find them."

Gray switched on his motor and took off with a squeal of tires. "Sorry. Look, they turned this way, they've got to be up ahead." He ran the car onto the crown in the center of the road and put their speed up to fifty. "They've *got* to be up ahead. There hasn't been any turnoff."

"How could you tell if there was? You're going too goddamn fast to see it."

"We'll find them," Gray said. "Damn it, they must be here somewhere."

Ahead, the dark sky seemed to be resting on the rounded top of another rise in the road.

"Well, Comrade?" Dmitri said.

"Well *what?*" Strawberry said. "Why are you saying *well* to me?"

They were sitting in the car at the bottom of the Venice-Mestre ramp off the A-4. Dmitri hiked up his sleeve and looked at his wristwatch. "It is now more than twenty minutes that we have been waiting."

"And what conclusion do you draw from that fact?"

"I conclude that we have lost her, that she did not take the A-4 after all."

"That is a correct deduction," Strawberry said, sighing. "You might as well go back to Padua."

"Perhaps if we had not tried such a daring and unusual maneuver—"

"I will quote you a very wise epigram," Strawberry said, "as follows: It is better to have tried and lost than never to have tried at all."

Dmitri was silent for a moment. "It is a fine epigram, Comrade."

"It should be, since it is Pushkin, as you very well know, of course."

"Pushkin? A great writer. Yes, of course it is Pushkin."

Dmitri started the engine of the BMW. Strawberry slid down low in his seat; the brim of his Stetson tipped forward over his eyes.

Shortly after the girl left the state road, Orlandi instructed the off-white car to drop away. There was a car in front of them, but it veered off at a fork. Now they were directly behind the girl.

Orlandi said, "Turn off your lights, Rabito."

"*Sì, dottore.*"

Everything was black now. Rabito moved over to the crown of the road. He was hunched forward, his head almost touching the windshield as he tried to gauge his path by steering a course between the darkness of trees and undergrowth marking the edges of the road. When he rounded a curve the racket of the *cinquecento* became audible, and they could place the girl's position by the forward cast of her headlights.

Juno said, "She doesn't seem to realize she's being followed."

"She hasn't acted that way."

They were deep in the countryside. Here and there, well back off the road, there was an occasional dim light from a house. But for the most part the road was a black undifferentiated tunnel that seemed to be leading endlessly to nowhere. There was another curve, two of them, a tight hairpin turn, and the girl seemed to have disappeared. Orlandi was breathing heavily. Then, suddenly, they picked up the forward throw of the *cinquecento's* headlights.

"*Bene,*" Rabito said.

The lights ahead disappeared again, but when they came around a curve, there were the lights. Then they vanished again.

"She's going faster now," Rabito said.

"Yes," Orlandi said. "Can you give us a bit more speed?"

"Speed, yes. Without putting us in a ditch, I don't know."

The car spurted. The lights ahead appeared only briefly before winking out. Rabito bent over the steering wheel, and put on more speed. He almost missed a curve and wrestled to keep their car on the road.

"Ah," he said. "But there she is, *va bene.*"

As he started to accelerate again, a large dark shape moved across the road in front of them. Rabito stamped on the brakes and the car slewed, wheels squealing. The braking threw Juno forward against the front seat. The car rocked to a halt, barely inches away from a van drawn up broadside in their path.

She saw Rabito produce a gun, and she was aware that Orlandi was reaching beneath his coat. She saw dark figures swarming around the car. Rabito pointed his gun at the window by his side. There was a blast, the sound of shattering glass, and Rabito threw up his arms. Dark liquid splattered the windshield, and Rabito fell forward, spouting blood.

The sound of gunfire was abrupt, brief, and sourceless. Gray stopped the car and they listened, but the echoes died away, and there was only a profound country silence.

Gray said, "I think it came from somewhere ahead and to the left."

Diebold was furious. "We should have been there. Find them. Go on, move it."

"Which way?"

Diebold didn't answer. He sat in a still, brooding silence. Gray went slowly ahead and stopped at a road branching off to his left. The roads were indistinguishable from each other—black macadam under lacy denuded branches arching over the road, stolid tree trunks, barriers of undergrowth lining the verge on both sides. He took the left turn, not with any idea of where he was going, but because he didn't want to give up. Even if he did, Diebold wouldn't permit it.

And so he drove on, feeling that he was permanently lost, that he would spend the rest of his life groping through the dark like some blind, unsentient, primitive organism. There was no logic to his turns, he had lost all sense of direction; it was simply a panicky run through an impenetrable maze, a dirty joke of a maze in which there was no way out.

Suddenly they had arrived back at the state road. He stopped the car. "Go on," Diebold said. "Go back in again. Keep going."

He started over, trying to take different turns than he had before, but never knowing for certain whether they were different or the same. He lost track of time and distances: they merged into a ghastly blur, a fusion of macadam, trees, undergrowth, and Diebold's glowering silence. And so, in his mood of hopelessness, when they finally came on it, he would have overrun it if Diebold hadn't shouted. He slammed on his brakes, not quite short of the long scorched track of skid marks.

Diebold was already out of the car, following the marks. By the time Gray reached him, Diebold was bent far forward, scouring the road in the cast of their headlights. They found an intermingling of blood and shattered glass, and then an erratic trail of red running off to the side of the road. Diebold got down on his knees to examine the body. It was lying on its back, its eyes staring, half of its neck blown away.

"Orlandi's driver," Diebold said. "Shotgun wound." He got to his feet. "Let's see if we can find their car."

A hundred yards or so along, a dirt road slanted off the macadam. Diebold told Gray to wait. He got out and trotted up the dirt incline. He was gone for only a minute or so. When he returned he started walking back to where they had left their car. Gray followed.

"The car is there," Diebold said. "Nobody in it. The driver was killed by shots through the window, probably fell out when they opened the door."

"Then they've taken them?"

Diebold nodded. "Pretty good haul for the bastards. Not the woman so much, but Orlandi. They've got the best-known antiterrorist cop in Italy in their hands. They'll have a picnic with it."

"Anything we can do?"

"Not now. They're long gone. Go home."

It took Gray another half hour to stumble on the state road.

Twenty

Juno's eyes fluttered open, and before they closed again she saw a blurred image of Michael's face hovering over her. Somewhere there was a disembodied murmur of low muted voices.

"Mother, can you hear me?"

She started to yawn, and in some mindless reflex of good manners brought her hand up to cover her mouth.

"Mother?"

She forced her eyes to open, shielding them against a sharp painful light somewhere above her. She realized she was lying on a bed, with a rough woolen blanket drawn up under her chin. Someone took her hand.

"Mother, it's me." The voice took on a familiar deadpan teasing tone. "It's Michael, Mother, your incredibly wonderful son."

Tears welled in her eyes and spilled over. She brought the hand to her lips. It was real, and it tickled; like Jerry, Michael had hairy knuckles. She put her arms around his neck and drew him down in a fierce crushing embrace. Then she held him off and looked at him; his black-bearded face wavered in the watery film that clouded her vision.

"Oh, Michael, Michael . . ."

The murmur of voices was stilled for a moment, then it resumed.

"It's Joe Bering," Michael said. "And the policeman, Orlandi."

She started to ask about Rabito, then remembered with a shudder. "Is Dr. Orlandi all right?"

"He's okay. He's been awake for a half hour. Would you kindly try not to choke me to death?"

She smiled and loosened her grip. "Where are we?"

"Venice. Don't try to sit up yet. You'll feel better in a little while."

"Adriana..."

His mouth was tight in its forest of beard. "Yeah, Adriana."

"I'm sorry, darling." I knew myself, once, what it means to be betrayed by a lover.

He shrugged, and then his beard opened up in a glistening smile. "You realize, don't you, that you're probably a leading candidate for Jewish Mother of the Year?"

"Make fun of me if you want to. All that counts is that I'm here with you."

"Yes," Michael said, his voice suddenly drained of humor. "Yes, you're here with me."

"Although we have been very successful and landed a very big fish, we must nevertheless review our errors and indiscretions so that they may be eliminated in the future."

If there was such a thing as a computer programmed for revolutionaries, Adriana thought, Federico would speak its language perfectly. The errors and indiscretions he was referring to were hers, of course, but like that theoretical computer he was impersonal. Not that she didn't deserve criticism: she *had* betrayed herself with her careless remark about Michael's beard; by the time she had realized her mistake, and the fact that Michael's mother was onto her, it had been too late to cover over the damage.

"The revolutionary course is beset with reefs and shoals and a single slip can lead to shipwreck."

Even his metaphors were boring, Adriana thought.

They were scattered about a large room with peeling paint and damp-streaked walls. It was cluttered with unwashed dishes, books, papers, articles of soiled clothing left where they had been dropped. Ugo and Barbara were slovenly housekeepers. The room served as parlor, kitchen, and meeting room. It was situated directly over the cellar, its unswept stone floor covered indifferently with a scattering of shabby throw rugs. Federico, as chairman, stood behind an old table; the others sat on a motley collection of chairs, two of which were canvas beach chairs somebody had stolen from a hotel on the Lido. Everyone seemed exhausted, spent, dispirited, as if coming down from the high peak of excitement had left them in a postcoital trough.

They did not present an appetizing spectacle, Adriana thought. Too bad one couldn't choose one's political bedfellows by conventional standards. In that case, she would have nothing to do with any of them, with the possible exception of Carlo, whose weak stomach for violence, however, made him the least dependable of all of them, even less than the young Giorgio, who lacked judgment but was admirably zealous. As for the unspeakable Gildo—baboon! And what could be said for Ugo, the intense, bony-faced ex-athlete whose revolutionary philosophy could be translated into a brutal desire to avenge the shattered knees that had sidelined him at the age of twenty-six? Or for Barbara, a re-formed soccer groupie who, before her conversion to more serious things and a monogamous relationship with Ugo, had been rumored to have taken on an entire team in a single night?

"... vigilance that must never be relaxed for a single moment. It is to explicate this theme, rather than to punish Adriana or hold her up to ridicule, that I must now refer concretely to Adriana's nearly fatal blunder—"

"I'd like to point out," Adriana said, "that it is past two o'clock, which is, as most other people know, an unacceptable hour for long speeches."

"I will not be hurried," Federico said, "until I have made all my points."

She tuned his oratory out. As she had often thought before, Federico should have been a pedagogue instead of a terrorist. And yet he was the ablest of all of them and the most experienced. If it had not been for him, his guidance, discipline, the fragile bonds that held them would long ago have ruptured, and they would have disintegrated.

Federico had set up tonight's ambush and orchestrated its details to perfection. Granted, it was pure luck that they had snared someone as important as Orlandi; he had become a national figure since his role in all but smashing the Brigate Rosse after the liberation of General Dozier. In effect, they had captured an archenemy. What was astonishing was that Orlandi had exposed himself as he had, doing such ordinary po-licework instead of relegating it to a subordinate. Could it be that his head had been turned by the attractive Signora Sultan? Love and sex among the middle-aged? Well, why not? Her mother, her own mother, that bitch, would fornicate beyond the grave if she could find some way of managing it.

Federico's voice droned on. Giorgio was circulating, refilling wine glasses. Adriana waved him away.

Technically, the operation had come off with a precision that satisfied even Federico's demanding nature. At just the right moment after she had driven by, the van had shot out and blocked the narrow road. She had heard the squealing brakes, and almost immediately thereafter the sound of gunfire. She put her car in reverse and by the time she reached the van, the police car was being driven onto a dirt road, Carlo at the wheel, Gildo kneeling on the front seat with his shotgun trained on Orlandi and the woman in back.

Her injection of the barbiturate, by the light of Federico's flashlight had gone smoothly enough after the start, when the woman, with a hand speed that had taken them by surprise, lashed out; Carlo had taken a blow across the bridge of his nose. Three of them had finally subdued her, mostly due to Orlandi, who, seeing the uselessness of resistance, and to spare her physical punishment, urged her to submit.

The woman, Adriana was forced to admit, had more spunk than the usual bourgeoise. As Adriana held the needle poised over her arm, she had not flinched but looked her squarely in the eye.

Their new way of getting to Venice had gone smoothly; it was far simpler than when they had brought Bering in. Giuseppe had dug up a cooperative watchman on a wharf on the Mestre waterfront who agreed to turn the other way. While she drove on to Venice and parked the *cinquecento*, the van rendezvoused with Giuseppe at the wharf. They loaded their captives onto Giuseppe's scow and then chugged sedately from the Laguna into the Canale Santa Chiara and thence into the Canale di Cannaregio. Gianni had been waiting on the embankment with his cart. Orlandi and the woman were piled into the cart under the tarpaulin, and hauled without incident to the house in the Ghetto.

"... the capture of Orlandi"—Federico's voice wafted back into her consciousness—"and the killing of his driver will increase the pressure upon us. Let us take it seriously—we do not, after all, have aspirations to martyrdom. Now, another consideration—as much as we will impress the population with our capture of Orlandi, so we will be condemned for the Signora Sultan. It cannot be helped."

Mamma, Adriana thought, the sainted figure of Italy. *Mamma*—the word itself was enough to reduce an Italian to tears. Well, just about now, down below, Michael and his mother would be having their reunion at last, if not under the circumstances either of them would have envisioned. And tonight she could cradle her little boy's head on her breast and croon him a lullaby until he slept.

You're jealous, Adriana, never having had a true mother of your own. *Mamma*—the word arouses in you the deepest of hatreds and the most inexpressible longings. *Basta*, Adriana! Enough of your sentimental maunderings!

"May I please have your full attention, Adriana?"

If Federico wore spectacles, Adriana thought, he would peer over their rims in the immemorial manner of the kindly pedant of children's stories. "Yes, Federico, you may."

"The question of Francesca. Someone might put two and two together, pull her in and sweat her."

They had depended too much on believing that angelic little Francesca wouldn't be suspected of having done anything more than a good deed when she told the signora about the night lectures. As to whether she could resist extreme pressure, it was an open question. And in any event, why take a chance?

"I'll phone her at the school tomorrow morning," Adriana said.

"Why not tonight?"

"I don't know where she lives. She has a nine o'clock lecture, I'll call her through the office. Look, the police have plenty to do, they'll be focusing most of their energy on the scene of the ambush. It'll be a while before they get around to checking out peripheral figures like Francesca."

"It's known you have had lunch together. She must go underground. Does she have a hiding place?"

"*We're* her hiding place."

"All right," Federico said. "Get to her as early as you can. And make sure she's careful."

Adriana nodded. So this was to be the end of Francesca's medical career, too. Well, she had another career waiting for her, as a full-time member of the Forze Scarlatte.

Who could possibly be domestic as a captive in a damp cellar in Venice? Juno Sultan, that was who. But it gave her something to do, it helped divert her mind from their predicament. So she made up the two cots, and neatly stacked the extra blankets and comforters that had been thrown down the stairs the night before. When that was finished, she got onto Michael about his teeth. It was better than brooding on the fact that this might be the last day of their lives. The deadline was midnight.

The sleeping arrangements had been devised partially by Michael and partially by everyone else's sense of modesty. Michael had insisted that she take his cot ("In this case," he had said when she protested, "age comes before the incorrigible maternal instinct") and there wasn't any point in arguing. Bering had offered his to Orlandi, who had refused rather bluntly. She was sure his mood came of his embarrassment— though a stronger word was called for: something like disgrace—at having been captured. He refused all solace; he had not been rude to her but withdrawn.

She had risen at seven o'clock in the morning by her watch, which

she had dutifully wound before going to bed; the light ir
cellar was the same, morning and night. There was som
the single bathroom— a reverse jockeying, with everyone a
her and each other. There was little conversation. Orlandi had w
her *buon giorno* and then gone off to study the iron gate in the far w
with Michael and Bering.

Two masked men, one holding an automatic weapon, brought breakfast. They left two trays at the top of the stairs. No word was said,
either by the masked men or by anyone in the cellar. They pushed the
cots together and ate with the trays balanced on their knees.

No one spoke until Juno said to Michael, "Have you been eating
decently? I'll bet not."

"Mother, for God's sake."

She was deliberately playing Jewish mother, hoping it might help
defuse the tension.

"The food is good," Bering said. "I'll say that much for these people.
Right, Mike?"

"Michael isn't eating," Juno said. "He looks like a scarecrow."

Michael made an exasperated face but said nothing. Orlandi was
picking at his food, his face grim, his eyes turned down. The cheer-
lessness was oppressive.

"You know," Juno said brightly, "this is the first time since Girl Scout
camp that I've had a breakfast without brushing my teeth."

"Come on, Mother," Michael said, "cut that stuff out."

"It's trivial, I know, but being clean—especially your teeth—makes
you feel better. It keeps your spirits up."

Orlandi looked up with a little smile. He knows what I'm doing, she
thought; I have an ally.

She said to Michael, "When did you look at your teeth last? They're
disgusting, all green and furry. Do you know what I'm going to do?"

"Something ridiculous," Michael said.

"I'm going to ask them to give us some salt."

Michael groaned.

"They might not want to give us a toothbrush and toothpaste, but
how could they begrudge us some salt?"

"She's right, you know," Orlandi said.

"Look," Michael said, "you're the new boy here, you're not entitled
to an opinion until you've put in a couple of weeks as a captive."

"Michael! You're being rude!"

Michael glared at her, then shook his head and smiled. "Never go
into captivity with your mother along. It cramps your style."

"I was captured in the war, a prisoner of the British," Orlandi said.

I was very young then. The commandant of prisoners—a colonel, our senior officer—set down a program to help keep our spirits up. We had games, sport, sings, lectures on various topics. But even more helpful was personal hygiene: shaving each day—and with some very dull razors, I can tell you—bathing, keeping our uniform in order by washing them, sewing them up when they became torn. At first I thought it was rot, but really it worked wonders for our morale. What reminded me of this—we asked the British for toothbrushes. They didn't have them, but they gave us as much salt as we wanted. Keeping our teeth clean and not green"—he smiled—"was a very valuable part of our regimen."

Michael said, "So you're in her thrall." He grinned. "It's the way she operates. She gets people to fall for her so she can make them clean their teeth."

Juno felt herself flush. Michael, I know you're joking, but... she risked a glance at Orlandi. He was smiling, in no way embarrassed or guilty. Guilty about what, for God's sake—a romance that existed entirely in her own head?

She faced Michael. "There's one thing I'll tell you, my dear son. When they come to pick up these things, I'm going to ask for salt."

Michael sighed.

"And I'll see to it that you use it."

She was satisfied; she felt that she had brightened things up a bit. After breakfast she stacked the dishes neatly on the trays. Michael went off and began to exercise, at the same time supervising Bering, whose efforts were halfhearted. Orlandi went over to the iron gate. After a while he returned and sat down on the opposite cot.

"I have been ashamed to speak to you," he said.

His face was somber. Behind him Michael was graceful as a dancer, doing a series of rapid push-ups. Bering was resting on his stomach, breathing hard.

"I am desolated by what took place last night. Professionally, yes, of course, but even more because of what I allowed to happen to you, signora. That I cannot forgive myself for."

She moved the dishes aimlessly on the trays. "It wasn't your fault. They were very clever. I insisted on coming, didn't I?"

"You made it difficult for me to refuse you, and for that reason I should have been especially firm." His smile was wan. "I should not have allowed it to happen to me, either, but that is different, risks are part of a policeman's brief."

"You're a big catch for them?"

"The biggest, I think, since Aldo Moro, though it's a poor distinction. Yes, they will make much of my capture."

"Moro was the former prime minister?"

"Yes. They killed him after holding him for many months. Very sad. He had a wife, children, to whom he was devoted. They allowed him to write. His letters were very moving, *patetico.*"

She abandoned the pretense of stacking the dishes. "I won't hear of your blaming yourself. Especially about me. Believe me, I would trust you in anything."

He gave her a long look, his eyes soft. "You are a very kind and good woman, signora." He took her hand, bowed his head, and kissed her fingers.

Beyond his bent head, the smooth black hair touched with gray, she saw Michael. He was resting on his stomach, staring at them. Relax, my son, it's an old European custom.

"The question now, of course," Orlandi said, "is what we can do to help ourselves." He spoke to Michael and Bering. "I have examined the gate. Without tools, impossible to do anything with it."

Michael was sitting up. "I tried sawing at the bars with a piece of glass. I barely scratched it."

"Where does it lead to?" Juno said.

"That I do not know," Orlandi said. "But in the old days of the Republic, the people who lived here might have used it as a route to bring out valuables, perhaps when the tax collectors came. Whether it is a strong room or a passageway of some kind, I cannot tell. In either case, it's impregnable. As for the rest of the cellar—"

"I've been over every inch of it," Michael said. "It's a cement box, top, bottom and sides."

"Except for the door at the top of the stairs," Orlandi said. "If we have any hope of escape it may be there, when they open the door to bring food."

"I thought of that too," Michael said. "And so did they. There are always two of them, and the second one stands well back with the gun."

"Yes, well," Orlandi said, "But it bears thinking about."

Above, the door opened suddenly. This time there were two masked men, both armed.

"Ah," Michael said, "the housemaids. The squatty one with the shotgun is Gildo, the Sicilian garlic king. The one with the burp gun is—"

"*Basta!*" Gildo said, with a menacing gesture of his short ugly shotgun. Then he spoke to Orlandi. "Most distinguished doctor, maybe we have the pleasure of your company up here?"

"And if I decline your invitation?"

Gildo's teeth showed in the opening of the mask. "In that case, most distinguished doctor, we will beat you unconscious with the butts of our guns, and carry you up. Which will it be?"

"The little bastard means it," Michael said. "Don't make an issue of it. Not worth it."

Orlandi nodded and climbed the steps. Both men drew back, watching his ascent alertly. On the small flat landing Gildo reached out, grabbed Orlandi by the arm, and pulled him through the doorway. Then the door slammed and they heard the bolts being shut.

Juno stood looking up at the thick blankness of the scarred door. Michael touched her arm.

"It's all right, Mother, he'll be all right."

She turned away. "They forgot to take the dishes. I'll wash them in that sink in the bathroom."

"Mother, for God's sake."

"Don't just stand there," she said. "Pick up a tray and bring it into the bathroom."

She put down her tray with a clatter and looked stricken.

"Mother," Michael said. "What happened?"

"Your father," she said. "He'll read about my being captured, and the shock, in his condition...oh, Michael."

Michael put his arm around her. "He's a tough old bird, he'll be all right, Mother. Don't look as if it's the end of the world."

Why I'm looking as if it's the end of the world, she thought, is because it took me twelve hours even to think of Jerry.

She said, "Pick up your tray. I'll wash and you can dry."

Driving against a fierce rain under black clouds, Fernald's plane set down at Malpensa Airport in Milan just before nine o'clock in the morning. He retrieved his bag and took a taxi to Linate, the Alitalia domestic flights airport some twenty-odd miles away. He checked in for a flight to Venice, the nearest viable airport to Padua, with an hour or so to spare before departure time, and then decided to look for Jerry Sultan.

He recognized him from the back, bent over an array of newspapers at a stand. Fernald watched him for a second, then walked over and spoke his name. Sultan turned around.

"How did you know I was here?"

Fernald studied him. He was wearing a sports jacket and flannel pants, and a crumpled white shirt with a soiled open collar. He looked pale, drained. But not so pale and drained as I must look, Fernald thought; after all, Sultan had doubtless spent a few hours in a bed in a hotel room in Milan.

He said, "We discovered that you had checked yourself out of the hospital, and that you weren't at home or in any of your known haunts—"

"I don't have any haunts."

"—so it wasn't hard to figure out where you had gone. Can't we get away from here and find someplace quiet?"

"You know some Italian, don't you?" Jerry didn't wait for a reply, but bought a newspaper. "Juno's on the front page—her picture and big headlines. Something has happened."

Jerry folded the paper under his arm. They found a corner that was relatively isolated from the busy flow of activity. Jerry handed the newspaper over. Fernald opened it. There were separate pictures of Juno Sultan and of a man; a caption identified the man as Orlandi.

Fernald read the streamer aloud: *"Orlandi e la signora Sultan Rapiti dai Terroristi...* Orlandi and Mrs. Sultan kidnapped by terrorists..."

"Jesus," Jerry said. "I thought it meant raped."

"Captured or kidnapped." He scanned the subheads quickly. *"Imboscata sulla strada isolata...* Ambush on isolated country road. *Un agente assassinato...* A policeman killed. I'm awfully sorry."

"Yeah," Jerry said. He was sweating, but he spoke calmly. "I had it more or less figured out myself, except for the *rapiti* part, thank God. You didn't know about this until just now?"

Fernald shook his head. "I've been on a plane all night. I'm glad to see that you're taking it so well."

"I'm not taking it well at all. I'm dying inside, but I'm trying to keep control of myself."

"You shouldn't have come here. You're a sick man."

"No, you are. I had a heart attack, but I've been all right for at least a week now. I think you got the doctors to lie to me about my condition."

"They felt the extra rest would do you good," Fernald said. "All right, it happened to fit our needs. Yes, we wanted you at the hospital, and since we were concerned about your health anyway..."

"All you were concerned about was that I would live long enough to go on betraying my wife."

"Not betrayal. We had to know what she was doing so that we could help. We needed a listening post. You were her husband, the perfect conduit."

"Conduit. It makes me feel like a tube of metal or concrete, it's dehumanizing. Before that, I was an asset, like Joe Bering. Asset, conduit—for Christ's sake!"

"Those are just a shorthand way of identifying things."

"But it equates people with *things*, did you ever stop to think about that?"

No, Fernald thought, I never did. He said, "Don't build it up, it's not important."

"Conduit," Jerry said. "Look what being a conduit got me—and Juno.

You want to know something, Fernald? You guys stink. I don't mean that personally, that goes without saying. I mean you're lousy spies, you're terrible fuckups."

His face was red and he had begun to sweat copiously. His jaw was thrust forward and his eyes were showing white. Careful, Fernald thought, it wouldn't take much to make him explode. He was a powerful man, he'd be a handful if he turned violent.

"We have an occasional setback," Fernald said neutrally. "We're only human."

"You flatter yourself."

Fernald scanned the newspaper column quickly. The cop who had been driving had been killed by a shotgun. There had been backup cars, but they had gotten lost. How could a competent policeman like Orlandi, on his record, have run such a clumsy operation?

"I believed you," Jerry said, "when you promised to protect Juno."

"I'll know better what to tell you when I get to Padua. We have some men there. You're taking the plane to Venice?"

"They better not hurt her," Jerry said. "If they do, I swear..." The fierceness drained out of him; in its place were bewilderment and pain.

"I'll be taking a taxi from Venice to Padua," Fernald said. "You're welcome to ride with me."

"So you can keep your eye on me?"

Exactly right, Fernald thought. But he shook his head and said, "What can you do on your own?"

"Yeah," Jerry said. "I'll ride with you." He circled his neck with his hand. "Any place here I can buy a tie?"

"I've got some extras. I'll lend you one when we get to Padua." Fernald listened to the public address system. "They're announcing the Venice flight."

As they started toward the gate Jerry said, "You want to know what I can do on my own?" His voice was pleasant. "What I can do—if anything happens to Juno—I can kill a couple of you fellows. You understand what I'm saying?"

"Here we are," Fernald said. "Gate seven."

Twenty-one

Orlandi sat on a wooden chair in the center of a large untidy catchall of a room, facing a semicircle of his captors like a prisoner in the dock. They all wore masks, including the girl, Adriana, although she was blown, and knew it.

Masks or no masks, he had drawn some rough conclusions about the group. Two had cultured, educated northern accents; another, who rarely spoke, was slight and boyish, surely still in his teens. The tall rawboned one, who winced when he crossed his legs (bad knees, Orlandi thought, it's something I know about), had a rough voice, an outdoor voice accustomed to being lifted in order to be heard against competing sounds. The second of the women mumbled, and her speech was slurred; Orlandi guessed she was doing drugs, perhaps pills. The one who kept the *lupara* trained unswervingly on his chest—it was he who had blown Rabito away through the windshield—was dark and squat, and his dialect was pure Sicilian. He was less solemn than the others, perhaps he didn't take himself with the same heavy seriousness, but he was the most immediately menacing; he seemed to be itching to pull the trigger.

The leader was professorial and chose his words with agonizing care, as if, Orlandi thought, he wanted to be well regarded even—or especially—by his enemy. His name was Federico. The second girl, the spaced-out one, had addressed him by name and had been furiously hissed at for a breach of security.

Orlandi sat quietly, with an air of calm gravity. But inwardly he seethed with shame and rage at having allowed himself to fall into the hands of such a ragtag gang. Whatever happened, his career was ruined.

The leader stood up. "It is by no accident," he said, "no mere bad luck, that you have fallen to us, Signor Orlandi. Instead, it is due to the determination, cleverness, passion, daring, and dedication of the Forze Scarlatte, all of these elements welded together by the irresistible flame of an ideology that the corrupt and diseased establishment can no more stand against than a grain of sand can resist the pull of the mighty ocean tides. If the *capo* of the so-called antiterrorist branch of the so-called governing body of our country has fallen, can the entire structure be far behind? Signor Orlandi—"

"Dottore," Orlandi said, not that he cared, but because he hoped for some relief from the oratory.

"—I am prepared to believe," Federico continued, "since I know you to be an intelligent man, that you can discern that what I say is true, and that before such truth you must tremble."

If not by a bullet, Orlandi thought, then they will surely kill me with boredom, with the blunt instrument of their incessant constipated rhetoric. He remained impassive.

"I will now turn," Federico said, "to the business at hand. You may have coffee if you wish."

The offer of coffee set off a debate. Was it fitting to offer the solace of coffee to a man who had tortured thousands in his vicious efforts to thwart the inevitable triumph of the revolution? Had he ever offered anything but blows and blood to his innocent victims? The man with the bad knees was the most determined to deprive him of coffee. The burden for what they called "politesse" was upheld by the one with the soft overcultivated voice. The girl, Adriana, took no part in any of it. Even behind her mask she seemed bored; the toe of her shoe tapped the worn linoleum flooring impatiently.

Orlandi declined the offer. His declaration didn't quite stop the argument—there was a principle beyond acceptance or rejection involved here, the man with the bad knees said—but it did take the wind out of its sails. So that, when Federico stamped his foot for silence, it finished.

Federico said, "Signore, has it crossed your mind to wonder why we did not shoot you out of hand like the other pig, the driver?"

"No. I didn't think about it."

"May I ask why you felt it was not worth a thought?"

Orlandi made a sour face. "If I had known I would undergo this childish catechism I might have begged you to shoot me."

"Soon enough," the Sicilian said cheerfully, aiming his *lupara*, "soon enough you'll have your wish."

"Then I will say it for you. Alive, you are worth more to us than dead."

"Yes," Orlandi said. "Newspaper headlines."

"No," Federico said with a little smile. "We'll get those, of course, but our main interest is to barter your life for the removal of a deadly and humiliating cancer from our soil."

"The government won't deal with you. You should know that by now."

"They'll simply allow a true and faithful servant of their interests to die without a qualm?"

Maybe not simply, Orlandi thought, and surely not without some qualms. There would be debate in the inner councils, in the parliament, some breast-beating, some cold-blooded calculation, much high-flown philosophy and profession of principle. But in the end there would be no choice. They would not deal, they would elect to let him die as they had let Moro die.

"Now I ask you another question," Federico said. "Do you accept that there are filthy germ warfare weapons emplaced on Italian soil?"

"I have no certain knowledge on the matter one way or another."

"Hypothesize. Suppose you had such proof. Then what would your view be?"

"I take that as an invitation for me to express a view that would agree with yours. I don't agree with anything."

"If you did, it might save your life."

"I have no more confidence in your being able to save my life than I do in the government's."

"Denounce the missiles—that is what we are asking you to do."

"A waste of time. Everyone will know that I did so under coercion."

"Ah," Federico said. "But you will write a letter of denunciation in your own hand and your very own words."

Enough of this bullshit, Orlandi thought wearily. He said, "All right, I will state my views on the missiles. I believe they are here and I am delighted that it is so."

In the outburst that followed he caught the words "fascist," perhaps a half dozen times, "pig," "rat," "idiot," "tool." Federico stood in grim silence, as did Adriana, who regarded him with her head tilted to the side skeptically.

Federico held up his hand and the invective died away gradually. "Do you wish to reconsider your statement?"

"No."

"You have said your last word on the matter?"

"I have stated my deeply held belief," Orlandi said solemnly. And what *is* my belief, he wondered. But he knew the answer: he was the obedient public servant, the good soldier; his only real interest in the politics of missiles was disinterest.

"Put a hot iron to his feet," the second girl said, "and we'll find out what he believes in, we'll have him screaming for his mama."

"You will not modify your view?" Federico said.

"It is unalterable."

"Very well. We shall not press you. To be candid, we had anticipated this stalemate. Nothing more need be said. You will be returned to the cellar. However, we do not wish to be gratuitously cruel. If you wish to write to your wife we will supply you with writing materials."

"I have no wife."

"Children?"

Orlandi shrugged.

"As you know, Aldo Moro was allowed to write from captivity. We would do no less for you."

He was astonished that they could be so insensitive as to invoke Moro. Did they believe he never read the newspapers? Moro's letters were eloquent, moving, touching, but they were finally unacceptable: because they contained a plea for his life (sometimes directly, sometimes by implication), they degraded him.

"No letters," Orlandi said.

"The hot iron," the second girl said. "Just a touch of it to his prick and he'll write in *terza rima* if we insist."

"No letters," Federico said. "Not even if by so doing you might save the life of some of your fellow captives?"

It was the last frayed string to his bow, Orlandi thought, and it was a lie, of course; nobody would be spared. He got to his feet. The *lupara* tracked him.

"Take me back to the cellar," he said.

They led him out of the room—the Sicilian with his shotgun, the bad knees fellow with an automatic rifle, both of them prodding him vindictively from behind. But if somehow they had meant their offer seriously, would he have agreed to do their bidding, at whatever cost to himself, in order to save the Signora Sultan? Never mind the others. The signora?

They opened the cellar door and pushed him violently from behind. He fell down the steps, out of control, landing in a sprawl at the bottom, feeling hurt in a half dozen places, and with the breath knocked out of him.

As he lay there, unable to move, the Signora Sultan was the first to reach him.

* * *

"The cream of the joke," Gildo said, when he and Ugo returned, "is that we didn't even stay to watch him go down. We locked the door at once. But we could hear him clatter. It took quite a lot of bumping for him to reach bottom."

Carlo said, "I don't think it's terribly funny. We're not hoodlums."

"Maybe you aren't, goldilocks," Gildo said, "but Ugo and me, we're real roughnecks. On the other hand, we don't piss our pants when we're required to pull a trigger."

"Ape," Adriana said.

Federico clapped his hands together sharply, continuing until he had a semblance of attention. "Now that we've had our period of childish play, perhaps we can settle down to the business before us. Are we agreed that we will take our prisoners to the Lido tonight and liquidate them?"

Gildo said lazily, "Why not wait until tomorrow? I hate to go out in the rain."

"It must be before midnight today," Federico said. "That was our pledge."

"They won't be found until tomorrow, anyway," Gildo said. "Who is to know the difference?"

"An autopsy will establish the time of death. It must be clear to all that we keep our word. There is a kind of omnipotence to timeliness. It proves our power, our unswerving determination, our iciness. It will enhance our stature, it will cause a great shiver of terror."

"If you say so," Gildo said. "I just don't like to get wet. The killing is nothing to me."

"Very well," Federico said. "Now the question of Orlandi."

"Kill him with the rest of them," Ugo said.

"The matter hinges on whether or not we are of the opinion that we can break him, and get him to plead for his life."

Carlo said, "I move we explore the matter in depth."

"See?" Gildo said. "No stomach for shooting."

"The point to consider," Federico went on, "is whether it's worth the risk. As long as he's alive, the police will be in a frenzy to find him. Dead, the urgency will diminish, he can't be brought back to life. As for breaking him, for all the softness of his looks, we must realize he's a tough hard-bitten cop."

"I say we try," Carlo said. "It seems to me that—"

"Your opinion is recorded," Federico said. "Barbara?"

"I say use the hot iron."

"Thank you. Adriana?"

"I think there's an outside possibility he could be convinced to play along in return for sparing someone else's life."

"You heard his answer to that, didn't you?"

"I saw him hesitate. He has eyes for the Signora Sultan. If he's enough of a romantic fool...No, I suppose not. Forget it."

"Now you're talking, *duchessa*. He's the one I want to pull the trigger on personally. Michael? Well, I'll leave Michael to you. Would you like that, *duchessa*?"

"You black Sicilian hyena, you African!"

Gildo laughed. "If you're a good girl you can do the signora, too, your mother-in-law."

"Quiet," Federico said. "Any further discussion?"

Adriana turned her smoldering gaze away from Gildo. "I don't see any need to include the signora, never mind what our ugly African says. She's entirely innocent."

"Nobody," Federico said, "is entirely innocent." He pondered for an instant. "Or even partially innocent."

"That's a wonderful epigram," Adriana said. "It's only flaw is that it doesn't make sense. I move we let the lady go."

"Do you ask for a vote?"

Adriana looked around the circle. "No," she said, "no vote."

"In deference to your sensibility," Gildo said with mock gravity, "you won't have to kill her. I'll do the honors myself. After I've had her, of course."

"You're very tiresome, ape," Adriana said. "I wish you were on the other side."

Federico looked at his watch. "What time can we expect Francesca to arrive?"

"It depends. She might want to finish out her class."

"It's her last day," Federico said. "What difference does it make?"

"You wouldn't understand," Adriana said. "She wanted very badly to be a physician and now it's over." She shrugged. "She'll be here."

Twenty-two

The rain might have begun as snow in the mountains. It swept down into the Veneto with icy force and velocity. It was the kind of wind-driven rain, Diebold thought, that swept city streets clean, not only of dog shit and debris but of people as well. Here in Padua, the low massed clouds seemed to draw up light from below; the few people who had ventured out leaned against the deadening chill of the slanted rain in a light that at slightly past midday seemed more suitable to twilight.

He had been waiting for over three hours now, he and Gray, in the streets near the university. They had used store entrances and doorways to get out of the rain occasionally, but they hadn't wanted to stay anywhere too long, so they were both soaked through. Diebold's topcoat was sodden, and the brim of his hat had gone floppy and out of shape. Gray, in his raincoat, was somewhat better off. They were both chilled to the bone. Although he was impervious to hardship—discomfort tempered a man's steel—Diebold would have appreciated knowing with some degree of certainty that he wasn't wasting his time.

When they had set out in the morning to watch the university it was mainly because, with the girl's disappearance the night before, the trail had gone cold. He knew that, after the kidnapping, the girl had burned her bridges; she couldn't return to the university. But there was always the chance that she might be careless or stupid, or that she hadn't known that there had been other police cars on her trail. He didn't really believe any of that, but he was prepared to explore any possibility, however remote. Or else admit failure, and it wasn't in his nature to give in.

He saw Gray pause at the corner before going on. He caught up with him halfway along the next street.

"Strawberry is here," Gray said. "He's been making circuits in the BMW. The same gorilla as last night is driving."

"He disappeared last night, he must have lost the trail. So he may not know about the ambush."

They turned to their left at the corner. The rain beat in their faces.

"He must know," Gray said. "It was on the radio. It's probably in the newspapers by now."

"You want me to assume he has some information we don't?"

Gray nodded. "Either that or he's here because *we* are, thinking that we have some information *he* doesn't."

Diebold bowed his head to allow water to spill off the brim of his hat. "You're serious about that?"

"Well, it would be funny if he thought we knew something, and we thought he did, and neither of us had *anything*."

Diebold gave Gray a slanting sideward look. "I don't see the humor."

"I didn't mean funny in the humorous sense," Gray said.

"I don't know how I missed him going by," Diebold said.

Gray said, "Shall I go back to my post?"

Diebold nodded. Gray turned and went toward the corner. Diebold continued, circling back to the Via Antenore.

A few minutes later, standing with his back to the street in the doorway of a shop, he saw a reflection of the BMW glide into view. After it had gone on he turned and followed it with his eyes. Its rear window was running with water, obscuring a view of the car's occupants, but there was no reason to doubt Gray's report. A half hour later, he saw Gray pausing at the head of the street again. He walked to meet him.

"He went by a while ago," Diebold said. "I saw him."

"That's changed now. He's in another car."

"Switched cars?"

"Not exactly." Gray knit his brow. "I think I'd better tell it seriatim."

"Seriatim?"

"The way it happened. I spotted him outside the BMW, walking fast, as if he was going someplace."

"Raining. Up to now he's been warm and dry in the BMW. He didn't like getting wet."

"I followed him," Gray said. "He went around to where the girl had been parked last night. He looked for the old fellow in charge of the parking, and spotted him standing in the doorway. He spoke to the old fellow for a while, making gestures with his hand, like this..." Gray held his hand out palm down below shoulder height. "Indicating somebody of short stature. The old fellow listened, then led Strawberry to a car—a little gray Renault. Strawberry gave him some money and the old guy went back into his doorway. About thirty seconds later the BMW showed up. Strawberry waved, and it pulled into a space near the Renault. All right. Then."

Gray had stopped walking. Diebold said impatiently, "Yes?"

"Then Strawberry picked the door lock of the Renault and got into the back seat and curled up so that he couldn't be seen. Not so easy for someone his size, but he did it."

Diebold thought for a moment, his hands deep in his waterlogged pockets, with his head tilted back so that water trickled off the brim of his hat and down his neck. "It's not the girl's car, Adriana?"

Gray shook his head. "Adriana's is a Fiat Five Hundred. This one is a Renault, the very small one. And it's a different color."

"All right. Find a phone and call the Medical School and ask to speak to Adriana Ferrara."

"And if she's there, if she comes to the phone?"

"Make something up, say it's a mistake."

"And if she's not there?"

"Then we'll stop waiting for her to come out, and we'll go watch Strawberry."

Orlandi lay on the cot with his legs drawn up. Juno had covered him with blankets. He made no sound, but she knew that he was in pain. He had drawn the blanket over his face, perhaps to hide his grimaces.

Michael said, "Leave him be, Mother, he'll be all right when he gets his breath back."

Michael and Bering moved away. They stood in front of the iron gate, talking in low tones. She tucked the blanket in around Orlandi's shoulders. Michael and Bering, with an air of purposiveness, went to the old wine bins. Presently, she heard the sounds of splintering wood.

"Now I can breathe."

Orlandi turned over on his back. His brow was furrowed, but the color was returning to his face and he was attempting to smile.

"At my age, signora," he said, "I no longer bounce. A few years ago I would have laughed at falling down a mere flight of steps."

But his attempt at humor was strained; it didn't reach his eyes, which were glazed with pain, and, Juno thought, the darker hurt of humiliation. She remembered what he had told her about kneecapping—that beyond the injury itself it inflicted the loss of dignity. Men had their own code of honor. From her point of view it was *mishegahss*, an irrelevance, but of course she wasn't a man.

He pushed himself into a sitting position, wincing, and swung his feet to the floor. Juno redraped the blanket over his shoulders. Michael and Bering came out of the wine bin enclosure. Michael was trailing a long tangled skein of wire. They came over to the cot.

"Feeling better?" Bering said.

"A few aches," Orlandi said, "but all in one piece."

"Filthy bastards," Michael said. "It was those animals Gildo and Ugo." He lifted his skein of wire and showed it to Orlandi. "I pulled this out of some boards back in the bins. We're going to try to cut the bars with it."

Bering said, "Michael thinks it might work." He looked doubtful.

Orlandi got to his feet. He was unsteady. Juno put out her hand, but he shook his head. He took a few wobbly steps.

"Michael," she said sharply, "help him."

"Mother, for God's sake, don't you see he doesn't want any help!"

Orlandi walked a few paces. "Thank you, signora, I can manage now." He bent forward tentatively, testing his back muscles.

"Would you like a glass of water?" Juno said.

"Chicken soup, Mother," Michael said.

"I'll thank you to mind your own business."

Michael laughed, then walked off toward the gate. Bering followed after him. Cautiously, Orlandi began to do simple flexing exercises.

"Shouldn't you rest up a bit first?" Juno said.

"Thank you, signora. I appreciate your solicitude more than I can say. But there is no great damage, I can tell. I am all right."

"When they pushed you," she said indignantly, "at that moment I could have committed murder."

"It is almost worth being hurt to earn your sympathy." He was looking at her levelly, holding her gaze, ardent and meaningful.

"Yes, well." She felt flustered. "I wonder what Michael is up to."

She walked away from him, and stood behind Michael at the gate. He had broken off two lengths of wire from his skein, each about a foot long, and given one to Bering. He had looped his own length behind one of the bars, and holding an end in each hand, was sawing it back and forth. Bering was doing the same thing, awkwardly and with half Michael's speed and force. A few flakes of rust and paint fluttered down.

Juno watched for a while, then said, "Take a look, Michael, see if it's doing anything."

Michael ignored her. Bering stopped sawing and ran his fingers over the back of the bar. "I don't think anything's happening." He was already breathing hard.

"Take a rest," Juno said to Michael. "You'll wear yourself out."

He threw her a furious look over his shoulder. She saw Orlandi coming back from the bathroom. His hair was wet and he had attempted to comb it with his fingers. She walked over to him.

"Can they accomplish anything?"

Orlandi shook his head. "Given much time, who knows? But I doubt it even then." Michael's wire suddenly snapped. He threw it away and began to untwist another piece from the skein. "The wire seems rough enough," Orlandi said, "but as you see, it heats up and breaks. Even if he succeeded after much labor, it would be only one bar. It would need to be at least three or four to make an opening large enough. Beyond the gate there is the wooden door, though perhaps that would not be so much of a problem."

"You mean it's really impossible?"

"Yes."

"Why don't you tell them so?"

"It makes them think they are trying to accomplish something, and they feel less helpless." He shrugged. "I will help them. Perhaps it will make me feel better, as well."

He joined the others at the gate. He broke off a length of wire, and began to saw at a bar. Bering let out a sharp little cry and the wire dropped from his hands.

Juno walked over to him. "What's the matter, Joe?"

He looked at his clawed hands. "Arthritis. I'll be all right in a second."

She picked up the piece of wire he had dropped, and nudged him away from the gate. "I'll fill in for a while. Michael, your hands are bleeding."

"Thanks for the information, Mother, I wasn't aware of it."

"You've been here for days. Why do you suddenly decide to do this now?"

Michael's bloody fingers seemed to redouble their speed. Orlandi gave her a sidelong glance, then turned away. She began to saw furiously at the bars.

In midafternoon, when two of the terrorists brought their meal, she noticed that neither of them was wearing a mask.

Diebold asked Gray to screen him from the street. Gray stood in front of him in the doorway and watched him fit a suppressor to the muzzle of his blunt .38, then reach beneath his sodden topcoat and slip the now elongated weapon into his belt.

Gray said, "I hope you don't intend to shoot anybody in broad daylight."

Diebold didn't reply; none was necessary. He was prepared to shoot any time of the night or day. Shooting—or at any rate, killing by whatever means—was his vocation. And if they might have to go up against Strawberry and the other Ivan, his driver, it was wise to be armed. Still, Gray thought, a silencer smacked of premeditation.

For that matter, it was by no means broad daylight unless you went strictly by the clock. The unrelenting downpour and the low leaden sky had turned the ancient city into something more nearly night than day. As for what was implied by "broad daylight," the presence of people, the streets were almost deserted. The few who were abroad, mostly students from the look of them, walked leaning against the wind, their heads down to keep the rain out of their faces.

Diebold said, "You're shivering. Go sit in the car."

Gray made an effort to stiffen his jaw; his teeth were chattering. "It's all right. Anyway, it won't be much warmer in the car."

"Do as I say, please."

The rain buffeted Gray when he left the shelter of the doorway. Their car was a half dozen spaces removed from the Renault. The BMW was on the far side of the Renault, two car spaces away. There was no sign of Strawberry in the Renault; he was well hidden.

Gray settled as comfortably as he could behind the wheel of the car. They were parked closer to the corner than Strawberry and the BMW, so they would have first look at the quarry, assuming they recognized it. There was no sign of Diebold in his doorway. The parking attendant appeared, running down the street, his feeble old man's body struggling against the wind. He disappeared into a sandwich shop.

Gray had stopped shivering. He played with the thought that it had been brought about less by the weather than by Diebold's malign presence, and admitted the possibility. Had Diebold guessed as much? Pointless to attempt to fathom Diebold's perceptions on a human scale; he was off the meter, or not on it. He marched to a different drummer, whose cachinnations made other people's teeth chatter.

He would have liked to turn on the car's heater, but starting the engine was out of the question. He felt waterlogged. His feet bothered him more than anything else. Rainwater had sloshed into his shoes, and his woolen socks were heavy and sodden. There was an unpleasant squishing sound whenever he shifted his feet on the floorboard. He considered removing his shoes and squeezing his socks out, weighing a degree of practical comfort against Diebold's disdain if he caught him at it. But the issue was settled for him when he heard the brief stuttering of a horn in the ranks of parked cars. He was certain it was a signal from the Russians' BMW.

A figure had come around the corner, a hurrying child in a red raincoat and matching hat.

But the walk was not a child's, nor the shape of the figure. It was a young woman, slight, tiny, but not a child. The girl hurried past; he caught a glimpse of a pretty face with an upturned nose, and then she was slanting in toward the Renault.

Later he was to be astonished that the train of events, surely less than a minute from the time the girl bent toward the lock of the Renault's door, could have unfolded with such ponderous slowness, as if normal time had been obliged to expand to encompass a violence so sudden and explosive, or itself explode, fragment.

The girl straightened up abruptly (Gray guessed that she had seen scratches around the lock), and after that everything seemed to take place at the same time, including his own belated part in it.

Strawberry was coming out of the Renault, his long arms and legs unfolding like a species of more limber praying mantis. The girl seemed to be transfixed, and by the time she turned to flee it was too late. Strawberry caught her by the collar of the red raincoat and her legs were both in the air, still in motion. Strawberry lost his grip, or she pulled away from it, and she fell to the pavement.

Strawberry bent over her. His cowboy hat fell off, incongruously landing on her head, actually settling there for an instant before it tumbled off. Gray fumbled for the handle of his door, and had it partially open when he saw Diebold running out of his doorway. Strawberry saw him coming and, still holding onto the girl, reached inside his fringed jacket with his free hand. But the end of Diebold's elongated gun was already trained on Strawberry's chest. Gray saw muzzle flash, three times in rapid succession. Strawberry folded over and fell heavily. If there was any sound at all, Gray had not heard it; it would have been covered by the drumming of the rain.

Diebold was signaling furiously toward the girl. She was sitting on the pavement, dazed, not making any effort to get up. Gray ran toward her as Diebold scuttled quickly between parked cars and disappeared from view. As Gray tried to lift the girl she began to struggle. He encircled her with his arms and heaved, and she came up weightlessly, helpless as a doll, her face bloodless and her eyes rolling in terror. He shifted her weight to one of his hips and felt the tenderness of her small breasts against his arm. Through a corner of his eye, or perhaps of his consciousness, he became aware of three more muzzle flashes. In a moment, Diebold appeared; his gun was out of sight.

Diebold yanked open the rear door of their car and ducked inside, holding his arms out. Gray passed the girl inside. Diebold received her on his lap and clapped one arm around her waist and the other over her mouth. Above his fingers her eyes were enormous, straining. Gray slammed the door shut and ran around to the driver's seat. At the corner there were two people, standing flat-footed, gaping.

He started the car with a roar, and pulled into the street without looking behind him. He heard squealing brakes and then the angry blasting of a horn. He paid no attention to it but shot off down the street. He turned on his windshield wipers. The blades flung off great gobs of water and the glass cleared.

"You remember how to get out of town?" Diebold said.

Gray nodded, fighting to maintain traction as he whipped around a corner. In the rearview mirror, everything seemed clear. Traffic was sparse. He headed to the north and east, the general direction he had taken the night before, following Adriana.

"Sit still," Diebold said in a conversational tone.

Gray risked a glance over his shoulder. The girl was moving in Diebold's lap, but not much; she was imprisoned by his hands and arms. She looked like a species of novelty doll in her red raincoat. Her hat had become dislodged. She had fine ash-blond hair.

"The other Ivan," Gray said. "The driver of the BMW?"

"I put him down," Diebold said.

What did I suppose those three flashes were, Gray thought—a cigarette lighter? After all, Diebold didn't smoke.

It might have been even more difficult, perhaps impossible, to kill the girl if she had been in mint condition. It would have been unthinkable to destroy that perfect small-scale replica of a grown woman, with those appealing eyes, the finely proportioned hips and breasts . . .

But they had dehumanized her. And Gray knew that, much as he was repelled by it, he would be able to pull it off. Her dress was bloody around the crotch where her nails had gouged at herself as if to root out her agony by main force. Her face was battered (Diebold's open palm was heavy enough to raise welts and draw blood from her nose and mouth), and running with a mixture of tears and mucus that the rain hadn't been able to wash away. Her blond hair was plastered to her skull.

She stumbled ahead of him through the fields, stubbly with the detritus of some summer crop, her miniature beauty a rebuke to the weather, to her predicament, to—Gray thought, surprising himself—to the irremediable wickedness of the whole sphere and everyone who lived upon it.

The rain beat down, spilling water faster than the sated earth could absorb it, forming muddy puddles for their feet to slosh into. Once the girl turned her head, and he thought she would plead for her life, but her eyes were empty, perhaps blinded by terror, and he wasn't even sure that she saw him. She stumbled on and would have fallen if he hadn't steadied her.

They were far enough away now from the dirt turnoff where he had parked the car. He had driven out of Padua, found the state road, and cut off into the country from there. He had twisted and turned at random through the drowned countryside until Diebold had been satisfied and told him to pull off the blacktop into a side road.

They were far enough into the fields now, and, he knew, had been for some time. There was no point in prolonging the girl's ordeal and his own. He overtook her with a single long step (worth two, two-and-a-half of the girl's little ones) and, holding the gun an inch or two away from the back of her head, pulled the trigger. The report was snatched away by the wind, doused by the rain. She went down as abruptly as a duck in a shooting gallery. He knelt in the muck and fired a second shot into her already shattered head.

He turned away and clumped back across the field to the dirt road. The hood of the car had been lowered into place, and the jumper cables, no doubt, stowed away in the trunk. He could see Diebold in the passenger's seat in front. Gray realized that he was still holding his own gun in his hand. Given that Diebold was looking straight ahead through the windshield, it would be no trick at all to circle behind the car, come up on Diebold's side, and shoot him dead through the window.

But he knew that—the way they defined rational in their business—Diebold's judgment was, on a rational basis, correct: there was no way to spare the girl after what they had done to her. She had put up some resistance, to her credit. But the third time they had given her a jolt, a sustained one (the engine revved up to keep the voltage high) she had screamed out what they wanted to hear, and what they knew, without any question, to be the truth.

The girl had to die. It was in the national interest that she had to die, Diebold had said. The national interest—an irresistible force, not to be subverted, not to be questioned, the gospel according to St. Patriotism. Such a little thing, he thought, to have died for such a big principle.

He slipped the gun into his pocket, skirted the car, and got in behind the wheel. His face was dripping with rain. And tears as well? How could he tell? Water was water.

"We're going to Venice," Diebold said.

* * *

"You're telling me," Fernald said, "that in the space of approximately one hour you terminated three people. Do I have that right?"

"Not exactly," Diebold said. "I did Strawberry and his driver. Gray did the girl."

"Decent of you to share," Fernald said.

Diebold was silent. But Gray, using the word "sir" a great deal, outlined the action in Padua in detail, and said that in his considered opinion the shooting was absolutely unavoidable. Strawberry had been reaching for his gun when Diebold had shot him, and after that, taking the driver out had been a prudent preemptive strike.

"Yes," Fernald said. "What was the overriding motive behind the killing of the girl?"

"The girl, sir?"

Gray turned to look at Diebold for guidance. Diebold's expression was a blank. No help there, Fernald thought, you're on your own, Gray.

"The girl," Fernald said. "Why did you kill her?"

They were gathered in Fernald's hotel room. It was rank with the musky animal smell of damp wool. Diebold and Gray had declined his invitation to take off their outer clothing and they sat steaming in their dampness. Through the windows the rain seemed to be coming down in wide perpendicular strips. Across the street, the ocher facade of a building, defying all logic, seemed to glow with sunlight.

Gray had a haunted look. He said, "The national interest. She had to be snuffed in the national interest."

"I see. And how did you parse the national interest in its application to the death of the girl?"

"I hated to do it but—"

Diebold intervened. "If we let her live, we would have been blown. If we were blown, it would have ended any chance of extricating Bering. In short, the national interest."

What bothers me, Fernald thought, is a moral concern over the value of three lives. But he had been trained to believe that such narrow issues had no standing in the equation of what might or might not be the national interest. Was his problem that of a desk man? He had accepted the belief more readily when he was in the field and his life had been at risk. And how much of his attitude owed to his dislike of Diebold?

"Back to the main point," he said. "You went to Venice and you saw the house yourself. There's no doubt at all that the girl was telling the truth?"

Diebold looked bored; they had already been over it. But Gray said, "None whatsoever, sir. She was a wreck. She just folded and blurted out the truth, and there's no doubt whatsoever."

Fernald knew they would recognize the truth when they heard it. "Nobody went in or came out of the house?"

"We didn't hang around and rouse suspicions," Diebold said. "All we were interested in was sizing the place up from the tactical point of view."

"And you did?"

"An old house that looks diseased," Diebold said with contempt. "The whole Ghetto looks like that. The back of the house gives on a narrow alley. No rear exit, and the whole back bricked up, not a single window in it. They either stay in or they come straight out the front door."

"No waterway front or back?"

"No. The front door is wood. There are locks, but the wood looks decayed. I'll guarantee that a good solid kick would pull the locks right out of the wood. And maybe the hinges as well."

"But such a frontal assault, no matter how quickly it was executed, would leave them sufficient time to kill their prisoners, wouldn't it?"

Diebold shrugged. "That would solve the extrication problem for us."

"It would also settle the hash of the other three. At risk of seeming overly nice about details, I'd like to save the others, if possible."

Diebold shrugged again. "The terrorists are going to kill them anyway. Tonight is their deadline."

And they could, Fernald thought, be dead already. But he didn't think so.

As if he had read Fernald's mind, Gray said, "They're still alive. At least they were as of a couple of hours ago. The girl said so."

"What I'd like to do," Diebold said, with a gesture that waved Gray's words aside as an irrelevancy, "is mount an operation to take the house."

"All by yourself? Single-handedly?"

Diebold ignored the sarcasm. "Send to Milan for some of our muscle, hoods, fly them in..."

The telephone rang. That would be Jerry Sultan, Fernald thought wearily. Earlier, with some difficulty, he had persuaded Sultan to go to his room down the hall and take a nap. Reluctantly, Sultan had agreed. He looked terrible, and probably knew it. Fernald picked up the phone.

Sultan's voice said, "I'm awake. Have your guys showed up?"

"Yes."

"I've got to take a shower. I stink. I'll just be ten or fifteen minutes. Keep them there." And then, in a different voice: "Any news?"

"Yes. But not over the phone. It'll keep until you get here."

"Just tell me—is it good?"

"Yes. Pretty good."

"Okay. You'll keep them there so I can talk to them?"

Fernald hung up. There would be blood on the ceiling, guaranteed, with Sultan and Diebold in the same room. He would have to get Diebold and Gray out as soon as possible. "The answer to your plan," he said to Diebold, "is no. In case you hadn't noticed, we're on foreign soil."

"You want to bring in the Italians?"

"It seems advisable."

"They'll fuck it up," Diebold said.

"Don't be so sure of that." Fernald picked up the phone. "Why don't you two go change your clothes, get a little rest, some hot food..."

Gray started toward the door. Diebold stood in place. "You think the Italians will just hand Bering over to us—not want to hold him and debrief him?"

"No, I don't think that."

"You think we can count on Bering not to spill the beans?"

"No, not that either."

Diebold seemed momentarily nonplussed. "If you mean that there's bound to be a lot of wild shooting, and I can manage to go in with the first wave of Italians..."

"Yes," Fernald said.

"That's more like it," Diebold said.

"I'm glad you approve. If you'll both excuse me now?"

When they had left the room, Fernald gave the operator the number of the Chief of Station in Milan. Terminating Bering was, without question, in the national interest, he thought as he waited. It wasn't Diebold who had made that determination, but he and Locksley. And he and Locksley were qualified spokesmen on behalf of the national interest, weren't they? Well, weren't they?

Twenty-three

They had flown in from Milan in two small planes, fighting turbulence all the way, and, after several swooping passes at a landing, managed to come to ground at Padua's small airport. There were a dozen of them, fit-looking in semimilitary regalia, and heavily armed with rifles, riot guns, automatic weapons, tear gas, and even fragmentation grenades, although it was beyond Fernald to imagine how a grenade could distinguish between the flesh of a terrorist and that of a captive.

In the muster room of the Padua Questura on the Via Santa Chiara, they looked pale and shaken as they sipped at hot coffee. A few of them admitted that they had spent the entire flight praying. They were the pick of the Milan antiterrorist squad. The man in charge was a *vice-questore* named Giordano—*Dottore* Giordano, of course—a tall handsome man wearing a battle jacket and combat boots, with iron-gray hair and very blue eyes which were icy when he spoke to Fernald in private.

"I tell you at the start, signore, that it is a form of extortion."

Fernald could hardly blame him for being irritated; and, in fact, his choice of words for what had transpired between him and the Milan Station Chief was hardly overstated. The Station Chief, acting on Fernald's explicit instructions, had told Giordano, flat out, that if Fernald and his small group were not permitted to be a part of the operation then he would simply withhold their information about the whereabouts of the Forze Scarlatte hideout. It was an outrageous proposition, any way you looked at it, but the Italian police were left without a choice. But it was a victory, Fernald knew, which would make future relations sticky.

He said, "I'm sorry, Dr. Giordano. Our man in Milan exceeded his instructions, which were merely to *request* that we be allowed to accompany your force. His behavior was deplorable, and he will be disciplined for it."

"Ah, I see," Giordano said without conviction. "Be that as it may, I have given my word. But it is to be clearly understood that you and your people will be directly under my command, and except in unforeseen circumstances will not be called upon—or allowed—to take part in the fighting, if there is to be such."

Fernald nodded. "We will be armed, however. Side arms only, and purely for defensive purposes."

Giordano hesitated before saying, "But you will not use them without my permission."

"Absolutely. Our presence is in no way intended to be a reflection on the Italian police, for whom we have the highest regard. All our presence boils down to is a proprietary interest because of the three Americans who are involved. That is all. We welcome the opportunity to serve under your command."

It was a nice little speech, Fernald thought, worthy of an Italian for style. Whether Giordano was mollified by it or because he was a pragmatist, he warmed up a bit. They returned to the muster room. Diebold, Gray, and Jerry Sultan were off by themselves in the back of the room.

Earlier, when Fernald had introduced Sultan to Gray and Diebold, Diebold had said, ignoring Sultan's outstretched hand, "Are you telling me that he's included in the operation?"

For once, Fernald sympathized with Diebold's view. He had tried everything in his power to dissuade Sultan, but to no avail. Sultan's stubbornness was monumental, obsessive, and he had threatened hysterically to rush off to the newspapers if he was excluded. He had to be taken seriously. No matter how much a raging lunatic he might appear, he was Michael's father, Juno's husband; the newspapers would listen to him. Not only would there be a danger, then, of the raid being tipped off, but, in his anger, Sultan might compromise Group Nine as well. And so Fernald had given in. Only on the question of Jerry's being armed had he been adamant: no.

To Diebold, now, he simply said, "Yes."

"What are his credentials for taking part in a field operation?"

"My credentials are that it's my wife and son," Jerry said. "What are yours?"

Diebold, without bothering to look at him, said, "Those credentials aren't worth shit."

Jerry's face reddened, but Fernald intervened. "The matter is settled. I won't tolerate any argument."

The matter wasn't settled, of course. Jerry smoldered silently and Diebold ignored him.

Giordano moved to the lectern at the head of the room and held up his hand for silence. The antiterrorist cops seemed to have recovered from the trauma of the airplane ride, and they were speaking volubly, gesturing broadly, keyed up for the coming action. A similar group of our own, Fernald thought, would have been quiet, understated, but he recognized the difference was purely one of style: the Italians looked tough and competent.

Giordano outlined the operation succinctly. There was to be nothing fancy about it. Because of the deadline—which they would have to assume would be no later than midnight; the FS had a certain nicety about such matters—it would have to be a straightforward investment of the objective with the hope of forcing a surrender when the FS saw that their position was hopeless. If, however, the FS chose to make a fight of it...

A cop raised his hand. "*Dottore*, if we announce our presence, we sacrifice the element of surprise. Why not burst in and overwhelm them?"

"Because their prisoners must be regarded as hostages. If we used *force majeure* they would undoubtedly kill them. We will therefore attempt to negotiate. Much depends on how much or little the FS want to die. On that point there is no reliable precedent. As always, the longer we can prolong negotiations the better our chances of a settlement will be."

"And if they refuse to negotiate?" one of the cops asked.

"In that case, you will have the opportunity to do some killing. But patience is called for, and no overt action will be taken unless I specifically order it. We may all be very wet by the time the matter is resolved."

Wet, Fernald thought, was a word with various levels of meaning. In the lexicon of spookdom it signified the shedding of blood. He looked over at Diebold, who was sitting up straight in his chair, his face expressionless. He wasn't listening to Giordano, but to himself, to some inner voice which undoubtedly addressed him in familiar tones of quiet fury.

"You have all participated in such operations before," Giordano said, "you know the routine. I comprehend that you have a low tolerance for terrorists, but you are to keep your emotions in check. That we will eventually take these FS bastards goes without saying. Our priority is to save the lives of the prisoners. *Capiscono?*"

There was a low murmuring chorus of assent: *Sì, d'accordo, capisco, capiamo.* Understood.

"We will be assisted by four American allies"—necks craned, and curious looks were directed to the rear seats—"who will be under my direct command. The house in the Ghetto has been under surveillance by detectives of the Venice Questura since early this evening. If our information is correct, the FS are still inside. We will also have assistance from a small detachment of Venice police as well as some *carabinieri.*"

Although nothing was said openly, Fernald gathered from the surprised, sometimes amused exchange of glances, that the announcement of the participation of the *carabinieri* was unusual.

"I expect the fullest cooperation from you. We must give the lie to the canard that the police and the *carabinieri* are always at odds. We must work smoothly and generously with our brother officers. The waters of the canals are the domain of the *carabinieri.* We will be transported from the Viale Roma by a *carabinieri* launch, which will then remain on patrol. The investment of the house, however, will be strictly an operation of the *polizia.* We will now proceed to Venice."

Fernald looked at his watch. Near eight thirty. By a bit past nine the operation would be in place and the chase would be over. Provided, of course, that their birds had not flown the nest.

As a soccer player Ugo had been highly disciplined, a man who preferred set plays to improvisation, which, of course, in a game where accidents play a major part in the flow of the action, somewhat limited his value to a team. He was much the same in his private life, so that, when he was told, earlier than originally planned, to go off and get the *motoscafo,* he groused about it. Suppose Piero wasn't drunk enough yet?

But everyone was worried because Francesca had not yet turned up, and they had decided to advance the schedule in the interest of caution. It made sense, of course, even though Ugo thought that Francesca might simply be shacked up for a last good-bye with a boyfriend. He put on a heavy *impermeabile* and a peaked nautical cap, and went out into the rain, which hadn't let up since early morning, and would doubtless have swelled the gray-green waters of the canals, which would by now have lapped into the ground floors of some of the more decrepit *palazzi* along the Grand Canal.

He wound his way through the alleys of the Ghetto to the Fondamenta Cannaregio, with the wind slashing the rain into his face, and thence to Calle Riello, near where Piero lived, a five-minute walk from the Cooperativa Veneziana water-taxi mooring at the foot of the railroad station steps, where he kept his boat. Ugo opened the ineffectual outer-door lock with the tip of his penknife and went up the stairs to Piero's room.

Piero was sitting in front of his television set, watching a musical extravaganza with glazed eyes, a glass in his hand, a bottle of Scotch on a table at his elbow. He was drunk enough; given the weather, he had probably packed it in early and retired to his room for his nightly bout with the bottle.

"I need your boat," Ugo said.

Piero refilled his glass. "Not a chance."

Ugo sighed inwardly. If Piero was going to be difficult it would take time to convince him, and Federico had urged him to be quick about it. True, there was a shortcut, which was a punch to Piero's sagging jaw, but that would be saved as a last resort.

"It's an important job," Ugo said.

"You know what it's like out there?" Piero pointed to the tightly drawn shutter over his window. "You'll get the boat all wet."

"It's getting wet sitting there at the dock."

"You can't see a foot in front of your eyes, this weather. You'll run it into a *vaporetto* or a fucking *carabinieri* launch, and then where will I be?"

"Listen," Ugo said, "this is a very special cargo. The pay is good and you'll get the usual fifty percent."

"Drugs," Piero said, shaking his head. "I don't want any part of it."

"No drugs, I don't fool around with that shit. It's booze."

Piero's eyes showed a flicker of interest. "What kind of booze?"

"There's an English boat sitting in the *laguna*, and one of the dining room stewards has got his hands on twenty-four cases of premium Scotch."

"Scotch? Ah."

"The real good stuff. Not the stuff for European export, but the real English stuff. There's good money in it."

"How much?"

"And besides, I can sneak a full case out specially for you."

Piero licked his lips. "How about two cases?"

"Two cases and you'll never come up for air. Give me the keys, okay?"

"Two cases," Piero said.

"*D'accordo*, two cases. You drive a hard bargain," Ugo said. "The keys?"

"Over there." Piero waved his hand vaguely.

Ugo found the keys on a cluttered table. "One more thing. I want you to lend me your poncho."

"What for? You're wearing a raincoat."

"It's lousy, it lets the rain in."

"It's one of a kind, that poncho."

"Shit, don't be such a stingy dog. All right, I'll throw in two extra bottles."

"Three."

Ugo nodded. He lifted the poncho off a hook and left. Before he went out he took off his raincoat and put the poncho on. It was the perfect touch. Assuming any of the water-taxi drivers were even out on a night like this, they wouldn't look twice when they saw a man in a poncho get into Piero's boat. He was famous for his poncho, no one else wore anything even remotely like it.

The Cooperativa Veneziana mooring platform was deserted except for one man, who was asleep in the cabin of his boat. A *vaporetto*, beating its way toward the bobbing landing platform, was almost empty. There were one or two figures standing forlornly at the top of the rain-blackened station steps, and that was it. Anyone arriving on a late train would have to take a *vaporetto* or else swim. Serve them right—nobody in his right mind was abroad in Venice tonight.

He started Piero's speedboat, revved it up, and then, standing at the helm, headed out into the Grand Canal.

The floor at Michael's feet was littered with discarded pieces of wire that had broken against the adamancy of the bars. Juno pleaded with him to stop, to let her attend to his hands, even speak to her. He ignored her, moving only to keep sawing away at the bars with his bloody hands, his breath hissing out through his teeth. When she touched his sweaty shoulder he shrugged her hand away irritably. She had given up her own efforts when she recognized how futile they were. Bering was sitting on the damp floor, his back against a wall. His moon face was furrowed with pain, his hands clasped under his armpits as though to comfort them with the warmth of his body.

She moved toward him. "Can I do something to help, Joe?"

Her presence brought out his salesman's smile. "I'm okay, Juno. Soon as the arthritis lets up I'll be fine."

"A warm compress—would that help them?"

He shook his head and turned jovial. He began to tell her the old story about the doctor whose patient asks him if, as her mother-in-law has suggested, a warm compress would help alleviate the pain in her sore shoulder. "So the doctor says"—Bering grinned and removed a clawed hand from under his arm in order to gesture. "So the doctor says to the patient, 'Gee, *my* mother-in-law says a *cold* compress.'"

She felt like a nurse in a casualty ward. She was the only able-bodied person there: Michael bleeding, Bering arthritic, Orlandi stiff and bruised....She saw Orlandi climbing the steps, moving slowly and awkwardly, whether because of his battered body or for stealth she couldn't tell. He crouched before the wooden door, gauging its strength, the margins at top, bottom, and sides. He shook his head and edged back down the stairs. When he saw that she was watching him, he tried to meliorate the somberness of his expression with a smile.

She said, "Did you find something up there?"

"I found what I did not want to find. The door is very thick wood, and it appears to be barricaded on the other side with metal bars. Even if we attempted to break through, the noise would bring them on the run. I am sorry."

She said falteringly, "Tell me what you think will happen now."

"Would you mind if we walked? It helps loosen my stiffness."

She fell in beside him and they began to circumambulate the cellar floor. Occasionally their shoulders brushed. They passed by Bering, whose head was back against the wall, then Michael, his broad back set uncompromisingly, his hands working relentlessly on the bars.

"As to your question," he said when they moved on, "you wish me to speculate?"

"I want your opinion," she said evenly, "an honest judgment."

He stopped walking, turned toward her, and looked at her squarely for a long moment. "They will probably shoot us all."

That she had expected it, that she had known what his answer must be, none of this helped. Her legs began to tremble. Orlandi held her by the arm to steady her. His eyes were sorrowful.

They began to walk again. With an effort to keep her voice from quavering, she said, "Yes, that's my opinion too."

Orlandi stopped. He was still holding her arm. "Signora, I wish to tell you something. It may be useless, even cruel in the circumstances." His arms fell to his sides helplessly. "I do not know how to say it . . ."

"No need to say it, Alfredo. And it is not useless, it can never be thought of as useless." She leaned toward him and kissed him on the lips. "Thank you. I must go to Michael now."

She crossed the cellar floor and stood behind Michael. She knew by the spasmodic movement of the muscles in his back that he was aware of her, but he didn't turn.

"Listen, you," she said, "stop that nonsense this second and look at your mother."

He made no response. His bloody fingers moved in a blur of extra effort.

"And don't tell me I don't understand. You blame yourself for my being here, and you think you can work out your guilt on that stupid bar that you've hardly made a scratch in. Well, I came to Italy of my own accord, nobody twisted my arm, so you've got nothing to expiate, and no reason to tear up your poor hands. Do you hear me?"

He glanced at her over his shoulder. "Listen, Mother, when I want psychology I'll consult my sister. Okay?"

"Michael, turn around."

"What for?"

"So I can hug you one last time."

He turned with agonizing slowness. His face was scrunched up, and she knew, remembering him as a young boy, that he was trying to keep from crying. Still slowly, he lowered his head until it rested on her shoulder. She embraced him fiercely and stroked his head.

"Afer all," she said, "you're still my baby. And when are you going to get a haircut?"

The door at the head of the stairs burst open. The two men who had pushed Orlandi down the steps appeared, their weapons leveled. They clattered down the steps, and behind them all the others followed in a rush, jostling each other in their haste.

"Attenti! Siamo la polizia..."

And then Giordano launched again into his spiel over the bullhorn: Attention. We are the police. The house is surrounded by a large heavily armed force. Your situation is hopeless. Throw out your weapons and emerge with your hands on your head...

Thus far, the only signs of life had come from a few neighboring houses, where black shutters had been slitted momentarily before closing again.

"Attenti! Siamo la polizia..."

The force, it struck Fernald, was like some waiting beast crouching in the dark forests of the black sodden Ghetto. They were spread in a semicircle before the house, taking such cover as they could find in doorways, in shop entrances, or, lacking anything better, lying flat in the puddles that had collected on the pavement. Even so, he feared that a wild volley of shots from the house might find an accidental target.

He stood beside Giordano in the partial shelter of an empty shop facing the house across the street obliquely. Not a satisfactory cover, but it would protect them from any fire that wasn't angled directly at their position.

Diebold was next to him, peering through the rain at the house, a decrepit building with shutters drawn, echoing with an unbroken, brooding silence. It was three or four minutes now, by Fernald's rough reckoning, since Giordano had first blasted the quiet of the Ghetto with his bullhorn. There had not been the slightest sign of life from the house.

As if reflecting both their doubts and his impatience, Giordano changed his tune. Fernald knew enough Italian to make sense of it.

"If it's a siege you want, you can have it. But you must realize that you're caught like rats in a trap..."

And we're just a different species of rat, Fernald thought, drowning in the ancient streets of this melancholy, desolate corner of history.... Giordano fell silent; there was a kind of bafflement to it, though Fernald couldn't see his face, could only hear the uneasy tempo of his breathing. Fernald sympathized with his problem: the fear that he and his small army were besieging an empty house. Defeat was bad enough, but to look ridiculous was far worse.

Diebold stirred beside him, and Fernald turned to see what he wanted, but by then Diebold was already out of the shelter of the doorway and pelting across the street toward the house, running all out in a straight line for the door.

Giordano was shouting in a fury, and he heard himself say, "Diebold, you sonofabitch," but it was too late. Diebold stooped at the door—to locate the doorknob, Fernald thought, to know where to attack—and then he raised his leg and brought his foot flat out against the door. There was a sound of cracking wood. Diebold kicked a second time and the door sagged inward. He backed off a few paces and ran into the door with his shoulder forward; it gave, swung open.

Diebold disappeared into the darkness of the house.

Giordano gave no signal, but there was no need for one. The damage, if that was what it was, was done. The policemen vacated their shelters, rose from their puddles, and charged raggedly through the broken door. Fernald was slow getting off the mark himself. Ahead he saw Jerry Sultan enter the house, the only one of them who wasn't armed, running very strongly for a man recovering from a heart attack. He was out of sight by the time Fernald went through the door.

The police were climbing the stairs, spreading through the house, shouting.

Diebold came clattering down the steps from an upper floor. Like Jerry Sultan, he was not carrying a weapon, but not for the same reason. He was so sure of himself, of his judgment, his instinct, Fernald thought, so certain the house was empty that he hadn't drawn his gun.

He saw Gray approach Diebold. Diebold pushed him aside and stood still for a moment, as if in deep thought, jostled by policemen, lit fitfully by their jouncing flashlights, and then he darted away to a wooden door that was partially ajar. He yanked it open and without a pause went through it.

A few policemen had followed him. Fernald went down a flight of wooden steps, his eye taking in the signs of recent habitation—two cots, blankets and comforters strewn about—before focusing on a gate that stood open against the far wall and through which the police were pouring. A second door, a wooden one, also stood open. He found himself in a low, dank, mephitic tunnel that allowed him to move only in a deep crouch. It ended at a rough-timbered staircase that slanted upward at a sharp angle.

It wasn't until he had climbed to the top that he understood that the tunnel had run through the next house in line, and come out in a vacant shop. The rear door of the shop was open, and police were pouring through it. They started running along a dark narrow alley. Fernald followed, laboring. The alley ended at a waterway—*rio*, they called these minor canals—flowing between ramshackle buildings looming over its banks.

Diebold stood at the very edge of the embankment, his hand up for silence, his face furious and intent. The police stopped chattering. Fernald heard the thrum of an engine, coming from somewhere around a bend in the waterway.

Diebold pointed and said, to no one in particular, in a choked voice, "There go your fucking terrorists."

Twenty-four

The *motoscafo* moved cautiously through the *rio*—one of hundreds of such canals that ran through Venice's circulatory system like a network of thin veins. Ancient scarred houses crowded the banks, some of them festooned with wash hanging limply on a swaying line anchored between buildings. Rain drummed on the roof of the speedboat's cabin.

It seemed to Juno to have been only a few minutes since the terrorists had rushed into the cellar. They had all carried arms, including Adriana and a second woman, and Juno had been certain they were going to be killed. But one of them had unlocked the iron gate—the Sicilian, grinning, had taken note of the discarded bits of wire and said to Michael, "You hoped for a miracle?"—and then the wooden door behind it. They were rousted, herded together into a group, and shoved roughly through the doors into a low tunnel. Had some wealthy Ghetto Jew, centuries ago, hollowed it out to escape a raid, or to conceal his few remaining possessions from the rapacious Republic of Venice?

The tunnel ended at a staircase of rough timbers. Someone pushed a trapdoor upward, and they were hurried into a vacant shop; a lingering smell of leather defined its nature before it had gone out of business. They were shunted through a door into a narrow alley and driven forward, prodded by blows from fists and gun butts. It was fast, brutal, ruthlessly efficient, and it made resistance impossible. It occurred to Juno that they might call out, but their voices would have been smothered by the wind and the steady drumbeat of the rain. They were as helpless as animals in a chute. When somebody beside her stumbled, she caught his arm and dragged his sagging weight erect. It was Bering. He was gasping for breath. They were given no chance to pause, to plant their feet. They simply stumbled forward blindly in the dark.

She didn't see the speedboat until they were almost on top of it. The alley had ended abruptly at an embankment, and the *motoscafo* was there waiting, bobbing on the choppy water. Ahead, someone was trying to pull back—she was sure it was Michael—but he was given a violent shove, and he fell sprawling into the boat. When her turn came, someone helped her aboard, and then pushed her into the cabin. The purring motor let out a roar, and the *motoscafo* nosed out into the *rio*.

The four of them were huddled inside the cabin on the padded benches, with the Sicilian and the second young woman facing them, their weapons trained.

Through a partially curtained window, Juno caught a glimpse of the man at the helm of the boat. He was wearing a poncho and standing up at the wheel behind the curved windshield, in the traditional way of the drivers of *motoscafi*. The rest of the terrorists were crouched down on the deck, more or less below the boat's gunwales. She picked out Adriana, bare-headed, her long hair plastered to her skull and face. The terrorists had apparently left in such a hurry that they hadn't been able to dress for the rain. Well, neither had their prisoners, so head colds would be apportioned without bias to both sides.

If one side lived that long.

She looked at Michael. He was slouched in his seat, his shoulders hunched forward, his eyes smoldering. Beside him, Orlandi was patting his knee, shaking his head slowly, as if to warn against any rashness. Bering's eyes were washed out; he blew warm breath on his curled-up hands. Orlandi caught her eye, gave her a tiny smile. His lips formed a word: *coraggio*. Courage.

The boat spurted forward into a wide body of water. A little while later, she saw the autostrada spanning the Laguna between Mestre and Venice. A train, its powerful headlight diffused by the rain, pulled slowly out of the station and onto the causeway. The boat, throbbing powerfully now, rocking with the turbulence of the waters, passed beneath the causeway, to the rear of the massive pile of the railroad station. Now she had her bearings. They turned into the Canale Santa Chiara, and then bore to the left, into the Grand Canal.

She could not recall ever having seen it so empty of traffic. There were neither gondolas nor *motoscafi*; almost everything seemed to have laid up for the night. A *vaporetto* was lumbering across the railroad waters on a diagonal, heading for its stop at the railroad station. They passed beneath the Ponte degli Scalzi, the last (or first) of the canal bridges. She knew the Grand Canal well; she had traveled its length often by gondola, by *vaporetto,* and by *motoscafo,* and even through the heavy weather she could discern the shapes of familiar landmarks.

At the junction of the Canale di Cannaregio with the Grand Canal, she realized that they had doubled back on themselves; a turn to the left would have returned them to the embankment near the Ghetto. The thought might have occurred to the driver; he coaxed a little more speed out of the boat. When the Grand Canal curved around to the right, she recognized the baroque facade of the Pesaro Palace, Venice's museum of modern art, and, presently, on the opposite bank, the marble-covered facade of the Ca D'Oro.

The Sicilian, grinning, said, "Take a good look, signora, it's your last."

Michael said, "Shut your mouth, you pig."

He shook off Orlandi's hand and struggled up from his seat. The Sicilian aimed his shotgun. Juno shouted out a warning to Michael, and then, suddenly, blindingly, the cabin was illuminated with a dazzling light. She heard the echoing sound of a bullhorn, and saw a speedboat in front, bearing down toward them. There were *carabinieri* on deck, one of them with a bullhorn. She didn't understand what the reverberating voice was saying, but it was clear from the man's gestures that he was ordering them to heave to.

There was a burst of gunfire. She saw the bullhorn shatter, and all three *carabinieri* fall to the deck. Behind the driver, the terrorists continued to fire. The driver of the *carabinieri* boat pitched forward against the windshield and his boat slued off and ran for the side of the canal. It crashed into the concrete *fondamenta* and burst into brilliant orange flames.

She put her hand over her eyes as they swept by. She heard a final burst of fire from their bow, and a wild chorus of triumph.

The police were crowded into the cabin of the launch, dripping water on the boards. On the foredeck, Fernald stood beside Giordano. Next to the driver, a *carabinieri* major, the commander of the launch, peered through the windshield. Diebold, standing off by himself, was taking the full brunt of the driving rain—for no good reason, Fernald thought, other than his need to test himself against every rigor. He had seen Jerry Sultan go into the cabin, which was just as well; he and Diebold were like a pair of competing alley cats.

The launch was plowing through the waters of the Canale di Cannaregio toward its confluence with the Grand Canal. It was a large, slow vessel, it had no chance of matching the speed of the terrorists' boat; nor did they have any idea of where their quarry might be. After

Diebold's discovery of the escape by boat in the Ghetto, they had pelted back through the alleys to the Fondamenta Cannaregio, where they had earlier left the launch near the arched entrance to the Ghetto. The *carabinieri* major had radioed an alert to all available patrol boats, but, lacking knowledge of what course the terrorists might take, the patrol force would be spread thin. The major theorized about the choices open to the terrorists: they would emerge into the Canale delle Sacche, beyond the northern boundary of the city. That much was clear, but afterwards they had many options open to them. They might go eastward around the northern rim of the city and thence into the Laguna Morta; they could go left into the great Laguna of Venice, after which they might bear toward Mestre; they could head into the Canale Santa Chiara, where they could choose either the Grand Canal to their left, or, to their right, the Canale Scomenzera into the Guidecca Canal or God knew where else.

Giordano instructed the major to head for the Grand Canal. While it was unlikely that the terrorists would have taken that route, at least the launch would be in a central position and might be able to join the battle if any of the *carabinieri* patrol boats spotted the quarry.

Giordano tilted his head toward Diebold. "I almost shot that man when he broke toward the house."

"I almost shot him myself," Fernald said.

"In the end, he did us a great service. But it was stupid. He could not know that the FS was not inside."

Couldn't know, Fernald thought, and yet, somehow, he did. It was too much of an effort to explain Diebold to a stranger, so he merely said, "He had a hunch. Those things sometimes work."

"We could still be there, surrounding an empty house," Giordano said. "It is embarrassing to think of that."

The launch bore to the left and entered the Grand Canal.

"If they came this way, we would not be far behind," Giordano said, hopefully. "Our route was a direct one."

"You believe they came here?"

"I don't know what to believe. In their place I would stay away from the Grand Canal. But perhaps they thought to fool us. It would be audacious, and that too is why they might have done so."

From somewhere ahead, they heard a clatter. There was a brief period of silence, while they all peered anxiously ahead of them through the rain and mist, and then there was a brilliant flash of light followed by an explosion that shook the boards beneath their feet.

"Move it," Giordano shouted at the driver. "Move this fucking tub!"

The driver spoke over his shoulder. "Unless we get out and push, *dottore*, this is as fast as the fucking tub will go."

* * *

The flames from the burning *carabinieri* boat were still visible when they passed under the Rialto Bridge, its shops darkened and boarded up for the night. There was a stunned silence inside the cabin, barring the two terrorists, who were exultant. Juno had seen two *carabinieri* go over the side of their boat into the water, hurled by the force of the explosion. One had been tossed high in the air, a blackened form spread-eagled against the brilliance of the flames before it fell back in the water and submerged.

Her horror had been for a moment supplanted by a helpless rage at the cheering of the terrorists. What kind of people were they who celebrated the destruction of life? Through tears she saw the others: they were numbed, shocked, disbelieving.

The *motoscafo* swept through the broad curve that straightened out as it approached the wooden Accademia bridge. She recognized the dining terrace of the Gritti Palace, and ahead, on the opposite side of the canal, the voluptuous capitoline domes of Santa Maria della Salute. Soon they would be coming into the Basin and Canal of San Marco.

Bering pointed to the Piazzetta, with the facade of the Ducal Palace just beyond, lit up and resembling some delicately fantastic confection. "If it's all the same to you, you can drop me off at Harry's Bar."

His joke fell flat. Nobody laughed; the two terrorists ignored him. Now that it had entered the unsheltered waters of the San Marco Canal, the boat had heavier going, pitching and rocking. The terrorists inside the cabin were alert, bracing themselves against the motion. Ashore, on the Molo, Juno could see gondolas, speedboats, and the larger cruisers being buffeted at their moorings, and the *vaporetto* landings were swaying erratically. At the top of the clock tower, Gog and Magog, in their eternally arthritic way, were striking the hour with their hammers. Seaward, the Giudecca, faintly lighted, looked like a beached ocean liner. Surging on, fighting the roiled waters, the *motoscafo* headed outward and away from Venice. Once they passed by the little island of San Giorgio Maggiore, there was nothing beyond except the resort island of the Lido to the southeast, and then only the open Adriatic.

Bering said, "Where do you guys think you're going?"

The terrorists looked at him blankly. Orlandi translated: "He asks where you are taking us."

The Sicilian scowled, but the young woman said, "Tell him to a funeral."

* * *

After the explosion the cops had poured out onto the deck of the launch and helped fish the *carabinieri*, or what was left of them, out of the water. Two were dead, horribly mangled, and a third had had an arm blown away. The driver was still aboard, aflame, his body curled in the fetal position.

Fernald, standing beside Giordano and the *carabinieri* major, noticed that Diebold was leaning casually against the cabin housing. Gray was speaking to him. Diebold seemed indifferent to whatever it was he was saying. In fact he seemed oblivious to the whole scene, to the flames, the smell of burning flesh, the excited shouts of the policemen. Unlike myself, Fernald thought, he is neither sickened nor horrified. Maybe that was what distinguished the desk officer from the agent in the field. No, he thought, taking note of Gray's pallor and obvious lack of composure, no, it was the difference between Diebold and the rest of mankind.

There was a signal on the major's radio. He spoke to Giordano, and relayed instructions. Then he began to argue heatedly with Giordano, gesturing to the *carabiniere* who had lost his arm. He was lying on the deck under a blanket. Giordano walked away from the major. He bent over the form of the *carabiniere* and put a hand to his throat. He straightened up and said, "*È morto.*"

The major's shoulders slumped. The launch moved forward. The waters ahead were flickering with reflections of the flames. Fernald looked at Giordano inquiringly.

"The radio call was from a *carabinieri* patrol that spotted them in the San Marco laguna," Giordano said. "We're going after them."

"What was going on with the major?"

"He wanted us to bring this one"—he nodded his chin minimally to the corpse on the deck—"to the hospital. I don't blame him, after all they are his men. Fortunately for interservice brotherhood, this one meanwhile died."

Fernald looked at the major. He was back talking on the radio. His face was splotched, his eyes were blinking as though to hold back tears.

"Any idea where they're heading?" Fernald said.

"Toward the Lido, according to the *carabinieri* who spotted them."

"They're going to put ashore there?"

"I don't know what else they can do. Behond the Lido is the Adriatic. They would be lunatics to go out into the sea in their little speedboat." Giordano looked behind him; the burning boat was no longer in sight. "I instructed the *carabinieri* patrols to avoid contact, just to follow out of range and keep in contact with us. We don't want another burning boat, do we?"

"If they land on the Lido," Fernald said, "we've got them."

"There is Santa Maria della Salute," Giordano said, pointing. "It is very beautiful."

Gray moved toward them. "What's going on?"

"We think they're going to land on the Lido."

"Ah," Gray said.

"You see that church on the right?" Fernald said. "The one with the cupolas? It's called Santa Maria della Salute. It's beautiful, isn't it?"

Abruptly, as though it had broken through some invisible barrier, the boat began to pitch and toss with a new violence. Steep waves slammed against the sides at an angle. Inside the cabin they were all buffeted, knocked about, and they clung to each other to keep from being thrown out of their seats.

Gildo, a worried scowl on his face, one hand splayed against the roof of the cabin to brace himself, was shouting and kicking at the door. The young woman, Barbara, looked ill. The boat veered sharply, and she staggered and fell to her knees. Gildo snarled at her, motioning to her to bring up the muzzle of her weapon and keep it trained on the prisoners.

"We're out in the sea," the girl screamed. "What are we doing in the sea?"

"How the fuck do I know?" Gildo said, and continued to drum his heel against the door.

The door opened, admitted a great wash of foaming water, and Federico ducked inside. Juno caught a glimpse of figures crouched in the bow, clinging desperately to the gunwales amid showers of spray.

"What the hell are we doing in the Adriatic?" Gildo shouted. "You want to drown us all?"

Although he was shouting to make himself heard and at the same time struggling to maintain his balance, Federico's voice was calm, his explanation economical and to the point. Back in the Laguna they had discovered that they were being tailed by a boat, obviously a *carabinieri* patrol.

"They were keeping their distance, not trying to close in, but so long as they stayed with us, they could monitor our position. So we tried to give them the slip by going around the island into the sea. We thought they wouldn't give us credit for so much audacity."

"Or lunacy. And?"

"They did. They followed us. They're out there behind us somewhere."

"Wonderful," Gildo said. "Then we'll all drown together."

The boat heeled, swerved, shipped water, raised high on the crest of a wave, fell sickeningly into the trough, then began to rise again.

"We're very close to shore," Federico said. "Ugo's going to try to run us up on the beach."

"And if we make it, then what are our plans?"

"I'll tell you them if we make it."

As Federico ducked through the door the boat plunged forward, rising and falling, pitching crazily.

"Hold tight," Gildo yelled.

The boat heeled far over to one side, seeming almost to be standing on edge, and Juno was certain they would capsize, but then it rolled back to a more or less even keel, lifted high, and rode down and forward as if on a toboggan slide. The bottom scraped, ripped, and the boat grounded on the beach.

There was a moment of stunned silence, and then Gildo let out a scream of triumph. "Everyone out for the Lido, playground of kings, dukes, imperialists, and other such garbage!"

He and the young woman backed up to the door, pushed it open, and gestured with their weapons. Some of the terrorists on the deck were dropping off into the water. In the cabin no one moved.

"Out!" The Sicilian brought his shotgun up into firing position. "Out," he shouted in a rage, "or I'll blow you to pieces."

Orlandi and Bering rose tentatively. Michael didn't move.

The Sicilian took a step back into the cabin and Juno felt something cold and hard against the back of her neck.

"You get up and move," the Sicilian yelled at Michael, "or I'll shoot her head off."

Michael leaped out of his seat.

The Sicilian slid his arm around her waist and pulled her backward, the gun still at her neck. "Slowly, slowly," he said to Michael. "Come along, lover."

He whirled Juno around and sent her spinning through the door. Someone grabbed her arm and sent her reeling toward the side of the boat. One of the figures in the water took her arm and helped her over the side. Freezing water lapped against her legs. She was pushed toward the shore. Her feet touched sand. A sheet of rain struck her full in the face, momentarily blinding her.

Somebody shouted, "*Alt!*"

Michael, Orlandi, and Bering were shoved forward, and a tight circle was formed around them. The sand was heavy and gluey, it clung to Juno's shoes and scuffed up grittily onto her ankles.

Michael said, "Mother, are you all right?"

She nodded. Bering, breathing heavily, said, "It always rains when you go to the beach, wouldn't you know it?"

Someone yelled furiously in English, "Shut up, all of you!"

Federico, kneeling in the center of the circle, was addressing his comrades, his voice raised against the roar of wind, rain, and surf. Juno, straining to hear, pieced together what he was saying: The *carabinieri* vessel, being bigger and heavier, hence more seaworthy than the *motoscafo*, could afford to stand offshore and wait for reinforcements to arrive. Thus they had five, perhaps ten minutes head start, and no matter how assiduous the pursuit, it would be next to impossible for anyone to find them under these weather conditions.

"Yes," Adriana said, "but where are we going? We're on an island. If they can't find us tonight, all they have to do is wait for daylight."

"By daylight we will no longer be on the Lido."

"We're going to sprout wings and fly away?"

Juno looked for Michael and Orlandi, but it was impossible to identify anyone beyond a few feet. Bering, at least, was still close by.

"We can still stick our finger in their eye," Federico said, "provided we can reach Santa Maria Elisabetta."

The Lido was a cigar-shaped—or, as Juno had once determined, paramecium-shaped—island with an airport at one end, a golf course at the other, and, in between, clusters of luxury hotels, beach clubs, and plush villas. Santa Maria Elisabetta, the main port of entry for ferries and pleasure boats, faced Venice a mile or so across the Laguna.

"It can't be more than a couple of kilometers away," Federico was saying. "At Santa Maria Elisabetta we can expropriate a boat from its mooring, work our way back through the Venetian waterways, which is the last place anyone would expect to find us, make for Mestre and the mainland, and then disappear. That is my plan. Any questions?"

The Sicilian screamed, "We'll drown in this fucking rain before we get halfway there, with these pigs slowing us down. Let's finish them off now so we can travel light."

"No," Federico said. "Now they have become hostages in a direct personal sense rather than the political one. If we are overtaken, we can use their lives as bargaining chips."

The Sicilian made a halfhearted attempt to pursue his argument, but he was shouted down.

"Very well," Federico said, "it's settled. Let's get moving."

Juno felt herself being prodded, and the group started forward, a ragged cumbersome entity, half blinded, into the wind-driven rain. Beside her, Bering stumbled. She caught his elbow and steadied him, then took his hand.

Everyone was laboring, prisoners and captors alike. The waterlogged sand sucked at their feet, the wind was a palpable force trying to push them back. The terrorists stopped to confer, altered their course somewhat, and slogged on again into the black rainswept void. Juno held tightly to Bering's hand, from time to time pressed it reassuringly. Once, one of the terrorists fell flat on his face and rose spitting sand. They stumbled on, their world narrowed down to the glutinous sand, the wind, the relentless rain, the unending darkness.

When the sound came, the FS hurled themselves down on the sand. Juno's first thought was that the eerie hollow noise was a trick of the wind, or even a stutter of thunder. But after a pause it repeated itself, resolving into a voice booming through a bullhorn.

"We are the police. You are trapped. Throw down your weapons..."

Bering was pulling at her, surprising her with his strength. She held back, but she was no match for his weight. Grasping her hand so tightly that it hurt, he dragged her after him. Behind them, there was a brief brilliant flare of light, and she heard a shot. Bering kept slogging ahead, pulling her, and she stumbled after him. There were more bright flashes, more shots, but she knew that the shots were wild, and that, except for an unlikely lucky hit, they had gotten away.

"Keep running, Juno." Bering's voice was a series of broken gasps, its tone a mixture of elation and hysteria. "Come on, keep going."

To their right, from the sea, with a suddenness that struck with the impact of a sharp blow, a brilliant concentrated beam of light pierced the darkness. It moved like an illuminated finger, probing, sweeping, and then it dipped down, ran across the sand, and found its quarry, transfixing them as if on the flaming tip of a needle. She couldn't distinguish Michael and Orlandi from the others, they were all dark shapes burrowing down like some species of giant sand-borers. Then several of them shifted position and a series of flashes and a staccato burst of firing broke out. They seemed to be aiming out to sea, toward the searchlight.

"Keep moving," Bering gasped. "We'll try to find the police."

But she was certain, as Bering pulled her along, that they were moving in the wrong direction.

Twenty-five

When the beam of the searchlight from the *carabinieri* speedboat offshore homed in on its target, Fernald clapped his hands together and said, "Good hunting."

Giordano lowered his bullhorn and watched the ragged stabs of light as a fusillade of fire broke out. "They're trying to shoot out the searchlight. Automatic weapons fire, pistols, a shotgun, they can't reach it with that stuff."

It had been no more than a few minutes since the police launch, guided by the radio of the *carabinieri* patrol boat, had come in a dozen paces from where the terrorists had beached their craft. The cops had piled out and waded ashore through the creaming surf. A few hundred feet inland, Giordano prudently spread his force, deploying them in a loose semicircle around an improvised command post consisting of himself, Fernald, and the *carabinieri* major.

When the firing out to sea stopped, Giordano spoke through the bullhorn again: "*Attenti! Attenti!*"

It occurred to Fernald that even if the terrorists had wanted to answer, it would be impossible to hear them over the roar of the elements. He watched the figures up the beach scatter, run a few paces before dropping to the sand again. The searchlight seemed uncertain of its role now that it had no central target, flitting nervously from one figure to another. He wondered why the FS didn't plunge inland, beyond the range of the searchlight. But they must have been afraid that the police would then begin to shoot, pick them off while they ran. Instead they were counting on the protection their hostages gave them as long as they weren't obviously seen to be escaping.

Giordano said, "You notice several pairs? Those would be an FS with a prisoner, and undoubtedly guns to their heads."

Jerry Sultan loomed up out of the darkness. He was hatless, and the rain was streaming down his face. He looked feverish.

"Tell him to be careful," Sultan shouted. "Tell him not to turn his men loose."

"It's not my show," Fernald said. "Mr. Giordano is in command."

Jerry turned to Giordano. "Don't try to rush them or they'll kill their prisoners."

Giordano glanced at him expressionlessly. He raised the bullhorn: "Give yourselves up. Throw down your arms and give yourself up and we will not harm you. You have my word for it."

Fernald tried to pick out Bering in the antic movement of the searchlight, but it was impossible to distinguish individuals. He looked around for a sight of Diebold or Gray, but the darkness was complete beyond a few feet in any direction.

"You might say that a stalemate was in our favor," Giordano said, "but I don't believe it is so. My men are like drowned rats, frustrated and very angry. I can't keep them lying out here much longer or I'll have a mutiny."

"Look, Mr. Giordano," Jerry Sultan said. "My wife and son are out there, and if there's any shooting..."

Giordano ignored him. He was speaking to the *carabinieri* major.

"You hear me?" Jerry yelled. He put his hand on Giordano's arm. Giordano scowled and shook him off. Jerry turned back to Fernald. "Will you for God's sake warn him about Juno and Michael? Tell him not to take chances."

Fernald said to Giordano, "You have only a few choices open to you."

"You sonofabitch!"

Jerry was wild-eyed, his fists clenched, and for a moment Fernald thought he was going to lash out. But then he turned abruptly and ran off into the darkness. Fernald called after him, but he was gone.

Giordano was speaking through the bullhorn. "We are giving you five minutes to surrender. After that, we are coming after you. We will shoot to kill. If you care for your lives, you will surrender. You have five minutes, that is all."

Gray loomed up. "What's going on, sir?"

"He says we're going to attack them." He jerked his head toward Giordano. "But I don't know whether he means it or not. Where's Diebold?"

"Diebold?"

"Yes, Diebold. I'd like to talk to him."

"Diebold," Gray said. "I don't know where he is."

"You were together, weren't you?"

"Yes sir, but then he disappeared."

Fernald stared at him.

"One moment he was standing beside me, and the next he was gone. Melted away, if you know what I mean."

"Yes. I believe I do."

"I appeal to you to spare the lives of everyone, your own and the hostages," Giordano said through the bullhorn. "You have five minutes..."

Or less, Fernald thought, depending on where Diebold was, and what reckless idea he had in mind.

As a child, fleeing Evil through the forest in daydreams inspired by storybooks, Juno had accepted as gospel that people who were lost were prone to travel in circles. The notion seemed convincing now as she and Bering plodded through the waterlogged sand into an impenetrable curtain of wind-driven rain. They had been trying to find the police by guiding on the sound of the bullhorn, but it had been some time since they had last heard it.

Bering seemed played out. Once he had tripped over an unseen hillock of sand, or simply over his own feet, and fallen straight forward. He had lain inert with the rain pounding down on his uncovered, sparsely haired head, and she had almost panicked, thinking that his heart had given out. But when she had knelt and screamed his name, he stirred and, with her help, managed to regain his feet. His face and clothing were glazed with a coating of wet sand.

She put her lips to his ear. "Let's try to rest a bit."

He shook his head. "Mustn't let them get us again, mustn't. Can't take any more of it."

There was no trace now of the normal sunniness of his nature; his ordeal had changed him, eroded his inveterate optimism.

She ran after him, and they plowed on, through the wind and rain and darkness, through the nightmare forest of being lost, through the bitter place where the ogre lurked.

Then the ogre caught up with them.

He materialized out of the storm that was his habitat. He stood squarely in front of them, sodden, dripping, wearing a drenched topcoat and a shapeless snap-brim hat. She saw a dim slash of horizontal whiteness, and realized that Evil was showing its teeth.

* * *

Carlo crawled over the sand to Federico. Uncharacteristically, Federico had been in a rage at the mindless burst of fire directed at the searchlight. So Carlo was hesitant about broaching his idea.

He said, "Federico, please listen to me. I would like your permission to try to hit the light with my rifle."

"No. That stupid shooting was a waste of ammunition, and further-more it made us look ridiculous."

"The rifle is entirely different, it has the range and accuracy."

The mechanical disembodied voice of the bullhorn rang out, remind-ing them that only four minutes remained before the proposal for a surrender expired.

Gildo, lying nearby, shouted into the void, "Fuck yourself!"

The searchlight shifted its beam a fraction and picked out Adriana and Michael. They were sitting on the sand, facing each other, as if in casual conversation, but Carlo caught a glint off the barrel of Adriana's pistol, aimed at Michael's head. Somewhere to the right, Ugo would be covering Orlandi in similar fashion.

When the noise of the bullhorn died away Federico said, "Carlo, it's too difficult a shot."

"But not impossible, I assure you."

Gildo, who had been listening, said, "Our *Dottore di Filosofia* wants to prove he's a marksman as well as a scholar."

"I am a marksman," Carlo said, "an expert. I've fired a rifle all my life, from the age of eight, when my father first took me hunting. In my judgment the light is within range and can be hit."

Federico looked at him appraisingly, then nodded.

"Very well. You may try."

"Thank you."

Carlo eased his rifle out from under his coat, where he had cradled it in an effort to keep it dry. He rolled onto his stomach, spreading his legs apart, wriggling them into the porous sand for purchase. When he was comfortable, he fitted the stock of the rifle securely to his shoulder.

"Pretend it's a rabbit," Gildo said. "Or have you never hunted big game like rabbits?"

Facing the light, searching for its core through the sights of the rifle, Carlo inhaled, let out his breath partway, and then slowly, delicately, squeezed the trigger. The rifle cracked wetly; in the brief muzzle flash his face was pale, studious.

With his cheek still against the smooth stock, Carlo turned his head to Federico. "The distance is a question of judgment, of guess. I must make several attempts to gauge it correctly so that I can adjust for elevation and for the force of the wind. I did not expect to hit it at the first shot, nor can I on the second or third, but as I adjust—"

"Don't talk so much," Federico said. "Shoot."
Carlo aimed, fired.
"Try again," Federico said.

Even without a watch, Fernald knew that more than five minutes had
elapsed, but Giordano was on the bullhorn again. "Attention, the time
is growing short, but there is still time for you to surrender..."
His voice tailed off. He lowered the bullhorn and looked at Fernald.
"You've got to go in," Fernald said.
"The hostages will die. Do you think I'm afraid to attack? It is the
hostages."
"Do you have any choice?"
"You don't care about the hostages, you're all business."
"Of course I care," Fernald said. "But they'll kill them sooner or later.
We may have a chance of surprising them and saving at least some of
the hostages." He paused when he heard the distinctive crack of a rifle
shot. "They're trying for the searchlight with a rifle."
"Let me think," Giordano said.
"Not for too long," Fernald said. "If they get the searchlight we're in
trouble."
There would be lives lost, Fernald thought, the hostages would die,
as well as the terrorists—though they didn't count, they were abstrac-
tions—and some of the police, too. But the only target that counted
was Bering. Bering represented the national interest, so you didn't count
the cost in other lives.
There was another rifle shot. It would take a very good shooter,
Fernald thought, or a very lucky one. He looked at Giordano, who stood
with his head bowed. He's really thinking, Fernald thought with surprise, weighing the pros and cons of the equation, trying to make the
accounts balance. He was an intelligent man, not that that was necessarily a virtue in a policeman.
One way or another, Fernald thought, the national interest would be
served. The odds were good that the FS would execute Bering if they
were attacked. But if they didn't, if they decided by some caprice to
surrender and deliver their captives to the police intact... In that case,
where the hell was Diebold, whose job it was to extricate Bering? Maybe
he had gotten lost, something as simple as that. In the event, then,
Fernald thought, if it comes to it, I'll have to do it myself. There was
Gray, of course, but no, he wouldn't entrust it to Gray.
"We're going after them," Giordano said. He began to issue crisp
orders on his radio.
The searchlight blinked out, and an instant later they heard the crack

of the rifle. A very good shot, Fernald thought. The police had risen from the sand and were moving forward. Before the searchlight was snuffed out they had had enough time to take a fix on the position of the terrorists, so the very good shot had come an instant too late.

He said, "Joseph Bering?" and then, as Bering moved toward him, he added, "My name is Diebold."

Juno wasn't aware of his gun until he had already fired it, and it occurred to her with monstrous irrelevancy that he was like a considerate dentist who concealed his instrument from a patient's view until the last instant before an extraction.

Diebold fired four times, twice after Bering had staggered backward and collapsed. He turned his head to glance appraisingly at Juno, as if to fix her position for future reference. She was immobilized, rooted by shock and disbelief. And it was only when Diebold crouched over Bering, hiking up his trousers at the knees, as a man does to preserve the crease of his pants, that she understood that he was groping for Bering's head. She screamed and leaped forward. She struck at Diebold's shoulder, jarred him, but not enough, and in the flash of his shot she saw Bering's head cave in.

Diebold straightened up. She recoiled. The pistol was nowhere in sight, but she was onto that trick, so she knew he was about to shoot her. Later she was to realize that reason snapped off at that moment and sparked her reflexes, a more primitive and reliable circuitry. She kicked out sharply at his kneecap. She heard a snapping sound.

He went down so abruptly that it astounded her, and she thought at first that it might be another trick in his repertory. But he was grabbing at his knee with both hands, and she saw the blackness of the pistol on the sand beside him. Except for a single involuntary gasp of pain he hadn't made another sound. She saw him groping for the pistol and she knew there was no time to back off and run. Instead, she took a step forward and brought her foot down on his hand with full force. She felt his fingers mash between her shoe and the hard steel of the gun. As she grabbed the gun he butted her in the stomach. She doubled over backward onto the sand in a sitting position. Diebold launched himself at her and knocked her flat. He fell full-length on top of her, and the rigid fingers of his uninjured hand stabbed at her eyes. She whipped her head around; the stiff fingers struck the side of her head and rebounded.

She swung the pistol upward in a short arc. It caught the side of his face with a crack, and as he pulled back she saw a smear of darkness spread on his cheekbone. He might have been stunned, because when she heaved her body upward she took him off balance and dislodged him. Diebold, for the moment, lay still. She rolled away, and scrambled to her feet. She might have run then, but it crossed her mind that Bering might still be alive. Diebold was stirring, but still lying flat. Quickly, she knelt beside Bering and probed with her hand; wherever it touched, it felt thick fluid and something even worse. She cried out in revulsion and dismay.

When she straightened up she saw that Diebold was on his feet, moving in a distorted way, barely touching the sand with his wounded leg before drawing it up again. He was hobbled, crippled, but he kept coming on. She raised the gun and pointed it at him.

"Stay where you are or I'll shoot."

He stopped, looked at the gun, and said in a conversational tone, "I don't think you will." She drew her arm back and threw the gun at him. He ducked, and it went by over his head, a dark blob turning in the air; it landed soundlessly somewhere behind him. He hesitated, as though contemplating going after it, but instead started toward her again.

And suddenly the spirit drained out of her, and she felt helpless. He was the ogre, Evil itself, unstoppable, impregnable, unkillable. Her only salvation lay in flight, back into the dark forest, and he was too hurt to catch her.

She started to run and tripped over Bering's body. She fell forward. With panic driving her, she scrambled to her feet. Diebold leaped off his good leg, and his outstretched hand caught her ankle. She fell full length. He was crawling toward her. She lashed out with her free foot, and felt it smash into his face. But he kept his grip and pulled himself on top of her, pinning her down with his weight. She twisted beneath him and managed to turn herself around. His good hand shot out and clamped around her throat. She clawed at his eyes, but he had anticipated her and lowered his head, and all she accomplished was the dislodgement of his ridiculous hat.

She gouged at his hand, feeling his skin crumple and tear, but she couldn't budge it. The fingers tightened around her neck. She tried to raise her head off the sand and for a moment succeeded. Her face rested against his in an obscene intimacy in which their sounds merged and flowed together: his grunt as he applied leverage, her wheezing as she desperately sucked in air. He forced her head back onto the sand. She tried to tear his hand away but she felt weak, her movements were very slow. She fought for breath; the cords of her neck were distended, she felt on the verge of blacking out...

She concentrated on preventing her eyes from shutting, as though that would somehow help her keep her senses, and so she was aware that a dark shape had smashed into Diebold. It took another moment to realize that she was free of his weight. She gasped for air, and heard herself wheeze in pain. Somewhere in the distance she heard the sustained sound of gunfire.

But there were closer sounds of violence. Two figures were locked in combat, rolling and thrashing on the sand, punishing each other's flesh. One of them was Diebold, and blind panic overtook her at the mere thought of him. She slid backward to put distance between herself and Diebold, but when she collided with Bering's body she recoiled in terror. She saw that the struggling figures had assumed another shape. One was above the other, shoulders bunched, arms extended downward.

There was barely any sound; the two figures seemed permanently welded into a hideous sculpture. One of them was Diebold, and she knew that Diebold was unstoppable. She pushed upward from the sand, very slowly, aware, now that her breathing was normal again, of the deep pain in the muscles and cords of her throat, the fiery burning of bruised skin. The two figures had not changed position, they seemed fixed in an eternal embrace, the terrible intimacy of two people trying to kill each other with bare hands.

The topmost of the figures, without changing the position of its arms or its muscular concentration, began to turn its head toward her, and she shrank back. But it was not Diebold. Instead, she realized with astonishment, it was Jerry.

Twenty-six

Fernald borrowed a flashlight from one of the policemen—snatched it away from him, really—and ran from one to another of the forms sprawled out on the beach, some dead, some alive and moaning, and crouched above them like a battlefield scavenger. The police, charged up on adrenaline, were making a fierce racket: uttering elated cries of victory, shouting congratulations to each other, cursing out the surviving members of the Forze Scarlatte, and occasionally cuffing or punching them.

The miniature battle had seemed endless, a kind of slowed-down ballet of violence, though Fernald knew that it had been all over in two or three minutes from the time Giordano had given the signal to attack. There had been nothing subtle about the charge of the police. Released from restraint, they had gone in yelling, lusting for action, for blood, for vengeance. The FS had fought back, but they had been overwhelmed by the superior force and savagery of the police.

Fernald had been slow off the mark himself—the policemen were young, eager to settle a score, and by the time he reached the scene of the battle it was half over. He had spotted Michael Sultan and headed toward him because he had reckoned that Bering might be close to him. In the fitful flares of muzzle flash he had seen the girl Adriana, with her pistol trained on Michael's head. He had shouted—a protest, a warning—although he knew that it was too late to save the boy from the infinitesimal tightening of the girl's finger on the trigger. The boy himself might have tried to save himself—as, a moment earlier, he had seen Orlandi doing, struggling for a gun with his captor—but he seemed immobilized, staring directly at the girl.

When she made a sudden motion of her arm, Fernald knew that the boy was finished. But the movement had been to redirect her aim from Michael's head to her own, and ended with the pulling of the trigger. In the flash of her gun, Fernald saw her face break apart before she fell away into darkness.

Fernald slipped off into the dark. It wouldn't be long before Giordano realized that two of the hostages were missing, and organized a search for them. So he plowed forward wearily through the heavy sand, leaning into the force of the wind, his pistol in his hand with a round in the chamber.

He felt weary, done in . . . and just a bit indifferent? No, no, never. He was a true servant of his country, a tropism turning its face to the sunlight of duty. Not his to question why. He moved on, dutiful servant, tropism, into the black heart of rain, wind, and the underlying beat of the surf.

When he stumbled upon them—the reward of doggedness, of faithfully pursuing the impossible because such was his duty—his eye sought out Bering. A glance at that unmoving lump, at its terrible inertia, told him that Bering had been successfully extricated.

Then he was free to give his full attention to what was going on a short distance away. Sorted out, it consisted of Jerry Sultan straddling somebody, his hands extended downward, his body a knot of concentrated power; and of Mrs. Sultan, screaming in a hoarse voice, pulling at his shoulders, trying vainly to dislodge him and keep him from committing murder.

As Fernald came up beside her, she recognized him without blinking an eye; by now he thought, she must be immune to surprise. She yelled, "Help me, he's going to kill him!" Fernald recognized Diebold's hat lying on the sand. He threw his arm around Jerry Sultan's neck, tightened his grip, and tugged, wondering as he did so why Mrs. Sultan would want to save Diebold's life, and deciding that she was either a fool or an angel.

Sultan's neck was like a pillar, unmovable. How could they ever have kept such a man in the hospital for two weeks? The back muscles remained bunched, the arms extended rigidly to Diebold's throat. But then, perhaps because his wife's pleading at last reached him, touched him, his fingers released their hold, and now, when Fernald pulled, Sultan went backward easily and fell onto the sand.

Fernald bent so far forward over Diebold that their faces almost touched. Diebold had died untidily, with his tongue hanging out, his eyes bulging, his face black and contorted. Still, he put his hand to Diebold's swollen throat; no pulse beat in the carotid artery.

He went over and knelt beside the Sultans. Pointing over his shoulder toward Diebold he said, "He's coming around. I'll take care of him."

Then he told them that the fighting was over and their son was alive and unhurt.

Ahead, flashlights flickered, and Juno could see the odd stroboscopic movement of figures in their fitful beams. She trudged through the sand toward those beckoning lights. Jerry tried to keep pace with her, and at the same time to explain his presence here. She told him not to bother, that it wasn't important now, that nothing mattered but Michael. Her long-legged gait left him behind.

She came into the center of the lights, and it seemed a madness, a witches' sabbath. Dozens of people were rushing about, most of them with flashlights. There were dark figures lying on the sand; some were very still, some moaned. Other figures stood over them, looking down, watching.

Where was Michael? She heard Jerry shouting her name, but she paid no attention, moving on, peering at each grouping. Had Fernald lied to her? She ran past someone sitting on the sand, holding his shoulder. She recognized Orlandi. Her pace slackened for an instant, but then she went on, and in the next grouping she found Michael. He too was sitting on the sand. Someone stood over him with a flashlight pointed downward, and she could see a head cradled in his lap. It was Adriana's head, and although it was distorted, a mass of blood, bone, and torn flesh, her honey-colored hair, spread out on the sand, glowed with life in the beam of the light.

She fell to her knees. "Michael. Oh, Michael, it's Mother."

He turned to her slowly. Tears were streaming down his face, mingling with the rain.

"Ah, Mother," he said in a detached voice, "see what's happened."

She held her arms out to him, and when he came into their circle she pressed his head to her breast. Someone was taking Adriana away, dragging her across the sand. Michael was sobbing. Juno stroked his wet hair.

"There, Michael, there, darling..." Her voice was a harsh croak, but he would hear the tenderness in it. "There, baby, there, there, baby..."

"It's all over, Head of Group," Fernald said.

There was a long pause in which Locksley said nothing. Whimsically, Fernald thought he could smell sherry on his breath, a neat trick over three thousand miles of telephone and through a scrambler, as well. The silence prolonged itself, and Fernald couldn't be sure whether Locksley had been surprised into silence or was merely inattentive. Or was he simply taking time out to light his pipe?

"Ah," Locksley said at last.

Fernald was phoning from an office in the Milan consulate. The rain was still coming down. It was four o'clock in the morning, 10 PM in Washington. He had flown from Venice in one of the police planes. Since his arrival, he had been jolting himself periodically with strong Italian coffee, unadulterated by either milk or hot water.

"Bering has been extricated," he said.

"Good-oh," Locksley said.

So much for a man's death, an innocent man, if you thought about it, a man who had been accidentally caught, through no fault of his own, in the teeth of the machinery of national interest.

Locksley said, "Diebold did the honors, of course?"

"Honors? Yes, Diebold snuffed him."

"We're going to look quite good around here, you know." There was an unaccustomed note of elation in Locksley's voice. "I suppose the details can wait. Are you coming home?"

"I'll be flying out of Milan, probably around noon. Yes, details can wait. There are a few untidy bits, however."

"Anything that compromises us?"

Quite a few things, Fernald thought, but they'll eventually be smoothed over by the grease of diplomacy. "Diebold is dead."

"Good Lord!"

The bodies had been stretched out in stiff rows on the sodden floor of a back room at the Venice Questura, Bering, Diebold, two policemen, four of the Forze Scarlatte, two men and two women. The bodies were all encrusted with sand—they had been dragged across the beach to the police launch—and they looked identical, like ossified mummies of a sort, like stone, like the crude underpinnings of a dolmen.

He said gravely, "Diebold died in line of duty, as he would have preferred to go." Was he laying it on too thick? For Locksley, never; probably not thick enough. So he added, "He wouldn't die, of course, until he had accomplished his mission."

"We shall miss him," Locksley said. "He was one of a kind."

For which, Fernald thought, give thanks to God.

"Who killed him?"

Locksley's voice was casual enough, but it contained an underlying note of purposiveness. Group Nine, taking its cue from the Marine Corps, which boasted that it always brought back its dead and wounded from the battlefield, regarded it as a sacred obligation to avenge its members who were killed in line of duty. Fernald was ready for him.

"He was killed by a terrorist," he said. "The terrorist is dead. I shot him myself."

"Oh, I say." Locksley controlled a gleefulness in his voice and simply said, "Well done."

"Diebold was shot in the back," Fernald said.

"Bahstards, oh the bahstards!"

Fernald placed himself back on the beach at that moment after the Sultans had gone off for reunion with their son. He had knelt beside Diebold and very carefully, like the most conscientious of doctors, double-checked to make sure that he was dead. Then he had rolled Diebold over on his face, and shot him in the back twice.

He had reckoned that he owed that much to Jerry Sultan, and to Mrs. Sultan, as well. As for Diebold, in whatever exotic sector of the afterlife he was destined for, he would at least be spared the humiliation of having been killed in hand-to-hand unarmed combat by a rank amateur. The bullet wounds were his passport to Valhalla.

"Fortunes of war," Fernald said solemnly.

"Oh yes, quite," Locksley said. "Quite."

Twenty-seven

"There was no bug at any time," Jerry said. "The bug was me. Everything you told me I passed on to them."

Juno said nothing, merely nodded, as if to acknowledge some casual piece of gossip.

"Juno—are you listening to me? No bugs on the telephone or in the room, just me. I gave you away, I betrayed you from the very start."

It might help him, she thought, if she made an outward show of being horrified or scornful; his self-loathing required some emotion to sharpen itself against. But she didn't want to be obliging, and in fact couldn't even look surprised, because surprise had lost its edge.

He said bitterly, "I was known as the Hospital Listening Post. That was my code name, it stood for a man who was snitching on his wife."

They were wearing white, sumptuously thick terry cloth robes that the hotel had provided. Jerry sat on the gold-and-black bedspread whose colors echoed the flocked wallpaper; she had drawn a petit-point-covered chair with gilt arms up beside the window, with its sweeping view of the Grand Canal, of the cupolas of Santa Maria della Salute on its boat-shaped spit of land.

Jerry had phoned the hotel from the Questura. When they walked into the elegant lobby, a pair of water-soaked, sand-bedaubed scarecrows, the staff had risen to the occasion with a brilliant display of suavity: Ah, Signor and Signora Sultan, how good to see you again, such an unexpected pleasure. By a stroke of luck we have available your favorite room, number 203, of course. Caught in the rain? Your baggage delayed? Unfortunate, but we will remedy. These clothes of yours must be immediately cleaned and laundered, and later, if it is necessary, we will help to replenish your wardrobe. . . .

She had luxuriated in the gorgeous marble shower; she had washed her hair thoroughly and watched the sand swirl down the drain. She wrapped herself in the white robe, wound a towel around her hair, and nudged Jerry awake. While he was showering, a porter appeared at the door to collect their clothing, which he had looked at despairingly. A few minutes later a charming lady from the manager's office appeared. Their discarded clothing would take a long time to be cleaned, perhaps was beyond salvage. So, when the shops opened, which would perhaps be in another half hour or so, she would consider it a pleasure to buy the signora a complete outfit. She discussed size, color, and materials with high enthusiasm, and went off, promising to send up an assistant manager to consult with the signore so his wardrobe too could be replaced.

When Jerry came out of the shower, he said, "Juno, there's something very important I have to tell you. What I tried to tell you on the beach? Sit down."

She had already been sitting, watching the sky over Santa Maria della Salute through the window. It had stopped raining, or almost, and there was a chance, she thought, that the scudding gray clouds might be on their way out to sea.

"Juno, I want you to listen carefully and with an open mind."

But he had been interrupted by the arrival of the assistant manager, who gravely noted Jerry's suit, shirt, shoe, and coat sizes, his preference in ties—a stripe, a foulard?—and then went off to the shops.

After he had left, Jerry told her all about what he called his "treachery."

His guilt was killing him; he was waiting for some hanging judge to pass sentence on him.

She said, "I understand what you've been telling me. What isn't clear is why you did it."

"Because I thought it was the best way to help both you and Michael. These people are professionals. I thought I was protecting you, giving you backup."

"What kind of word is backup?"

"I knew how they worked. I knew them personally, you know, some of them, at least. When Fernald walked into our apartment that night, he was by no means a stranger."

"You both pretended to be meeting for the first time."

Jerry said, "It's the way you do things. You don't talk about it, and you conceal it wherever possible."

"Conceal *what?*"

"That I worked for them."

"*You?* You worked for the CIA?"

"I've been associated with them for the past five years or so, on an occasional basis. I was what they call an asset."

"And I was what they call a liability?"

"There was nothing wrong with it," Jerry said with a touch of defiance. "I just did some odd jobs for them, not as many or as important as Joe Bering." He stopped. "Yeah, Joe Bering was an asset, too. Look, Juno, people tend to have the wrong idea about the CIA. Sure, there are some bad apples—"

"Like the man who shot Joe Bering?"

"Diebold. A bad apple . . . You know, Juno, I went out of my head when I saw what he was doing to you. If Fernald hadn't pulled me off him, I would have killed him. He deserved killing."

She said, "Jerry, the CIA isn't the issue between you and me."

"You feel that I sold you out. But can't you see I did it because I thought it would help you and Michael?" He got up and began to pace the floor. "I'm not even asking you to forgive me, Juno, just understand what my motives were."

"I'll think about it."

"Juno, for God's sake, we've been married for twenty-six years—"

"Twenty-four."

"And when I ask you for understanding, you say you'll think about it?"

"You're getting overexcited. It's bad for your heart." But choking a man half to death was soothing? She went into the bathroom for the sleeping pills the young doctor at the Questura had given her. She handed one to Jerry. "Swallow this and get some sleep. We'll talk later."

"Juno, you don't go to sleep when the stakes are a good marriage, two people who love each other—"

"We both need sleep." She put one of the pills in his palm. "I'll take mine and bring you some water." She went back into the bathroom, put her pill in the pocket of her robe, and filled a water glass. "Okay, now take your pill."

"I want to talk."

"It's too late. I'll be asleep in two minutes."

After he swallowed his pill she stripped the spread off the beds. She patted one of the beds. Reluctantly, Jerry lay down. She pulled the cover over him and gave him a light kiss.

"What was in that pill?"

"Dalmane, thirty milligrams."

"Oh, God, I'll be out for the rest of the day."

He was highly susceptible to sedatives. She said, "I'll wake you."

"Juno—won't you try to understand?"

She knew that understanding narrowed down to believing that Jerry had acted on behalf of her and Michael's interests, and that was something she could never doubt. Jerry's loyalty to his family was fierce and abiding. So, however much his betrayal of her hurt, she knew his motives could not be questioned. And what she understood she could forgive.

After Jerry fell asleep she went back to the chair beside the window. The sky was full of scudding clouds. The gray-green roiled waters of the Grand Canal were busy with traffic: water taxis, *vaporetti* heavily laden with people going to their jobs, even gondolas.

By rights she should take her sleeping pill; at the very least it would give her some relief from the pain of her throat and bruised neck. But she couldn't sleep, maybe didn't want to. It seemed more important, in this quiet moment, to sort out the events of the night, to try to understand what they meant, if indeed there was any meaning to them at all.

What she recalled most clearly of the long hours of violence, shock, and revelation was the stunning epiphany of cradling Michael to her breast, and trying to resolve his fears purely by her presence.

Beyond that moment, her impressions were vague. She knew that the dead and wounded had been loaded into several ambulance boats. Bering's body was included, and Diebold's as well. But Jerry had not killed him, thank God. Fernald had pointed out that he had been shot, after the battle was over, by mistake, an unfortunate matter of confused identity. Young Giorgio had survived, and seeing him trembling, ashen with fear, it had crossed her mind that, given half a chance, she might have comforted him as she had Michael.

At the Questura, the din was deafening. People were running off in all directions. When she lost sight of Michael, she gave in to hysteria. A young doctor, one of several from the hospital who had come to the Questura, calmed her down. He also examined her throat and neck, gave her something for the pain, and advised her to have herself examined at the hospital tomorrow as a precaution.

She had been told that she was free to go. She asked to see Michael, but was told that he was being debriefed. Neither Orlandi nor Fernald was visible in the main room. At last, at Jerry's urging, she allowed herself to be led out of the Questura. Silently, they walked through the dark alleys of Venice to their hotel.

Someone was knocking at the door. Jerry, lying flat on his back, was sleeping deeply. She opened the door to the young woman from the manager's office, her arms full of packages. She apologized when she saw Jerry and started to back out of the room.

"It's all right," Juno said. "He won't wake up."

The young woman began to unwrap her packages. A beautiful lime-colored silk blouse ("perfect with the hair and eyes, signora"), a tweed jacket, a camel's hair coat, a skirt and a pair of tailored navy slacks, stockings, shoes for walking and shoes for show, and underwear which could be best described as frisky.

Juno thanked her and complimented her on her taste. The young woman was delighted. "I have no money, but when my husband wakes—"

"Nothing to worry, signora." She turned to the door. "Such a pleasure to buy such beautiful clothes, signora. *Grazie.*"

Juno looked at her new clothing, spread out on a sofa and the chairs, and thought of dressing and going out to the Questura to look for Michael. But they had said they would call her, and she had begun to feel tired, so she decided to wait. She went into the bathroom for water so that she could take her Dalmane. But before she could swallow the pill, the phone rang.

It was Orlandi. He told her that Michael had been arrested and was being flown to Rome.

When Juno left the hotel the sun was out, high in the blue sky, touching up the ancient glories of Venice with an immemorial glow. *La Serenissima,* arisen smiling from the waters. In St. Mark's Square the tide had receded from the floor of the piazza, the boardwalk was being dismantled, and the pigeons and the tourists were out in full force. At a gondola station near the baroque facade of the church of San Moisè, *gondolieri* were playing their inevitable game of cards and raising their hoarse bantering voices.

In her new clothing, Juno walked the streets toward the Ospedale Civile. She had not waked Jerry; he would learn the news all too soon, so let him enjoy a few hours of peaceful sleep. She entered the Campo San Zanipolo, dominated by Verrocchio's fierce equestrian statue of Colleoni. The hospital was a Renaissance structure with decorative cornices and capitals, and at its top a series of graceful lunettes. She had often thought that it would be a pleasure to spend a short painless period of convalescence in so beautiful a hospital, but that, of course, had been in the past, when silly jokes were possible.

She entered through the arched doorway into an anteroom with marble floors and frescoed walls. A receptionist telephoned, then directed

her to the stairs. Orlandi's room looked down on the square. He was
propped up in bed, wearing a hospital gown. His left shoulder was
heavily bandaged.

"Good morning, signora."

His face was somber, unsmiling. He gestured to a chair beside the
bed. She pulled it forward and sat down. She asked about his wound.
He made light of it. The bullet had gone through, tearing the flesh a
bit, but the bone was untouched. And then, with the ghost of a smile,
"After a kneecapping, it is only a mosquito bite. And you, signora, the
throat..."

She tried to match his mood. "Aside from croaking like a frog, I'm
all right."

"I am very relieved."

"Yes," Juno said. "About Michael?"

He sighed, and with some effort pushed himself to a more upright
sitting position. "Michael asked specifically that I must tell you the news.
I do not know why he chose me."

But she knew that in the cellar room Michael had been aware of the
emotional interplay between Orlandi and herself. He had guessed that
Orlandi would be gentle, considerate, when he broke the news to her.

She said, "How did you find out about Michael?" And then, in a show
of spirit, "Assuming that it's true."

"It is true, signora, I am sorry to say. We did not ourselves find out.
Michael confessed—to working with the Forze Scarlatte, to assisting in
the kidnapping of Signor Bering—"

A little cry escaped her. Orlandi paused. She said, "Go on, please."

"I am causing you pain, signora. It must be hard to learn that one's
son is a criminal—"

"No!"

"Yes, signora, that is the word. Even if I were not a policeman I could
not use any other term."

She said, "Michael told you that—about Joe Bering?"

"Yes. And more. Beginning with how he had been drawn into the
FS because of his deep feelings for the girl, Adriana. How he conspired
to ambush Signor Bering."

"But they made him a prisoner, too."

"Not at first, but later, yes, with Adriana's acquiescence." He shrugged
his good shoulder. "Your son was infatuated by the girl, he was perhaps
not himself. But this does not excuse him. Many people have died,
signora."

And I have died, too, Juno thought, or some part of me, some blind
and loving trust that can never again be resurrected.

"I wish you to know something, signora. When your son began to confess, I warned him that what he was saying was irrevocable. I did advise him that barring the two surviving members of the Forze Scarlatte—whose word nobody would accept—the only witness to his crime was Signor Bering."

"But he's dead," Juno said.

"Exactly. And therefore, if Michael remained silent, and denied all, it would be difficult to incriminate him."

"It was generous of you."

"Too generous, perhaps. It was because of you, signora." There were two spots of red glowing in his pale cheeks. "Surely you must know that I have certain feelings for you? Your courage, your determination... what am I saying? It is more than admiration for courage, much more. I had hoped not to speak of this, it is the wrong time, but..." He placed his hand over his heart.

It is the wrong time, Juno thought, and now there can never be a right time. She said calmly, "And when you told Michael that he might go free if he didn't confess?"

"He said he understood. He said he wished to confess. I asked him if he was prepared to stand trial. He said yes. 'But you are guilty out of your own mouth,' I said. 'Yes,' he said, 'that is why.'"

In some little way, she thought, she could still be proud of him.

As if echoing her thoughts, Orlandi said, "He is in that way courageous, even honorable. It is something to be comforted by."

"Where is Michael now?"

"In Rome. There he will be questioned further."

"And then?"

"Then he will be put in prison and he will be remanded for trial."

She lowered her head and said nothing.

"But I see some hope of leniency. He faced the music, refusing to take advantage of the circumstances. There is great style, even dignity, to such behavior, and always we Italians love the grand gesture. He will not be forgiven, I do not go that far, but it may not go too badly for him."

She stood up. "I appreciate the consideration you have shown Michael and me, Dr. Orlandi. I must go back to the hotel now. I'm sorry about your wound. I hope it heals quickly."

"What will you do now, signora?"

She looked at him in surprise. "I'll go to Rome so that I can be near Michael. Whatever he has done—and I can't excuse it—he is my son, my child. More than ever he needs me to be near to him, to comfort him."

"Thank you for coming here, signora."

She moved toward the door. "Good-bye."

"*Ciao*. Perhaps then, in Rome, we might see each other?"

"Perhaps."

But she knew, as she walked down the marble steps, that she would not see him again. It was finished. Whatever it was, or might have been, it was over now. There was only one cause, one priority, and that was Michael.

Outside, she paused and looked back, squinting up into the sun. There was a shadowy figure at a window, looking out. *Ciao*, Alfredo. But with your wound you should stay in bed. *Ciao. Ciao.*

She turned away and strode briskly through the bright square toward the hotel and Jerry.